8<u>00</u>

THE MEMORY OF WHITENESS

K S Robinson

KIM STANLEY ROBINSON
THE MEMORY OF WHITENESS

A SCIENTIFIC ROMANCE

for Justine,

w/best from

Stan (& NAMASTE)

Other Change,

1993

TOR

A TOM DOHERTY ASSOCIATES BOOK

THE MEMORY OF WHITENESS

Copyright © 1985 by Kim Stanley Robinson

First printing: September 1985

A TOR Book

Published by Tom Doherty Associates
49 West 24 Street
New York, N.Y. 10010

Cover art by Joe Bergeron

ISBN: 0-312-93467-X

Printed in the United States of America

It is the theory which decides
what we can observe.

—ALBERT EINSTEIN

Table
of
CONTENTS

Prelude

‖: THE VISIONARY :‖ AWAKES

Now all my life forces my flight through the streets of Lowell, and I run from alley to commons to alley like a rat pursued through a maze. It is dark night and the commons are eerie, empty fields. In the darkness the city's enveloping hemisphere is invisible, and beyond one alley's abrupt ending Pluto's Tartarus Plain stretches like a black ocean. I cast dim shadows, my upper arms slide wetly against my sides, I feel my heart's allegro thumping. An interior chorus demands the drug nepanathol.

I will see him sober, I promise myself again. My hand shakes, I shove it in my pocket. Familiar back alleys now, I am nearing the Institute; I slow down as if the air is thickening. It is past time for my next crystal. I have not slept for days, I am continuing on the drive of . . . my   destiny.

Home. Across the dark tree-filled commons stands a big square building with a tall door; over the door in carved letters is written HOLYWELKIN INSTITUTE OF MUSIC. I cross the commons, open the door, slip in, sneak across the foyer. Holywelkin's hologrammic statue stares down at me, a short figure semitransparent in the low light. I circle him warily, alive to his presence in the shadows between me and the ceiling. Kin of the Holy Well, Master of our world, could you possibly have intended it to be this way? Halls determine my path, then another door, *the* door: *sanctum sanctorum*. A deep bell clangs from the main hall and I jump. Midnight, time for the breaking of vows. I knock on the door, which is a mistake; I have the privilege of entering without knocking; but no, I have lost all that, I have revoked all that. An indistinct shout arrives from inside. Oh. . . . Time to face him. Take a deep breath.

I push the door open and a slice of white light cuts into the hallway. In I go, blinking.

The Master is under the Orchestra, on his back, tapping away cautiously at a dent the tuba bell suffered during the last Grand Tour.

The Master looks up, gray eyebrows rising like a bird's crest. "Johannes," he says mildly. "Why did you knock?"

"Master," I say shakily, my resolve still firm: "I can no longer be your apprentice."

Watch that sink in, oh, oh. . . . The autocrat edges out from under the Orchestra, stands up, all slowly, very slowly. He is so old. "What is this, Johannes?"

I swallow. I have a lie all prepared, I have considered it for days; it is absurd, impossible. Suddenly I am impelled to tell him the truth. "I am addicted to nepanathol."

Right before my eyes his face turns a deep red, his blue eyes stand out. "You what?" he says, then almost shouts, "I don't understand?"

"The drug," I explain. "I'm hooked."

Has the shock been too much for him? Oh, old man, old man that I love. . . . He trembles, says, "Why?"

It is all so complex—too complex to say. "Master," I say, "I'm sorry."

With a convulsive jerk he throws the hammers in his hand,

and I flinch; they hit the foam lining of the wall without a sound, then click against each other as they fall. "You're sorry," he hisses, and I can feel his contempt. "You're sorry! By God, you'd better be more than sorry! Three centuries and eight Masters of the Orchestra, you to be the ninth and you break the line for a drug? This is history's greatest musical achievement"—he waves toward the Orchestra, but I refuse to look at it—"you choose nepanathol above it? How could you? I'm an old man—I'll die in a few years—there isn't time to train another musician like you. And you'll be dead before I will." True enough, in all probability. "I will be the last Master," he cries, "and the Orchestra will be silenced!"

With the thought of it he twists and sits down cross-legged on the floor, crying. I have never seen the Master cry before, never thought I would. He is not an emotional man.

"What have I done?" he moans. "The Orchestra will end with me and Ekern and the rest will say it was my fault. That I was a bad Master."

Ekern, Chairman of the Institute's board of directors, has always disagreed with the Master's choice of me as apprentice, has always hated me—this will vindicate his judgment. "You are the best of them," I get out.

He turns on me. "Then why? *Why?* Johannes, how could you do this?"

I would have been the ninth Master of Holywelkin's Orchestra. I was the heir to the throne, the crown prince. Why indeed? "I . . . couldn't help it."

He only cries.

Then, as from a great distance, I hear myself. "Master," I say, "I will stop taking the drug."

I close my eyes as I say it. For an old man's sake I will go through the bitter withdrawal from nepanathol. I shake my head, surprised at myself. What moves us to act, where are the springs of action?

He looks up at me with—what is it, craftiness? Is he

manipulating me? No. It's just contempt. "You can't," he mutters, angrily. "It would kill you."

"No," I say, though I am not sure of this. "I haven't been using it long enough. A few hours—eight, maybe—then it will be over." It will be short; that is my only comfort. The interior chorus is protesting loudly: what are you doing! Pain . . . cramps, memory confusion, memory loss, nausea, hallucinations, and a strong possibility of sensory damage, especially to the ears, palate, and eyes: I do not want to go blind.

"Truly?" the old man is saying. "When will you do this?"

"Now," I say, ignoring the chorus. "I'll stay here, I think," gesturing toward the Orchestra that I still refuse to look at.

"I too will stay—"

"No. Not here. In the recording booth, or one of the practice rooms. Or better yet, go up to your chambers, and come back in the morning."

We look at each other then, old Richard and young Johannes, and finally he nods. He walks to the door, pulls it open, looks back. "Be careful, Johannes."

I nearly laugh, but am too appalled. The door clicks shut, and I stand alone with Holywelkin's Orchestra.

♪

I recall the first time I saw it, in the Institute's performance hall, in a special program for young people. My mother and I had come by train from the far side of Pluto to hear the concert, invited because my teachers at the Vancouver Conservatory had recommended me. The Master—the same one, Richard Yablonski, an old man even then—played pieces to delight the young mind: Moussorgsky's *Pictures at an Exhibition*, De Bruik's *Night Sea*, her *Biologic Symphony*,

Shimatu's *Concerto for Digeree-doo*. The last piece was a revelation to me; the Master started each phrase hesitantly, and exaggerated the rests, and the solo instrument's mournful honks and hoots sounded like music played for the first time, improvised, filling space beyond the hall, beyond music itself, as if the fantastic tower of blue circles and glints was creating a texture of transcendent vibration all on its own.

After the performance a few children, the ones already being considered for the apprenticeship, came forward to speak with the Master. I walked down the aisle in a daze, my mother's palm firm in the middle of my back, barely able to pull my gaze from the baroque statue of wood and metal and glass, to the mere mortal who played the thing.

Yablonski spoke quietly to us of the glories of playing an entire orchestra by oneself. As he spoke he watched our faces. "And which did you like better," he asked, *"Pictures at an Exhibition* played on the piano, or with the full orchestral arrangement?"

"Orchestra!" cried a score of voices.

"Piano," I said, hitting a rest.

"Why?" he asked politely, focusing on me for the first time. I shrugged nervously; I couldn't think, I truly didn't know; fingers digging into my back, I searched for it—

"Because it was written for piano," I said.

Simple. "But don't you like Ravel's orchestration?" he inquired, interested now.

"Ravel smoothed a rough Russian piano score into a lush French piece. He changed it." I was dogmatic then, a precocious child who even before the move to the conservatory had spent five hours a day at the keyboard and three in the books—and one in the streets, one desperately short hour, six o'clock to seven every day in the streets burning up a day's pent energy—

"Have you compared the scores?" the Master asked me, blue eyes piercing mine.

"Yes, Master. The notes are nearly the same, but the

textures are wrong. The timbre is wrong. And timbre is—'' I was going to say *everything*, but instead I said, "important."

Yablonski nodded, seeming to consider this. "I believe I agree with you."

Then the talk was over and we were on our way home. Years would pass before I saw the Master and his Orchestra again, but I knew something had happened. I felt sick to my stomach. "You did well," my mother said. I was nine years old.

♪

And here I am ten years later, sick to my stomach again. It is difficult to tell what is happening in my body—past time for the next nepanathol crystal. The little twinges of dependence are giving me their warning, in the backs of my upper arms. At least it will be short.

I turn to the Orchestra at last. "Imagine all of the instruments of a modern orchestra caught in a small tornado," an early detractor wrote of it, "and you will have Holywelkin's invention." But there are few detractors left. Age equals respectability, and the Orchestra is now three hundred years old. An institution.

And imposing enough: eleven meters of musical instruments soaring in air, eleven meters of twisted metal and curved wood, suspended from a complex armature of glass rods only visible because of the blue and red spotlights glinting from them. The cloud of violas, the broken staircase of trombones, the bulbous mercury drum; the comical balloon flutes, sleek lyricon, sinuous godzilla . . . all the world's soundmakers hanging like fruit in a giant glass tree. It is a beautiful statue, truly. But Holywelkin, architect of our age, was a mathematician as well as a sculptor, a musician as well as an inventor, and this particular result of his synthesizing mind was, in my opinion, unfortunate. Unmusical. Dangerous.

I stride to the piano entrance and slide onto the bench. The glassy depression rods cover the keys so that it is impossible to play the piano from its bench; and that symbolizes the whole. I continue up to the control booth, using the glass steps behind the cellos. Even the steps are inlaid with tiny figures, of French horns, lyres, serpentines. . . . It is as if I see everything in the Orchestra for the first time. The control booth, suspended in the center of the thing, nearly hidden from the outside: I am astounded by it. I sit on the revolving stool and look at it. Computer consoles, keyboards, foot pedals, chord knobs, ensemble tabs, volume stops, percussion buttons, tape machines, amp controls, keyboards: strings yellow, woodwinds blue, brass red, percussion brown, synthetics green. . . . I hit the tympani roll tab with my toe, hit tempo and sustain keys and *boom*, suddenly the B flat tympani fills the room, sticks a blur in the glass arms holding them. I long to hold the sticks and become the rhythm myself, to see the vibrations in the round surface and feel them in the pit of my stomach, for *that* is what music is, that *feeling*; but to play that roll in Holywelkin's Orchestra I just slide a tab to a certain position and push another one down with my toe, so I stop pushing the tab down and there is instant silence. "No, Holywelkin, no! Don't you see what you've done? Don't you see how you've stripped from music the human component, the human act that allows it to move us? This damned orchestrina. . . ." I don't know what to say to it. I shake my fist around me. I climb out the glass arms of the statue to the mercury drum, seize it in a bearhug and pull it to and fro; inside the liquid sloshes over the pickups, and the eerie oscillation of silver sound cuts at me . . . but I can't control it. Starts of pain flare like matchheads in my arms and legs and neck. I struggle back to the control booth, defeated. Out with a yellow keyboard, down with ensemble tabs: the left hand plays, and sixty violins burst into life, in a rich, vibrant

tone—another mark for Holywelkin. Add a fast big toe to the
lower yellow keyboards and the basses join from below, and
I'm off, into De Bruik's *Winds of Utopia*. Some adroit taping
and the right foot can splay out through the brass, leaving the
right hand free for the arching oboe cries, full of pain,
denying the name of those endless plains, ah De Bruik!
—Such performance requires intense concentration, which I
am not capable of at the moment; it is necessary to split the
attention four or five ways, a truly spiritual discipline. Still,
four or five ways is not one hundred and fifty ways; this
machine is no orchestra, and orchestral music suffers in it, is
condensed, recorded, rearranged. . . .

Quit. Only the double basses, lugubrioso. I indulge myself
and watch my feet bounding over the yellow keys and creating the low bowed notes that expand out of the rising spiral
of big, dark bodies below me, primal vibration, hidden right
hand tickling the synthesized bass to take the notes down,
down, below twenty hertz, a trembling in the stomach below
hearing— Both arches cramp, and in my guts something twists.
I can't remember the De Bruik, the conductor's score that
threaded through my head is gone, the basses saw away like
industrial machinery. Sweat breaks out on my face and arms,
and the Orchestra is slowly spinning, spinning, as it does in
concerts—

. . . I am waiting for Mikel and Joanne to arrive so we can
leave for the concert. I sit at the battered old upright piano
that I brought from Mother's house right after her funeral,
playing Ravel's *Pavanne pour une Infante defunt* and feeling
lonely. Tears fall and I laugh bitterly at my ability to act for
myself, unsure as always if my emotions are real or feigned
for some imaginary audience in a theater wrapped around my
head; ignoring the evidence blinking before me, I think, I can
call them up at will when I'm miserable enough!

Mikel and Joanne arrive, laughing like wind chimes. They
are both singers from the conservatory I have left, true
artists, friends who are sad I no longer study with them. I

compose myself, greet them, we sit in a circle, laugh, talk
about Thomson's Gazelle, the balloon-flute quintet we are
going to hear. The conversation slows, Mikel and Joanne
look at each other:
  "Johannes," Mikel says slowly. "Joanne and I are going
to eat crystals for the concert." He holds out his hand. In his
palm is a small clear crystal that looks like nothing so much
as a diamond. He flips it into the air, catches it in his mouth,
swallows it, grins. "Want to join us?" Joanne takes one
from him and swallows it with the same casual, defiant toss.
She offers one to me, between her fingers. I look at her,
remembering what I have heard. Nepanathol. I do not want
to go blind.
  "Are you addicted?" I ask.
  They shake their heads. "We restrict ourselves to special
occasions," Joanne explains. They laugh. Happy people.
  "Oh," I say, and once again all my life is behind me
pushing, Mother's lessons, the years at the conservatory, the
winning of the apprenticeship, her death, the Orchestra and
the Master and Ekern looming behind it all, "Oh," I say,
"give it to me." I don't care—it seems a solution, even—
and—I cannot help it. I place the crystal on my tongue.
It has no taste. I swallow—

♪

  Hallucinations. For a moment there I was confused. I
climb back onto the stool and regret moving so quickly.
Nausea weakens me. Pulling keyboards out is a bit of an
effort. I try the *St. Louis Blues*; impossible to play the seven
instruments all at once, so I tape passages, replay them in
loops, playing the Orchestra with the sound engineering skills
so crucial to it, setting it all up in a compilation fugue, then
concentrating on the front line. The trombone is hilarity

itself; unable to anticipate the notes as human players do, the glass arms of the Orchestra move the slide about with a tremendously rapid, mechanical, inhuman precision. The trombone solo from *St. Louis Blues* becomes the clarinet solo from *Rampart Street Parade* (see how they fit together?) and I quit in resignation. I hate to play poorly. And that, after all, is the whole point; the whole problem.

♪

All you have to do to stop this, the interior chorus says, is go home and swallow a crystal. Without a moment's thought I slip off the stool; my knees buckle like closing penknives and I crash into a bank of keyboards, fall to the floor of the booth. In the glassy floor are inlaid bass and treble clef signs, swimming under me, reproaching me. After a while I pull myself up and am sick in the booth's drinking fountain. Then I drop back to the floor. I feel as sick after vomiting as before, which is frightening. "Do something!" Do what? This cobra tree entrancing me . . . I pull out the celesta keyboard just before my face, the bottom one in the bank. Far above is the ornate white box that is the instrument, suspended in the air, dwarfed by the godzilla beside it. The celesta: a piano whose hammers hit steel plates rather than wires. I run my finger along a few octaves and a spray of quick bell notes echoes through the chamber. (No echoes in this room.)

I try a Shimatu Two-Part Invention, a masterpiece of elegance that properly belongs on the piano bar. My hands begin to play at different tempos and I can't stop them; frightening! I stop, and to aid my timing I reach a shaky right hand up and start the metronome, an antique mechanical box that struck Holywelkin's fancy. It's an upside down pendulum, a visual surprise because it seems to defy gravity.

I begin the Invention again, but the tempo is too fast for me and the notes become a confused mass, sounding like church bells recorded and replayed at a much higher speed. The gold weight on the metronome's arm reflects a part of my face (my eyes) as it comes to its lowest point on the left side. And my heart—my heart is beating in time with the metronome's penetrating, woodblock-struck, rhythmic tock.

And the metronome is speeding up. Impossible, for the weight has not moved; yet true. At first it was an andante *tock . . . tock*, and now it is a good march tempo, *tock, tock*; and my heartbeat with it all the way. With each pulse small specks of light are exploding and drifting like tiny Chinese lanterns across my eyes. I can feel the quick pulses of blood in my throat and fingers, the tocks are now an allegretto *tocktocktock*, and frightened I lift a finger, a terrible weight, and stick it into the flashing silver arc with the gold band across its center. The metronome stops.

I begin to breathe again. My heart slows down. A true hallucination, I think to myself, is very disturbing. After a time I push the celesta keyboard back into its nook and try to stand. My legs explode. I grasp the stool. Cramps, I think in some cold corner of my mind, watching the limbs flail about. I knead the bulging muscles with one hand and keep shifting to find a more comfortable position; it occurs to me that this is what the phrase "writhing in agony" describes. The cold corner of my mind disappears, and that was all that was left. . . .

I come to and the cramps are gone. They feel like they are on the verge of recurrence, though. If I don't move I think I will be all right. I wish it were closer to the end. How long was I gone? Time expands with my breath, deflates in my exhalation. How long have I lived? I no longer believe in time, the metronome is broken, the moment here is all that is, the moment and the only moment.

I can see my reflection in the tuba's dented bell. A sorry-looking spectacle, disheveled and pale. The features are architecturally distinct. I can see quite clearly the veins below my eyes. The reflection wavers, each time presenting me with a different version of my face. Some are dome-foreheaded and weak-chinned; some have giant hooked noses; others are lantern-jawed and have pointy heads.

I reach up to the stool and grab it; my hand closes on nothing and I look again; at least six inches off. I must get up on the stool. Arms move up, feet grope for purchase, all very slowly. I move with infinitesimal slowness, as a child does when escaping his house at night to run the streets. Head to seat, knee to footbar, I stop to get used to the height, watching the broken light explode in my eyes.

Now I am up and seated on the stool. I remember a holo in which a man was buried to the neck in tidal flats at low tide. Ancient torture of our primitive ancestors on old Earth. A head sitting on wet, gleaming sand, looking outward to sea: the image is acid-etched on the inside of my eyelids.

Do something. I pull out the French horn and oboe keyboards, play the soaring, ethereal duet of De Bruik's *Garden Prayer*. "These are the instruments with colds," the Master once said to me in a light moment. "The horn has a chest cold, the oboe a head cold." Timbre, the heart of music. The prayer is too slow, the instruments cannot play the glissando, mistakes intrude and I switch to scales, C, F, B flat, E flat, A flat, D flat; bead, bead, every good boy deserves favor, each good boy does fine; then the minors, harmonic and melodic—

. . . "Drop that sixth," she yells from the kitchen, "harmonic, not melodic. Play me the harmonic now."

Again—

"Harmonic!"

Again.

She comes in, grabs my right hand in hers, hits the notes. "Third down, sixth down, see how it sounds spooky? Do it, now." I do it, I see the difference, it is like a light bursting over me, a whole world revealed, suddenly a realm of feeling is available to me that before didn't exist, and I feel I am floating over the bench, lifted by sound. "Okay, do that twenty times, then we'll try the melodic."

♪

I stop playing minor scales, my heart pounding. I collect the oddball keyboards seldom played—glockenspiel, contra-bassoon, slide clarinet, digeree-doo, glass harp—and become bored with the quintet even as I gather them. I am sick again in the drinking fountain. Matchheads in muscle; it hurts to breathe; and time flutters like an anenome, in a tide of pain. Certainly I have been in the Orchestra for a long time. A walk around the room would be nice, but I fear it is beyond me. I am very near the end, one way or another. The tide is rising. De Quincey and Cocteau, Burroughs and Nguyen, Kirpal and Tucci, you lied to me—there is no romance in withdrawal, in the experience itself, none at all. It is no fun. It hurts.

♪

There is a knock at the door. In it swings, slow as the arm of the metronome when the weight is highest. A short man struts through the doorway. Tied to his middle is a small bass drum, and welded to the top of the drum is a battered trumpet, its mouthpiece waving about in front of his face. Beside the mouthpiece is a harmonica, held in place by stiff wires wrapped around his neck. In his right hand is a drum-stick, in his left an ancient clacking device (canasta?) and between his knees are tarnished cymbals, hanging at odd angles. He looks as scruffy as I feel. He marches to a spot just below me, lightly beating the drum, then halts and brings his knees together sharply. When the clanging dies down he looks up and grins. His face has a reddish tint to it, and I can see through him.

"Who are you?" I ask.

"Arthur Holywelkin," he replies, "at your service." Suddenly I see the resemblance between the disreputable character below me and the imposing statue high in the foyer.

"And you?" he says to me.

"Johannes Wright."

"Ah! A musician."

"No," I tell him. "I just operate your machine."

He looks puzzled. "Surely it takes a musician to operate my machine."

"Just an engineer." We are speaking in a dead silence, a perfect stillness. "Did you really build this thing?"

"I did."

"Then it's all your fault. You're the cause of all my troubles," I say down to him, "you and your stupid vulgar monstrosity! When you assembled this joke," I ask him, kicking a glass upright, "were you serious?"

"Most serious." He nods gravely. "Young man," he says, emphasizing certain words with drum beats, "you have Completely Missed the Point. My Invention is Not an Orchestra."

"But it *is* an orchestra," I say. "It's an imitation orchestra—an orchestrion, an orchestrina—whatever you call it, it does a terrible job! All you've done is turn a sublime group achievement, a *human* act, into an inferior egotistical solo—"

"No, no, no, no, no," he exclaims, drum beats for every *no*. "The invention is an imitation of an orchestra only in the same way a one-man band was an imitation of a band, eh?" He winks suggestively. "In other words, not at all. It is a fallacy to become comparative." He takes off and makes a revolution around the Orchestra, playing "Dixie" on the trumpet and pounding the bass drum, and filling all the rests with cymbals. It sounds awful. Back again. "Wonderful, eh? Thank you."

"You have proved my point," I say viciously. "This instrument is a joke. Nothing but showmanship. I am an *artist*"—voice hurting—"and I cannot abide it."

Slowly the grin on his face disappears. He grows in stature, pulls the bass drum around to the side so that he can lean into the Orchestra and scowl at me. "My invention is no better or worse than any other instrument. No further from human action than any other step away from the voice." Now his face is shoved far into the Orchestra, it glares at me from between the tape recorders and the neck of a cello. Low voice, whispering: "If you are ever to learn to play my instrument properly, you must change the way you think of yourself. . . ."

"You can't change the way you are."

"Certainly you can. What could be simpler?"

The silence stretches out. Red and blue lights reflect in the glass.

"Listen," he commands in the whispery voice. "*The Orchestra has been misnamed.* I did not build it to play symphonic music of the past; in that regard the Masters have mistaught you. The instrument has its own purpose, and you must find it. You must look around, think anew. You must write its music yourself. That is what I did. They never thought of me as a composer; but they were wrong. All of my work was music."

"You were a mathematician."

"Exactly. And because of that I built this instrument. And you must *learn* it to understand me. To understand its purpose." He puts up a hand to stall my protest. "You don't know it very well yet." His small smile is frightening. "I took nineteen years to build it, yet it would only take two or three to put it together. Haven't you ever wondered about that? There is more to it than meets the eye." Now his voice becomes portentous, deep, ominous, and his red face is as tall as the control booth; it appears he is crouching down to stare in at me, and a giant finger waggles at me from the top of the keyboards: *"There is more to it than meets the eye. You must learn it completely. Then compose for it. Then play it; play it with everything in you. And then—"* He pulls away from the Orchestra, shrinks back to his original size. He turns, walks to the door, clink clink clink. A dull drum beat, a finger pointed like a gun. He leaves. The door closes.

♪

So here I am, a young man sizzling in a hallucinatory withdrawal, suspended in this contraption like a fly trapped in the web of a spider sizzling in a hallucinatory withdrawal. . . . You've seen pictures of those poor tangled webs that drugged spiders make in labs? That is what Holywelkin's Orchestra would look like in two dimensions, from any side. Glassy arms holding out bright brass and wood instruments like Christmas tree ornaments, like strange fruit. A glass hand, a tree reaching up in a swirl of rich browns and silvers and prisms. The Yggdrasil of sound. Music doesn't grow on trees you know. The cymbals are edged with rainbows.

Most certainly I have been suffering delusions. It is easy afterward to say that a conversation with a man three centuries dead is a delusion, but while it is happening, quite definitely happening, it is hard to discount one's senses. We only know the world by our senses, after all; or if not, if we know the world by more than our senses, it is a difficult thing to prove. The senses . . . damage is being done in my brain; it is as if I can feel the individual cells swelling and popping. I am very sick, very sick. There is little to do but sit and wait it out. Surely it is near the end.

I wait. Time passes. *Pop pop pop* . . . like swollen grains of rice. Oh, no—no!—not my mind. Something must be

done. Might as well play the thing. Set out to learn—to start
to learn.

I'm not convinced by you, Holywelkin! Not a bit!

♪

My   destiny.

♪

I arrange the keyboards in concert position, my hands
shoving them about like tugboats pushing big ships. Dispas-
sionately I watch my hands shake. The cold corner of my
mind has taken over and somehow I am outside the nausea. I
see things with the clarity you have when you are extremely
hungry, or tired past the point of being tired. Everything is
quite clear, quite in focus. I have heard that drowning men
experience a last period of great calm and clarity before
losing consciousness. Perhaps the tide is that high now. I
cannot tell. Oh, I am tired of this! Why can't it be over?
Bach's "Jesu, Joy of Man's Desiring," the baritone playing
the high line. So nice, the way 9/8 time rolls over and over.
The passages come to me clean and sharp-edged. I find it
hard to keep my balance; everything is over-exposed. I sway.
I close my eyes. A Shimatu fantasia. Against the black field
of my eyelids' insides there is a marvelous show of altered
light, little colored worms that burst into existence, crawl
across my vision and disappear. Behind the lights are barely
discernable patterns, geometric tapestries that flare and contract under the pressure of my eyelids. The music is inter-
twined with this odd mandala; when I clamp my eyes hard
there is a sudden rush of blue geometry with a black center,

with it a roll of tympani, swirl of mercury drum, wail of woodwinds, all fitting surely into the fantastic blue patterns that blossom before me. De Bruik's monumental Tenth Symphony, as effortlessly as if I were the conductor and not the performer. My interior field of vision clears and becomes a neutral color, grey or dull purple. Ten clear lines run across it in sets of five. The score. As I play the notes they appear, in long vertical sets as in a conductor's score. They move off to the left as on a computer screen. Excellent. Half-notes, quarter-notes in the bass clef; in the treble, long runs of sixteenth-notes, all like the sun shining through pinholes in dark paper. As far as I can tell the score is perfectly accurate. It is more than one person can play and I don't remember commanding the tape of the Symphony that might be on file to join in, but when I think, "it would be nice to have the aeolia howl through this passage," the airy whistling courses through the music, picking it up as a scrap of paper is picked up in a gale. My fingers are doing it, and yet my mind is not. Play it with everything in you: now every single instrument in the statue is giving voice, the Orchestra spins, the glass arms fiddle and finger and jerk about madly, the great finale of De Bruik's greatest symphony tears about the room, carrying me with it so that my heart beats like a child inside me, trapped and fighting to get out. Nineteen years, Holywelkin, is this what you meant? My mind is doing it, and yet my fingers are not.

The Orchestra plays what I want to hear.

I move into realms of my own, shifting from passage to passage, playing the music I have always searched for, the half-remembered snatches and majestic chords that I have woken up from in the middle of the night, and wished I could recapture; and now the lost time has returned, the lost music is mine. The architecture of Bach, the power of Beethoven, the overwhelming beauty of De Bruik, all confused into a marvel of thought: think it and hear the Orchestra play it at that very instant. The performer the instrument, so that my hands fly about the control booth, my feet, elbows, forehead, all playing, while the essential *I* floats out of the body to observe and to listen, astonished to rapture.

Music. If you are at all alive to it, you will have heard passages that bring a chill to your spine and a flush of blood to your cheeks; a rush of blood through all your skin; and this is a physical response to beauty. The music I am playing now is the very distillation of that feeling, oh, *hear it!*—it soars out and out, I close my eyes, but the rolling score no longer consists of musical notation, it is an impressionist fantasy of a musical score, the background a deep blood red, the notes sudden clusters of jewels or long flows of colors I can't identify even as I see them; yet see them anyway—drums pounding, strings rushing and jumbling, awash in a wave of fortissimo brass shouts, brass floating, triumphant—

. . . triumphant she is as I ascend the dais I can see her face and she is strained and ecstatic as if in labor for to her I am being born again and through the investiture all I can see is her bright face before me unto her a Master is born—

. . . and masterful, chaotic yet perfectly calculated. The score is a *mille fleurs* of twisted colors, falling, falling, the notes are falling in great thirds. I open my eyes and find that they are already stretched wide open; a rush, a rush of red, red is all I see, a blinding waterfall of molten glass cascading down, behind it a thousand suns.

♪

I awake from a dream in which I was . . . in which I was . . . running down alleys. Talking with someone. Perceiving a destiny. I cannot remember.

♪

I am lying on the glass floor of the booth, I can feel the bas-relief of the clef signs. My mouth feels as if it has been washed in acids, which I suppose it has. My legs. My left hand is asleep. I have been poured from my container, my skeleton is gone, I am a lump of flesh. I move my arm. An achievement.

"Johannes," comes the Master's voice, high-pitched in its anxiety. It is probably what awakened me. His hand is on my shoulder. He babbles without pause as he helps me out of the Orchestra, "I just got here, you're all right, you're all right, the music you were playing, my God, here, here, watch out, you're all right, my son—"

"I am blind," I croak. There is a pause, a gasp. He holds me in his arms, half carries me onto a cot of some sort, muttering in a strained voice as he moves me about.

"Horrible, horrible," he keeps saying. "Horrible." It is age old. Lose your sight, and learn to see. Or learn . . . something. I blink away tears for my lost vision, and cannot see myself blink.

"You will make a great Master," he says firmly.

I do not answer.

"The blindness will not make any difference at all."

And after a long pause—

"Yes," I say, wishing he understood, wishing there was someone who understood, "I think it will."

Chapter One

||: **THE MUSIC** :||
OF THE SPHERES

the exemplar of contemplation

Dear Reader, two whitsuns orbit the planet Uranus; one is called Puck, the other, Bottom. They burn just above the swirling clouds of that giant planet, and with the help of the planet's soft green light they illuminate all that dark corner of the solar system. Basking in the green glow of this trio are a host of worlds—little worlds, to be sure, worlds no bigger (and many smaller) than the asteroid Vesta—but worlds, nevertheless, each of them encased in a clear sphere of air like little villages in glass paperweights, and each of them a culture and society unto itself. These worlds orbit in ellipses just outside the narrow white bands of Uranus's rings; you might say that the band of worlds forms a new ring in the planet's old girdle: the first dozen made of ice chunks held in smooth planes, the newest made of an irregular string of soap bubbles, filled with life. And what holds all these various worlds together, what is their *lingua franca*? Music.

Our story, then, has its beginning—one of its beginnings—on one of these worlds, the one called Holland. Holland is a somewhat irregular moonlet, verdant in its lowlands, bare and moorish on its hilltops, which the locals call tors. And in a heather-floored dell, near a pebble-bottomed stream, under one of the tallest of these tors, there stands a lone cottage, sheltered by a single yew tree. Over this cottage, in the spring of the year 3229, a clear dawn pulsed with a pure light; a shaft of this dawn, a Puckish gleam, peered in the cottage window, and inside Dent Ios awoke.

Dent came to consciousness still entangled in a dream, and so he sat up groggy and apprehensive. He had been dreaming that Holland had caught fire, and that it was his job to warn all his neighbors. He had run down the path with a big club in his hands, shouting like Paul Revere and tripping over every stone and root; pounding on doors until they opened and his final blows struck the inhabitants; running from the angry victims, and calling out to houses that they passed as they ran; grabbing canisters to quench small patches of the blaze, and finding he had picked up gasoline; until at last he was felled by a low blow from his own club, so that he sprawled panting in the dust, surrounded by fire.

Cursing the random neuronal firing that produced such visions, Dent climbed out of bed and doused his head under the kitchen tap. Still on the stove top was a big black pan, caked with a layer of hardened bacon grease. Dent wrinkled his nose. It was cool; he stepped into pants, and pulled a thick blouse over his head. Returning from his outhouse, he heard music from the path leading up the dell to his house. Someone was coming. He hurried inside to clean up a bit.

His cottage was a mess. Dirty dishes were stacked on every surface of the kitchen nook, discarded clothing covered the floor, and books and holo cubes were scattered every-where. Dent was one of those on Holland who affected the pastoral style of life popular there, although a close look at his home, crowded as it was with books, musical instruments, sheet music, prints, holo cubes, and computer consoles, revealed his many refined (some on Holland would say over-refined) interests. Though his cottage was nominally a farm, no sign of farming marked its interior—and few signs of farming marked its exterior, if the truth were told. Unlike most of his neighbors, Dent hiked to the local village and bought most of his food, and his neglected tomato patch struggled under an onslaught of weeds. Now he stumbled hastily around his unmade bed, and despaired of ordering the place in time to greet his visitors properly. He resolved to meet them in the yard.

Over the shadowed hills to the east Puck gleamed from the very center of Uranus, so that the planet seemed an immense opal around the diamond chip of the whitsun. This added to the yellow dawn a touch of green that made the dewy heather glow. From the last set of switchbacks on the trail up the dell came the sound of voices. Dent took his long moustaches between soft delicate fingers, and pulled on them desperately: uninvited guests—and in the morning! A crisis!

Three figures appeared over the steepest part of the trail, and Dent relaxed. Approaching were three of his good friends: June Winthrop, Irdar Komin, and Andrew Allendale. June was playing a piano bar, and Irdar and Andrew sang with her. When they saw Dent standing in his yard they waved. "Hill dweller!" June sang. "Three wise ones approach, bearing news!" And the two men flanking her sang peals of harmonized laughter.

Dent led them to the benches under the yew tree, and rubbed dew into the planking. "What brings you here so early? You must have left the village before sunrise."

"Well," June said, "you missed last night's meeting!" And Andrew and Irdar laughed. All four of them were part of the collective that published *Thistledown*, a monthly journal of music criticism and commentary that was considered the best in the Uranus system; the collective met at irregular intervals in the village nestling in the valley below Dent's little dell.

"I'm sorry," Dent said, at a loss. "One of my tapirs was calving."

June laughed sardonically. "I hope you had some assistance! I was with Dent the last time one of his ewes birthed," she told the others, "and he had a vet come and do everything, while he hopped about white as a sheet!"

"I suppose your many past and future marriages make you a qualified *midwife*," Dent said, to the groans of his friends. "Anyway, I'm sorry about the meeting. I hope I didn't miss anything important?"

And his three friends burst into gales of laughter! Annoyed, Dent said, "Please! What happened?"

June played the beginning of Beethoven's Fifth: Fate knocking at the door. "After a long discussion it was decided that *Thistledown* should have a correspondent covering the Grand Tour of Holywelkin's Orchestra."

"Oh my," Dent said distastefully. "I should have thought it beneath us. . . ." Then he saw the looks on his friends' faces, and came to a halt. "Wait a minute—you don't mean—" He stood up. "You don't mean you want me—"

June nodded. "We decided unanimously that you would do the best job."

"No!" Dent cried. He circled the yew in agitation, said simply, "I won't do it."

"You must!" said Andrew cheerfully. "It's just like the presidency—whoever isn't at the meeting gets stuck with it."

"But this is far worse," Dent said. "No, no. It won't do. I simply couldn't." He appealed to June, who currently served as the collective's president. "That Orchestra is nothing but a toy, really, a bauble used to take money away from the ignorant. Why should we cover any sort of tour made with such a thing?"

"There's a new Master of the Orchestra," Irdar said. "Haven't you followed his work?"

"As I say, I have no interest whatsoever in Holywelkin's Orchestra."

"But this Wright is something different. He has been the Master for five years now, and in all that time he hasn't made a single public performance."

"Very wise of him, I'm sure."

"He has only published compositions—etudes, he calls them."

June said, "You reviewed one of them yourself, Dent. I looked it up last night. One of Wright's etudes was published in the Lowell Piano Guild journal, and you praised it highly. Original and strange, you called it."

"Ah," said Dent, remembering the piece. "That was Wright? How unfortunate that he is yoked to such a monstrous instrument."

"But he may change the instrument," Andrew said.

"No," Dent said, "the Institute that owns it will make sure that nothing but light classics are played on it. That's its business. The Master is just the lackey of the board of directors—"

"Not true," June objected. "The Masters are responsible for the repertory. It's just that Yablonski and his predecessor played what the board of directors suggested. But that may change as well. I've heard rumors of friction between Wright and the board, and our Lowell correspondent tells me that Wright was pressured into making this Grand Tour, and that he agreed to only when promised complete artistic control."

"Irrelevant, with that thing," Dent said contemptuously. "What is it after all, some sort of player piano? An orchestrionetta, didn't they call them in Europe? It's preposterous."

June sighed. "You're not being fair. Like it or not, Holywelkin's Orchestra is one of the most famous musical . . . phenomena in all the solar system—in all of history, for that matter. These Grand Tours are one of the few times that music from the outer worlds is performed for the inner planets, so during them modern music is revealed to cultures that are centuries behind, musically. And the results are always interesting. *Thistledown* is the best journal of modern music, and so it follows we must cover this tour.''

"And you're the best man for the job," Andrew exclaimed.

"Nonsense," Dent replied angrily. "My tapir calves, and I am cast across the solar system."

"But that should be an attraction for you," June said. "Have you visited the inner planets?"

"No. And I don't want to."

"Have you ever visited Pluto?" Irdar asked.

"No."

June shook her head. "Where *have* you traveled?"

Dent tucked his chin down defensively. "I've been to Titania and Oberon—"

But he was interrupted by his friends' laughter. "How old are you?" June inquired.

"I am twenty-six."

"Twenty-six, and already an old homebody! Dent. Don't be silly. The chance to travel downsystem doesn't come often."

"But I like it *here*."

"You're the same age as Johannes Wright," Andrew said. "That should make it especially interesting for you."

"At least leaving Holland would get me away from your smirk," Dent said, irritated. "What if they had asked *you* to leave your home for months and months?"

"Come now," June said. "The collective has decided, and we know you are a true Thistledowner, willing to abide by the will of the majority. Go get yourself an instrument, and we'll play some music. You'll get used to the idea, and then you'll be excited by it."

"I will not," Dent said stiffly, and walked up to his cottage to collect himself. Abstractedly he picked up a voicebox, and returned to the yew tree. Puck's light bounced from the lumpy, dewy grass, giving his untended lawn a gray sheen. A flock of New Guinea lories descended on the yew and landed in it, transforming the tree into a statue filled with multi-colored ornaments. Dent looked around his high little valley and groaned.

Sullenly he sat on one of the benches and tuned up with the others. Andrew and Irdar both had flutes, and they blew up and down the C scale merrily. June played a set of seed chords on the piano bar, and they began to improvise a quartet. For all of them music was a language as subtle and expressive as any collection of words, and as they played within the simple sonata form Dent's three friends attempted to create a mood of lightness, of harmony, encouragement and enthusiasm. But as everyone knows, harmony is a matter of consensus; one dissenter, and all is discord. And Dent had the instrumental advantage as well. Over the pleasant clear tones of the piano bar and the two flutes, he cast a hoarse, high voice, keening "noooooo, oh noooooo, nooooo, noooo-ooooooooo," until the others were laughing too hard to continue.

"We'll try again later," June said. "Now Dent, the Grand Tour begins in Lowell during the Outer Worlds May Festival, which is only a month away. You should be off as soon as possible—by tomorrow, in fact. So you'd better start packing. We'll come by later this afternoon with a cart, and help you carry your bags over to the spaceport. And cheer up! I've been downsystem myself, and I know it will be good for you." Irdar and Andrew added their mocking congratulations, and the three of them departed.

Muttering to himself Dent re-entered his cottage, which had suddenly taken on an indescribable charm, and for a while he just stood in it, stunned. Then he went to the sink and scraped bacon grease from his pan. The smell of it filled his nostrils; out his east window, on the green hillside across the creek, a stand of eucalyptus trees blinked olive and rust

and gold. Above them the sky was the color named Holland
blue. His tapirs were hooting for feed—he would have to get
the collective to care for them—

"Damn!" he said, and smacked the pan on the stove,
clang!

♪

the third millennium: a symphony

First movement: *Allegro.* Colonists landed on Mars in
2052. Most of them came from America and the Soviet
Union, and the tension generated by this fusion of the terran
empires helped give the colony its driving energy, its ceaseless conflicts, its utopian spirit. The colonists found enough
water to make Mars an independent world, and that became
the colony's ultimate goal. The terraforming engineers were
given tasks that would take generations to accomplish, and
the rest of Martian society structured itself to do what was
necessary to forward the great project. No colony in history
ever exhibited such initiative; it was a society with a dream.

Ritard: moderato. In 2175 the first permanent settlement
was built on and under the ice of Europa. Again the colonists
went at the task of making a home with a will; but they had
less light, less gravity, and fewer resources of every kind,
including the spiritual. The colonies on Europa, Callisto,
Ganymede and Io never lost the character of outposts, habi-
tats on the edge of the possible. This character was even
more pronounced in the colonies of the Saturnian system. A
settlement was established on Iapetus in 2220, and the other
moons were soon colonized as well. But these colonies resembled grounded spaceships, and their cultures grew strange.
Further expansion to the outer planets seemed a fruitless

enterprise; the Jovian and Saturnian colonies turned inward, and music, the most abstract of the arts, became the center of their lives.

Second movement: *Adagissimo*. Meanwhile, Earth entered a new dark age of upheaval and disaster, famine and conflict. This immense crisis threatened all humanity, as the crushing overpopulation of the home world stressed the resources of the entire solar system. Even with the cooperative efforts of all the nations it was impossible to avoid devastating famines. All the energy of humanity had to be devoted to saving Earth's billions. This was no simple project, and it required centuries of grim retrenchment. The world economic system had to be restructured to more closely resemble a closed ecology; this entailed severe hardships for all. And so the race hunkered down for survival, and the space colonies anxiously watched the dark age plod on. Only Mars, continually working at its great project, made any significant progress.

Third movement: *Intermezzo agitato*. All during this long dark age, however, science advanced, particularly on Mercury. There the physicists of the rolling city of Terminator provided an immense influx of energy to Earth and Mars, and in the orbit of Mercury subatomic studies were advancing toward the construction of the Great Synchrotron. The Synchrotron and the Orbital Gevatron yielded uncanny results which left the physicists in a confused, excited ferment of theory. . . .

Fourth movement: *Accelerando*. Arthur Holywelkin wrote his *Ten Forms of Change*, a grand unified theory that proved to be tremendously powerful. Physicists took his work and applied it to the unprecedented amounts of energy available just above the coronal flare zone of the sun. And they found that with their new understanding they could concentrate and transfer that energy from one point to another. And they could contract it to singularities that, within the confines of a spherical discontinuity, pulled inward with gravitational force beyond their apparent mass. Discontinuity physics was the

key; the door to the solar system was unlocked. One gee
colonies illuminated by projected flares of the sun were
established on hundreds of moons and asteroids, and the
organic world bloomed everywhere. Millions of people left
Earth and Mars for the new worlds, and the age known as the
Accelerando began.

♪

first crossing

Come then, Reader, whose spirit I love for embarking on
this voyage, and follow Dent Ios across the vacuum to Pluto,
the ninth planet. The plane of the planets is divided into three
hundred and sixty degrees, with 0 degrees lying in the direction of Pisces. In the spring of 3229, Uranus is at 188
degrees, Pluto at 225. (Neptune and its great satellite Triton
are across the system at 110 degrees, and therefore will not
be visited by this Grand Tour.) So we have a voyage of over
twelve astronomical units to make, in less than a month:
accelerate, dear Reader! Dent Ios travels on the spaceliner
Pauline; we trail behind, pure spirits in the impure vacuum.

As we approach Pluto we must dodge hundreds of ships
like the *Pauline*, for the Outer Worlds May Festival has
begun, and as the outer planets (except for Neptune), and
therefore many of the outer terras, are in the same quadrant
this year, there are many celebrants attending. Spaceships
orbit the planet in broad strings, following the moon Charon;
shuttle craft descend to the black crater-shocked surface of
Pluto, and then rise again. The planet seems at first to display
only its bleak, primordial surface, but there against the black
horizon, see a greenish hemisphere of light. There a Holywelkin
sphere extends half above, half below the surface; and there

under the upper half of the invisible discontinuity is air, light, warmth, and all the bustle of human existence; a city under a clear dome, there on the dead surface of Pluto. Further inspection reveals a number of these green bulbs of life, some set on high plateaus, some set in craters so that crater walls serve as a low "foundation" for their bubble domes, others set in rift valleys, in strings of hemispheres so that short rivers can run. The largest of these cities, tucked under a set of hemispheres on the Tartarus Planitia, is Lowell, the home of the festival. Down there, when we cross the discontinuity, we will find a million celebrants, a thousand stages; we will find the Holywelkin Institute of Music, and Holywelkin's Orchestra, and the Orchestra's board of directors and its chairman Ernst Ekern, and the road crew for the Orchestra's Grand Tour, and Johannes Wright; and, although currently he is delayed and orbiting outside Charon, we will soon find Dent Ios. Let us descend and break into that soap bubble of a world.

♪

the exemplar of action

Lowell, the largest city on Pluto, is a rough and scattered place, once described as "five hundred concrete blocks dropped on a cow pasture." On the roof of Lowell's power plant—the tallest building in the city—the road crew for the Grand Tour scrambled to ready the Orchestra for its first concert. Margaret Nevis, crew manager, discussed the city's acoustic problems with Delia Rosario, her sound chief; each city's combination of overlapping hemispheres, like a multi-domed cathedral, had resonances all its own, and the amplifiers had to be adjusted accordingly.

Margaret brushed long black hair out of her eyes, and wiped the sweat from her brow onto her workpants. She was a tall woman, broad-shouldered and strong. When a bank of Collidoscope lights beside her burst on, bathing the Orchestra in its disorienting patchwork of colors, annihilating distances, she shouted, "Turn that off!" She originated from Saturn's moon Iapetus, where Russian is the primary language, and her English was idiomatic but harshly accented. "How are we supposed to see?"

"But Margaret," a voice whined peevishly. It was Anton Vaccero, her new lighting chief. In the light his red hair looked like a crown of flame. "How will I know what the show will look like?"

"You'd better know already," Margaret said. "Now turn those off. Other people have work to do." She walked over to the thin plastic partitions that had been set up around the perimeter of the roof to hide the Orchestra from the crowd below. Anton followed her, and pointed between two panels. There one segment of Lowell pulsed under banks of lazed light, packed light, bent light, broken light . . . Margaret disliked the effect. "It hurts the eyes," she said.

"You'd better get used to it."

"I will never get used to it. Look at all those people." The city below shifted and heaved like a honeycomb under bees: people everywhere. Each rooftop patio was packed, and the grassy open land between the clumps of buildings was mobbed.

"Have you been to the May festival before?" Anton asked.

"Yes. I was the manager for Yablonski's last tour. But I liked it no better then."

"You don't have crowds like this on Iapetus?"

"I suppose. But they are different. You Plutonians are strange edgefolk. Even your cities show this. On the terras you can forget where you are—all is green, the sky is blue— they are like little Earths. Iapetus is different, but even there great continents of life have been created. Here, every town is like an oasis, overlooking some black abyss."

"It's deliberate," Anton said. "We do it to remind ourselves where we really are."

Margaret gestured out at the city's edge, where the hemisphere of air and light ended abruptly and the crater-ringed surface of Tartarus began. "And that is strange."

The Planck Double Reed squawked loudly. "There's something wrong with that amp," Margaret said.

"Or with the Orchestra."

"No—there's seldom a problem with the Orchestra itself, I've found." Margaret called for Delia, fitting her shouts in between squawks. "Delia!" *EhhnnnnnRAHN!*—"Delia!"

Then there was a flurry at the elevator door, and several people appeared there. Anton stepped back against the panel. Margaret walked over to greet Karnasingh Godavari, her security chief. He smiled at her briefly, then looked about the roof, frowning slightly at the dark and the bustle. He was as tall as Margaret, black-haired and dark-skinned. As his people spread out to search the roof the two of them conferred. "How does it look?" Margaret said.

Karna shook his head nervously and didn't reply. Margaret had hired him as security chief for her last four tours, and she knew that his silence meant he was at work. He gestured at the elevator.

Two of his employees emerged, flanking a short, slight man. A certain hush fell over the workers, so that the din from the city below was more evident. There was a smattering of applause, and Margaret said loudly, "Get to work." Johannes Wright did not appear to notice either the applause or her command. He headed straight for the Orchestra, tilted his head back to peer into it. Margaret went to his side and he looked up at her.

"Hello, Margaret. Will we be ready on time?"

"We're ready now, almost. But Delia is having trouble with the Double Reed's amp. Maybe you could help her."

He nodded. The photoptic cells that had replaced his eyes glinted, reflecting Anton's enprism lights. They did a good job with the cells, Margaret thought, they looked like real eyes; still, when you are looking into the face of a man with two artificial eyes, you know it.

Delia appeared and Wright led her into the Orchestra. Around Margaret people were arguing over electrical connections, pounding with hammers, firing away with staple guns. She wiped sweat from her forehead and grinned, enjoying the work. She returned to Karna's side.

"How did he seem to you?" she asked.

Karna shrugged. "Quiet. I don't know what that means. Do you know him well?"

"No. I met him when I managed Yablonski's last tour, but only briefly. As apprentice he didn't come along."

"Ah." Karna was distracted. "Listen, Margaret." He guided her to a corner of the roof. Frowning, he said, "My people have heard things down on the street that I don't like. Someone said that Wright will be killed on this tour."

"*What?*"

"I know. It's bad news. It makes me nervous."

"But it's absurd!"

"Yes. It may just be part of the festival craziness—nothing to it. But Marie-Jeanne was on the street when a man came up to her and said, 'The Greys are going to kill the Master this time.' "

The Double Reed honked mournfully, like a foghorn. "The Greys," Margaret said. She knew little of them; they were one of the more obscure religions, and tended, she thought, to congregate downsystem. "But how would anybody but a Grey know about it?"

Karna shrugged. "True."

"And someone just said this out of the vacuum to Marie-Jeanne?"

"It was probably just nonsense. But . . ."

"We'll have to keep an eye out," Margaret said.

"Yes." Karna peered anxiously up into the glass arms of

the Orchestra, which under the lights were an autumn blaze of gold and red, brown and silver.

♪

ernst ekern

Ernst Ekern stood on the roof of the Holywelkin Institute, apart from the small group of acquaintances who had joined him for the concert. Some of his guests were members of the Orchestra's board of directors; others were fellows of his secret order, and they mingled with the unknowing board members with ease, as if to mock Ekern with the incongruity. He ignored them and peered out over the commons below. The banks of light set on certain public rooftops around the city were conspiring to make the rooftops appear islands in a wave-filled sea of light, a rainbow ocean. The heads of the people rippled like sea-cabbage under a surging tide. All manner of bizarre and pathetic hopes were represented in those drowned heads below. And on the rooftop islands in that sea of madness stood concert parties, chattering in their gardens—the aristocracy, waiting for his Orchestra to be revealed. Between the two crowds patterns of relationship swirled; shouts exchanged could be jovial or insulting. In his group the tangled pattern of relationship shifted continuously as fellows of his order circled the roof and engaged board members in conversation. The Magus herself explained to the board's senior vice president the nature of her friendship with Ekern; all a complex lie. And Atargatis stood alone in the corner by a lemon tree, his bright eyes observing all. Diana might be the Magus, but it was Atargatis whom Ekern respected (and therefore feared)—Atargatis of the bright looks and the subtle mind.

But, he thought, it was Ekern who controlled all the patterns that swirled around him: the concert and the crowd, the garden party and his fellows. He stared across the town through disorienting light to the top of the power plant. There an octet of panels lowered like a blossom unfolding, and standing like the complex pistil of the flower was Holywelkin's Orchestra. It began very slowly to rotate, and the crowd roared. Interwoven with the roar was the beginning of the music, an imitation of the crowd's shouting that rose out of it into song. Chromatic clickings crossed and crossed again, and Ekern's company stopped talking. Many of them fell into the half trance necessary to follow the intricacies of the typically thick Plutonian musical style, a polymelodic mesh of sound in which one had to seek for the patterns in a weave as dense as chaos. . . . Almost automatically Ekern began to fall into this listening trance, although he did not want to; he wanted to observe his party and the whole city, to see the effect of the music on them, and so he struggled back up from the impact of the music's beginning as from a sudden immersion under water. Clear of it now, and with that freedom came the usual surge of elation, at the feeling of control; for he controlled not only his own mind, but also that *omphalos* of the city that everyone else now helplessly attended: he was the true Master of the Orchestra. And yet—the music, there—and there—and there—the phrases were like premonitions in sound, they were the forms of premonitions without the content, and Ekern shuddered as his memory was brushed ever so lightly by images of the end of the concert—of concerts to come. . . . He shook off these vague impressions and regained control by forcing the music into a single thing, a lump of inchoate sound irrevocably outside him. There: success. His power was greater than Wright's—and yet listen to that!—a sudden wash of music over him; he shook himself free of it again. Emotions roiled in him, forming a wild confluence. *He* was in control, the power to conduct, to point at the crowd and say *move now, shout now, cry now* was his,

his and no one else's. (And yet—) He determined all the conditions that had created this music, and the puppet in the machine was only playing what he, Ekern, maneuvered him to. (A great falling screech from the Planck Reed) but to think of Wright instantly brought to Ekern's flailing imagination the image of Wright in the Orchestra, at that moment, playing before all: and the terror of performance raced through his blood. In this panic Atargatis's steady eye pierced him most acutely. The great live oak tree spun, throwing out running clicking tension, strands of melody melting away the moment his ear acknowledged them . . . keeping a stoic front for Atargatis helped him to resist this assault, as it tended to distract him entirely. Must show nothing, must display complete control . . . not an easy thing to do in this tempest of sound. That Wright was a bad one, all right. Ekern had opposed him all down the line, his original investiture, the decision to keep him after he destroyed his eyes, the suicidal fool—and since then. . . . But there! Down in the streets the masses were battling! A tall figure in a green coat darted through the crowd like a bottom fish, leaving swirls of anger, shouts that fit the music's powerful pulse. All sound was stripped away to the wail of the godzilla, the low ominous canon of basses and triple basses. His guests stood like statues of Lot's wife, all but Atargatis, who like Ekern himself now paced the garden in a nervous, undirected walk. Bass waves flirted with the subsonic, twenty hertz oscillating in the stomach, and all of Ekern's fierce resistance disappeared: this music was *terror*. Each new basal distortion rent the air, struck at the swirling crowd, brought Ekern to such peaks of fear and despair that he had to pace about to counter them, thinking it's only music, only sound. But there . . . "No!" he cried out, and immediately felt humiliated. But no one could hear him. Then he saw that while the directors of the Institute still stood frozen at attention, all the members of his order were free of the music, it was just noise to them now, they were from downsystem and didn't understand; and as he saw this his own understanding fell away as well, the sounds became only an unnatural rapid tumbling of bass tones. The storm-tossed crowd shrieked and screamed, the fellows of the order watched him and he met their eyes, he nodded, feeling his control return in an exhilarating rush, he pointed up at the Orchestra, saying against the din, Yes, yes, this is the start of it. This is the start of my performance in the art without a stage. The opening act. The others attempted no response; there was none to make. Ekern's conception was gigantic, his execution flawless. Groups in the mass below jumped up and down rhythmically. Fists pummelled bodies frozen in the strobe of broken light. All on their own Ekern's fists clenched as well, and he longed to leap into the crowd and flail away, oh, this Johannes Wright was evil! His music was dangerous—destructive—worthy of destruction. It was fitting to Ekern's higher art, the art that would contain it; it made a stunning opening burst to the play that his order was here to witness. How the Magus rolled her eyes! How the others shivered, plugged their ears, glanced in awe toward Ekern! Great storm waves pulsed in the crowd below, the noise was a force battering at all, it was an ambient fluid they swam in, Atargatis spoke to Ekern and Ekern saw only the ironic mouth, moving. One could shriek like the damned in this assault and it would mean nothing to the man beside you. Ekern ignored Atargatis's disturbing mouth, he said, "I will end you. I will finish you," as if thinking to himself. Turning his back on all the rooftop audience he burst into strained laughter. The rainbow ocean made its tidal surge, the lights turned everywhere upward, lazing, splitting, prisming, chroming the air; the coda of Wright's formless roar echoed from the discontinuity of the spheres. Ekern's senses were overwhelmed, he burned in a blaze of triumph; he held onto the roof patio railing for support, feeling like Iago on the battlements of Cyprus.

♪

retrogradation

Unfortunately for Dent Ios, there was a mistake in the scheduling of the shuttle flight from the transCharon orbits to Lowell, and a subsequent delay of an hour or two. When the shuttle came to a halt Dent ran down the tunnel to Lowell's terminal and hurried to a small festival information booth.

"When will Holywelkin's Orchestra perform?" he asked.

The guide in the booth looked surprised. "It's just over, friend. You're late."

"It's *over*?"

"Ended half an hour ago."

Dent struck his head with the palm of his hand. "Late! Late! Damn this tour!" Dent cursed June and his collective, his spaceliner and the shuttle crews, Johannes Wright and his stupid Orchestra: "Exiled to Pluto to witness this spectacle, and then kept from seeing it! And the next concert of the Grand Tour is right back home on Titania." It was too much.

Still seething, Dent walked down a corridor to the space-port's tall entrance, where it opened out onto a broad boulevard of some sort. Altered light of all kind pulsed over the city, making it a jumble of color. And it was very noisy. "Oh my," Dent said. "Impossible. I'm not going out there." He returned to the information booth. "When does the next shuttle leave for the transCharon orbits?"

The guide consulted a schedule. "At about six tomorrow morning, sir. That's about eight hours from now."

"Eight hours!"

"Yes. The last one just left, so it'll be a while before the next one goes."

"Of course." Dent stormed off to a waiting room adjacent to the corridor. "I will wait here," he declared to the empty room. "I'll be damned if I go out into that chaos when the whole reason for being here is gone." And he plumped down in a thickly upholstered chair.

Nearly an hour passed. From outside came faint shouts and howls of revelry; bent light bounced around the corners and bathed the chamber from time to time in its ghastly blue glow; and the seconds on the wall clock made their slow plod round to sixty, again and again. Dent had nothing to read, and his nails were already tended to. Boredom crept up on him. And from outside came brief snatches of music, conflicting strains from what he assumed were competing concerts. Slowly but surely Dent's curiosity overcame his fastidiousness; besides, if he toured the streets after Wright's concert, he could reproach his collective with whatever meager news he could gather.

So he got up and went outside. The air was warm and humid, thick with the smoke of bonfires and the smell of sweat. Packed light dazzled his vision and shouts struck his eardrums like fists. "My," he said, blood stirring. "This is awful!"

He started walking toward what appeared to be the center of town, where the buildings were the tallest. The irregular streets of Lowell were paved with a tough grass, and they were flanked by oddly spaced three- and four-story buildings; most of the streets were as wide as boulevards, and seemed to function as parks, at least during the festival. Big pits in certain intersections held bonfires, and everywhere parties of people stood or sat in clumps and circles, so that Dent had to weave his way through the crowd, slipping into streams of celebrants taking the same route. Eventually they led him to what someone said was Tombaugh Square, a big park in the city's center; the utilities building stood on one side of this square, and apparently the Orchestra had been placed on it during the concert, so that the park was still jammed. In all the commotion Dent didn't know what to do next. A very large woman ran into him, knocking him down. As he got up he cried, "What was the concert like?" The woman

only laughed, revealing teeth that had been stained bright
red. "Too drugged to remember it, are you?" she shouted.
"No!" Dent replied, but she was gone. He cursed her back
angrily.

Still, the exchange had given him a method. He wandered
between groups, looking for single individuals who appeared
congenial. In the altered light it was difficult to tell; shafts of
packed inthrob light made people appear living flames, clothed
in leaves of fire. Dent walked on. Across the park two oak
trees bracketed a small bonfire; in the light of the blaze it
might be possible to distinguish real features. Keeping his
hands out as bumpers, Dent slowly crossed the square. Beams
of spectralite, ultra, rodercone, and enprism assaulted him;
even with his eyes closed he saw some of these lights, and
walked through a kaleidoscope of shattered color.

Beyond the oak trees a brace of water buffalo lowed
uneasily, tugging at their tethers. The bonfire between the
trees was rendered invisible by a sudden burst of inthrob. A
friendly looking man with a beard stood contemplating the
phenomenon. "What did you think of the performance?"
Dent asked him.

The man pulled his beard and grinned. "Sir, that young
man lazed us! He packed us, he lazed us, he bent us, and
then he shattered us!"

"You're a light technician, I take it."

"Not at all. But that young Master certainly is. And he'll
bring us all back to the white light of the godhead, you mark
my words."

Dent walked away, shaking his head. Perhaps these inter-
views were not going to be of help after all.

Suddenly he noticed a curious thing. There was no music
being played anywhere in the square. This was so unusual as
to be freakish. Typically after a concert of this sort soloists or
small groups would be recreating by memory various parts of
the performance, transposing them for the instrument they
played; at a festival like this there would be so many street

groups that the competition for sound spheres would be fierce. But tonight . . . nothing. The oscillant chatter of hundreds of voices in conversation—but no music. Dent bit his lip, stared about uncomfortably. What had Wright played, to cause such silence?

He approached a smallish woman standing alone. "What did you think of the concert?"

A bank of polychrom lights snapped on and suddenly the woman's round face and long braids were broken into primary colors, as if Dent had stepped too close to a pointillist painting. She looked awful, and Dent supposed he looked the same. "Truly a disgrace to the Orchestra," the woman said. "Wright's technique was sloppy and he overused the tape systems dreadfully. It's a sad contrast to Yablonski, who played every instrument live. And the music was no more than reworked De Bruikian polyphony." She nodded emphatically, shifting her facial colors in a way that made Dent almost sick. He marvelled that there was so much green in flesh tone.

A trio of Martian bagpipers ran from the building behind the trees, skreeling like banshees. With a howl members of the crowd raced after them, chasing them around the trees and into Dent and the woman. Dent leaped back. The trio's assailants were attempting to stop them, but the Martians were half again as tall as their hunters, and they kicked out in a Highland dance made martial art, keeping the crowd at bay. Then one was tackled and the other two went to his aid, and the piping stopped. A woman in a long red coat broke into a wild Arabic ululation, and dove into the melee swinging her fists. "My God!" Dent cried, and skittered away, startled by the violence. Something was wrong with this festival—he bumped into someone and turned, ready to run. He was facing a tall skinny man with a bony face, on which were painted red "whiskers." The man grinned wolfishly and the red lines across his cheeks folded in.

Dent stepped back nervously. "What did you think of the concert, sir?"

"Why do you want to know?" the man said.

"Well—I missed it, and it's left me in sort of a gray area. I am a correspondent—"

"You are not," the man growled. "Why do you want to know!" he shouted, and pushed Dent hard in the chest.

Dent tumbled backwards onto the grass. "Excuse me," he said, crawling rapidly away. "Just curious—I have a right to ask—"

And was shoved off his knees onto his side. A kick to the midriff and his breath was gone. While he lay gasping rough hands pulled at his coat, searched the pockets, tore his wallet away. "We'll find out who you are right enough." "Gaaa—" Another kick and he was beyond speech.

After a while he sat up. Enprism lights scattered the scene before him into several illusory dimensions. The oak trees seemed leaved with emeralds. Someone was pulling at his arm. "Are you all right?"

"Need police," Dent said.

"There are no police on Lowell," said the bearded man he had spoken to earlier.

"But—how do you get help?"

"I'm helping you, aren't I?"

"But what if you're attacked?"

"Then you defend yourself. What, lose a fight?"

"I was robbed."

"Ah." The man pulled him up by his elbow, and Dent stood, hunched over. "That's bad. Here, need a hand somewhere?"

"Thanks. I'm all right." Dent took a few exploratory steps.

"They'll be able to identify you at the spaceport. You shouldn't have any problem. You weren't carrying anything valuable?"

"No. Thanks again." Dent hobbled off. He tacked back

down the boulevard like a boat in a storm: voices howled like the wind, shouts cracked like thunder, banks of light burst over him like bolts of lightning. A Martian in a purple dress loomed over him and chanted, "Holywelkin didn't mold it for play, there's too much chance in music today!" A man behind her pointed at Dent and shouted, "He's the one who did it! He's the one!"

"Not me," Dent bleated, and staggered into a side street. Here alleys were coiled like the tracks of positrons, and he lost himself. It seemed hours of walking and dodging passed before he could relocate the boulevard. By the time he saw the spaceport entrance he could barely walk. Persephone, Pluto's whitsun, broke over the eastern horizon like another bank of lights. Suddenly the air of the city glowed a real blue, and one by one the banks of altered light were shut down. Looking north Dent could see all the way to Tombaugh Square. Everyone around him spoke in a language he didn't recognize. It was dawn: only bonfires and the limpid blue sky lit the town now. A great roar of protesting voices washed over them all. Exhausted, hurt, Dent hobbled to the spaceport; its facade flickered under the dusky yellow light of a dying bonfire. In the doorway he turned for one last look. The shouting was like the roar of high seas on a beach.

♪

inversion

Johannes Wright—remember him, dear Reader?—the musician who glimpsed his destiny?—Johannes Wright was tired. He sank back into the couch against the wall of a lounge in the power plant, and let everything wash over him. Voices of Marie-Jeanne and Rudyard, chatting quietly with Margaret.

His old friend Anton Vaccero, laughing nervously over a game of cups, played with two of Karna's security people. Grainy texture of light as he allowed the photoptic cells to unfocus. He looked at the blur that was Margaret: raven blue-black hair tossed in a reflexive gesture over a shoulder. The ophthalmologists had told him the photoptic cells would enable him to distinguish about a thousand colors, as opposed to the six million gradations visible to the natural eye. The cell was as sensitive as the retina, they said, but the connection to the optic nerve was inferior. A poster world: it could be beautiful. Even if seven or eight hundred of the thousand colors were some shade of blue. He faded into the grainy blue-out drowsily. The wall behind Margaret yellow, yellow-green, aquamarine, and yet on it a dark blue stain . . . her shadow, of course. A certain processing problem there. Some time during his seven months of blindness, he thought, he had forgotten how to see; and now eyes meant nothing to him, sight was an alien sense. What if you could suddenly distinguish the gases in the air around you, or feel magnetism like static electricity, or see the gravity created at the center of a sphere? It wouldn't do you any good, not without a teacher. Looking at the world of the wall Johannes saw that inanimate objects were formed always as false parallels, while all living things were stacks of intersected ellipses. Or else he had been reading too much Mauring geometry in his attempt to understand Holywelkin. Margaret's powerful shoulders, a field of ellipses, slumped against the couch back: in the extremity of blue-out he felt he could see all her veins. He drifted off toward sleep, the shutter of all the senses.

Anton's familiar laugh cut off abruptly. Wright focused his eyes.

Ernst Ekern stood in the doorway. The room was silent. Wright struggled up out of the couch and stood. ''Yes?''

Ekern stepped farther into the room, looked around. He was nearly as short as Wright, a thick man running to fat. To

Johannes he jumped out of the grainy blue because of his coloring: curly white hair on top of his head shaded to white-gray curls at the back, and whitish sideburns shaded to a reddish-brown beard. Redbeard, Johannes had called him in the days of his apprenticeship. Round puffy nose, sharp intelligent brown eyes.

Redbeard said, "I want to speak with you, Johannes."

His crew roused themselves as if to leave. "No," Ekern said to them. "Stay here." He said to Johannes, "There's another lounge across the hall."

Johannes followed him, and together they entered an empty, dim lounge. A rustle came from behind a large mirror and in his poster vision, blue on blue, he saw clearly that it was a window as well. He turned to face Ekern. He was too tired for the passions, and their stormy history seemed silly to him now, the squabbling of children for dominance. He had never understood Ekern's dislike of him; it had no cause, no motive. Ekern paced the other side of the room, wall to wall, slowly as if to some adagio march. All his ellipses were squashed to a near perfect circularity, the effect of tremendous control exerted. Yet such an effort could never be successful, and Johannes almost laughed: hernia as the elliptical result of crushing ellipses to roundness. Then Ekern stopped and faced him, and smiled. And that smile was the crack in the wall, it split all the pretenses of civility; through it seeped all Ekern's long-tended hatred. Johannes stiffened and woke up fully at last.

"So you have begun your first Grand Tour," Ekern said quietly, and commenced pacing again. His voice was a fine baritone, exquisitely modulated, with a touch of roughness in its timbre. It had the sound of a great cat's purr.

"Yes," Johannes said, fumbling. "Yes."

"And it was quite a beginning."

Meaning what? Johannes shook his head. Fragments, the barest part of the whole. He had a lot of work to do. It would take more study, and some sort of . . . key. Yet even now he pushed at the edge of his understanding.

"You were not satisfied?" Ekern asked.

"No."

"Then we have something in common," Ekern purred, and paced. In the dim blue light his red beard glowed. Johannes felt a draft, and shivered. What was this man in the shadows after?

"You play only your own compositions," Ekern said, with a quick glance.

"That is what the Orchestra is for."

"You play only your own compositions. Work unknown to the public. You base your compositions on Holywelkin's mathematics—on his *Ten Forms of Change*, in fact."

"Yes," said Johannes, surprised. "How did you know?"

"I have studied you." Ekern stopped pacing, stared at Johannes curiously. "I have had to study you, Johannes Wright, to know what to do with you. And now I know more about you than you do."

Johannes shook his head, annoyed and fearful. "You know nothing," he said. "No one knows anything of me." Yet he had thought the basis of his work was known to himself alone. His notes—Ekern must have had his notebooks searched. There the broken twigs of his passage could be found, but what would they signify to an outsider? Nothing.

"So you attempt what De Bruik attempted, in her *Free Radical Binds to Macromolecule*."

"We all attempt what De Bruik attempted, in one way or another." In *Free Radical* De Bruik had represented the macromolecule, an RNA strand, as a passacaglia, a ground base repeated again and again, in patterns of four that alternated regularly. This was a simple icon, a metaphor in which the repeated ground base stood for the repeated proteins in the RNA; fine. And the free radical's part was a test for any trumpet player. But the problem always returned to the question of how to yoke together the two terms of the metaphor.

What was the analogy between certain pitches of a certain duration, and strings of protein molecules? For De Bruik it had been no more than an impression, an instinctive meta- phor made from scattered readings of, and the one crucial meeting with, the elderly Holywelkin—a matter of feeling. But Johannes was convinced it was possible to be more exact; he wanted to make a musical analogy for the world that was precisely accurate. . . .

". . . Music based on physics," Ekern said. He had been speaking for some time, but Johannes had been distracted, and now he was at a loss. "It certainly *sounds* disturbing enough," Ekern said. "It drove the crowd mad." He cocked his head, as if understanding the music by that remark. "And here you are commencing a Grand Tour. With nothing famil- iar in your repertory. An unprecedented program."

"Hull the third Master and Mayaklosov the sixth Master played only their own work," Johannes said. From behind the mirror-window, a rustle, a muffled cough.

"Every third a sport, eh? But those were considered nadirs in the Orchestra's history."

"Not by me."

Ekern smiled; another crack, another seepage. Johannes shook his head apprehensively. What did he want?

Again Ekern paced. "You make your first Grand Tour. The Orchestra is famous everywhere, people will flock to hear you. Through the layers of history back to ancient Earth you will travel, playing your new composition, changing it as you go along, revising and completing it. On Mars there will be a festival to make Lowell's look like a tea party; all the planet will gather at Olympus Mons for their Areology. And you will play music they have never heard. Then to ancient Earth and the awe of those capitals, in the homes of our minds; a triumph, certainly. But for whom? What will they make of you? What will become of the Grand Tours to come, of Holywelkin's Orchestra?"

Johannes shrugged, stepped toward the door, away from

the darkness surrounding Ekern, red patch in the blues. "I choose the music played," he said, feeling Ekern's message in the oblique description.

"So you do," Ekern said. "You choose it. You compose it, and not the spirit of Holywelkin. Not the spirit of Holywelkin, do you understand me?"

"No," Johannes said, feeling a stab of fear.

"Holywelkin's influence would change your mind."

"No!" Johannes said. "I know Holywelkin better than you."

"Ah!" And Ekern paced in the gloom, back and forth, back and forth. Johannes felt the ominous silence. Shivering, he tensed his eye muscles to try to *see* his foe better. Red beard dull in the dark.

"You have studied Holywelkin, then?" said the rough baritone voice.

"Very well."

"Then you know."

"Know what?"

A long pause, two turns, a sudden stop. Redbeard staring straight at him, shadowed eyes intent. "You know."

A shiver rippled up the skin over Johannes's spine. What had he missed? What did Ekern mean, what did he know, thus to assume Johannes's understanding? Holywelkin had been a strange man, secretive, eccentric, unpredictable—the Kepler of the Thirtieth century; everything one knew about him contradicted some other fact of his biography. It could be anything—

Unless he meant the heart of things. The meaning of Holywelkin's work.

Johannes came to and saw that in the course of his pacing Ekern had approached him. He took a step back. Moved to the mirror, touched it. In the mirror world Ekern's beard was a dull green, the room was flattened and the air was gray. Too much obscurity—he turned—

Ekern pointed at him, finger like a gun. "I will change you," he said, and hopped past Johannes out the door.

Heart pulsing like a knock at the door. Johannes rubbed a cold hand over his chest. The dim room still seemed quite occupied. He left it with a shudder and walked down the hall, unwilling to face his road crew in this state of amorphous dread. Hallways, quiet and dim. All those years of dissension with Ekern . . . from the very first meeting he had been a bitter antagonist. Yablonski had introduced him, and Ekern had sneered: "So *this* is your apprentice." And for *no reason*. There had been no *cause* for his hostility. The memory of it was so disturbing that Johannes willed himself to think of something else.

He recalled his evening's performance. He had programmed into the Orchestra's computer the equations of two of Holywelkin's ten forms, and then chosen tones in the bass to represent lazed glints, leaving the singularity sphere of one of the power stations orbiting the sun. The effect of two of the forms of change on these glints, scored for the bass instruments: inversion and retrogradation, vertical and horizontal reversals, made repeatedly until the score was sufficiently complicated. And very important forms of change they were, too. But until all of the forms were brought to bear simultaneously—as they were in reality—he would not be satisfied. There had been too many centuries of partial music already. Holywelkin had struggled with this problem before him; in his last notebook he had written, *in the complete glint mechanics all apparent motion must be taken into account.* . . .

Considering these matters Johannes walked by the door to the storage room, where the Orchestra waited for the voyage to Uranus. He paused, but did not enter.

♪

the orchestra's song

And by not entering, missed what occurred inside: such turns, such unnoticed forks in unnoticed paths, determine all our lives.

It was almost dark in the storage room; only a red light high on one wall illuminated the Orchestra, which nearly filled the chamber. Against the door stood a tall figure, limbs taut and ready for flight. When the footsteps in the hall outside receded, the figure moved into the room, toward the Orchestra. The red light accentuated the color of his curly hair; it was Anton Vaccero, the lighting chief for the tour. In his left hand was a small bag, and on his face was a blank expression. He circled the Orchestra warily, found the entrance through the piano bench gap. Up and inside, then, and following the glass steps that made a twisting path to the control booth. But once there he continued to climb, past the row of saxophones, and the quartet of tympanis, up into the twisting glass branches where people rarely visited. At that height there were few steps, and Vaccero's long, lithe arms and legs served him well as he stretched from foothold to foothold, spreadeagling as he climbed higher. The cloud of violas formed an obstacle that was difficult to get past; the big brown fiddles rested in delicate glassy carriages composed of bow-arms, finger tabs, *pizzicatta* pluckers, and tuning dials, so that they appeared oddly shaped fruit encased in a rime of reddish frost. Vaccero descended, took an easier path up. He shifted the bag from hand to hand according to need, and grasped the thick clear struts carefully. He was wearing thin gloves.

Eventually he came to the celesta, with its white soundbox and its elegant ivory keyboard, encrusted with glass finger tabs. The arms holding the instrument were thick, and Vaccero stood on two of them to complete his work. The top panel of the soundbox rose easily, revealing the narrow steel plates

that the instrument's hammers struck. Vaccero put the bag on
the plates and drew from it a pair of brackets and a short
hammer. From his blouse pocket he took nails just bigger
than tacks, and reaching into the soundbox he tapped away
awkwardly until the brackets were nailed to the inside of the
box. Then he took from the bag a small notebook, with stiff
plastic covers. He glanced at the pages with a quick riffle;
they were filled with a spidery handwriting. He slid the
notebook into the brackets, shook it to make sure it was
firmly in place. Then he let the top of the soundbox down,
and descended as quickly as he could through the maze of
glass.

The door was a test; what to say, if he emerged and
somebody saw him? Screw your courage to the sticking
place: a musical metaphor, referring to the mandolin. Holding
his breath he slipped out. No one saw him.

And the Orchestra was alone. A glass tree ten meters high,
growing in a dim red room. See it now, dear Reader, from
top to bottom: five flutes, five clarinets, two Ganymede
bugles, five oboes, three balloon flutes, two piccolos, five
bassoons, two saxophones at each pitch; six trumpets, a
balilaika, bagpipes, a choirbox, three guitarps, six French
horns, the celesta, a harpsichord; thirty violins, ten violas,
six trombones, two alto clarinets, a digeree-doo, two bari-
tones, fifteen cellos, two bass trombones, two tubas; (note
the glass arms and fingers on the wind instruments, the
airhoses, the plastic-and-wire lips enveloping every mouthpiece); around the control booth in the middle, a piano, the
spiral of organ pipes, two harps, four mandolins, four tympanis,
snare drum, bass drum, wood blocks, several guitars, a
banjo, the godzilla, the mercury drum, eight double basses;
then near the bottom, the big boxes: the master computer, a
Planck Double Reed, four Klein bottle-drums, and an aeolia,
all forming a broad base for the rest. All held in glassy arms,
or set on glassy struts; all wired to the control booth, the
cocoon at the heart of the tree.

See it now as the storage room jerks and then slowly drops down the shaft in the center of the power plant; the room is an elevator. Thus begins the laborious process of moving the Orchestra to the site of its next performance; workers wait on the ground floor to shift the statue onto an equipment bus that will take it to the spaceport. As the Orchestra was not made to be moved, it is a delicate operation. Even the slow stop of the elevator room causes a slight stress in the many branches of the glass tree; some of them bend millimeters, then return to their rightful positions; and by this movement small sounds are created, little clinks, and creaks, and bings, a tiny tintinnabulation that is the Orchestra's own song. . . .

Onward, Reader, out of the darkness and silence.

Chapter Two

‖: A MIDSUMMER :‖ NIGHT

holywelkin

I know. Who, you ask, is this ubiquitous Holywelkin? Reader, he is the Euclid, the Newton, the Einstein, the Mauring of our age. Humanity moves from one model of reality to the next; and often, as the anomalies accumulate, it is a genius who looks at the shaky structure of observation and theory, and lays a new foundation for us to build our stories on. And who can explain genius? Genius is not a matter of intelligence, but of spirit; and we cannot speak accurately of the spirit in any language but music.

Not that this has prevented the hundreds of studies of Arthur Holywelkin from being written, filmed, hologrammed. In them you can learn all that one human can know of another: all the details of the birth in 2956 on Deimos, the childhood on Mars, the youthful work in the high energy physics laboratories in Mercury's orbit, the Year of the Thought

62

Experiments; the involvement in the plans for the Great Synchrotron, which created subatomic events with energies never before imagined possible, introducing the flood of new data that piled onto the tottering structure of Thirtieth century physics; the quiet years on Ganymede, when the *Ten Forms of Change* was written; and the last years of exile on Pluto, where the Orchestra was built, and where Holywelkin turned his back on the technological developments based on his work, which were altering the whole of civilization. You can learn all this and more: his childhood fears, his youthful excesses, his sexual preferences, his numerological superstitions, his arcane religious views . . . you name it: that aspect of Holywelkin has been intensively studied.

And yet all of this has done nothing to explain Holywelkin. Except for the work done, his biography could be that of any lab technician, nightclub musician, lay preacher, traveling salesman. Nothing in his life explains his work. Nothing in the life of any genius explains their work.

But we can *describe* the work—to a certain extent. You, dear Reader, may live in a culture that believes that gods inhabit every object, or in another that believes the speed of light to be an absolute limit, or in a third that understands the world to be composed of tiny balls bouncing against each other. Who knows? After I place this tale in a whiteline jump, it might end up anywhere (or nowhere). So there are certain difficulties. But know this: physics had ground to a halt in the Thirtieth century. After the atomists of classical physics, with their gridwork of absolute space and absolute time; and after the quantum mechanists, with all their relativities of the spacetime continuum; and after the multidimensional cosmologists, with their compactified curved dimensions, wormholes, and spacetime discontinua—after each of these, there came the time when physics was stumped. Experimental results from the Great Synchrotron and the Orbital Gevatron yielded glimpses into the five microdimensions, and provided a rich wilderness of data from which no good general theory could be made. Particles were smashed together at trillions of electron volts, results were captured on plates as far away as the asteroid belt, and even at the small sunwatch station on Pluto; in essence the whole solar system was one large physics laboratory. And these experiments showed that quarks were made of smaller "particles" ("events" might be a better term), which existed in the sixth, seventh, eighth, ninth, and tenth dimensions, each of which was curved more tightly than the last. Thus quarks were contained in the "bags" of the higher dimensions, so that quarks behaved differently depending on their constituent parts and the different properties of their "bags"; and there were hundreds and hundreds of these combinations to be found and named. For almost a century physics was reduced to a kind of taxonomy, as new events in the higher dimensions were continually found and labelled. But a larger system that might explain their activity was nowhere offered; the math used to describe these marks on the plates was fractal in its structure, except that it was a fractal pattern without the central core, branches without the tree.

Then Holywelkin, in his twenty-third year, the "Year of the Thought Experiments," postulated that all the myriad events that made up quarks were caused by even smaller "particles," which in varying combinations in the realms of the ten dimensions (five macro-dimensions and five tightly curved micro-dimensions, Holywelkin said) created the confusing welter of behavior seen at the level above it. Using Mauring's micro-dimensional geometry, Holywelkin made certain predictions about broken quark behavior that were borne out by experiment. He was given time on the Great Synchrotron, and directed a series of experiments designed to confirm his theories concerning these uniform, basic "subparticles," which he called *glints*. The theories were confirmed, and enough data collected for Holywelkin to begin the formulation of the equations governing the movement of these "sub-particles." These were published as the *Ten Forms of Change*, and Holywelkin's own version of the grail-like grand unified theory was given to the world.

Which made much of it. But that, dear Reader, is History, not physics. And History you will read on every other page of this tale.

♪

second crossing

Because of Pluto's May festival, the planet's space was crowded with ships; they circled the planet like strings of tiny pearls against the black velvet of space. The catch of one of these strings, you might say, was the great spaceliner *Orion*, perhaps the most famous ship in the solar system. For over two hundred years the *Orion* had conveyed the Grand Tours of Holywelkin's Orchestra downsystem, and now the Orchestra, its traveling crew, and several hundred devoted followers from all over the outer worlds were aboard, ready for the passage to Uranus.

Dent Ios, however, was not one of those on the *Orion*. Booking passage had been no easy task; by the time his collective had sent money, cabins were available only on the *Caliban*, a second-rate ship that had just arrived in Pluto's space. The exhausted and discouraged Dent had shuttled up to find that his room was no more than a sleeping closet. Even so he would not have left it, but there was no room service, and hunger drove him to the dining commons. On the way he passed a small porthole. Bitterly he stared out at the *Orion*, which floated just five or six vessels ahead of his. Everything of interest during the crossing would occur over there, with Wright and his crew, the critics and the devout, while Dent might as well sleep for the next month. He cursed his collective again—they were ill-organized, manipulative, domineering, inefficient, cheap. . . .

Then the catch of the necklace broke away and curved out of the orbit away from Pluto, and the entire string of pearls followed it. Fine image of humanity! For are not most of us on strings, following the few who in matters of the spirit lead us: little *Calibans* and *Paulines*, sailing in the wake of the infrequent *Orion*. . . . But now, the Grand Tour was off! —And Dent Ios only heaved a piteous sigh, and went to get something to eat.

In the dining commons he sat next to a couple speaking a Scandinavian language. He ordered Szechuan beef and bean curd from the table console, and quickly it appeared in the console slot, steaming. He ate voraciously. Midway through his meal two men sat down across from him. One was tall, bulky, swarthy, and quick of movement; Dent guessed he was Indian, which meant that he probably originated in the Jupiter system. The other man was short and slight, with odd eyes. They spoke together in Hindi. Dent understood a little of the language, and looked down at his food, embarrassed to be eavesdropping. The two men exchanged a banter almost too rapid for Dent to follow—he only understood that they were discussing the ship and its occupants. The short one spoke at length in a lilting tone; exaggerated shifts in pitch and rhythm made his Hindi a sort of singing. The tall man laughed from time to time. They were joking about the Scandinavians, and even Dent. Something about the smaller man drew attention; even diners at other tables turned to look at him, and listen to his babbling. Soon their table was full, and the small man included them all in his conversation, although no one there seemed to understand Hindi. He was just playing with them. Then he took a radish from his salad, and using his chopsticks as a catapult attempted to shoot it at a passenger entering the commons; but the radish slipped, and struck Dent on the collarbone.

Perhaps it reminded him of the blows he had received in

Lowell. Dent scraped his chair back angrily, fist raised. But the tall man stood very quickly indeed, and said in English, "We're sorry. A misfire. My friend is—"

"Your friend is rude," Dent said in Hindi. "These people and I, they do not"—he searched for the word—"they do not need bad words."

Now the short man stood. "I'm sorry. I'm being the fool tonight." He offered a hand, and reluctantly Dent took it: a small, strong, long-fingered hand. The man's English was as lilting as his Hindi.

Dent felt embarrassed again; his outburst was out of proportion to its cause. "It was nothing," he muttered. "I've had a long couple of days."

"You didn't enjoy the May Festival?" the short man asked.

"No," Dent said. "Not at all."

"Will you play with us tonight?" the man said.

"I—I don't know."

"Please. You play guitar."

"Why yes, I do."

"I knew by your calluses." The man's smile was slight, inward. In some ways he seemed to be conversing only with himself—listening to himself very carefully. "We're going to play Schiapella's Sixth Guitar Quartet, and we need a fourth."

"I don't know those by heart."

"None of us do. We're having scores printed."

"All right, then," Dent said uncertainly. Usually he played with friends—

"Good. In a couple of hours, then, in the first practice room."

Leaving the commons Dent looked back; the two men were surrounded by a group of people, and the slight young man was laughing at his tall companion, holding the attention of all with a strange force—with his luminous voice, his odd blank face.

Two hours later Dent entered the music room, guitar case

in hand. The room was almost full; people stood in small knots talking. To one side a woman performed on a large godzilla, tapping its hollow arms and rocking it gently, seeming to coax by caresses a series of metallic, lazily oscillating tones. In the room's center Dent's new acquaintances were setting sheet music on metal stands. They greeted Dent and introduced a Marie-Jeanne, their fourth, without naming themselves. Dent tried to scan the score as they tuned, but they were ready before he had skimmed more than the first several bars. The woman with the godzilla stopped, and at a nod from the short man they began playing. Dent concentrated. His part was simple enough, but it was hard to put life into sight-reading, and he worked at it. The others were good. The short man was playing with great power and expressiveness; Dent began to enjoy watching the man's long fingers and their spatulate, callused fingertips, that looked as round and flat as a tree frog's. His eyes were artificial—Dent saw that in a flash. That accounted for the curious blank intensity of his gaze. Dent lost his place, then a strong run from the short man showed him where they were, and he saw in the score that the man had played Dent's part for a second to reorient him. Dent confined his attention to the development of the second theme. Now he only heard the others, and he realized that the tall man was a relatively weak player, the woman not much better. But the radish tosser—he was a musician. The room was full of listeners, he could tell by the acoustics. Dent glanced up and saw they were watching the short man. He thought, *That's Johannes Wright.* He almost lost his place again, but forced himself to concentrate. The eyes—that was Wright's situation, he remembered. And the audience. No one would gather to listen to a pick-up quartet; they would be too busy making their own music. No, it all seemed to fit. Traveling on a smaller ship for privacy, security, whatever. And playing counterpoint with him, Dent felt Wright's power. When the finale ended the room rang with applause and looping whistles.

"You haven't told me your name," Dent said to the man.
"Johannes," he said, folding up his sheet music.
Dent grinned, suddenly feeling that he had known all
along. "Dent Ios," he said. "Happy to meet you."
The crossing to Uranus had taken on a new light.

♪

the traitor

On board great *Orion* the hallways were tall and broad,
carpeted here with plush fabric, there with rich mosses. It
was night in the giant ship, and the light strips running high
along the walls were dimmed, the long passageways nearly
empty.

Down the hallway to the communications rooms walked
Anton Vaccero. A message had roused him with the news
that a holo caller was waiting in live transmission for him; he
knew who the caller was. He felt hot and light-headed. In his
bed he had considered ignoring the message, but he had been
afraid to. And now he hurried, afraid of keeping his caller
waiting too long. In the communications complex the woman
in charge led him to one of the holo chambers. "Your call's
from Pluto," she said. "There'll be about a twenty-second
delay."

She left. Vaccero felt weak and faint, as if he had not
eaten for days. The room went dark and he tried to batten
down his fear, to pull himself together. When the light came
on again Ernst Ekern stood before him like a ghost, solid and
well-lit, but somehow wrong. Prepared for the shock of the
sight, Vaccero stood as stiff as a soldier. For what seemed a
minute the apparition of Ekern only stood there. Then it
nodded.

"Where is Wright?" The room's speaker was near the ceiling.

Anton took a deep breath. "He's on another ship, with Godavari. I don't know which one."

The twenty seconds seemed like another minute. Sweat slid down the insides of Anton's arms.

"Find out," Ekern said. "You should have known that I would want to know this, you should have anticipated. Why isn't he on *Orion*?"

"They were afraid. Godavari's agents heard Wright was in danger."

Twenty seconds.

"Good. Thus it begins. You understand: in the beginning of the drama the motif is fear."

I understand that all too well, Anton thought.

"First he frightened the crowd, and then we reverse the terms. The crowd frightens him. When Wright is afraid, he is ready for the next act. Now to help create the Aura of Unfocused Danger, we must frighten the crew as well. I want you to arrange for their floor to be emptied, for an entire evening within the next few days."

"I can search it for you if you like," Anton offered.

Another twenty seconds.

"You just play your part," Ekern said, frowning slightly. "You are my apprentice, you make no suggestions to me. You play your part and play it well. Clear the floor, and if that proves impossible, gather the crew into a single room. Call room 3773 on *Orion* and leave the message 'X' on the evening before this is to occur. Do you understand?"

"Yes, master."

Ekern's bearded face frowned; he was slightly cross-eyed as he waited for Vaccero's reply. Then he nodded, and said, "Very good. Remember, Anton, within the larger framework of the metadrama, small scenes such as this one are partly yours to direct. Once accomplished they become one thread of the weave. We will both be watched by the Magus and all

the members of our order, and it will help your rise in the
fellowship to use your esthetic sensibility here. And remember—find out which ship Wright is on. This is something you
should have known." Ekern's expression twisted and instinctively Anton recoiled. "This is something I should know!
To have the actor disappear—it has made the others doubt
me, and Atargatis laughed. I will not have it! And you,
Anton, you my beloved apprentice—but why do you look so
pale, my boy? Ha! Why do you fear me?"

Anton swallowed. "You control my destiny, master."

Twenty seconds.

"You should not fear your destiny, boy. Do as I command, and all will be well. End transmission."

And he disappeared. The room went dark. When the light
came back on Anton stood in an empty room. He heaved
several breaths into his chest. He was damp with sweat, his
heart was racing. He fled the room.

♪

inclusion: interpolation

And so, dear Reader, you will not be surprised to learn of
the following events; this is how they occurred. One evening
on the great *Orion*, Anton Vaccero gathered the Orchestra's
traveling crew into its suite's window lounge, where he read
the tarot for each one of them. All agreed that Anton's
readings exhibited an accuracy that was uncanny, and all
became absorbed in the reading.

Margaret, who took no interest in the tarot, spent the
evening playing with the *Orion*'s passenger orchestra. She
was assigned one of the second cello parts in De Bruik's *If
. . . Then*, and as she took the elevator up to the crew's suite

she hummed the famous cello part of the response, which she had played that night with particular fire.

The elevator door opened onto their suite, and she stepped out. The central hall was empty and silent. Walking down it she passed several empty rooms, and the window lounge had its door shut. Margaret heard a faint shout from within. She tried the door, but it was locked, and her keytab had no effect on it. Inside someone shouted "Help!" She knocked, which produced a chorus of shouts.

She called ship security on the phone and described the situation tersely. Very little time passed before several of the ship's security people hurried out of the elevator, and they went to work on the lounge door.

When they opened it Anton and Delia and Marie-Jeanne and the rest of the crew burst out, all talking at once. "Shut up!" Margaret said loudly.

"We were locked in!" cried Vaccero.

"We know," Margaret snapped. "Did you see who did it?"

"No," several of them said at once. The door had slammed in the midst of a reading, and their keytabs had been useless to free them. The room was without intercoms, and they had been forced to sit and wait.

"Check all the rooms," Margaret said to the security people.

The woman in charge nodded briefly. "Don't touch anything," she told the crew.

"I thought you told me no one but us could get to this suite," Margaret said angrily.

The woman nodded. "You can't get the elevator to stop here without one of your keytabs. And the vents are connected to alarms."

"Well, someone found a way."

"Maybe." The woman ignored Margaret's hard look. "It's more likely one of your keys got them here."

Delia shrieked. "*Ah!* Oh, my God . . ." She backed out of one of the corner lounges, hands at her mouth.

Margaret ran after the security people to the lounge.

It was a shambles, furniture scattered everywhere. And there was a large red drawing on one of the lounge's beige walls, painted in thick red brush-strokes. It consisted of three figures. The largest was a bull, drawn in an imitation of the Cro-Magnon cave painting style, with an elongated body and long curving horns. Over the bull a human figure stood; one of his hands held the bull's head up, and the other reached across the bull's shoulder and slashed its throat. Another figure crouched under the slash and held a cup to collect the falling blood; but the paint ran right through the cup to the floor.

Someone cleared her throat awkwardly. Margaret looked away from the painting and noticed that the room's furniture, rather than being tossed around, had been carefully upended: tables and chairs pointed leg up, lamps and stands and bookcases were placed upside down. Nothing had been damaged.

Vaccero, face pale, crossed the room to inspect the drawing. He turned to look at Margaret. "Blood of some kind," he said. "It's real blood."

"Everyone get out of here," Margaret said. "Let security go to work." She addressed the agent in charge. "I want one of your people here at the elevator all the time, from now on. And cameras set up in the halls."

The woman nodded. "Sorry about this. But remember—what I said about access to this suite still holds."

"And I want a guard with the Orchestra itself," Margaret went on. "Full time." She left the room, went back to the window lounge door to pick up her cello in its black case. "And get that wall cleaned, too!" she shouted down the hall. Rudyard and Sean were comforting Delia, whose face was still pinched with fear. Margaret stalked to her room and kicked open the door. It slammed against the inside wall and bounced back, and she kicked it again.

♪

the anxiety of influence

It was apparent to Johannes that his new acquaintance Dent Ios was interested in him, but for a few days—during which Ios stared at him in passageways, conspicuously eavesdropped on his dinner conversation, and even followed him—Johannes did not understand why. One evening as Ios was twisting his long awkward body to hear what was being said at their table, Johannes leaned back and said, "Why don't you join us?"

Ios jumped and then blushed, mumbled a thank you and struggled around to their table with a wary, nervous look, as if he might be plunked with another radish, or something bigger. Johannes compressed a smile to nothing, and shared only the briefest flicker of a glance with Karna, whose face said all too plainly, This man is a rabbit!

But once he was settled at their table he behaved normally. When asked about Titania he gave a description of the Smithson anarchy that made them all laugh, and the story of his adventure in Lowell was also entertaining, in a way. "I hope my music didn't inspire the attack on you," Johannes said, concerned.

"No. The man was criminal in some way, alas. Music had nothing to do with it."

Later Karna excused himself with a polite and straightforward farewell to the man, and Johannes was left alone with him. "Why do you follow the Grand Tour?" Johannes asked.

Ios smiled crookedly. "It's my job."

"And your job is?"

"I am the correspondent for the journal *Thistledown*."

"You report the events of the tour?"

"I write only about the music."

Johannes said, "You make your living writing about music?"

"Actually I breed tapirs for a living. But I do write about music, yes."

Johannes laughed. Then he saw he had offended the man: ellipses of sealed lips, cheeks flaring red . . . "Sorry," Johannes said. "But—writing about music!"

"Now wait a minute," said Dent Ios. "It's not as funny as all that, Mr. Wright."

"Call me Johannes."

"Certainly. And you call me Dent. But you must allow me to defend the act of writing about music."

"Of course," Johannes said. "It needs defending, if you ask me. I can't imagine anything more futile."

"Well—nevertheless—follow along, if you will. You will agree that there are two ways that we know the world—by acquaintance, and discursively."

"At least two. I agree."

"Knowledge by acquaintance is the direct apprehension of something through the senses—the primary way of knowing. But discursive knowledge includes all that language does—"

"Not the sound of it."

"No. But the meaning. The ability to know what is not present is discursive. So discourse is as important as acquaintance, even if it isn't primary."

Johannes paused to think about it. "Maybe," he granted.

"In our time, I don't see how you could disagree. It is a discursive age. Now, music itself is known both by acquaintance and discursively. Musical phrases refer the listener to other phrases, and to things outside music—they are part of a discourse."

"Agreed." Johannes began to attend to this rabbit-man with some interest. "But writing . . . ?"

"Language allows us to discuss what we know by acquaintance or discursively. Without language, we could not say what music meant."

"But even *with* language we cannot say what music means," Johannes said, laughing. "What about all the criticism we see—you know: this is the greatest work since De Bruik died, it dazzles with glittering tongues of flame, some dark, others wounding to the eye, while every phrase is as remarkable as summer's first light on a spring day, its sheen is as brittle as icicles of almost naked exaltation. . . ."

"Please!" Dent cried. "Not funny!" But he had laughed.

"That's just bad writing. And there's a lot more bad writing about music than good. Because it's hard to do. Music is a dynamic, polyphonic process, while writing is linear and static. But that doesn't mean writing about music is never accurate, or useful."

"I suppose." Johannes tried to recall some example of useful writing about music. *Handbook of Musical Notations*, perhaps. "But these dubious metaphors and all the rest . . ."

"I know. Often it's as bad as the example you recited. That was for real?"

"Yes! I memorized it."

"Amazing. But think about it. Music has qualities which are also known by the other senses. This cross-sensory participation is called *sensory isomorphism*, and the words that describe properties perceived by more than one sense are called *universals*. Our response is universal, while the stimulus is particular, you see. So that if I were to call a melody rough, I would be naming a response to a particular stimulus—a response I might make to other stimuli as well. Use of these universals is not only valid, it's necessary! Otherwise we couldn't talk about music at all."

"I'm still not sure we can," Johannes said. But Dent's words had stimulated a response in him; certain problems he had imagined for the reception of his new work might not be problems at all, if the audiences could make analogies to their sense of sight and touch. He might actually be able to reveal to them the world. . . .

Dent said, "What about De Bruik's writings, her notebooks?"

"Rubbish!" Johannes cried. "Have you read them? They're craziness."

Dent laughed again. "I always thought it was me."

"No. Unless it was both of us. De Bruik—her music is a huge achievement, it hangs over us all, but . . . music was her language, not words. She wrote as if she barely understood English."

Dent pounded the table with delight; but at the end of his mirth a finger pointed up out of one fist at Johannes. "Still, no composer can be trusted when talking about De Bruik. It's bound to be blasphemy, right?"

"Yes," Johannes sighed. "I suppose so."

"Like the Romantics after Beethoven. What was it Tchaikovsky said about him? Like listening to Jehovah—no love, only fear."

"I enjoy listening to De Bruik," Johannes objected mildly.

"But as you said, her achievement hangs over us all. It intimidates the artists who follow."

"Perhaps," Johannes said. "She wrote a lot of music that we cannot write, now."

"Exactly! Do you know Bloom's books on influence?"

Johannes shook his head. "Someone has written about this?"

"Oh yes. Long ago. Old alchemical texts, very bizarre. But the basic ideas are good. He outlines strategies that the younger artist uses to deal with the overwhelming presence of the precursor artist."

"You do it better than they did."

"Ha! But if you have a precursor like De Bruik?"

Johannes shrugged. "Perhaps this is something that critics worry about more than composers." He saw Dent frown. "You know—the truth is, I'm not doing what De Bruik did. She was great, but it doesn't affect me. There's always new music to write."

"But that is one of Bloom's strategies. You make a *clinamen*, a swerve away from the precursor. *Clinamen* from Lucretius's term for the swerve in atoms that makes change in the universe possible."

"What a strategy—a *universal* like that would describe

any artist's relation to any earlier artist, wouldn't it? Very convenient for the critic.'' But he thought, *Makes change in the universe possible*. . . . Holywelkin would say, there is no such thing as a *clinamen*; each swerve in the sub-subatomic realm could be accounted for in Holywelkin physics, and if his equations were applied completely to the macroscopic world, presumably they could account for all change there as well. This disturbing thought was one that had recently occurred to Johannes during his studies of Holywelkin. . . .

So this man Dent could make him think! It was a surprise. Because of his isolation as Master of the Orchestra, he had not really talked with anyone in a serious way about music since . . . well, since Yablonski died. And Yablonski had been no theorist. So, since his days in the conservatory: how they had argued over composition there! And perhaps he missed those talks, even though he had forgotten the language for them. Once he had been yoked to the Orchestra, no one on Pluto had ever really talked with him again.

The realization made him feel lonely, and he avoided the feeling. His thoughts wandered to his composition and its relation to De Bruik's body of work, and they became lost in it, so that music filled his mind. He did not know how much time had passed when Dent spoke again.

''What?'' he said.

''What about you, Johannes? It's been over two hundred years since De Bruik, and composers since then have been— well, at a loss, say.''

''I don't know.''

''No, but you must tell me. Not about how your work relates to hers, if you don't want to. But what do you think of De Bruik?''

''Well . . .'' He made an effort to converse with this man who had sparked his interest. ''You know. De Bruik lived just as Holywelkin's work was becoming known. A process that has still not ended, I might add! And everything shifted with Holywelkin, including music. Music depends on the world view of the time, as you probably know—you see the corpuscular-kinetic view of reality expressed in classical music, relativity and the uncertainty principle expressed in the aleatoric music that came in the centuries after Einstein. And De Bruik did the same for the new Holywelkin age, or tried to. But she was an instinctive artist, she composed in a frenzy, hardly reflecting on what she had done . . . so . . . she reacted to Holywelkin, but she didn't understand him. Neither the physics nor her reaction. She just composed. All that work—*The Floor of Time, Muon Meets Gluon Meets Quark, The Glint in Your Eye*—beautiful music, all of it, but not . . . accurate. Impressionistic only. And the whole range of De Bruik's work—three thousand compositions, was it? Well, it was genius. But the whole body of work was one giant impression. She was a great explorer, and much was seen, but little . . . understood. Because it's not just a matter of feeling, there's a more direct connection, something more accurate, more rigorous. There can be a music that sings the world precisely, do you see?''

Dent shook his head. "How have you gone about your work, then?"

"I? I have been studying Holywelkin.''

"But nobody really *understands* Holywelkin, do they?''

"Certainly." He observed the man curiously; odd that people remained so far from physics, when it was the whole foundation of their world. "The people who do understand him keep our worlds in existence. And I understand something about him. I—met him—" But the frown of consternation on Dent's face showed he had gone further than the man was prepared for. ''—in a way. And I have been studying the geometer Mauring, who preceded him. She is easier, and gives me an entry, and . . . well. I don't want to get into that." Spiraling down into the micro-universe where each *clinamen* could be charted by Holywelkin's equations, by Mauring's strange postulates. . . . "But De Bruik did some-

thing instinctively that I will do with my full intelligence.
And the result will be something *entirely new.*''

♪

titania

Time passed, and the crossing to the Uranian system came
to an end. *Orion* and its comet tail of followers spun down
into orbit around Titania, the system's largest moon. Margaret Nevis was on the first shuttle to Titania's spaceport, and
once there she waited impatiently for the arrival of Wright
and Godavari.

The spaceport was splayed out over the tableland adjoining
the rim of a giant rift called the Titania Gap, which marked
where Titania had once almost broken apart. The terminal's
outdoor patio stretched along the rim of the Gap, and there
Margaret paced the length of the railing. She stared moodily
down into the kilometer-deep gouge of the canyon, at the city
of Titania contained in it. From her prospect it appeared an
architect's model of a city: buildings like blocks, parks like
green postage stamps, trees like miniature bonsais. But no
sane architect would have designed such a city. Titania was
the meeting place for all the worlds of the Uranian system,
and under its long string of hemispheres people were free to
build what they would, where they would. The result was a
crazed jumble of styles: here were green mounds covering
underground dwellings, there a white marble villa, farther on
a neighborhood of geodesic domes, beyond them a line of old
space bunkers, across the Gap a line of Martian skyscrapers.
Margaret pursed her mouth at the disorganized spectacle and
scanned the skies overhead for a sight of the next shuttle.
Nothing but the blue-black of the air under the hemisphere,

and the stars, with Uranus like a greenish opal flanked by the two diamonds of Bottom and Puck. She took a turn at the end of the terminal, and started another lap.

By the time their shuttle arrived impatience had driven Margaret into a foul mood. Karna was the first out of the shuttle, followed by Johannes and a tall spindly man who was deep in conversation with him. Johannes waved his hands, talking as fast as he could, not watching where he was going, and the other man nodded like a marionette with its head on a spring, nod, nod, nod, nod, nod. She walked to them and shook hands with Karna. "We've had an eventful flight," she said curtly.

"Uh oh." Karna's glance was sharp, worried.

"I'll tell you about it. Hello, Johannes."

"Hello Margaret." The artificial eyes looked up at her. "Margaret, this is Dent Ios, our traveling companion on the crossing, and a writer for *Thistledown*."

Margaret had never heard of *Thistledown*. She shook the man's hand; he had the limpest handshake she had ever felt. "Hello," she said. "I hope you write well of us."

"I do too," the man said, smiling nervously. He shuffled in an uncoordinated way, and his gaze flickered to Johannes, who said,

"Dent and I have been talking during the trip, and I want to be able to continue the conversation. I'd like to offer Dent a room with us, if we have one available."

Margaret looked at Karna, who made a minute shrug with his eyebrows. No help at all there; Karna had a tendency to leave policy decisions to her, which usually she appreciated. And Johannes was staring at the city below. Suspiciously she looked the man over, thinking of the vandalism of their suite. "You write for what?"

"*Thistledown*. It's a journal published on Holland, in this system. The rest of my collective will be here for the concert, and they can . . . vouch for me."

"Good," Margaret said brusquely. This lanky man with

his watery gaze was getting on her nerves; she didn't like hangers-on. "We've had some trouble, and I don't want anyone in our suite that we can't trust."

"I trust him," said Johannes, returning abruptly from his reverie.

"Fine," Margaret said. Just what they needed. "You have arrangements for the stay here?"

"Yes," Dent said. "With my collective."

"We'll see you after the concert, then." Margaret waved the man off, took Karna and Johannes in tow. As they crossed the terminal patio she told them about the crossing's incident. "So we've increased security. And now that it's known that Johannes traveled by another ship, it would be easy to find him. From now on I think we can do a better job of protecting Johannes on *Orion* itself."

"I agree," Karna said.

"Good." At the terminal patio's farthest edge a long set of escalators began, and they stepped onto it. It zigzagged down one of the spines of the rift wall, and as they descended they had a fine view of the city. As they walked around a switchback Margaret said, "The tradition in Titania is that the Master of the Orchestra comes down this escalator at the start of the concert, and then plays from the last switchback platform down there. On the way down there's music amplified all over the city, with lights and so forth."

Johannes nodded. "We'll abide by the tradition."

♪

the head of an ass

One of the *Thistledown* collective had a brother who lived in Titania, in one of the eastern hemispheres of the city near the cliff and the escalators leading up to the spaceport. On the night of the concert the whole collective was there, on the roof patio drinking and singing and watching the crowd in the open parklike ground under the cliff. Dent Ios was the hero of the hour. He was toasted collectively and by each shifting knot of celebrants, and he initiated a fair share of toasts himself. Several times he was entreated to repeat the story of his trip, which he did with ever-increasing enthusiasm. "The funny thing is," he declared once again to June, Irdar, and Andrew, "I didn't even *see* the Lowell concert!"

June laughed. "This we know already. But on that tramp of a ship we managed to book you on—"

"On that ridiculous little ship I met and became friends with Johannes Wright, yes." Dent toasted the notion with another sip of champagne. "And he is quite an extraordinary fellow. *Strange.* Oh my yes. You can talk to him and he'll be right in the conversation, and then—something you say, no doubt—and he's gone. Those glass eyes of his roll like marbles. Then all of a sudden, bang—he's back again and wants to know what you've been saying. We talked for hours. And it looks like we'll talk for hours more, if I can get past that tour manager. What a dragon she is! Like a general in charge of her troops. But she let me on board *Orion.* And so I'll see the Orchestra—I never saw it at all—there it is, see?"

Andrew, Irdar and June laughed long and hard. "Yes, Dent, we see it."

The Orchestra stood on the lowest platform of the downward escalator ridge, where the escalator made its last switchback. It was about twenty meters above them, and half a kilometer away, and so far it was lit only by the beams of light aimed by curious neighbors. "Bizarre object," Dent said. "To think of it as an instrument—well—I can hardly wait to hear this." From the park below came a roar of voices. Dent looked over the roof's edge and saw a bright field of flesh and clothing. Every rooftop held a party similar to theirs, and a nearby group threw sparkling fireworks at the crowd. Even the randomly placed trees were filled with spectators, and Dent laughed loudly to see a large olive tree collapse under the weight of its climbers. "It reminds me of Lowell," he said happily.

"Do you think there'll be a riot, then?" Andrew asked.

"It wasn't exactly a riot in Lowell," Dent said, frowning as he tried to make the distinction. "More of a . . . bacchanalia. A Dionysian festival, in fact."

"I see," said Andrew, exchanging glances with Irdar and June.

Intrigued by the sight of the Orchestra, Dent did not notice. Beams of bent and broken and split light fenced in the air over the Orchestra. The brown expanse of the cliffside served as the palette for hundreds of ellipses of bright color, all jumping about erratically. Many of the beams of light converged on the Orchestra itself, creating a white talcum of light around that omphalos. "It looks like the insides of an antique clock," Dent said, staring at it owlishly.

As if in response to his words it began to revolve. The shouts rose to howls and the mass of people on the floor of the Gap surged toward it. Lights ran up and down the escalator ridge, which seamed the cliff-face like a bright metal zipper. From the amplifiers set around the base of the Orchestra came a low, oscillant hum. Dent recognized it; the *intermezzo* before the last movement of De Bruik's *Human Biology*. The finale of the symphony was a standard concert opener in the outer worlds. Soon the crackling of superamplified muscle contractions and the rush of adrenaline into the bloodstream announced the shift to the finale, and the crowd cheered wildly; Dent could feel his blood surging through him—

Johannes Wright appeared on the rim of the canyon, a tiny figure in a bright blue cape. He stepped onto the escalator and it conveyed him slowly down the ridge of the canyon wall. *Thump, thump, thump,* pounded the pulse at the heart of the music, and long *portamento* slides of alpha and beta waves crossed to form the movement's famous first theme, one of the anthems of the outer worlds; and with each thump and glissand Wright dropped closer to his Orchestra. Dent felt his pulse synchronize with the musical heartbeat, and knowing of the accelerando to come he hopped up and down on his toes, dancing with the rest of his collective. Wright was at the switchback above the Orchestra's platform—

With a sizzling *snap snap snap* a beam of painfully bright red light burst into existence, stretching from the half-buried geodesic structure next to their house, up to the escalator just below Wright. "It's hot!" someone shouted. Unable to hear himself over the ensuing blast of noise, Dent shouted "Oh my God! Hot light! Look out!" It seared his eyes to stare up at the escalator, but he watched anyway, clutching at the roof railing and moaning. The escalator stairs just down the ridge from Wright glowed a fiery red, sagged, Wright leaped from the escalator, which buckled out into free fall, still pushed from above. "Oh no, *oh no, oh no*—" No sign of Wright. The burning ruby beam blinked off, and the building housing its source exploded into flame. Dent jumped up and down frantically, squinting through the bright green bars marring his vision. "Come on!" he heard June yell in his ear, and he was jerked by the arm toward the stairwell. Awkwardly he clumped down after her. In the street he hopped and skipped through the gaps between clumps of people, trying to keep up with June and Andrew. The confusion reminded him of Lowell and suddenly he was afraid. He slowed down. The general movement of the crowd was toward the Orchestra; he was cutting across that flow. June and the rest of the collective were gone, lost in the mass of bodies. People crashed into him, he saw round mouths wide open, eyes covered by hands, all through a prison window of green bars. He found himself across an open stretch of ground from the burning geodesic building. He blinked, gasped heavily. No sight of the others. What to do? Why was he here?

Something about the crowd—there, near the wall of the

building next to the burning one—a tall man, a bony face—
red whiskers painted on his cheeks. Dent started, turned and
pretended to look up at the cliff, looked over his shoulder
briefly. It was the man from Lowell, his assailant. Edging
away Dent saw that he had been noticed—the man was
pointing him out to two companions, and they were starting
to move toward him. . . .

Dent pointed at them. "They did it!" he shrieked at the
top of his lungs. "They did it! They killed Wright! Over
there! Them! They did it!"

Red Whiskers and his two men turned and ran. Dent
struggled forward through the crowd, making slow progress;
no one was chasing the assassins but him. When he realized
this he slowed his pace considerably. Red Whiskers was
looking back often, and Dent kept his head lowered. His
shoulders crashed into other shoulders; he brushed a fist aside
and stopped running. I'll tell Karna all about it, he thought to
himself, I'll give him the best description possible, it's the
best I can do. Yet all the while he was shuffling between
people, unwilling to let Red Whiskers and his men out of
sight. He was elbowed as he hunched over to keep his head
below the top of the crowd: "Ow!" he cried. "Excuse me!
Excuse me!" What was he to do? If he caught up with the
assassins he surely would be beaten, or worse. It only made
sense to give up and return to the collective's house. Up
ahead Red Whiskers turned another corner, a grin splitting
his face. Grimly Dent put his head down and barreled forward. The street he turned onto was narrow but relatively
unoccupied; he saw he would have to run if he expected to
keep up with his quarry.

He ran.

He followed only two men now; Red Whiskers was one of
them. They were fast, and Dent had to hurry. His lungs
burned, and he could feel all that champagne sloshing in his
belly as his feet pounded over the cobblestoned street. The
street opened onto a small square with a fountain, surrounded

by wedge-shaped hotels and boarding houses, which fitted between the dozen streets that converged on the square. Drinking peacefully at the fountain was a big flock of sheep, blocking the way across the square. Dent struggled across flagstones, kicking at the sheep and waving them away with his hands. His foes were likewise obstructed by the flock, and their curses were audible. Trying to kick and run simultaneously Dent slipped on sheep dung and fell onto a terrified ewe, which collapsed under him bleating in panic. A sharp little hoof struck Dent in the cheek as he struggled up. Holding his cheek he staggered on, crying "Ow! Shit! Murderer! Stop them!" The two assassins were still in the flock, slipping and cursing.

"Dent! *Dent Ios!*" It was Karna Godavari, standing on the rim of the fountain. Dent jumped up and down madly, holding his cheek with one hand and pointing with the other. Karna leaped off the fountain, and Dent resumed the chase.

They met at the mouth of the alley the two men had chosen. "It's them," Dent gasped. "The man who beat me on Pluto. And they came out of the house." Karna took off and Dent followed as fast as he could, running pell-mell down the cobblestoned alleyway. Breaths rasped in and out of him. "What are you doing here?" he said.

Karna said over his shoulder, "One of my men saw you chasing someone this way. Whoops—they've gone in that building—" Karna ran up a stoop into an apartment, and Dent followed him unsteadily. Inside Karna checked the rooms on the first floor, pointed up a narrow staircase and took them two at a time. The next floor was dark, and Karna had just begun his search when they heard scuffling on the floor above. Dent slipped on the first step of the stairs, and tripped Karna neatly. Together they struggled up the flight of stairs, Karna half supporting Dent, half pushing him away. "Dent, for God's sake—there—watch it—"

A light shone on the next floor, and voices came from behind one door; Karna opened it with a bang, and they saw a man holding a girl's shoulder as she sat at a kitchen table. The man pointed up, toward the roof. They dashed up the last flight onto the flat roof patio.

Beams of light still stitched the night air. Across the alleyway on the roof of the next building there was movement, and a grin framed by red whiskers shone from the stairwell doorway. "That's him," Dent said. They ran to the roof's edge. A wooden walkway that had connected the two roofs dangled from their side, smoking slightly.

"Come on," Karna said. He stepped back, got a running start and leaped across the alleyway onto the other roof. "You're kidding," Dent said. He hurried to the back side of the roof, knees shaking. Without pausing to permit himself any more thought he ran forward and jumped into space. A moment of whistling stillness, like eternity; then he crashed onto the opposite roof, tumbling heavily onto his right forearm and over onto his back. He struggled to his feet, disentangling himself from the lounge chair he had landed on. Karna had already disappeared down the stairwell. Dent hobbled down the stairs after him, sucking air in and out like a bellows. "Ow!"

When he got to the ground floor Karna was standing in the street, staring back the way they had come. He saw Dent and made a chopping motion. "No sign of them," he said, voice rich with disgust. "I don't know which way to go."

"Ahhh," Dent said, and sat down on the doorstep. After a while, when his breath had returned, he said, "And Wright?"

Karna gestured at his ear, which apparently contained an intercom. "They say he's barely hurt. He landed on the platform and rolled." He stared at Dent curiously. "He's probably in better shape than you are. What did you do, fall down the stairs?"

"Ah . . . landed on a chair, I believe." Dent concentrated on his breathing; he was feeling a bit sick. But the news about Wright was a tremendous relief. When the wave of nausea passed he felt immeasurably better. "Well. Quite a chase."

Karna laughed shortly.

"That was them, I'm sure."

"They ran like they were."

Dent nodded dizzily. "We almost caught them."

"Yes," Karna said, looking at Dent curiously. "We almost caught them. You cut your face on a chair?"

"No. A sheep kicked me." Dent did not see Karna's smile. His ankle, arm and face throbbed fiercely; he felt—he did not know how he felt. He had never felt this particular emotion in his entire life, and he did not know how to name it. But, dear Reader, observing this bloodied, sweaty, gawky, weak-chinned, long-moustached figure, we see a slightly different man than we did at the beginning of this tale; a transformation makes its small beginning, its *clinamen*.

♪

The next day when Margaret Nevis met with Titania's highest official, the Chief of Traffic and Utilities Maintenance, she was still furious. "You should look worried," she said to the man, whose big round face was red and stubble-jawed.

"The only thing I'm worried about is Johannes Wright," the man said huffily. "How is he?"

"Scraped and bruised. Sprained ankle." She walked to the railing of the spaceport patio and looked over the rim at the city below.

The traffic chief followed her. "That's good to hear. Perhaps we can reschedule the concert for next week?"

"We won't be rescheduling it," Margaret said. "You don't have enough security here to police a concert. You should hire a force."

"We don't need police in Titania."

"You did last night." Margaret shook her head bitterly. "You damned anarchists. Look at that." She gestured at the city below. "No plan to it—no rhyme or reason—streets all circling around like cow paths, and no one in charge—"

"That's the way we like it," the man said defensively. "I think it's beautiful."

"But you can't control it. A concert is just an invitation to disaster. Someone means harm to Wright, and you can't protect him."

"That's your job," said the traffic chief, setting his big underslung jaw like a bulldog. "There are no hot-light generators in this city, so your assassins came down with the rest of your off-world audience. You should have brought your own police as well."

"We have twenty securities traveling with us," Margaret said. "When they're working with a local force, that's enough."

"But some of us don't have local forces," the man said. "We don't need them, do you understand? We get along fine without them."

"Except that Titania is known to be the most dangerous city in the outer worlds," Margaret retorted. "Open city anarchism—do what you want, but if you're attacked, you're looking out for yourself."

"It rarely happens. Listen, you come here from offworld and give a concert, some other offworlder tries to kill you—don't blame us for it."

"All right," Margaret said. "But it's too dangerous here to try it again."

"You made a commitment—"

"Not at the risk of our performer's life! How could you guarantee it wouldn't happen again?"

The traffic chief's face reddened, and he walked in a small circle. "You can't guarantee that *anywhere*. You might as well cancel the whole tour."

"Security is adequate when the local authorities cooperate."
Now the man was as angry as Margaret. "You're making
a bad mistake," he said. "Downsystem you'll be just another
novelty act from the rimworlds. You won't mean a thing to
them. It's out here that you mean something. You should be
playing for the people who care about the Orchestra—about
music! You should care about these people who came to see
you!"

Margaret gestured at the city again. "This is the only place
people could try to kill Wright knowing there was no chance
they would be caught. We can't operate where there is no
law, not when we're in danger."

Over at the terminal entrance Marie-Jeanne was waving at
her. "I have to leave. Listen, we'll beam you a holo of the
next performance, you can play it from the platform if you
like."

The traffic chief shook his head. "You're making a mistake. You should stay up in the rimworlds where the Orchestra is loved. Downsystem you're nothing."

"We'll beam you a performance. Sometimes you need
law," she said, pointing a finger as she turned away.

"Damned socialist! You're a damned fool! Downsystem—
you'll see!"

Chapter Three

𝄆   # TERRA INCOGNITA   𝄇

motiveless malignity

Ekern's fear began in a dream. One night before a performance—just a little recital for all the students of his teacher—he had gone to bed fine. And then in the dream it had all gone wrong. He was alone on a big dark drafty backstage, with acoustic dampers hanging overhead like the blades of guillotines, and through the wings and chinks in the stage curtains the voice of the audience poured like a thick liquid. Frightened by the babble he opened his flute case and found the top section missing. He put the other two sections together and searched frantically in the bare wooden corners of the backstage, but there was nothing there but dust and wood and the thick liquid sound of the watchers, and he was being called to perform. They grabbed him by the arms and pulled him toward the stage as he struggled and fought. . . .

But that was just a dream, and dreams rarely impinge on

the real. The next day, however, as the actual performance drew closer, his unease grew and grew, until he stepped out onto their little practice stage rigid with fright. Though his flute was whole he could barely play it. The dream had been like the tree of knowledge; and now he knew enough to be afraid. "A very nerve-racked performance," his perfectionist father had said severely. And two weeks later at a festival performance it was worse.

Tearfully Ekern cursed the dream, and wondered why it had come to him. It had been an act out of his control, he never would have willed it; and as his fear grew with every attempt to play, it seemed to him that he had been destined to suffer the curse of stage fright, in a world where performance was all.

Years later, playing to himself in a stairwell full of echoes, it occurred to him that most of the times we are betrayed, it is by ourselves—by some part of the self impervious to the will, beyond will. That there was such a part of his "self" amazed and appalled him, and he wondered if it were really so. Do Titans war within us, as the alchemist Jung said? And if so, why should one Titan prevail, another fall? Do our "selves" have any control whatsoever over our lives?

♪

the convocation of the magi

These questions and others like them still gnawed at Ekern during the course of the Grand Tour, as he and the other fellows of his order fired through the vacuum ahead of the tour, from Titania to the little terra Grimaldi. They descended on the terra like the falling angels on the lake of fire, intent on secret conquest. Diana stood at the center of a small clearing, and Ekern stood facing her, part of the circle of twelve around her. Beside the circle was a low concrete blockhouse, its only entrance a heavy steel door. Surrounding the blockhouse and the group of playwrights was a circle of baobabs, standing like an outer circle of listeners; beyond the trees, verdant savannah extended to the chocolate hills on the horizon. The steep-sided dome of the sky was a dark blue, and under the light of the low whitsun the trees gleamed like dusty gold leaf, casting long shadows all the way to the eastern hills.

Diana called them to order with her chant:

> "Go under the real
> To the heart of the real,
> Where what we can trust
> Is not what we feel,
> But what we then *know*,"

and so on. Ekern barely listened, impatient for her to finish. She was deceptive, their Magus; appearing simple made her dangerous, and Ekern kept his expression perfectly attentive. He had been apprenticed to her, and knew her temper. She had introduced him to metadrama, wandering the edge of Lowell's hemisphere one day (observing that it was a much smaller section than a hemisphere, that the sphere's center must be far underground, that the surface of the city bowed up in the center of town, like the surface of a much larger buried sphere, so that everywhere in the city the pull of the underground gravity generator felt [almost] properly down; observing that one could stick one's hand through the discontinuity of the invisible dome, and freeze it) —wandering in the melancholy humiliated life destined to be his, he had been struck by a young woman running for the discontinuity itself. "Watch out!" he had cried aloud, and held her by the arm as she struggled to free herself and dash through the barrier into Pluto's black night. "Hey!" he had cried, and then two men were pummeling them, attempting to free the woman so she could kill herself! In a confused frenzy he struck them both sprawling and trapped the woman under him. And then she had started to laugh. Oh, it was a crude metadrama, no doubt of it. "You were magnificent," she said. And when the two men had explained themselves, and his anger had subsided, he had considered it. Performance without the stage, without the exposure. "No matter how angry you are at us," the woman said, "we pulled a performance from you that you couldn't have made otherwise. And at the same time you were plunged straight to the heart of yourself, of your reality. Think about it." For some time he thought of nothing else; and then he went to see her.

So began Ekern's involvement with metadrama. And having looked back at the course of his life, in an attempt to explain this involvement, you may marvel at the paucity of causes: a dream, a fear of stages, a driving father—another child might have laughed at these influences, become someone kind, bold, generous. So I have failed; to explain Ernst Ekern is to dive deeper than I can go. But do not blame me, Reader. We emerge from the womb with our characters formed, our destinies written; can you explain yourself to yourself? If not, forgive me.

Now Diana finished her chant, and nodded to Ekern. Here, he thought, before this group, some of whom never gave their names, never even spoke, he could command. These people lived in fear always, but Ekern was free of fear. All life was a performance, a deception. Each person had a hundred performances a day to get through. And before his craven fellows he was the supreme performer. He stepped forward and captured all their gazes with a single sweeping look.

" 'Here we shall see, If power change Purpose, what our seemers be.' " So the Duke of Vienna had begun, in *Measure for Measure*. Ekern pointed at the blockhouse. "I know the code to this little terra, this piece of the flesh of the goddess lost. So we will descend through that door to the center of this terra, where the gravity generator resides. Down there you will witness the next scene of my drama, but you will also be my players. In this you are actors and audience at once, observing your audience to see his performance."

Atargatis looked over Diana's broad shoulder at him. "And what will we see, master?"

"That I will not tell you," Ekern said easily. "You have seen the play thus far: first Wright frightened the crowd, and then the crowd frightened him. You should be able to see the synthesis of this. We now offer, not without ambiguity, a guide, an explanation." In the eastern sky, just over the horizon, slate clouds flickered with soundless lightning. Ekern let his silence extend for a time. "You know of the Greys. They have a terra of their own, and it is said that downsystem they are seen often. Yet in essence they are a secret order, like ours. No one knows their purpose."

At this Atargatis smiled a crooked smile.

"We will subsume the Greys," Ekern continued. "They will become no more than the shell for our own purposes. Where it leads Wright, you will see. As the Duke of Vienna said, 'If his own life answer the straightness of his proceeding, it shall become him well; wherein if he choose to fail, he hath sentenced himself.' "

And with that he waved a hand, dispersing them. "We meet again at my calling." Off between the baobabs they weaved, talking among themselves. Atargatis waited for Ekern, eyes bright with curiosity. They left the grove together.

"What made you choose the Greys as your disguise?" asked Atargatis.

Ekern shrugged. "They suit certain needs of mine. Why do you ask?"

"I will tell you when I have seen more," Atargatis replied, smiling. Out on the open hillside there was more light;

Grimaldi's whitsun blazed in the evening sky like the little chip of Sol it was. To the east against the slate clouds arched a small rainbow, one especially bright in its violet, green and yellow bands. Atargatis pointed at it. "It is a good image of your drama, is it not? The rainbow is not there without us, and as we walk toward it it moves ahead of us, never getting closer. . . ."

"The image fits only a fraction of the drama I conceive," Ekern said sharply. Atargatis was too bright, too cunning, too interested. Ekern wanted him only to witness and remain silent. "This is nothing but a bow of color, a natural manifestation of split light."

"Natural, yet arranged by the weather people of Grimaldi," Atargatis said, smiling.

♪

the music of the spheres

Great *Orion* approached Grimaldi more slowly, and on board life fell uncertainly into the patterns of shipboard existence: long hours of sleep, extended meals, promenades before the broad windows, frequent concerts, endless talk. Johannes Wright spent the first part of the flight in the hospital; after that he kept to himself, spending his time in the Orchestra. His concentration was impaired, however, and often he found himself imagining the terrifying moment when the red streaks had burst up at him out of the city of blues, melting the section of escalator below him, forcing him to jump out into empty space; it was only luck that the platform had been there—he hadn't even seen it. Shuddering he would come to in his Orchestra, safe, and attempt to calm down and return to his music . . . it was hard. He avoided conversation with Margaret, who wanted to talk security, and with every-one else as well, except for Dent Ios. Ios only wanted to talk music, and Johannes liked that.

So the two of them limped along the corridors, Johannes favoring his left ankle, Dent favoring his right. The comic sight became the talk of the ship, but they didn't notice. One morning Dent caught up with him on his way to work, and Johannes invited him along.

The Orchestra was kept in a large dimly lit storage cham-ber, a room not much taller than the Orchestra itself, but much broader. Johannes switched on a light, and they limped over to look up at it. "Come up to the control booth," Johannes said.

"Is there room?" Dent asked.

"Oh yes." Johannes climbed in over the piano bench and began to make his way up the glass steps, through all the blue shadows. "Yablonski and I spent hours here together." He settled on the Master's stool, and Dent ducked into one corner, rubbernecking to see all the booth's interior.

But after a time he said, "Don't you find this distancing from the instruments a problem? Isn't it . . . bad for the music?"

Johannes laughed shortly. "How I used to think so! And how it cost me." A moment to fend off those memories. "But it is more a player piano than an organ, if you see what I mean. One shouldn't attempt to play all of a piece live— there Yablonski and most of the earlier Masters were wrong. You need to take advantage of the thing's taping abilities."

"But that takes you even further from live performance, right? Recording music that is mechanically played?"

"It's true," Johannes admitted. These questions of his youth were painful to recall. "But the controls are much more delicate than you might imagine. Here." He pulled out a clarinet keyboard. "Pressure on the keys partly determines volume, and pushing one side of the key or the other raises or lowers the tone. You have to have a fine touch, but with practice you can play slurs, vibrato, tremolo, crescendo and decrescendo . . . and the embouchures, the bowing, they're all superior. It is truly an astonishing instrument, but not exactly a performance instrument. Rather a composing instrument—a very good one. I could make tapes and you couldn't tell the difference between the Orchestra's instruments and their counterparts played directly by a musician."

Dent peered into one tall bank of keyboards. "I believe you." He stopped his inspection and straightened up. "And what will you compose with this instrument? What is this large work I have heard people speak of?"

Johannes considered how to say it, and became confused. "I call it *The Ten Forms of Change*. After Holywelkin's book."

"And the music is based on Holywelkin's mathematics?"

"Well—" Johannes stopped, searched for words. "Every quality of sound can be a sign. Pitch, timbre, duration, intensity—these tonal qualities constitute the sounds themselves, which are arranged in rhythmic patterns. Tensing, emphasizing, relaxing, tensing again, this sequence repeated in various pulses is the essence of rhythm. Sounds in rhythm create sonorous motion, and the simultaneous sounding of tones creates harmony, characterized by mass, volume, density, and tension . . . and what is needed is a harmonic texture as dense as the fabric of the real; not notes at every possible pitch all at once, for that is not the way of the world, but chords of immense volume, containing nodal points where subsidiary chords are clustered. . . ."

Dent was looking confused. "These are the elements of music, yes?"

"—chords woven as densely as glints in spacetime," Johannes said.

"I see," Dent said slowly. "I take it your composition is . . . complex."

"All music is complex."

"I see." Dent fumbled for words. "But you were saying something about Holywelkin?"

"Yes, and this is where the two came together for me. Once you have made a musical phrase, you have a sort of variable, a form that can be manipulated by equation."

"So you do," Dent said, squinting with concentration.

"Now—this is what struck me—there are ten operations by which one can change a phrase, or develop it, to use composing terms. *Change has ten forms.* And Holywelkin, do you see, in his equations describing the changes in microdimensional events, do you see, formulated *ten* big sets of equations. This is no shocking surprise, as the changes correspond in both cases to basic forms of change postulated in symbolic logic."

"I see?" Dent said.

"But the two are not just related. They are the same! Inversion, retrogradation, retrograde inversion, augmentation, diminution, partition, interversion, exclusion, inclusion, and textural change—these *composing operations* are the very ones described by Holywelkin's equations!"

"And so that means . . ." Dent said, and stopped, eyebrows raised.

"It means that the structure of our thinking and the structure of reality have an actual correspondence. Think about it," Johannes urged him. "When the big cyclic accelerators were set up in the 2900s in Mercury's orbit, they fired particles at higher energies than ever before. At those levels of energy *everything* appeared random, the results were so strange. Mauring postulated compactified curved dimensions to quantize gravity and explain certain features of particle physics, but she worked in isolation and the experimental physicists never saw a way of using her geometry—they thought it was just an abstract exercise. Do you see the problem?"

Dent cleared his throat, said carefully, "I can see there *must* have been a problem."

"Holywelkin, you see, came along at a time when the paradigm had topped out. This is always the great moment in physics, when the theoretical paradigm begins to break down under the weight of experimental data, because *someone's* got to make the break, in a lateral drift to a new paradigm.

"And Holywelkin did it. He studied Mauring's geometry and explained the data from the Great Synchrotrons in her terms: five macro-dimensions, five micro-dimensions, vanishing points, discontinuities and bubble discontinuities, pocket gravities, whitelines—all her strange system. He said that the shortest events were all the same—he called them glints, and postulated that they were moving according to the basic forms of change described in symbolic logic. Then he integrated Mauring's geometry and these principles of symbolic logic, down at this level where the events occurred chiefly in the sixth through the tenth dimensions—where particles per se had disappeared entirely."

"Disappeared entirely," Dent said.

"So with quantum mechanics fitting inside Holywelkin's more comprehensive physics, what do the equations describe? Very short-lived events, in waves with certain characteristics of form, amplitude, and frequency, changing by inversion, retrogradation, et cetera—"

"*Ah!*" Dent said, his deep frown replaced by a raised forefinger. "Like music!"

Johannes nodded. "Exactly. We exist in the middle world. The universe is about ten to the fortieth times bigger than us, and glints are about ten to the fortieth times smaller than us. This strikes me as suspicious, and I suspect it may be an artifact of our perceptual limits, but never mind that, the important thing is, most of existence is beyond our senses. We can know it discursively, to use your terms, but we can't know it by acquaintance. Thus it has no real meaning for us. Particularly when it gets as difficult and contrary to common sense as Holywelkin physics. To know the real nature of the universe by acquaintance—"

"By acquaintance with an analogy, you mean," Dent said, tugging hard on a moustache.

"Yes," Johannes agreed, nodding in approval, pleased that he was being understood to an extent, "but an accurate analogy, you see, an exact one. Using short tones of a certain pitch and timbre to represent glints, we can program Holywelkin's equations into the Orchestra's computer, and trace the progress of the glints musically—thus tracing the history of whatever substance the glints compose, no matter how large. We might then truly *understand* the nature of reality. . . ."

"And is this the music that you played on Lowell?" Dent asked.

"No no. Only a study for it."

"And people went mad."

"So I've been told." Because the accuracy of Holywelkin's physics might make it possible to predict the future. . . . "I don't want to talk about that. The important thing is, I'm not finished. There's the question of timbre, and of the origin of the first phrase. It's proving difficult." Because he wasn't ready to face the implications. Because there was no obvious starting point. Because . . . "Because I don't know enough yet."

Dent nodded, looking thoroughly confused. "I look forward to hearing this composition."

♪

the convocation of the irregulars

As they approached Grimaldi Margaret called a meeting of her security staff, and because of his adventures Dent Ios was allowed to join them. Margaret, Karna, Yananda, Marie-

Jeanne and Dent gathered in the Alnilam Chamber, a large clear bubble protruding from the side of *Orion*, and sat in one of the little nests of chairs out against the dome, where no one could hear them, or approach without being seen. The great clouds of the Milky Way spilled across the spangled blanket of stars, so that it seemed there was almost as much white in the vacuum as black.

"I want to know who is attacking Johannes," Margaret said.

Karna shrugged. "We all want to know that. But how?"

"What about this thing you heard in Lowell about the Greys?"

Marie-Jeanne spoke. "I was just outside the power plant, checking to make sure we had people at all the entrances. A man wearing a grey tunic and grey pants approached me. I've only seen a few Greys, and I didn't really think anything about his dress at first. He said, 'Are you with the Grand Tour?' and I said yes, and then he said, 'The Greys will kill the Master this time.' "

Dent, who was hearing this for the first time, gulped and said, "Oh my."

"So who are these Greys?" Margaret demanded.

Karna looked to Yananda. Yananda, a small swarthy Indian who had worked with Karna for years, shrugged apologetically and said, "Very little is known about them. Their world is Icarus, a natural asteroid with an irregular orbit that comes very close to the sun. In fact it's said in the Jupiter system that they are sun worshippers, and I think it may be true. But no one knows for certain. There are a lot of them on Mercury, I've heard, and some around Jupiter." He shrugged again. "Another of the secret religions, like the Phoenixes, or the Magi, or the Rosicrucians."

"But why would they want to kill Johannes?" Margaret said.

No one ventured a response.

"And if they did want to kill him, why would one of them tell us about it?"

"There may be different factions within the Greys," Yananda said. "I heard a woman on Callisto claim that, a few years ago. She said the whole cult was in the midst of a civil war."

"Or it could be part of something else," Margaret said. "A threat."

"It does seem like they're trying to scare us, more than kill him," Karna said. "That hot light on Titania—all they would have had to do was aim it right, and Johannes would have been dead. Missing him like that—it almost had to have been deliberate."

"Unless there was a struggle at the source of the hot light," Yananda said.

Margaret shook her head. "More likely it was deliberate. And that vandalism in our lounge—it's all calculated to terrorize. But to what end? Dent, tell us again what happened to you."

Hesitantly Dent described his first encounter with Red Whiskers in Lowell, and then how he had caught sight of the man again in Titania. "I'm sure he didn't mean to be seen by me," Dent said. "He was slipping away when I saw him, and there's no way he could have known I would be watching."

"Perhaps," Margaret said. They considered what little they knew in silence. Then Margaret said, "We have to act. We can't sit back passively and wait for the next attack, and then try to defend ourselves. We have to find out who they are, and what they're after, and deal with them. Pre-empt them."

Karna and Marie-Jeanne were nodding. "Let's go after them," Karna said. "But we won't be able to do that cooped on this ship."

"Unless they're aboard," Dent said, looking around the Alnilam Chamber.

"That's true," said Margaret. "The vandalism shows they were aboard once."

"But it would help to get an outside investigation started," Karna said. "There's a ship leaving Grimaldi for the Jupiter system direct. I was already going to send down some people to look into security on Ganymede."

"All right," Margaret said. "You'd better stay here and help me coordinate things. Yananda, you go down to Jupiter and learn what you can."

"Good," said Yananda. "I've got friends there who will help."

"I'd like to help as well," Dent said timidly.

Margaret regarded him with skepticism. His face was still misshapen from the cut and bruise on his cheek, and Margaret thought, here's an offer of help from a man beaten up by a sheep. But she said, "You can help us here. Maybe we can arrange some kind of trap for whoever is aboard." She thought about it, looking disgusted, and suddenly she struck the arm of her chair. "On a tour like this *we are our own police*. No one plays games with me and gets away with it."

♪

floating worlds

Meanwhile great *Orion* blazed onward, leading its comet's tail of followers, and as they shot across the vacuum they passed many of the scores of terras that orbited in the huge ring between the orbits of Uranus and Saturn. From the Rigel Room or the Alnilam Chamber, or through the roof of Bellatrix Hall, the passengers of *Orion* could occasionally spot three or four of them at once: whitsuns like stars, in a binary twirl with a little light blue soap bubble; and in each bubble discontinuity, a green world. Some of the terras grew to the size of lamps in the windows of their spaceship, where they could be closely observed by the curious travelers. Marveling in this way the voyagers rocketed past Da Vinci, which displayed a geography reminiscent of Ptolemy's world map, in that the long boot of Italy curved over the middle of the world, and the rest of the Mediterranean surrounded it, so that the people there could live in a replica of the Renaissance; and they sped past Dvorak, whose people were steadily preparing the terra to become a starship, by stockpiling goods and creating ecospheres until their world was a little Earth, and they were ready to spin out of the solar system to meet the universe, linked only by their whiteline to home; and past The Fortunate Isles, a water world whose ocean was broken only a few times by archipelagoes, so that hardy seafarers sailed from island to island perpetually, trading under a tropical whitsun, telling the solar system's greatest tales, and avoiding the worldwide storms that spun about the terra and whipped up waves that could even swamp the isles, and certainly could sink ships, so that one could die in The Fortunate Isles; and past Samadhi, a terra of devout Buddhists who had sculpted their land to resemble the steep misty mountains of Chinese landscape paintings, where they could sit in pavilions and drink rice wine as they contemplated the source of the peach-blossom stream; past Lebedyan, a terra founded by the utopian Anya Lebedyan, where the wishes of children were paramount in the affairs of state, and the people shared communal dorms or ventured to isolated cabins, at the whim of their children; past Reiphantasy, where the citizens grafted themselves to machines, forming cybernetic creatures that even in the Jupiter system would have been thought perverted, for very few people anywhere wanted their humanity tampered with; and past Tycho, where a people who called themselves the natchvolk expiated some ancient sin by living without a whitsun, in huts on a bare rock asteroid, in perpetual night; and past Sappho, or While-away, or An-Athos, where a civilization of women lived by themselves.

These terras the passengers on *Orion* were able to recognize; others passed in the distance like marbles thrown by their faces. Little worlds, separated from the void by invisible bubbles, simple discontinuities—I suppose you, dear Reader, coming as you may from a civilization that believes in phlogiston, or from a civilization that speculates that action at a distance is accomplished by the vibration of the ether, or from a civilization that imagines it impossible to determine simultaneously both the location and the velocity of an electron—I suppose you may find such a discontinuity in the fabric of the real difficult to believe in. But consider it, Reader: do we not often see discontinuities as radical as this? Between hopes and achievements—pasts and futures—lives and deaths? And consider it, Reader: inside your skull is another bubble called the dura, a tough bag enwrapping your brain. Inside this shell is your consciousness; outside this shell is the world; methinks there is no discontinuity more radical or strange than that. Are we not all little terras, separated from the universe by bubble discontinuities? And so you see the technological achievements of our Holywelkin Age are not without a match in the world you know.

♪

grimaldi

Then came the day when the soap bubble world circling its whitsun was Grimaldi. *Orion* braked in a fiery burst, and its passengers shuttled through Grimaldi's bubble discontinuity to the terra's surface.

Anticipation filling him, Dent Ios walked out of the tiny

terminal into bright sunlight. He led the tour crew and even the local guide to one of the Grimaldi villages, a stand of thirty-two pruned and shaped baobab trees, planted in a star-shaped pattern of Grimaldi's design. Long ago on Mars the utopian philosopher had had a vision of starfolk living in the environment of the African savannah, in tribal groups; here Grimaldi's followers had made it real. In his heightened mood Dent immediately felt the rightness of the philosopher's vision. The intense blue sky, the bright whitsun, the burnt yellow grass on a broad plain, the stands of baobab, the dark hills in the distance, the far-off herds of antelope or zebra—something about the sight was instantly familiar, instantly reassuring. The eons of human evolution had grown brains connected to this landscape, so that people's neural patterns were aligned to it; so Grimaldi had claimed, and Dent could only nod his agreement and skip to the baobab habitat happily. He could live here. And to hear Johannes Wright in such a place . . .

The crew and a group of locals ate a meal together on a deck set in the interwoven branches of two trees. From there they could see villages in the distance, against the dark brown hills. On the savannah foraged herds of zebra and gazelle, and the villagers told them of giraffes, elephants, baboons, and lions. After the meal the others went out to the granite amphitheater to prepare for the concert, and Dent was left in the milling crowd of offworlders. He wandered under the village, looked up at catwalks and open decks and box rooms set in the very highest branches of the trees. The treehouse village had the sort of intricacy that would please a child; it was all on the surface, ingeniously entwined with the trees.

Out on the savannah the big sink holding the amphitheater was filling with people: offworlders in their variety of height, coloring and costume; the local residents small, dark, sunburnt, and dressed in bright clothes that included liberal amounts of red. They danced to the tunes of pan pipes, and spoke English with a broad flat inflection. Four villages were visible from the edge of the ravine containing the amphitheater. In his wandering, absorbed by the sights and sounds of the crowd, Dent was scarcely aware of time passing. The rain-washed air conveyed images with perfect clarity; each blade of yellow grass called for Dent's attention, and he stared at the clouds and people's clothes as if newly alive. Quickly it was late in the day. People pointed at the stage of the amphitheater; Johannes was climbing into the Orchestra, into his own baobab, the tree where man was born. Dim yellow lights illuminated the glass statue, and in the twilight it stood forth clearly, in a fuzzy sphere of amber in the dusk. When Grimaldi's whitsun touched the western horizon the Orchestra began very slowly to spin: and Johannes Wright played.

♪

How does music mean? Not, you can be sure, in words. Music is a language untranslatable, it is too direct, too subtle, too . . . *other* for words. Music moves directly from the inner ear to the lower brain stem, where our emotional lives are generated; and nothing can stimulate the complex response that music does, except music itself.

So Dent sat on his knoll above the amphitheater and listened to Johannes Wright play, as the late afternoon shaded into evening; he listened with all his mind focused, his flesh quivering slightly in the cooling air. But you, dear Reader, cannot be *told* what Dent *heard*. Words cannot describe this music.

Still, be not annoyed with me. All is not lost. The mind is always singing, and somewhere inside each one of us pure music always flows. It flows from our bodies, the biologic symphony—heart pumping, blood pulsing, breath filling and then leaving us; it flows from the wave motion of the brain's electrochemical activity, as thoughts fire synapses and engender their own pitch, timbre, duration, motion; it flows from the spirit's transcendant reach, for the world beyond the world. The lush chords as you fall out of dream, the chants you hum to get you through work, the melodies spinning you off to sleep, they are greater than you know; listen to the embryo De Bruik within you, Reader, listen at last! Hear your music—hear it singing, in unforced creation—and know then that the music vibrating the twilight air on Grimaldi was somewhat like that interior majesty.

♪

So Dent listened, and when the concert was done, too full of thought to talk, too full of energy to sit, he hiked off into the hills. In the cool air faces rushed by. The people of Grimaldi had watched the performance in perfect silence, and when it was over they had applauded and headed back to their villages; the offworlders were subdued by the example of the locals, and were equally quiet. Dent followed small groups through the blue-violet dusk, over nearly invisible paths. The villages were dark groves against the silvery starlit savannah grass. Voices called out softly. Fireflies blinked and left their trails of light. The pattern of village, farm, and savannah gave way to a range of low hills; here the curving trail was lighter than the surrounding ground, and Dent followed it easily. Overhead the map of the stars was dominated by a big bright one—Sol itself—and by its dim illumination Dent could see over the dark hills for kilometers. He looked at the blazing star as he climbed a low knoll. "The sun," he said, in a voice choked with the questions only God could answer. He was completely alone now, and there was no sound but the low sough of the wind in the grass. There had been a moment in the concert, godzilla whistling over a bass susurrus, that fit this moment precisely. . . .

Had it been a dream? What had happened to him down on that primeval landscape? What you give to music, music gives back tenfold; while he listened time had curved to fit the rhythm, there had been intervals when duration had expanded to infinity, and in concentrating with all his being on the dense texture of sound he had fallen into seconds as long as years. In some of those stretches he had lost all sense of self, in others he had become acutely aware of his place, he had *felt* himself stuck by artificial gravity to the side of a tiny asteroid orbiting the sun far beyond Saturn, in the thirty-third century after Christ. . . . Had it finally happened? After all the years of toil and pain, war and waste, at this late date in history, had someone finally made a music that spoke the eternal?

The questions overwhelmed Dent, and he sat among rocks. He tried to recall what Johannes had said about his music. Dent had found the musician's theories obscure at best, and in his confusion he had nodded and pretended to understand in order to draw Johannes on; but at the time he had assumed this was merely another sort of program music. Rather than representing the sea or the starlight or some human drama, the music was meant to represent the micro-universe, a realm understood only by the most brilliant physicists. It had not seemed to Dent an important difference. Now he recalled what Johannes had said about accurate analogy, about using Holywelkin's actual equations to help generate the score for the music. "If that is the way the world works," he whispered, "then it is *beautiful*." Beautiful right down to its fundament. Beautiful, and something more disturbing than that—something that he couldn't grasp in words.

Down where the hills levelled into plain lay a village, looking like the last remnant of some great world-circling forest. There were a few lanterns lit in its trees, creating irregular globes of lit green leaves. A child's laugh wafted by on the breeze. Dent stood and stared at the grove curiously. They had taken in the concert with such equanimity! He wanted to run down to the village and shout to them the import of what they had heard, to exhort them into the hills to dance and rejoice, to glory in the sight of the distant Sol—

Voices from the nearby trail startled him. A group of four were traversing the hills. Their red capes looked black in the gloom. One of them carried a flashlight pointed down, bobbing a beam before them.

"There's someone up there," he heard one of them say. A woman's voice. They stopped, and the flashlight beam leaped up to shine on him.

"Hello!" he called.

"Hello," the woman answered, after a pause. The flashlight beam swept down, and the four approached. "Are you lost?" the woman asked.

"No," Dent replied. "I thought I'd hike up where I could get a view."

The boy holding the flashlight turned it up and covered it with his hand. In the ruddy glow Dent could make out the faces of the four, watching him curiously.

"Not much to see at night," a short, thick man said. "You're from offworld?"

"Yes. I'm here with the Orchestra."

"Thought so." The man's eyes gleamed. "Have you got a dartgun?"

"No!" Dent said. "Why?"

The man's teeth flashed as he grinned. "There are leopards in these hills, man. At night we cross in groups, with tranquilizer dartguns. You'd better take one of ours. You don't want to get eaten up here."

"True," Dent said. "But I don't want to take your gun. I wouldn't know how to get it back to you."

"It's not mine," the man said. "Just turn it in at the village when you get back. And don't stay up here too long alone like this. Leopards are fierce beasts."

"I won't," Dent said, looking over his shoulder. The man handed him a small pistol, and the group turned back toward the trail.

"We enjoyed the music," the woman who had first seen him said.

"Did you?" Dent said curiously, following them down the hillside.

"I like the Orchestra," the child said.

"We did indeed," said the woman. "We were talking about it before we saw you. It reminded me very much of dawn in our village. We have big flocks of doves, and crows, and mockingbirds, and—well—" She laughed uncertainly. "Tell us, does he play something different for every terra?"

"I'm not sure," Dent said. "I think he's still working out what he wants to play."

"Tell him, if you will, that what he played here was perfect for us."

"I will," Dent said. "I certainly will."

The group took off down the trail. The boy holding the flashlight called back, "I liked the Orchestra!" And they were gone.

Dent stood there, wind ruffling his hair. The gun in his hand was a constant reminder of the danger he was in, dashing his contemplations. The wind in the grass disguised a host of lesser sounds, and it was chill enough to give him goosebumps. Windy, dark, chill, vast . . . When his night vision returned he began to hike back down the path to his village. Near the plains he heard some beast's eerie cough, and he spun around with the gun at the ready. Leopard? Perhaps it had been a hyena. But hyenas were carnivores too. With a fearful shiver he hurried down the trail, stumbling and tripping awkwardly. The village that had been below him now bulged in the gloom to his right. He stopped momentarily to observe it in its slumber. Like a tree village at dawn: why not? In every thing the dance of glints was present. Dent felt once again the scope of Wright's music, its power.

Inaccurately he hummed and whistled snatches of the great composition; he needed a hundred voices, and with his one warbled up and through all of them. The ten forms of change. Seeing stars through the upper branches of the village gave him an idea, and he took a small notepad from his breast pocket and scribbled a triplet in it hastily, holding the dartgun delicately between his teeth.

A music leads the mind through the starry night
And the brain must expand to contain the flight
Like a tree growing branches at the speed of light

♪

the convocation of the greys

Once again Johannes found himself dropping further into the blue fugal state, in which instants of blue clarity overlapped, or reversed their order. . . . To simplify matters Johannes left the small party in Margaret's room. Among the top branches of the baobab they were housed in was a small deck, reached only by a single long rope-railed ladder. Ascending it Johannes felt the exhaustion in his limbs. On the deck he stood in the wind and looked out at the dark earth, the midnight sky black overhead, blue on the horizons. Villages in the distance sparked like clouds of fireflies. Breezes rustled the baobab leaves in tight ellipses of movement; Johannes leaned out over the rope railing to pull a leaf down to him, luxuriating in the multifarious clicking of the rustle. He stared long at the veins in the waxy surface, as if they were a score that could tell him his music. A leaf of life, patterned so clearly in shades of blue, what was it telling him?

A head popped over the edge of the ladder-hole in the platform. Old schoolmate Anton Vaccero, red hair spiraling in tight curls. "Strange thing, Johannes," he said, scrambling onto the platform. "A man wanted to give you a message, but he refused to come up in the tree. He was a Grey, I think."

Greys always watched him with a curious intensity. "What did he say?"

"He said, the Greys meet on Grimaldi's gravity generator tonight, and—because of Holywelkin, he said—you should attend. I don't know what he meant. He said the code for the elevator doors is Grimaldi."

"Holywelkin went to Icarus once."

"What's that?"

"I said, Holywelkin went to Icarus once. Did you know that?"

"No," Anton said. "I didn't."

"Greys on Grimaldi . . . this is peculiar, Anton. Perhaps I will visit these mysterious Greys, and learn what I can of them."

"Perhaps I should come with you."

"Perhaps *I* should come with you," said Karna Godavari, sticking his head out of the ladder-hole. Anton jumped at his voice. Karna rose through the hole smoothly, like a dark spirit. "What did this messenger look like, Anton?"

Vaccero cleared his throat. "He was short, light-haired, dressed in ordinary traveling clothes, a one-piece, but it was the cult's grey. I don't know. Nothing distinctive."

"You are to report all incidents of this kind directly to me, Anton," Karna said softly. "Do you understand?"

Vaccero nodded, looking down.

"I want to see them," Johannes told Karna.

"But they could be the ones who attacked you in Titania."

"What makes you think so?"

". . . People have said the Greys are interested in you."

Johannes thought, That is true.

"Somebody wishes you harm," Karna continued. "It may be them."

"I want to see them anyway," Johannes said. "Come with me; you can protect me. You may learn something too."

"I'll join you," Vaccero said.

"No," said Karna sharply. "I only want to guard one person."

Johannes descended the steep steps of the stair ladder. "Come along," he said up to Karna. "Anton, I'll tell you what happens tomorrow." Down steps of wood whose grain was etched in long ellipses, through the shadows in the mesh of branches, onto the broad catwalk that bulged into a promenade, down the broad staircase spiraling about the thick knobby treetrunk. Across the infinite complexity of the blue grass. In the center of the village was a low concrete blockhouse, with a single steel door. By the light of a few lanterns in the trees around, Johannes and Karna inspected a panel displaying the letters of the alphabet. Karna tapped out GRIMALDI and the door chimed. He turned the handle and pulled it open.

"Simple enough," Johannes said.

"The lock must be to keep strangers out." Karna entered, and Johannes followed him. Darkness. A narrow cone of light from Karna's flashlight illuminated another panel. He tapped out the eight letters again, and the door of a well-lit elevator slid open, spilling yellow all through the chamber. Inside there were only two buttons, UP and DOWN. Karna pushed DOWN, the door closed, and they felt the initial drop.

"Journey to the center of the earth," Johannes whispered. The descent took a long time. Then they came to a halt, and the door slid open, spilling light over a dim hallway. Karna stepped out, a small pistol held in his right hand. "Come on. Nobody home."

Johannes stepped into a hall that curved down sharply, over the relatively small sphere that they now walked on.

Floor, walls and ceiling were made of some dull metal, and all showed the curve of the two spheres they walked between. Square orange lights were set high in the walls every ten or twelve meters. The air was hot and humid, and the only sounds were their metallic footfalls and the distant whoosh of an air duct, sounding like the breeze on the terra's surface. The sharp downward curve of the hallway prevented them from seeing very far in either direction.

Karna led the way forward, gesturing with the pistol for Johannes to follow. Johannes hesitated, and noticed that although only a few meters away Karna stood upright at a slightly different angle than he did. Suddenly he felt how near to the gravity station they were; their hallway must be just over the cavity that contained the generator.

Some distance along the curve in the hallway the floor changed to a thick clear glassy material. Now below their feet they saw the planetoid's heart: a big spherical cavern, carved out when Grimaldi was settled. The rough nickel-iron walls of the cavern were ribbed with thick, curved steel bands; from these bands massive steel girders extended in to the center of the cavern, holding there a large sphere of banded concrete. Inside the hollow ball of the terra, the hollow ball of the concrete sphere; and inside the concrete sphere, the gravity generator. In that generator a singularity was created, controlled, sustained; and the singularity drew this whole little world to it with one gee, pulling with that force all the way out to the bubble discontinuity that was another of the generator's effects, where it ended abruptly.

A few orange lights were set into the wall of the cavern, and by the dim light Johannes saw that their floor opened up ahead of them, dropping by steps to a clear platform that ended in a steep metal staircase, which descended (looking like a steel strut that had buckled under the stress) to the surface of the concrete sphere. And down there—marching around from the other side of the concrete shell, marching sideways as it seemed to Johannes and Karna—came figures, people in robes that appeared dull orange. Ten of them appeared, marching with a long slow stride until they had formed a circle around the bottom of the staircase that led up to Johannes and Karna. Greys, Johannes thought. And they knew he would be there.

Karna was looking at him. "What should we do?" he whispered.

"If we can hear them, let's stay up here." They edged forward to the clear platform, stepped down onto it. They were well in sight of those below, but none of them were looking up. Warm air rising out of the cavern carried a scent like cinnamon. Johannes put his hand on Karna's arm, feeling a bit dizzy. Dim orange light in a dark blue cavity, thick girders extending across curved space; it was disorienting. Only the powerful pull of the concrete globe kept him from spinning.

One more Grey appeared around the curvature of the globe, weaving upside down between the girders. When the others saw him they began to sing a chant of vowels, in low tones. Echoes gave the chant thick metallic overtones, as if the girders were resonating with the sound. The new figure raised a hand over his head (almost pointing up at Johannes) and from the inner wall of the planetoid a thin beam of packed light burst on, appearing like one of the massive girders turned to fire. A whole forest of shadows sprang to life, redefining the dimensions of the entire cavern. The beam sizzled between the lamp and the pointing figure, whose robe now glowed in an ivory blaze. Under a deep ivory hood the figure wore a flat black mask; it made him only the outline of a human figure, standing like white stone while the figures around him chanted the vowels, and bitter cinnamon swirled in the air. The brilliantly lit cavern pulsed in a sharp chiascuro, and once again Johannes lost his sense of spatial relationships. Echoes from the chant were more reliable for basic orientation than the black-and-white vibrations reported by his photoptic cells, and Johannes thought, You're a blind man, depend on your strong sense.

Two women dressed in grey robes appeared around the globe, holding a big red rooster by neck and feet. The chanting grew in volume and split into a dense polyphony, in which words of a language unknown to Johannes were perhaps being sung; or perhaps it was just glossolalia. A man in a bright blue robe came next, holding a large glass bowl.

The figure caught in the beam of packed light moved to the two women; the rooster flapped desperately in the hands of its captors. With a sudden quick movement the fowl's head was neatly cut off. Light red blood fountained into the glass bowl; the women held it over the bowl until the body had drained. Then the bowl was held overhead by the lit figure. Over the confused chanting he sang like a cantor, "*Te Cauterizo, i Saturn, i Atar, i Opi, amesha spentas.*" The cavern's acoustics were strange, the chant washed over the lead figure's voice from time to time, and Johannes could not be certain what he heard, what he missed, what he imagined. "And end aforeknowlia," the figure warbled in falsetto, "an end to aforeknowlia, by which we see a symmetry of time." Or had he said "asymmetry of time"? "*Felix qui potuit rerum cognisceri causos. Causa aequat effectum.* Ahura-Mazda be with us now, Ahura-Mazda be praised before all."

The bowl was passed among the figures, and each drank from it. Johannes swallowed convulsively, imagining the taste of the blood. And the lead figure, with the beam of packed light following him, began to step up the stairway toward Karna and Johannes. Karna stiffened.

The figure stopped; his head tilted back, and the flat black mask appeared to be looking straight at them. The chanting dropped to a pianissimo murmur.

"Master of Holywelkin's Orchestra!" the figure called, in a muffled voice. "Master of Holywelkin's Orchestra!"

Johannes took a step forward; Karna held him by the

shoulder, restraining him. Everyone stopped; time stood still; Johannes, knowing not what to say, remained silent.

"Master of the Orchestra, grace us with your presence."

"I do," Johannes said.

"Master, you search for Holywelkin . . . you search for Holywelkin. We knew him on Iapetus, at Fairfax House . . . Fairfax House, look there. Holywelkin whom Ahura-Mazda blessed remains there still. Master of the Orchestra, with your presence grace us. Ahura-Mazda follows you."

And the figures answered, "Aaaaaaa—eeeeeee—ooooo-ooo—uuuuuuu."

With that the ceremony, or communion, was over. The Greys marched sideways around the globe, the leader retreated down the steps and walked upside down around the globe. The packed light disappeared, leaving the dim orange glow no more than a kind of darkness.

Karna took a deep breath. "Could you hear what he said? I couldn't understand a word of it in all that chanting."

"Most of it," said Johannes, deep in thought. Holywelkin had met the Greys on Iapetus, at one of that world's great old mansions. And he was there still? In some symmetry of time?

"So they knew you would be here," Karna said. "I don't like that."

"They told me to come."

"I don't like that either."

"Let's get back to the surface. I can't see down here. Everything looks wrong."

The curving metal hallway was empty; apparently the Greys had taken another exit from the generator's cavity. Just as the elevator doors closed, however, a man in a grey tunic ran by, staring into their little elevator chamber wildly. But they were on their way up, and could not stop the process. The elevator pulled them away from the singularity like a rocket.

The Greys had something to do with the sun. Had something to do with Holywelkin. Had something to do with Johannes Wright. He could not understand it. Happy are those who can know causes? Or *not* know causes? He wasn't sure. Causes equal effects, he was sure of that phrase. And Ahura-Mazda was a name for Sol. But in the universe of his ignorance, diffuse galaxies of the known, scattered at random, told him only so much and no more.

"Always bring me along for anything of that sort," Karna was saying. "These Greys could be dangerous."

"Yes."

And then they were on the surface. Under the trees it was chilly. Johannes ascended the circling stairs of his baobab, more tired than ever, black cracks in the blue, round and round ascending as in the spiral of life. . . . He was high among the main branches when he nearly collided with Dent Ios. He scarcely recognized him. They stood for a moment still as stones, each staring as if the other were a ghost; then without a word Johannes walked on and climbed to bed.

♪

the irregulars disperse

"All right," Margaret said, when Karna had reported the previous night's events to her. "Now we act." She pointed a finger at Karna. "See if you can find these Greys, on Grimaldi or in the ships following us."

Karna nodded, and behind him Yananda, Marie-Jeanne and Dent nodded attentively.

"Yananda, when you get to Ganymede, do whatever you can to learn more about the Greys. Join them if you have to."

Yananda said, "I will."

"They want something from Wright," Karna said. "And that wall drawing in our suite, of the bull being sacrificed— that sounds like their work as well."

"What about the attack on Titania?" Dent said.

Karna nodded. "It's possible. They're a religious cult of some kind—"

"Sun worshippers," Yananda said.

"And they make animal sacrifices. Maybe they were trying to sacrifice Johannes on Titania. Or doing it symbolically. Anyway if they're sun worshippers they may use Holywelkin in their religion somehow, and so Johannes is brought into it because of the Orchestra. We can't be sure until we know more about them."

"Enough," Margaret said. "The truth is we don't know enough to speculate. But we know enough to act, because you can act in ignorance. Yananda, get on that shuttle to Jupiter. The rest of you get to work finding out what you can about the Greys. I know every one of you has a network of some sort of information."

Her listeners nodded their agreement, feeling heartened by her determination. Then Dent said, "Remember, the Greys are so secretive—it would be easy to *pretend* to be Grey."

And the irregulars stared grimly at him.

Chapter Four

‖: THROUGH THE :‖ DISCONTINUITY

anton's whiteline

In his dream the ship was dark, figures rustled as they scurried past him in the halls, in one black corner Ekern seized him by the elbow and told him to murder everyone on the tour. But how? he croaked. And why?

Someone was calling his name. Better hide! He pulled his pillow over his head and that taught him where he was. Groggily he sat up, his stomach filled, as it was every morning, with a big knot.

"Anton!" His assistant Sara Eagleton stuck her head in the doorway.

"What?" He pulled the sheet up to his chest.

"We're passing Spandel's whiteline, and we have a good view from our suite window. You said you wanted to see it."

"Last thing I want to see," Vaccero muttered.

"What?"

123

"Be there in a minute."

His crew laughed affectionately as he staggered past them
to the bathroom. "You shouldn't get so bent every night,"
Rudyard called. Anton nodded, smiled briefly at them. Good
crew, all comfortable with each other and with him. The
stomach knot began to untie. Back from the bathroom he
joined the lighting crew in the suite lounge, where one wall
was a window. Sean and Ngaio were fiddling with a small
telescope on a stand. Sara handed Anton a cup of steaming
lemon tea. The window was still packed with stars, but
Rudyard and Angela were sure the whiteline would appear
soon.

"There is what's left of Vermeer," Sean said quietly.

Out in the vacuum, tumbling in the middle distance between them and the stars, were chunks of rock, some big,
some small, all jagged: a little school of fresh rough asteroids. Anton didn't want to think about Spandel and his
incredible revenge, but his crew discussed the case with
relish. Spandel had been kicked off his terra Vermeer for
opposing the state; it had been a sort of Fourier communal-
ism, and Spandel had insisted upon raising his own child. For
that he had been exiled, into a decade of bitterness and insane
plotting: long voyage downsystem, complicated sabotage at
Vulcan Station, and Vermeer's whitsun had veered into the
little world's center, destroying it and its hundred thousand
inhabitants instantly. Spandel had committed suicide at the
same moment.

It was a minor affair compared to the big accident, of
course, but this had been deliberate, and in the outer terras
the shock of the news eventually shifted to a morbid fascina-
tion: Spandel of Vermeer was remembered ever after in
songs, programmatic symphonies (pogrommatic symphonies,
Vaccero called them sourly), operas. . . .

"And here's the whiteline that did it," Sean said, pointing
at the bottom of the window.

"You'd think they'd have shut it off for good," said Sara.

"It provides the whitsun for Tortuga as well," Sean replied. "There, see it?"

Whitelines are so named for the distortion of the stars seen through them; the lines themselves are invisible pencil beams of higher dimensions, in which the laws of the macro-world no longer obtain. Inside the beam they now looked at, free glints escaped the tight curvature of the higher dimensions and snapped to their moment of fiery emergence in the whitsun at the end of the beam. But starlight seen through the beam stretched with it, in an effect similar to a gravitational lens, so that the beam appeared a transparent white line, and as the ship moved, shifting the crew's viewpoint, stars nearing the line suddenly stretched and disappeared into it, while other stars suddenly coalesced out of the line and popped back into the network of constellations. Strange sights. Perhaps it was the strangeness of whitelines that caused the constant speculation concerning them; or perhaps it was their evident power. For whatever reason, tales concerning the powers of whitelines were common. Some said that too close an approach to a whiteline would duplicate the spaceship and everyone on it; others said that material objects placed in an uncapped whiteline would be instantly transported an immense distance across the universe—a theory that was actually being tested on Mars; while others said that if this latter story were true, it meant that the objects were being projected into the past. . . .

"I'm going to get something to eat," Vaccero said, disturbed at the visible proof of such discontinuities in the real. He left the suite, walked down the halls toward the elevator. He wasn't really hungry. Passing one of the practice rooms a voice called him—"Anton!"

It was Johannes. Vaccero stopped in the doorway, and watched the slight powerful hands bounding up the keyboard of a black piano. Johannes smiled at him. Always the same, Vaccero thought, cheerful and unconcerned, friendly, not

very perceptive. . . . Johannes waved at the empty piano
backing his. "Anton! Do you want to play?"

Vaccero swallowed convulsively, shook his head. "Work
to do, Johan, I'm on my way to it."

"Ach," Johannes said, but Vaccero was already off down
the hall, the knot tighter than ever in his stomach, pursued by
quick descending arpeggios that mocked his retreat; and he
heard again, in two voices, the child's and the man's, *"Anton! Do you want to play?"*

For they had been schoolmates. Childhood friends.

They had both attended the Vancouver Conservatory, in
the town of Vancouver on the far side of Pluto, up at the
head of the Plenka Valley. Vancouver was a pleasant string
of green half-globes, a quiet town on the edge of the night, as
far away from Lowell as one could get on Pluto. At the
conservatory they were very serious and thorough; everyone
on Pluto learned music in their home, often under quite
rigorous instruction, and so to justify its existence the school
had to do more. Learning several instruments, and the elements of composition, was just the beginning. It was an old
school with a long tradition (the third Master of Holywelkin's
Orchestra had been trained there, as they always said) and the
work was hard. Anton, one of the lucky children accepted to
the school, had gone planning to become the next De Bruik;
he was certain he had in him a whole world of new music.
He had arrived on the same day as Johannes Wright, and so
they were given adjacent rooms in the dorm. In the next
room was a girl named Elyse.

In the years that followed they became fast friends. But
early on the work began to oppress Anton; he found he was
barely up to it, and he became frightened sometimes. His
friends were a comfort. In the evenings when they each
practiced alone in their soundproofed rooms it occurred to
him that they were actually composing trios in some tele-
pathic way. He was sure the trios were beautiful. When he
mentioned the idea to the other two, Johannes insisted they

tape their practices and then play the tapes all at once; they did it, and Johannes and Elyse laughed madly the whole hour.

Then Anton changed, and found he was in love with Elyse. He gave her significant looks and self-conscious caresses, and her response was accommodating enough to allow him to think she felt as he did, although it took some imagination. Johannes, now, was still in love with music only. Anton imagined Elyse and him performing together during the annual recital week; playing the principles in that year's opera, *The Lovers of Phobos;* being acknowledged a serious couple.

It hadn't turned out that way. One day after their deeplearning class they were led onto the roof porch, still disoriented by the drugs and the subliminal imagery. Anton had determined to ask Elyse to play with him during the recital week, and he followed her. Persephone's light shattered in her thick yellow hair, and in his ears the chattering voices still sounded, as they were meant to: *Music is the relation between the sound, the listener, the emotion evoked, and the context. We call the sound the sign, the emotion the signification; but all parts contribute to the whole. . . .* As always when the deeplearning drugs were used, Anton was in a highly wrought state in which everything was striking and significant; the whole world sang to him. A stiff breeze raked the rooftop, one of Vancouver's innumerable flocks of swallows turned all at once in the air over him—magic!—and his fellow students' faces were wide-eyed, attentive to inner trains of thought, to the voices. Beyond the hemisphere of air over Vancouver the surface of Pluto was blacker than the night sky. Anton approached Elyse, asked her, "W-will you play a duet with me during recital week? I've written a four-handed thing for us."

"I can't," she said. "Johan and I are playing, and that will take up all my turns."

The pit of his stomach had risen to clutch at his heart. He turned away. Johannes stood on a rooftop corner, facing the wind and singing nonsense syllables, up and down, up and down. Persephone blared on them, the other students wandered in circles, the wind made his eyes water and suddenly everything was stripped clear, the flagstones of the rooftop sharply individuated, everything painfully bright.

And so the recital week occurred just as he had imagined it, only it was Johannes with Elyse, at every point. Anton hated them both; but it was a piteous hatred, mixed with envy and jealousy, and the desire that things return to the way they had been, and it made him miserable.

But that was just the start. Everyone suffers disappointments of this sort, in the throes of adolescence; a year or two later and Anton hardly remembered it, although underlying all of his interactions with Johannes there was now an undercurrent of dislike. And this was reinforced by something even more serious than the affair with Elyse; for musically Johannes was surging off into realms of his own, astonishing classmates and teachers alike; while Anton could barely keep up with the required work. Anton knew he had the greater potential, but this knowledge began to slip under the pressure of the real. Subtleties of compositional theory escaped him, and he began to recall with great bitterness his childhood certainty that he would become the next De Bruik. It had been, apparently, only a foolish dream. And at the same time he had to watch the meteoric progress of his hated friend! He felt as though his music were being stolen from him. He got so far behind in his work that the school took him in hand and forced him through the deeplearning classes that would allow them to graduate him. They gave him a degree and sent him away.

After that he was sick of music, and he became a lighting technician in Lowell. New problems beset him. He heard that Johannes had been named apprentice to the Master of Holywelkin's Orchestra, and even at his remove in time and space the news cut him. He entertained black fantasies of musical revenge, of becoming the renegade genius, the Partch of the age. When he heard of Johannes's troubles with the Orchestra's board of directors he realized that Johannes had usurped that role as well. It seemed nothing was left for Anton to be! One day he was reading a life of Keats (he loved Keats for his burst of genius, for his darkly romantic end; he felt he was a Keats of sorts, living beyond his own death), and he came across a passage in one of the poet's letters:

> *My dear fellow I must let you know that as there is ever the same quantity of matter constituting this habitable globe—as the ocean notwithstanding the enormous changes and revolutions taking place in some or other of its demesnes—notwithstanding Waterspouts whirlpools and mighty Rivers emptying themselves into it, it still is made up of the same bulk—nor ever varies the number of its Atoms—And as a certain bulk of Water was instituted at the Creation—so very likely a certain portion of intellect was spun forth into the thin Air for the Brains of Man to prey upon it—You will see my drift without any unnecessary parenthesis. That which is contained in the Pacific and lie in the hollow of the Caspian— that which was in Miltons head could not find room in Charles the seconds—he like a Moon attracted Intellect to its flow—it has not ebbed yet—but has left the shore pebble all bare—I mean all authors of the present day— who without Miltons gormandizing might have been all wise Men.*

Thus Anton realized what had happened to him. He had been born into the Age of Johannes Wright—Johannes had drawn to himself all the available creative genius of the time, like a singularity bursting all its bubbles and sucking everything in—and there was nothing left for Anton to do but to try to forget all his dreams, all his hopes.

This strand of thought never left him, even when it was

overlaid with more adult problems and disappointments, which threatened to overwhelm him in their turn. The disastrous marriage to Janet, her desertion, these had to be coped with, and it was hard. One day talking to Janet on the holo he had truly forgotten the medium and tried to embrace her, to hold her to him; falling through her he suffered a breakdown of a kind, and had to be helped away.

Then one day on the commons of Lowell he had seen Janet, whom he had thought on Triton. He had chased her, and when he caught her and pulled her around by the arm she had melted before his eyes into Johannes Wright, breathing fire at him. The apparition had run off laughing, and Anton had collapsed, the fear of insanity stabbing through him. Then soon after that, in another holo room, he had sat like a stone, delaying his responses so that that awful Olga would think he had left Lowell for Copernicus, as he claimed to have done . . . delaying all of his responses the full ten seconds, and then when he did speak he told her that he loved her and that she should come to Copernicus to be with him . . . So that when Olga *had* left Lowell for Copernicus and he was out of danger (the woman had been mad!), he had felt the power of the lie, the exhilaration of deception; and when the bearded stranger approached him and explained that he had been deceived into practicing the deception, that Olga had acted her part . . . along with his anger he had felt an incredulous admiration. Here was a deception even more powerful than his, an art of it. . . . That was his introduction into metadrama, made for him by Master Ekern. The vision of Janet becoming Johannes had been metadrama as well. He had been supposed to learn that Janet was evil for him, Johannes as well. "And you see it was an act to flay you to *life,*" Ekern said intently. "In this world we live behind veil after veil of illusion, we cushion ourselves from reality in great tissues of lies, until we live like mummies, already dead. The work of the order is to trick these lies away, to strip away all illusions and sorrows and make all these poor players *see* what a world they live in.''

So Anton had become apprentice to Master Ekern, in the secret art; and so began another sequence of wrenching, bitter, anxious days.

. . . In the hallway of the great *Orion* Vaccero shook his head hard, clearing it of shadows. Out a little hall window he could still see the whiteline, bending starlight. And there was the whitsun burning at its end, illuminating the faery lamp of Tortuga's blue bubble, there amongst the stars in the pulsing blackness of space. What a world they lived in, how strange and mysterious!—and yet suddenly Vaccero saw the analogy on which it had all been constructed. For the giant Sol was like the greatness of the human heart, bursting with heat and life; and whitelines were like human desires, firing invisibly away from the heart; and the scattering of whitsuns were like human goals, blazing off in the distance, illuminating the perfect little worlds of our dreams. And with an inchoate solar flare of pain arching out of the sun in his chest, Anton Vaccero realized that for him the whiteline machinery was broken beyond repair.

♪

ten dimensions

"What about these ten dimensions," Dent said to Johannes one day. "Just what does Holywelkin mean by them?"

They were in the Alnilam Chamber, looking at the broad tapestry of stars; the constellation that was their ship's namesake stood before them, perpetually taking aim with the arrow that would never fly. Johannes pursed his lips at Dent's phrasing.

"It's not just what Holywelkin means by them," he said. "They really exist, you know."

"So I'm told."

"And you see the evidence for them all around you. You have lived in them all your life."

"The whitsuns, you mean."

"The whitsuns and all the other manipulations of the higher dimensions."

"But what are they? And how did we discover them?"

Johannes shoved his hands in his pockets, looked at the floor. "It began long ago, when a mathematician named Theodor Kaluza tried to explain electromagnetism by introducing the idea of a fifth dimension to the geometry of spacetime. Mathematically it was interesting, but as no fifth dimension could be found, the idea was abandoned. Then a Swedish physicist named Oskar Klein proposed that the fifth dimension was so tightly curved that any particle that moved in that direction would return to its starting place after moving only a microscopic distance. This would explain why we did not perceive the fifth dimension, and mathematically it also helped very much to explain quantum jumps of various kinds."

"You mean particles were jumping in the fifth dimension."

"Yes—or to be more exact, they would take short flights in the fifth dimension, and return in a slightly different place, and so look as if they had pulsed from one position to the next."

"I see."

"Well, mathematically, if one dimension like that could be postulated, any number could, and all sorts of movement on the subatomic scale could be explained as something more than an arbitrary given of Nature. In those early years there were mathematicians who proposed that there were as many as nine hundred and fifty dimensions! But for the physicists, as the years passed, the number necessary to explain subatomic motion was pared down. Mauring finally made the fullest theoretical model with her geometry of ten dimensions, five macro and five micro. But all this time, remember, it was uncertain whether these dimensions really existed, or were just useful mathematical tools. Only the immense energies made available to the Great Synchrotron and the Orbital Gevatron made it possible to find actual evidence of the micro-dimensions. And even then only Holywelkin recognized the data for what it was. But he did, and so here we are. Those whitelines we pass are discontinuities where, to put it simply, the sixth and seventh dimensions are penetrating our familiar four. A Holywelkin sphere is a bubble of the eighth dimension interacting with ours, and a whitsun is the energy of Sol bursting out of the higher dimensions into our world. And by these signs we know those dimensions are real.''

"Amazing," Dent said. "But what about the fifth macro-dimension? Why can we perceive the other four macro-dimensions, and not that one?''

"An interesting question," Johannes said with his inward smile. "And one with no clear answer. Mathematically, the fifth dimension is fairly straightforward, or so I am told. But explaining it in words has proved very difficult, and sometimes the explanations contradict each other. But what Mauring said, and Holywelkin generally agreed with her, is that the fifth dimension is a sort of reverse time. The fourth dimension, time as we usually think of it, moves in one direction, while the fifth, which Mauring called Antichronos, moves in the opposite direction, and it is the *interaction* of the two that gives time as we know it its particular pace, from moment to moment.''

"So that if the fifth dimension were stronger, time would be . . . slower?''

"Yes, it's not an impossible concept, the speed of time. Physicists have a smallest quantum unit of time flow, called the hadon—there are about ten to the twenty-fourth of them in every second. Presumably if time were slower, hadons would be longer, or something like that. The perceptual difficulties here are tremendous, and that is one reason discussion of the fifth dimension is so problematic. Holywelkin became quite mystical about it at the end, you know. He claimed that the peculiar force exerted within the discontinuity of a whiteline was such that the balance between the fourth and fifth dimensions was upset, so that a whitsun's fire appeared before it was generated in the power station.''

"But that's crazy!" Dent objected.

"True," Johannes said, nodding. "Still, if a physicist's mathematics work so well in the real world, one has to wonder if their metaphysical ideas might not be equally accurate. Or at least, more accurate than anyone else's."

"But effects appearing before their causes act!"

"I know. But people are testing aspects of the idea on Mars, with these whiteline probes—hoping to discover a mode of faster-than-light travel, and in my opinion murdering people in the attempt. . . ."

"I've heard of that," Dent said. "I'm surprised anyone would act on such an insane idea."

Johannes shrugged. "Mathematically, you see, it is not so crazy. The structure of our thinking and the structure of reality need not *always* correspond. Mauring herself said that it was the pressure of the two time dimensions working against each other that caused change to occur in the other dimensions—that entropy was the work of their contrary action . . . Chronos overcoming Antichronos, but also grinding up the world in the attempt."

Dent sighed. "I don't think I have the temperament to grasp these things. . . ."

Johannes smiled again. "And Holywelkin! He said that when we dream, we are living in the fifth dimension, in the realm of Antichronos, and claimed that this explained the scrambled nature of our dreaming consciousness, and the curious frequency of precognitive dreams."

"Holywelkin sounds like a raving lunatic," Dent said.

Johannes nodded. "But look at the proof of his work." He gestured out at the pure black ground of the constellations, where the spangling of stars was punctuated by the first magnitude pinpoints of several whitsuns. "Such results in the real world are hard to argue with."

For a long time they stared out at space. Such an intense, perfect black, pierced so very often by the jewelry of the stars; as always when Dent contemplated the sky for too long, he became a little giddy.

"It is so vast and . . . all-encompassing," Dent said, waving out at the sight incoherently. "It is almost as if . . . space itself is God."

The inward smile. "A man named Henry More wrote the same thing in 1671, in a book called *Enchiridion Metaphysicum*. He noted that the attributes of space are the same as those that the Scholastics had always assigned to the Supreme Being. 'One, simple, immovable, eternal, complete, independent, existing by itself, existing through itself, incorruptible, necessary, measureless, uncreated, unbounded, incomprehensible, omnipresent, incorporeal, all-pervading, all-embracing, Being in essence, Being in act, pure act, pure Being.' "

Dent shook his head. "I don't understand most of those. Why is space *necessary,* for instance?"

"I'm not sure it is. And I don't know that it must be incomprehensible, either." Johannes turned from the view to observe a group of people entering the chamber. Three people were stumbling over each other, giggling. Small wire-covered helmets encased their heads, leaving their vacant faces open to the world. "More proof of Holywelkin's work," he said sarcastically.

When Dent saw them he gasped. "What are they?"

"They are dreamwalkers," Johannes said. He looked at Dent curiously. "You really didn't know?"

Dent blushed. "I've never really paid much attention to the worlds outside the Uranus system. . . ."

"These are probably Jovians. The helmets keep their brainwaves in the delta state, where they will dream continuously. See their eyes."

Dent watched one woman and saw that her eyes were jerking back and forth violently, like a little pair of beings trying to break free. He shuddered.

"So we all appear while dreaming," Johannes said. "But the helmets can be programmed to feed the brain certain sensory stimuli, so that these people are partially awake, and their dreams are guided by the stimuli. Thus they send themselves on surrealistic voyages—perhaps into the fifth dimension, eh?" He laughed, waved back at the stars behind them. "Retreating into their pitiful fantasies, while all the while they are being carried by great winds across the sky."

♪

augmentation, diminution

Margaret Nevis was happy to land on Iapetus, her little home world. Every familiar sight made her smile: the large rundown space terminal, the big broad boulevards outside, the green tram cars, the frosty comet remnants dusting the rocky plains outside the hemispheres, reflecting in bright highlights the glow from the city; and ringed Saturn, floating big and beautiful in the sky above. Yes, Port Iapetus was the same as ever. The sound of Russian made her smile. And she liked the sense of order. Not for her the anarchic chaos of the outer terras, where nothing about the cities made sense. Long after she left it she had learned to appreciate Port, where the rectangular pattern of streets and avenues, paved with hard black composite, intersected in a completely predictable way with the radiating boulevards, which were paved with whitish basalt. And traffic directors aiding the flow of electric cars through every complex intersection. Yes, it was an intelligent design for a city. As the crew took a car through the crowded streets to the Port Concourse she said complacently to Dent, "I'm a socialist at heart, you know. Those outer terras aren't my style."

"Why do you live out there, then?" Dent asked.

Margaret didn't reply; she didn't really know. Instead she said, "There's something here about the feel between the people, of cooperation. Like we're all part of the same team, you see? Ah, you edgefolk—I doubt you'd understand."

"It seems rather dull, actually," Dent said. "All these stone buildings placed so regularly . . . not very spontaneous," he explained, seeing Margaret's expression.

"No," Margaret said. "But I like it. I was going to work here, you know." She pointed. "Like her. I was going to be a traffic cop."

Dent smiled. "You got your wish, in a way."

In the two days before the Iapetus concert Margaret enjoyed herself, renewing acquaintances with old friends, visiting parks and museums that she remembered liking, showing the curious Dent (whom she liked better for his curiosity) what their version of Martian socialism could achieve, and speaking Russian again. It made her quite unexpectedly happy, and she wondered at herself; it had been fifteen years since she had last been on Iapetus—when she had left she was twenty-four, now she was thirty-nine—and she supposed that the explanation was that she had forgotten what it was to have a home, in her outer world of roving isolatoes. The very concept had escaped her.

But on the day of the concert when she went to the old Port Concourse, the managers brought her bad news. Computer fraud was suspected in the sale of some tickets for the concert; it could be that some seats had been sold twice.

"The Concourse's capacity is twenty-five thousand?" Margaret asked, though she knew the figure.

The manager confirmed it.

"Get me Gregor Kammerer in the Office of Fire and Safety, down at the Government Complex," Margaret ordered, and hurried off to the gates.

The Concourse was a big indoor arena, oval in shape, with entrances at both of the long ends of the oval. The main entrance, where people were now filing in to hear the concert, was a curve of tall panels of stained glass, with the doors at the bottom of the middle panels. Margaret went to the head ticket-taker and checked her little master counter, which clicked over rapidly. Already the counter registered sixteen thousand, and looking out the open doors Margaret could see six lines of people stretching off across Port Plaza and down Westport Boulevard; no end of them in sight. Karna was across the foyer overseeing the security checks and Margaret told him to send her Marie-Jeanne. When Marie-Jeanne arrived Margaret said, "Get out there and estimate how many people are left in the lines. I want it within a hundred—close as you can make it." Marie-Jeanne nodded and hurried away.

The concourse manager waved her over to his phone. "I've got Kammerer on the line."

Margaret took the phone and looked into it. "Gregor, we've got a problem down here at the Concourse. I need your help."

"What is it?"

"Apparently the Concourse people have oversold our concert by some significant figure. People are piling into the Plaza, and the Concourse is almost full. When it fills and there's still a lot of people out there with tickets, it's going to get ugly."

"What do you want me to do?"

"You'll have to approve filling the place beyond the normal safety code."

Her old schoolmate's face wrinkled with displeasure. "I

don't have the authority to do that, Margaret. Particularly with this concert."

Margaret scowled. "Who do you need to okay it?"

"Probably the Minister of Public Works. Or the Mayor, I'm not sure. How much is it oversold?"

"They don't know yet," Margaret said. The manager tapped her on the shoulder, and Margaret turned to her. "We think there were fifteen thousand tickets duplicated." Margaret swore. "And you find out now." She looked into the phone at Kammerer. "They say fifteen thousand."

The man whistled. "That's a lot. I don't know where they'd all fit."

"Just get me the minister, Gregor. I know that's the best you can do, but you'd better get on it and do *something*. If fifteen thousand people with tickets are shut out they'll wreck the whole plaza area—there's a lot of offworlders out there who came a long way to see this, and they don't give a damn about Port. And everyone paid a fortune for those tickets." Kammerer nodded. "The minister is still Johnson?"

"Yes," Kammerer said.

"Get him over here." Margaret clicked off. "How did you ever sell *fifteen thousand* extra tickets?" she demanded savagely.

The manager blanched. "It was sabotage. One of the terminals had its guard broken into without keying off the security network. I don't know exactly how it was done, but it happened, and they've just been finding the duplicates and tracing the selling source today."

Margaret pounded a fist against one hip, wondering if the tour had been attacked by its unknown enemy yet again. "You shouldn't have sold through computers. This concert is too important for computers, didn't you know that?"

"How else?" the man asked, baffled.

Margaret sighed. "You print up a finite number of physical tickets ahead of time, and sell those. Like cash, understand?"

The manager nodded. "We've never done that."

Margaret blew out a long breath, went to take a look at the counter. Twenty-three thousand. Still no end to the lines outside. She went to discuss the matter with Karna, but as she approached him Marie-Jeanne joined them.

"There's about twenty thousand people out there!" Marie-Jeanne said, looking flushed. "I hurried at the end, and the lines all bulged out into a big crowd that filled the boulevard, but I *know* there are at least that many."

Karna said, "If Wright gets the reaction he did in Lowell . . ."

Margaret pursed her lips, thinking hard.

"Usually I love these indoor things," Karna said. "Security is so much easier. . . ."

"I wonder who actually oversold this thing," Margaret said absently. "You know."

Karna nodded. "The manager's got some people for you over there."

Margaret went to greet them, and shifted back to Russian; Kammerer introduced her to Johnson, the Minister of Public Works, a portly man who squinted about him suspiciously. The foyer was very crowded. "We can't overfill the facility," Johnson said. "It's against the law, and in this case it's an obvious danger. We've heard about what happened in Lowell and Titania. If that happened here it would be catastrophic."

"We had a very peaceful show on Grimaldi," Margaret said. "Things are calming down."

"Grimaldi is just a bunch of treehouses. This is a city like Lowell and Titania, with a mixed audience from all over the Saturn system. There are a lot of ship workers out there, and if they riot—"

"Look," Margaret said, pointing out the doors, "they might riot inside, but they are sure to riot outside if you keep them out when they've got tickets."

"The worst scenario results from trapping forty thousand

people into a twenty-five thousand person venue and then subjecting them to Wright's type of music."

"You're jumping to conclusions about Wright's music," Margaret said. "Wright plays a different program every concert. If I explain the situation to him he'll respond accordingly. And you could announce the situation to the crowd and urge everyone to cooperate." The doubting look on the minister's face made Margaret angry. "Look, you're the ones who oversold the place. All I'm trying to do is trying to save your city from a beating."

The minister hesitated. "Well," he said, "this really goes outside my authority. . . ."

"Who does have the authority?" Margaret demanded, moving toward the phones.

"We should hear the Prime Minister's opinion, I suppose."

"You're going to ask the *Prime Minister* about—okay—never mind—let's get him, then. We don't have a whole lot of time here."

So they went to the phones and began making calls, threading their way up through the bureaucracy. When they got the Prime Minister's administrative assistant, she took in the situation and made a quick chopping motion with her hand. "Ms. Nevis, can you guarantee a program that will keep things calm in the Concourse?"

"Wright will play an appropriate program," she said, mouth suddenly dry. "I promise."

The administrative assistant looked past Margaret to Johnson. "Let everyone with tickets in. Broadcast the situation inside and at the doors, and call in all the reinforcements you can."

Johnson nodded, and Margaret took off, running around the oval of the outer halls to the backstage doors. There one of Karna's people let her in, and she hurried through the backstage rooms, cursing heartily. She had really stuck her neck out this time: if anything went wrong, it would be her fault. She passed Vaccero and his lighting crew at their main console, and stepped onto the tall, broad wings of the stage. The Orchestra filled the backstage; dim lights broke on its curved surfaces. It was set on a platform that would roll on tracks out onto the main stage. Johannes paced the edge of the platform, staring up at his instrument. When Margaret blocked his way he looked at her; she wondered for a moment if he recognized her.

"Johannes," she said, "there's a problem tonight!" She explained the situation. When she finished he stared at the Orchestra as if he hadn't heard her. "Johannes!" she cried. "People are jammed together out there!" He continued to stare. She shivered; she hated to talk to him before concerts, he was always like this. But tonight it wouldn't do. Angrily she grabbed him by the arm and yanked him around, put her face a few centimeters from his. "People will die tonight," she said distinctly.

"What's this?" he said. "People . . . in the audience?"

She explained the situation again, very loudly. "There'll be no room for movement out there. They have to remain calm, or it will be deadly. Do you understand?"

"Yes, Margaret. Will the show be canceled?"

"No! What I'm saying is, you have to play something calm, something different than you have so far. They can't react like they did in Lowell."

"Ah," he said, and walked over to the Orchestra.

"So you'll do it?" Margaret said, following him. "You understand what we need?"

"Yes," he said sharply. "Stop talking to me like I'm deaf!" He laughed at her expression. "I have to change a lot of the tapes, that's all. I'll need some time."

"Oh. But you can do it?"

"Trust me, Margaret," he said, looking at her with his non-eyes.

She shivered again. "Good," she said, backing away. "I'll go tell the officials."

She ran back to the entrance to the Concourse. The knot of

officials around Kammerer and Johnson had grown to a crowd. That was bureaucracy for you, Margaret thought; but at least it was something, at least there was a system there to deal with, however timid and redundant it was. The Minister of Public Works nodded wisely at her news, and instructed the Concourse manager to let everyone with tickets in. Loud-speakers inside were announcing the facts of the situation, and security people were seating people in the aisles, and in every passageway inside.

Margaret returned backstage, and went to the wings. When she looked out at the concourse her heart pounded; the rising oval of humanity was jammed together so tightly that it was one great wave of heads. When the time came for the concert to begin, and the house lights dimmed, and the Orchestra rolled onstage in a great blaze of split light, she found herself holding her breath. But the thunderous applause died down, the sea of heads stayed in place; no one had room to rush the stage. She took a deep breath and tried to relax.

Johannes played. Margaret could just catch glimpses of him moving about in the control booth; once she saw his face, and he looked blind. He was working more than he usually did, she thought. Soft tones filled the hall; he was playing in a chordal style, and all the chords were consonant, thirds, fifths, octaves, major sevenths, dominant ninths: up and down and up and down and up and down and up and down and up and down and up and down, until Margaret found her heartbeat was in pace with the rise and fall. Clear tones only, viola, clarinet, trumpet, flute, serving as the overtones for each other, but each playing as sweetly and clearly as the instruments were capable of playing. Johannes had understood. She saw his face again, blank as a mask, the strange eyes like the marble eyes of a statue, thrust into a human face. He looked very young. How old was he, she thought, twenty-six? Too young to know this much.

The Planck Synthesizer began a duet with the godzilla, and the mercury tones slid in and out of the simple harmonics, alpha waves, theta waves, the brain seduced by the weave of sound. Margaret let it roll over her like a blanket. She had never listened to Johannes's music with pleasure; in the concerts played so far the music had struck her as madness, more or less, except in certain passages. The *Ten Forms of Change?* Give her De Bruik any day. Everyone since had been scrabbling about in her remains, if you asked Margaret. But this . . . she realized that the crowd was as mesmerized as she was, and as the music grew more complex and difficult, it still retained a serenity that made her happy. As if for her in particular, the cellos swept to prominence, playing one of the melodies you feel must always have existed, and over it rose the sweet cutting descant of an oboe. Mercury drum and its oscillant keening . . .

Afterwards, when the building was safely emptied, she was her usual self. Perhaps a bit less irascible than usual. She laughed at Dent as they looked out at the giant oval of empty seats.

"Music to soothe the breast, eh Margaret?" Dent said.

"Thank God they were socialists," Margaret said. "There's no one else so sensible."

"It wasn't them," Dent said quietly. "It was Johannes."

Margaret laughed. "I don't know. I'd like to see him try doing that program with you edgefolk." But she hadn't forgotten that passage with the cellos and the single oboe, and she acknowledged the truth of Dent's words with a big grin. "We could have been in serious trouble," she said, wiping her brow.

♪

inclusion: corrective interjection

Blue and indigo clashed before him, and walking backstage was difficult; so much to run into that was not real at all. The concert had left him in a particularly light state, as if he alone in all Port Iapetus was exempt from the singularity's pull, so that if he did not hold onto things—light stands, railings, Anton's shoulder, the wall—he might step up and float away. Hold steady, Johannes. Already he could not remember what he had played. "Did you get this one on tape?" he asked Delia. "Delia is over there, Johannes." Marie-Jeanne? Of course. So much taller. "Delia, did you tape this one?" "Of course we did, Johannes, it was lovely. Was that part of the *Ten Forms?*" "I don't know. I'll have to listen to it." "We tape everything of yours, you know." "I suppose I did. Have it scored for me as well, then, will you?" "Of course."

A couple of hours later his sight and sense of balance were almost entirely returned. He wanted to go look at the Fairfax House. They had only a few more days on Iapetus, and he was curious. Raven-wing hair across the hall in the next room; must be Margaret. He crossed to her. "Margaret, you're from Iapetus, yes?"

"That's right."

"I need your help. I want to go out and visit one of the old mansions. The Fairfax House."

Margaret lifted an eyebrow, nodded. "I know the museum's superintendant, she's another old school friend of mine. We can get the key codes from her."

"Good. And ask her if the house records are intact."

"I will. When do you want to go?"

"Now . . . ?"

Finally she smiled, and he realized that he was a little afraid of Margaret. "All right. I'll have to finish up here and make some calls, but then we'll go. If I can get Anna Villanova on the phone. Go get some rest in the dressing room, and I'll call you if I get her."

"Thanks."

And a couple of hours after that they were at the edge of the city, where Margaret rented a track car at the surface transport station. Her friend Anna Villanova arrived to give them keys and directions, and they were off—into the car and out of the city, sliding on a single track that wound over the frosty broken surface of Iapetus. "Do you know the way?" Johannes asked uncertainly, peering ahead at the big patch of ground lit by their headlight.

"Yes," Margaret said. "It's simple."

Margaret was so good at things, he thought. What would have become of them even up to this point, without her? And from here on—

"I liked what you played tonight," she said, all in a rush as if the sentence had been pent up inside her. "Was it part of your big piece?"

Johannes settled back in his seat and closed his eyes. "Not really part of it. More an extension of one small section, I guess. I can't really remember."

"Too bad. I liked it better than your earlier concerts."

"Yes? Interesting. But the *Ten Forms* isn't finished yet, so I hope you'll keep listening. What I did tonight—well, you know, I'm glad you liked it. But anyone can do lullabies. I want to do something more than hypnotize people."

She looked at him curiously. "What do you want to do?"

He was in the mood to speak plainly. "I want to show people the real. I want people to hear the true nature of reality just as clearly as the sound of their own name."

Margaret had a little wry smile that appeared rarely. "There's a certain difficulty there, if you ask me. When it comes to the true nature of reality, it seems to me that we're too much like the chimpanzees on Titan, who look up into the smog and imagine they see the whole universe. . . ."

"Perhaps." There was another track branching off from theirs. "Is that the way?"

"No. We have a long way to go on this one, first. We're crossing the Disraeli Plain here, a big one."

"So this is your world," Johannes said.

"Yes." A funny laugh. "To the extent I have a world."

"But you grew up here."

"Yes. I grew up in Port, actually. But the track craft are cheap to rent, and all the mansions and spas are public property, now. And I did a fair amount of trekking as well, crossing Delta Chasma and some tremendous wilderness plateaus. You get out on the dark side of the moon and Saturn is so big and bright you can hardly believe it."

"Why did you leave?"

She shrugged. "I was curious. At first I stayed in the Saturn system, on the Ring stations, but all the cities are modeled on Titan's socialism, and I was still curious. So I went out. Then I got into management, and started traveling full time. I haven't really stopped since then."

"That's one way to satisfy curiosity."

She laughed. "Oh it was satisfied long ago, believe me. And I think I prefer Iapetus in a lot of ways. This is a special place, made in a special moment of history. As soon as the spheres became available the revolutionaries on Titan seized the chance—Saturn was at 280 and Jupiter was near 90, so it was good timing—and they overthrew the landowners. That was early in the Accelerando, so that their socialism was fairly conservative, but now that I've lived on the anarchic terras, I wonder if that isn't to the good. Certainly I was happy here."

"You like things orderly," Johannes said.

"Perhaps. I like to know what's what."

They lapsed into silence and Johannes observed the chiascuro expanse of the plain. When the track curved the headlight beam caught tall contorted boulders, with frost patterns on them resembling animal faces, figures, runes, signposts pointing across the waste. Perhaps they had been carved. One looked like the Orchestra turned to stone, and he almost said something, but the beam left it and in the starry light it looked like any other lump.

After a while: "Here's our turn." He had been dozing, dreaming of leopards high on a hill. Margaret was flicking the switches that would put them on this new track. They clicked through the intersection and veered left. Far across the frosty plain there was a gleam of reddish light, from what appeared to be a faceted outcropping. "Is that it?" he asked.

"That's Laurenti House."

"Strange architecture. It looks like one of the strings of sugar crystals that children make. Colored sugar crystals."

"You should have seen them when they were occupied. They were lit from within so that all the facets glowed; you could see them for kilometers, and they lit up all the surrounding plain so that the frost was the color of the nearest House." She laughed. "The rich. Here they were building completely self-sufficient palaces, while the shipbuilding facilities were still tin cans. No wonder they were disenfranchised."

Johannes stared at the dim structure. "It's odd to think of such extravagance before Holywelkin. And now they're just curios."

"You can rent them for parties." Margaret pointed ahead. "There's the Fairfax."

As they approached the mansion Johannes saw that it was big—ten or twelve stories tall, a collection of cubes melted into each other in a vaguely crystalline way; no doors or windows were visible; each facet was an unmarked plane of blue glassy material.

"No windows?"

"There are, but you can't tell from outside." Margaret turned the craft up the tracks that led directly to the mansion. The craft slid directly up to a blank wall. Looking closer Johannes saw small knobs in it, but because the wall was blue his resolution was poor. With a jolt track craft and mansion locked together.

"Will there be air inside?"

"No," Margaret said. "We'll have to suit up. Anna told me how to turn on the electricity, though, so you'll be able to check the house records."

They got into the thin daysuits, and Margaret pushed buttons on the control panel of the craft. Doors slid open in both craft and building, and the craft's air escaped with a tiny tug at them. They entered the Fairfax House, and Margaret crouched by a box near the door. Lights came on.

The room they had entered, Johannes thought, was about three rooms tall. The walls were painted a pale blue, and it made him dizzy to look at them. A three-tiered chandelier descended from the faraway blue ceiling, breaking the light into a thousand hanging prisms. Johannes followed Margaret into a hall shaped like a pack of cards placed on end. "They seem to have liked tall ceilings."

"They were rich," Margaret said. "Let's see—I got directions from Anna—records chamber on the sixth floor. Go down the main hall to the ballroom and take the staircase up." They proceeded down the tall hallway, and came to a circular room that appeared to have no ceiling; an upright cylinder. Lit only by the undissipated light from behind, it was a patchwork of blues. Margaret found the lights and turned them on. More chandeliers. Five or six balconies stood out in rings from the circular wall, and spiraling up through the balconies was a wide, gradual staircase. "It's like being inside Archimedes' screw," Margaret said. She led Johannes up the stairs. Disoriented by the proportions and the ubiquitous blue light, by the silence and the stillness, Johannes took her hand and followed her step by step. Near the top they stopped to inspect one balcony; a small alcove in the wall was filled with round windows, which bent inward like lenses.

"Lindsay windows," Margaret said. "Look."

Through one they saw the Earth, a big blue and white ball, the cloud patterns perfectly visible, the end of South America pointing up like a horn. "How did they do that?"

"Ask Lindsay."

They continued up the stairs. The blue silence made Johannes nervous. On the sixth floor Margaret led the way to a

small room containing a medium-sized holo projector. One
wall was filled by the control console. Margaret switched on
the light, checked the power. "Everything's ready to go."

Johannes inspected the console. "So this bank has holos of
all the human activity that ever happened in this House, in
every room?"

"That's right."

"But why?"

"It was the thing to do. Every House had such a system. It
made them holo stars, I guess. Immortal."

"Immortal little figurines of light."

"Yes. But it's a common mistake, don't you think? To try
for immortality by leaving something of you behind?"

"Oh yes," Johannes said absently, poking about at the
console. "Very common. Now . . . Holywelkin was an acquaintance of the Fairfax of his time, and he visited here in
3008. So how do I find holos of him?"

Margaret laughed. "We'll just have to look. There's no
index. But for Holywelkin we can look in the best guest
rooms, and run through the year 3008 at high speed. That's
the only way."

She typed in instructions, and the holo flicked on with a
quick snap of red light, followed by the image of a room,
wall-less and without ceiling. It was about half as tall as
Johannes, so that the rich walnut furniture and thick Persian
rugs looked like the accessories of a doll house. Doll people
stood hand-high, with faces as clear as thumbprints. Margaret
turned a dial and the figurines sped about the room like bars
of light, like fairies visible in the first four dimensions.
Margaret slowed the figures when new ones appeared, and
soon they identified Fairfax and his family, introducing guest
after guest to the room. Guests put belongings in a closet
outside the holo; visited a bathroom also outside the image;
dressed, undressed, looked in mirrors, groomed, slept, made
love . . . Visitor after visitor made the space his or her lair,
then left it.

And then the visitor was Holywelkin. Short and stout, barrel-chested and broad-shouldered, in a black coat, with a wide, pug-nosed face: a Holywelkin doll, looking as familiar to Johannes as any face he knew.

"That's him," Johannes said hoarsely. "Take it back a bit."

"That's Holywelkin?"

"Sure. Don't you recognize him?"

"Well, he's so . . . small." They laughed. "I've only seen holos of him a few times, as I can recall."

"Hard to imagine," Johannes said. "There, start it here. I had a holo of him in my home for years and years."

"That would explain it."

"Yes. He—" Johannes hesitated, looked up at Margaret, looked back at the frozen figurines in the shimmery doll room. "He talked to me once. We had an argument."

"Ah," Margaret said carefully, inspecting him. "Well . . . you'll recognize his voice, then."

They laughed again. Margaret slowed the holo to real time and turned up the sound. Holywelkin and Fairfax walked about the room and Holywelkin unpacked his bag, and their voices faded and grew as they moved. "Two microphones," Johannes said, "one by the bed, the other over the door." It was odd to have normal human voices paired with the figurines, who should have squeaked like mice.

"The reception will be tomorrow evening," Fairfax said. His coat was the green of peacock feathers. "I'm sure everyone will be interested to hear about your travels."

"I'm not going to want to talk about my travels," Holywelkin said in a scratchy, tired voice. Johannes trembled; it was almost the voice he had heard in the control booth during his withdrawal, seven years before. He leaned over until his face was at the very upper edge of the cube, stared at the figure as hard as he could. Tiny translucent face, twisted with distress of some kind. . . .

"Why not?" asked Fairfax loudly. "Arthur, you are the

first outsider ever to visit Icarus! How could you not tell us
about it?''

"With silence," Holywelkin said. "No, Simon," he said,
forestalling an objection. "You want to know *why* I cannot
speak of it, I know. It is because I . . . because something
happened out there." He sat on the bed. "I can't talk about
it." Voice hoarse.

Over the cube Margaret and Johannes stared at each other.

Fairfax sat beside him. "I'm sorry, Arthur. I misunderstood. So this cult—this religion, the grey ones—they are—
dangerous, somehow?''

Holywelkin shook his head, tiny face wrinkled with unhap-
piness. "I can't talk about it."

"I see. Well." A long pause. "Perhaps we should make
something up, to satisfy people's curiosity at the reception?''

A long silence, while Holywelkin got up and paced the
room. "Yes. I think that would be best."

The image of Fairfax watched his guest for a time. "What
was it, Arthur?''

"I," Holywelkin said, and waved an arm. "They *know
things.*"

A long silence.

Fairfax stood, took Holywelkin by the arm. "Tell me
about it later, Arthur. I can see you haven't come to terms
with it yet.''

Holywelkin shook his head violently. "True. Very true.''

"Let's get your stuff put away.''

They unpacked Holywelkin's bag. Margaret speeded them
up, and tracked Holywelkin from room to room, stopping to
check every conversation. Holywelkin ate, talked small talk
with the Fairfax family, played with the children, slept.
Margaret moved on to the reception the following night. In
the holos of the ballroom people were no taller than thumb-
nails, and there were a few dozen of them scurrying around
the room; the holo resembled a box of colorful insects. The
soundtrack was filled with music and the tumbling beach

sound of party conversation. Even Johannes's intensely trained hearing could not distinguish Holywelkin's voice from the others'. Holywelkin was the center of several groups, and he appeared to talk, but he never smiled.

More small talk, eating, sleeping; then back in the guest room, packing his things, with Simon Fairfax. "He's about to leave," Margaret said. Johannes nodded, leaned over the cube once again.

"They did teach me," Holywelkin said, answering a question.

"Stop and run that back," Johannes said. "What happened to the earlier part of the conversation?"

"It must have happened in the hall outside," Margaret said. "No cameras in the halls."

Johannes clicked his tongue. "I'll bet that's where everything important in this mansion happened. Okay, let it go."

"They did teach me," Holywelkin said. "But I'm not sure I understand what they taught me. I've got to go do some work on it back home on my own. Need my programs and a lab."

"So *they* taught *you* mathematics?" Fairfax cried. "I can't believe it. There's no one alive who could teach you anything of math, I would have thought."

"Yes, well, this has to do with singularity physics. A sort of logic of the micro-universe. I've been working on a model for the motion of the particles discovered in the Great Synchrotron, and these Greys . . . well . . . it's not so simple. And besides I don't know how to describe what it was outside the mathematics involved, anyway. I don't know what it *means* in other terms, you understand?" Fairfax shook his head. "But I have . . . fears."

Fairfax said, "Will you phone me later, when you've worked this out?"

Holywelkin nodded. "Or I'll write it down. But these Greys . . . there's more to them than anyone suspects."

"Does anyone else know?"

"I'm not sure. No one else knows the details of my trip."

"I won't tell anyone even the little I know, then. Now, is your baggage together?" They began to pack.

Soon they were joined by the Fairfax children, and they left the room. Holywelkin left the mansion by the track craft door.

Margaret shrugged, turned the holo off. "So that was Holywelkin's visit."

Johannes nodded. He thought, the Greys watch me as I play Holywelkin's Orchestra. And the Greys were a part of the coming to the world of Holywelkin's mathematics. . . .

"Did all that tell you anything?" Margaret said, breaking a long silence.

"I need to know more about the Greys," Johannes said.

"We're already working on that," said Margaret. "Karna has sent an agent down to Jupiter to learn more about them."

Johannes shook his head. "I wonder if it will be possible on Jupiter."

Margaret regarded him. "Come on, let's go home. You look tired."

♪

And on the drive back home, as Margaret guided the craft and thought about the long night's action, Johannes slumped over and fell asleep, tilting until his head was resting firmly on Margaret's broad shoulder. She smiled a little, and left it there. Up to this point she had thought of Johannes as a prima donna, a problem, quiet enough but very difficult in his own way: absent-minded, distant, demanding by his very assumptions, obscure and pretentious in his art. Now. . . . The music he had played in Port echoed in her memory. She slowed the craft to a crawl so that when it clicked onto the

Disraeli track, his head wouldn't be pulled off her shoulder.
And smiled at herself.

♪

the gaze of the greek chorus

Now leave the Grand Tour for a while, Reader, and come
with me to Jupiter, King of the Planets. Light is provided by
the many whitsuns directed into Jupiter's space, and by the
ruddy light of the planet itself; and by Sol; in the Jupiter
system it is always day. And this Olympus of space is
jammed with courtiers: Io, Europa, Ganymede and Callisto
make their orbits, each a full world in its own right; all of the
smaller moons have gravity generators at their centers, bubbles encasing them, whitsuns following them; and great numbers of asteroids have been drawn closer to the king's fire, to
become terras in its system; so that all in Zeus's court is
activity and light.

Now imagine a gravity generator, orbiting the banded gas
giant somewhere outside Callisto. The concrete shell has been
painted the black of space, and even specked with "stars,"
so that it is almost impossible to see. The bubble encasing it
is invisible. Struts of clear glass hold three broad platforms of
clear glass a short distance off the black generator, so that the
only things clearly visible in this area of space are people,
dressed in robes of the seven primary colors, standing (it
appears) freely in space, on three different levels. Ernst
Ekern and the fellows of his order stand on this invisible
platform, and survey the spangled scene, preparing to add
one more ceremony to the system of ceremonies knitting the
vacuum slopes of the new Olympus.

Ekern paced on the middle platform and stared up at the

swirled bands of the Jovian surface, hoping to distract himself. Jupiter, its surface textured like thick oil paint, filled a big chunk of the sky. But Ekern could not keep his attention on it. This meeting of the dramatists had been called to hear his prospectus; it was his performance.

Atargatis stepped down the wide clear staircase, greeting Ekern with a broad smile. Atargatis was dressed in grey, *the grey* of the cult; he was the only Magus not dressed in a primary color. Ekern frowned. "Why are you so garbed? I will not have my drama mocked, Atargatis."

"I am a Grey, Ernst," Atargatis said, his bright brown eyes gleaming with mirth. "I am the Lion of Jupiter, in fact, and in this space I wear the cloak."

So Atargatis would know how Ekern's drama shaped the Greys . . . Ekern's mind spun with the ramifications of this shocking news, the difficulties and dangers: "But you are a playwright as well," he said, making the statement a host of questions.

Atargatis understood. "There are many different kinds of Greys, Ernst. For me the metadrama is life itself."

"And so—" Ekern stopped; perhaps he should consider the situation further, but in the lightning flux of metadrama it was often necessary to act on impulse, to let the instincts determine what course to take. This man could perhaps be co-opted into the drama, and thus controlled. And Ekern wanted to control this mysterious, irritating rival. "And so you will help me?"

Atargatis nodded. "I will do what I can for you. The Greys are appropriate to your drama."

"I know."

"They are more appropriate than you know." That small wry smile. "But Zervan, the Father of Fathers, lives on Icarus. And here I am ignorant; I do not know if anything can be done there without his awareness of it." Ekern stared at him, scorning the notion of clairvoyance. Atargatis lifted his eyebrows, shrugged. "I do not know. I will do what I can.

Now come give your metalogue. The rest are waiting, and you know what a poor audience the Magi are—so impatient, so critical.''

Spurs, deliberately applied. Ekern brushed the barbs away. "Go join them, and I will follow.''

Atargatis climbed back up the barely visible glassy steps. After a suitable interval Ekern hitched up his red robe, thinking, all life is a performance, a hundred performances a day, I am the Duke of Vienna, in secret control of all my kingdom, I rule those poor fearful fools above me. As he ascended the clear staircase he started to feel faint. He concentrated on the red gleam in the glass, walked more deliberately, breathed more deeply. Wright, Atargatis, Vaccero, Nevis, surely this was the hardest thing any of them had to do in the drama: to speak before the Magus Diana and her order. . . .

Once on the upper platform he looked around. Six men, six women; the twelve members of the order stood in a crescent, facing a glassy dais. Ekern's mouth tasted bitter. He cleared his throat, quietly. Diana waited until he was on the dais, then said in a clear voice, "Go under the real to the heart of the real: metalogue for a play in progress.''

Ekern saw the metalogue in his mind. It took the form of a sestina, the most highly controlled stanzaic form; six end words revolved in a strict pattern, so that each six-line stanza was determined by the pattern of the first one; thus he meshed form and content, in a principle of all life: "The early phases of acts imply the later phases.'' Retrodictive, predictive, his metalogue would shape all their lives; and so he was in control. Calmed, he spoke in a clear firm baritone.

"Glints sail from point to point like boats on water,
Thrust here and there by winds and current—No.
Like nothing else. Glints are where the change
Takes place, the ten forms on them act
In strictest combination—musically,
It might be said glints dance to tunes through time.

"It's hard to say there's no such thing as time,
For if not what moves there across the water
At dusk, what moves downstream so musically?
It is no leaf, no paper boat, no—no—
It is an endless line and not an act,
And so there is no chance, no choice, no change.

"You wish those scenes could be undone, you change
The past each night in dreams, that darkling time
You sang your song as if it were an act:
Your eye saw light break onto water
At that second, and you forgot to know
A single thing but that; light dancing musically.

"Not that the world is murdered musically.
Note follows note—the score will never change—
In this same way synapses trigger, no
Plan planned, control exerted; glints in time
Determined like a wave's sweet flow through water.
You think your thoughts like ocean currents act.

"You saw the curtain rise to start an act,
A woman crossed the stage quite musically
And paused to dash her brow with steaming water,
And though there was no sign to mark the change,
You suddenly remembered Earth—the time
They turned their heads and said, distinctly, 'No.'

"But did you choose to recollect? Oh no?
And did you ever really choose to act?
That all belongs to 'Once upon a time,'
Doesn't it now? It works more musically
Than that, it's not a thing your thoughts can change.
Look at it closely. Take a drink of water.

"Ten laws know glints, musically
They ring, it's time to note the always-change
That makes you act like boats held fast to water."

He was done. The euphoria of power filled him, power like a drug, a bursting free of all restraint. The poem determined the play. The play determined Wright. Wright determined the music. And the music—

"We will attend this drama to its close," Diana called, and the fellows of the order moved together until their spectrum of robes was unbroken (a patch of grey). The ceremony was done.

Chapter Five

|: **THE SUN ON OLYMPUS** :|

kang la

Back to the Grand Tour, which piled into great *Orion* and its pilot fish, and swam across the space between Saturn and Jupiter, and descended upon Europa.

Reader, know that Europa is an ice-encrusted moon; up to one hundred kilometers of water ice covers its rocky core. Spheres generated a short distance under Europa's surface created hemispheres of discontinuous ice, which were then melted and partially drained, leaving behind round lakes of liquid water, held in great bowls in the ice. Above and below the surface of a hundred of these lakes the cities of Europa were built, on floating islands and in submarine chambers. Kang La was one of the biggest of these new Venices: a great mass of moored islands, bridges, waterways, raft neighborhoods, submarine power plants, and lake bottom villas, all surrounded by a circular city wall of white ice, all sloshing about in the tides created by the giant banded planet that dominated the sky.

In Kang La they played the first Jovian concert to a crowd of two hundred thousand roaring fans, who, deafened by their own shouting, could not have heard more than a few notes played by the Orchestra. When the concert was over Dent Ios wandered backstage at the city stadium (an island unto itself), disturbed by the music's reception, and by what he had seen of Kang La. In one corner dressing room Karna and Margaret were in conference, and Dent joined them. "I'm off to meet Yananda," Karna told them. "He says he's got a contact in the Greys, and we're to meet him out in our old neighborhood on one of the western islands."

"Why there?" Margaret said.

"I'm going to keep Yananda away from the tour," Karna said. "In case we're being watched. I think it's important that he be able to do his work without whoever is opposing us knowing it."

Margaret nodded.

"Can I come with you?" Dent asked. Karna and Margaret looked surprised; Dent was a little surprised himself. But the memory of Titania spurred him, and he wanted to do something.

"Sure," Karna said. He stood up. "Are you ready?"

Dent nodded resolutely, and ignoring Margaret's quick grin (she thought so poorly of him!) he followed Karna out of the room.

Outside the stadium it was still crowded. The stadium was a gigantic cement oval structure, and against one long side wall was an elevated train station, its metal floors black with grime and cluttered with trash, its air hot and noisy. They got into one of the many lines and looked at the raucous crowd around them until let on one of the train cars. When the line finally moved, people filled the car until no one else could get on. Some of the passengers were dreamwalking, their heads encased in helmets, their eyes jerking wildly. The two women next to Dent had plug-in jacks surgically implanted in the sides of their necks, and the pupils of their eyes were no bigger than pinholes. With a jerk the train was off and rolling through Kang La.

Out the train window Dent caught glimpses of the city: far below their tracks the water in the canals shimmered under packed light, and the tops of heads were everywhere. The buildings were filled with windows, each skyscraper a glass house, and the lower windows were filled with pulsing displays of goods for sale. "Commercial district," Karna said, looking down. The skyscrapers extended right up to the sphere above them, and sometimes broke through it. Their track wound through a latticework which extended five or ten stories above and below them; other trains, looking like thin dirty worms, zipped by in other directions, and occasionally Dent caught sight of a face in another train window, looking across at him impassively. . . .

"It's enormous," he said. "How big . . . ?"

Karna shrugged. "It's big. We Indians, we build cities until they collapse in on themselves. And then we keep on building."

Dent nodded, staring down into the street canyon to the canal at the bottom. Below the water's surface he could see the lit windows of submarine buildings. Waving beams of bent light sent ellipses of red and green roving over the skyscrapers and their glass windows. "And this is where you grew up?" he said.

"No. On one of the outer islands. Not really the same, as you'll see."

The train entered a tunnel—a building, Dent surmised—and only the train's cabin lights shone on them. Old men in seedy clothes slumped in the ripped seats of their car. Youths in trailing robes prowled from car to car restlessly. Dent wrinkled his nose, disturbed by the smell of poverty and desperation. Again he noticed the dreamwalking passengers sprawled in the seats across from him. Then lazed light fractured the gloom and they were over an industrial island of the city, where networks of tanks and tubes connected long, low factories. On the water surrounding the island light danced in long squiggles.

Past the factories the train ran on a long pontoon bridge just above the roofs of hundreds of flat long rooftops, set on big square islands. "Here's my Kang La," Karna said. "The neighborhood. Several million here, working all over Europa. The indentured, you know."

They rattled over the long dormitories as if over big track ties, stopping every fifty or so. At one stop Karna rose to leave the train, and Dent followed him. Out on the streets he was assaulted by hot air that smelled strongly of spices and grease. The narrow streets between the dorms were concrete, covered here and there with a scruffy green plastic turf. Karna walked down the middle of one of these streets easily, negotiating a path between the clumps of loiterers with ease. He even smiled at Dent, though his eyes were not amused. "It never changes. This is the oldest part of Kang. They even put the old Tin Can here, as a museum thing. See that building over on the corner?"

Dent saw where the usual collection of corner shops was replaced by a low black plastic dome, badly pitted. "That's the first Jovian colony," Karna said.

"Is it really?" Dent cried. "Is it open? Can we take a look inside?"

"Sure." Karna consulted his watch. "A quick look, then." They approached it. "See, it says here by the door. Established 2175, occupied until the activation of the sphere in 2985. Average population eight thousand."

"But it's so small."

"A lot of it was taken apart, and besides, it's mostly below the surface."

"Still!" The whole population of his terra Holland did not exceed eight thousand. "It is terribly small."

"True. They really packed in."

They entered the little dome. Inside there were no windows; just rooms, low-ceilinged and narrow. Dent could hardly believe how cramped and drear it looked. Even the shabby streets above were filled with air and light . . . And here, he thought, in this grounded space tug and others like it, human beings had lived out their existences for nearly eight hundred years. Over eight hundred years. It was beyond belief.

Dent stopped moving from room to room and just stared into one closetlike bedroom. A whole life spent in this chamber, establishing the foothold in space. In these compartments every representative art brought memories of Earth, and therefore they brought pain. Music was the only art that did not remind them of their sensory deprivation; music, the expansion of the one sense left to them. Looking around Dent could *feel* the importance music must have had, he could *feel* the intensity of those strange Jovian composers, with their tiny foregrounds and their vast backgrounds. . . . "No wonder," he said to Karna. "No wonder the Accelerando burst out of here with such manic force. Imagine living in such an attenuated culture, and then being given all those worlds." Karna nodded. Dent felt a quiver of claustrophobia. "This explains a lot."

"It explains the Accelerando, that's for sure," Karna said, leading the way out. "Now let's go meet Yananda."

Back on the bright hot street Dent said, "After that even these dorms look spacious."

Karna laughed sourly. "That's why they leave the old Tin Can there."

They crossed a narrow canal and turned up a street more crowded than the rest. Men and women in cheap one-piece oversuits carried parcels wrapped in plastic. Children darted around laughing and shrieking, jumped off dorm steps, chased each other. Empty plastic bags tumbled across the intersections, propelled by air shoved out of street vents. The smell of spicy fried food filled the air. A group of young men and women stood in a circle, plugged into each other via the computer jacks surgically implanted in their necks. And here and there bodies lay like corpses in the gutters, their heads completely encased in plain metal boxes: an obscene sight. "Sensoriums," Karna said, seeing Dent's expression. Dent stared at them, still shocked by the sight of people who allowed their bodies to be mechanically invaded. Cyborgs— they were no more than sensational rumors in the outer terras. Looking back at one he almost tripped over an old woman in a long black coat, sitting in the gutter. Hastily he caught up with Karna.

At one intersection there was an open area, too small to be called a plaza. It was ringed by cafes and small markets, and people sat in circles on the old green plastic carpet. Karna led Dent into one of the cafes, and they sat down and ordered drinks. "See anyone you know?" Dent asked.

"No." A small smile stayed tucked under Karna's black moustache. "I left Europa twenty years ago. Broke my indenture. By now everyone I know will have been transferred to different cities."

"Why?"

"They do it to disrupt the communities. Look—there's Yananda, outside with someone. Here, Dent, sit at this next table and watch us. Pretend you're not with us. Just drink your White Brother and listen until they go or until I tell you differently. And if all three of us leave together, follow."

Dent plopped down at the table behind Karna's. Yananda came in with another man and greeted Karna warmly. "Karna, this is Charles. Charles is a Grey."

A moment of silence. Dent had to force himself to keep looking down at his table.

"How come you aren't wearing the right clothes?" Karna asked.

"I have a dispensation," Charles said hoarsely, and sat. "I am to observe, to be eyes, to seek out corruption."

"Well, you've found it here," Yananda said easily, ordering a drink as he sat beside Charles.

"Where else have you found it?" Karna asked.

"In the Greys themselves," the man croaked. "There is corruption in the Greys, and who shall I then report to? Zervan is too far removed, I cannot reach him. Yananda here suggested I report to you, that you might be able to do something."

"I might," Karna said. "I can certainly help you. Tell us about this corruption." He ordered a bottle of the White Brother, and the waiter brought over three little glasses and a bottle filled with the milky fluid that Dent was already drinking.

"The Greys are Mithraists," Charles croaked, and wiped his mouth. "We are sun worshippers, and our religion has its roots in the dawn of history, in Persia. We believe Sol to be a god, an all-powerful sentient being who creates us from his own essence and then controls us, and everything else in the system."

"I thought Mithraism died out under the Roman empire," Yananda said, "when the emperors became Christian."

"Into hiding we went," said Charles. "From the fall of Rome to the establishment of the Mercury colony, we were hidden. Thus one source of our trouble; parts are hidden from other parts still. But on Mercury we came out into the open again."

"Pythagoreans, Phoenixes, Kirlians—all these secret religions," Karna said. "Why did you choose to join the Greys, Charles?"

"I was called." Voice hoarse, low, croaking with pain. "So I joined and I thought, I will learn their secrets and sell them on the outside. Like I am to you now. But now my motive has changed. I am truly a Grey, now, and I am . . . disturbed at the corruption, outraged by the perversion of the order. There are hierarchies, levels on levels . . . the highest is on Icarus, but no fox will ever reach Icarus. Everywhere else, disruption of what should be. This worship of your musician Wright—"

"What's this?" Yananda said. Karna silenced him with a sharp glance.

"There are two manifestations of the sun among us, Mithras and Sol. Mithras is Zervan, the Father of Fathers, who rules Icarus. Sol—his is a secret task, he wanders from being to being. Now the Lion of Jupiter and the exiled Lion of Mars and their followers say that your musician is Sol. The rank and file Foxes—we must obey and follow, although we have very wise leaders of our own who tell us this worldly involvement is foolish, and dangerous. Some of the Foxes tried to kill Wright to save our religion from this. . . . The Lion of Oberon had them executed."

"Hmmm." Karna and Yananda took sips of the White Brother. Dent nervously ordered another glass for himself from a passing waiter, and when it came he drank some of the fiery liquor in a big gulp.

"So some important Greys think Wright is Sol," Karna said. "And they're following him downsystem. To what end?"

Charles said, "I only know I am part of a contingent of Greys ordered to Mars. I am to learn more on Mars."

"Can we meet you there?"

"I know not. I believe we will attend the concert on Mars; this will take us to Olympus Mons."

"We'd like to see you before that."

"The Greys have no home on Mars. I know not where we'll be."

"Could you call us?"

"Perhaps."

"Good enough. This will be our number in Burroughs. If we don't hear from you before, we'll expect to see you at the Festival."

Scraping chairs, they all stood. Dent glanced up and saw that Charles was a portly long-haired man, his black hair shot with strands of white. The three said farewells. Then Karna said out of the corner of his mouth, "Follow him, Dent."

"What?"

"Follow him"—with a hard kick at his chair. Dent stood, found the White Brother had quite a punch. "We'll pay your bill," Karna said, lips still motionless. "Get after him."

How far? Dent wanted to ask, but the look in Karna's eye discouraged idle curiosity. He left the cafe and looked around the little square. Shock of black and white hair—he hurried after the man, saw it was a long straight street, crossed it and followed the man at a slower pace, looking down or at the buildings beside him as much as he dared. Observing the man while not looking at him: Dent could not quite get the hang of it, and his head swivelled in ceaseless motion, down at the pavement, up at Charles, then quickly away to other passersby, to the windows facing him, quickly back to Charles, and so on. Anyone watching him would have suspected something immediately. And Charles did take a few looks back, especially after making turns at intersections. But he appeared not to notice Dent.

They crossed a bridge and were on the long pontoon island of the elevated train. Inside the train station Dent got into line just eight people behind Charles, and bought a ticket for the commercial district. Up on the trash-littered, noisy waiting platform Dent sat down against a wall, where old circles of spit dripped hard dry tailings over the faces of advertising celebrities. Dent had just noticed this and was busy sitting upright when Charles was joined by a tall man. After a quick glance around, Charles began to tell the man something, gesturing back at the slums. The man nodded and spoke, and as Dent watched him he felt a terrible jolt of recognition. Tall, bony face; if the man had red whiskers painted across his cheeks—yes! It was him! Dent slumped over and stared intently at his shoes. A train rumbled in, rolling the lighter rubbish over the dirty decking. Dent ventured a single eyeball-wrenching look up, and saw Charles and the tall men get on the train. When the train had whooshed out of the station Dent breathed at last, stood up and hurried back down to street level. He would have to tell Karna *immediately*.

Then it struck him that the street he was walking down looked just like all the other streets in this district. No street signs, either. Just dorm after dorm after dorm, all covered by the harsh smell of burning pepper oil. How would he find them?

And this street—it wasn't as crowded as the rest had been. Only small knots of men standing on stoops here and there, watching Dent walk by. Dent picked up his pace, and noticed that one of the groups was now trailing down the block after him. In these regular streets he could never outrun them— besides, now three of them stood ahead of him. Dent swallowed hard, his pulse racing. He glanced from side to side, without a plan, and was forced to a halt by the three men in front of him. They were linked by cords that ran from neck to neck, and two of them had metal boxes for hands. The men behind him fanned out.

"What are you doing here?" one of them said.

Dent cleared his throat. "I came here with a man who lived here. Karnasingh Godavari. We were going to look at the Tin Can."

"We show you another Tin Can."

"But I thought there was only one," Dent said.

"We show you another," the man said, but stopped, distracted by something behind Dent. Dent turned, and relief rushed into him like air; Karna was hurrying up to them. Still, there must have been ten or twelve men surrounding him. . . . Karna just walked through them to Dent's side, and surveyed them one by one. They stepped back. Dent glanced up at his friend, and understood. It wasn't just that Karna was big; at this moment he also looked distinctly insane, his gaze cross-eyed or somehow unfocused (or focused on all of them at once), with a foolish little smile lighting all his features. . . . These men had to respect the possibility that he might be one of those machine humans, death rays in his fingertips, painkiller for blood . . . they were fairly common in this most degraded planetary system, and these men had probably seen such cybernetic killers in action before. Only Dent knew that it was just plain old human Karna beside him, flexing his fingers and grinning like a moron berserker to keep the little band of thugs at bay. With another chilling look around Karna led Dent out of the group and down the street. At the next intersection Yananda ran up—"He found you!" he panted—and they continued on to the train station. Dent stammered out what he had seen. "It was Red Whiskers! That Charles met Red Whiskers, only the whiskers are gone now, but it was him—I recognized him."

Karna frowned. "We'll talk about it when we get back." He looked mystified. "Good work, Dent."

♪

When the three men reported what they had seen and heard to Margaret, she scratched her head. "Yananda, how did you meet this Charles? In detail."

"I came to Kang La and went to the home the Greys keep out on one of the dorm islands. They have enough people to control a block and the little square at the intersection, and when I was there they were having some sort of ceremony in the square. When they were done they all started to leave the square. One of them that passed me was crying, so I thought, here's one that's upset, maybe he'll want to talk. He said the meeting had been very upsetting. That Greys were killing Greys in the Uranus system, and that he feared for the order. He said, 'It's breaking into factions.' I told him I was very curious and wanted to hear more—I told him I had a friend who would pay very highly to hear more, because he was concerned about the Greys too, as apparently they had tried to kill his friend Johannes Wright. At that he declared that the attack had been heresy, and we deserved an explanation.

So I called up Karna and set up the meeting for when you all got here.''

"And then he went off with the man who robbed Dent.'' Margaret shook her head. "I don't like it. But this man Charles is our key, no matter who he's working for. He's our entry point, understand?''

"Exactly,'' Karna said.

"So make sure you find him on Mars, and follow him all the way back to his source.''

♪

inclusion: free absorption

For Johannes the tour of the Jovian moons was a blur of broken light over broken sound. He tinkered with the taped portions of his work during the long hours off, worked on the programs and read Holywelkin's notebooks, and tried to figure out just what was missing. During the concerts he could scarcely hear, and his live contribution consisted of desultory, almost random explorations, until he roused himself and exerted some discipline. One did not have to be able to hear to compose music; there were enough examples of the deaf composers who had come before him, dealing with theoretical patterns weaving through time. Glints: as they blew away from each other in the ultra-high energy collisions in the Great Synchrotron, they left patterns on the plates like nautilus spirals, or hyperbolas, or knuckleballs. Take the plates as the score and the progression of notes was clear; a composition could be written that was the precise musical analogy of the experiment. But that was only a start. The real task was to compose the precise musical analogy of glints in the real world, outside the experiments. He could program the computer with Holywelkin's interminable equations, without understanding the equations themselves. And then certain initial situations could be programmed, such as solar energy hitting one of the power stations, being transformed to a whiteline, emerging in a whitsun, casting light on one of the outer worlds. The result was quite a beautiful score. But what instrumentation was called for? What was the sound of a glint? Tonal qualities, range of pitches, what did this mean on the sub-subatomic scale? Every concert he gave was a meditation on the topic, and it angered him that the roars of the crowds altered the acoustics so drastically. Something was wrong with the response to music around Jupiter: desperate dionysiacs, they had lost that balance with the apollonian that made Pluto the ideal musical culture. Still, this round of concerts gave him a chance to work intensively, and he felt he was closer to the method to be used in the *Ten Forms of Change,* even though he was not sure what more he needed to do, what else the work required of him. He was tired.

But by and by the tour came to Ganymede, Holywelkin's moon; before Holywelkin moved to Pluto in 3013, he had lived in a little house hidden by a garden off the Hapsburgstrasse in Wien, Ganymede. Now the house was a dusty museum, and as Master of the Orchestra Johannes was welcomed and given the run of the place. In one of the back rooms were stacks of notebooks, the actual artifacts themselves. Margaret sat and waited for him in the sunny kitchen, playing with some kittens and the red silk-tasselled rope that kept visitors from handling the various crockery and utensils of the great man. Johannes sat down at a table and picked up the first pile of notebooks. "A lot of Orchestra people have been here to see the place," said the ancient woman who served as curator. Margaret looked into the room curiously. "What's that?" Margaret said.

"Are all these notebooks transcribed into the data banks?" Johannes asked urgently, looking at the stacks.

"All of them, yes. Took twenty years."

Johannes's head ached with the effort of focusing the photoptic cells. "And all of them were transcribed."

"Yes. There's scribbling on the covers, though—see there? —patterns, holophone numbers, little faces, appointment times. Now most of that was left out of the computer record, naturally. Here—they fit the slip covers perfectly if you're careful. Is there one in particular you want to look at?"

"No. I want to browse a bit. Do they have titles?"

"Some do. Others only have numbers. We've catalogued them ourselves, you see. Arthur just left them piled in here when he moved to Pluto."

"In a hurry, no doubt."

"Oh no," the old woman said. "At least—I don't think so."

"Just joking." He set to the task of looking through them. Checking the catalogue, digging the appropriate notebook from its case, going through it; it took time. There was no listing for Fairfax in the catalogue, no listing for Icarus. Under *Travels* he found several notebooks filled with what appeared to be close descriptions of life on Mars. Nothing about Icarus. He replaced those notebooks and went back to the catalogue. In this kitchen doorway he saw Margaret's foot, tapping slowly in the air as she patiently waited. Already it had been hours.

He looked up the Orchestra, and again was referred to several notebooks. The first on the shelf was free of dust. Inside were descriptions and pictures of old orchestrions, orchestrinas, player pianos, *synthesizers mechanique*. Then notes, instruction to the glassworks, programs, sketches. Hundreds of sketches. Once Holywelkin had thought to place the control booth outside the thing. In other sketches the keyboards were arrayed around a crow's nest in the statue's top. Finally it came to the form Johannes knew. Electrical blueprints looked like drawings of the nervous system of some mythological creature, a dragon or medusa. Then a thick file of correspondence with the Telemann Works, the Terran

instrument makers Holywelkin had dealt with. Johannes began to understand that the greater part of Holywelkin's fortune had gone to the construction of the Orchestra. This kind
of material could have kept him occupied for days; but it was
in the computer, and he had a specific story to search for. He
closed the notebook.

There on the cover—*Master 9,* in a big solid inky scrawl.
He felt the skin of his neck goosepimple, and shivered convulsively. Above it: *How To Tell,* and a long scrawl leading
down to that large Master 9. This among random words and
numbers scribbled on the cover; in that it resembled all the
other covers, for they were Holywelkin's reminder pads,
palimpsests of the daily routine. But this one—in darker
letters:

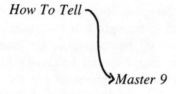

In Orchestrion—
one of the boxes

Destiny
give him time
that will be

Johannes roused Margaret from a catnap, and they left the
museum after thanking the old woman. "Find anything?"
Margaret asked.

"No." He was afraid to talk about it; he wished Margaret
didn't even know of his search, he wished he had never
started it. Margaret took his arm to help him along the street,
as he was missing curbs. How many years had passed since
Holywelkin had scribbled that message on his notebook's

cover, there among the appointments and numbers and odd phrases he had scratched down? Three hundred years, almost to the year. Writing a note to a man three hundred years in the future. . . .

"Watch out, Johannes," Margaret snapped. "You're going to get bowled over if you don't."

"Aren't we almost there?"

"Yes. Here."

"Thanks, Margaret. I'll join you in a while." He hurried through the bright yellow and chrome halls of their hotel. Blast of bent light from one chromatic room; someone inside, reading the tarot. Onto the tour floor, where there was some singing, and a chess game. Around back of the hotel was the big basement storage chamber. Marie-Jeanne and several other security people were at the doorway, sitting against the wall or standing around.

Johannes said, "Don't let anyone else in."

It was almost dark inside, and Johannes stretched the muscles that would help the photosensitive opening of the apertures of his eyes. Orchestra in the center of the room, reaching at the ceiling. Tree growing up through the cellar, break into the house, strangle the inhabitants, steal their lives, live their lives for them. He approached and climbed through the piano bench entrance. After all the schools and all the traveling, this was the doorway to his one true home. He had spent more hours here than anywhere else. Glass tree the material counterpart of his tangled soul. Up the glass steps, twisting and ducking at all the right places, not seeing the tiny bass and treble clef signs inlaid in every step. . . .

But this time there was something unknown there, in one of the boxes. Transmission box, full of transmitters and microchip boards and wires; the piano, harpsichord, celesta; three synthesizers, the choirbox, the godzilla. Other than that, only the little pulley boxes at the joints in the glass branches, holding wires so that they looked like the bridges of cellos. No room there.

He climbed up out of the control booth, up the small footholds on one of the main arms. Out over the forest of basses; a fall could be dangerous. He opened the top of the harpsichord and found it empty. Back down, then, to the piano, the synthesizers. Nothing in the piano, no room for anything in the synthesizers. He climbed again, up beyond the control booth, the thick glass arms, up into the network of delicate branchings, where a dim night light reflected from a thousand surfaces. The celesta: white box of polished wood, cast among the flutes and clarinets as a sort of counterbalance to the big instruments below. Opening the soundbox revealed a shortening row of metal bars, there for the hammers' striking. No one would ever tune those bars: a good hiding place. And there it was, held against the side of the box by two small brackets. A notebook very like the ones at the museum.

Johannes took it down to the control booth, turned on a reading light, opened the notebook. He read for a while, skipped pages, read, skipped pages, read again, all helplessly. Pages of spare black handwriting:

. . . proceeded from Mercury to intercept Icarus on its approach to perihelion, when it will halve the distance from sun to Mercury, and spin only thirty million kilometers from the star. This close approach is apparently what drew these people here. And I? Drawn by these strange people, and their invitation: "seen close enough Sol provides the solution to your problem," this followed by exactly the formulations that stopped me for over four years. How did they know? Could they be working along similar lines?

At first sight the asteroid seems uninhabited. Roughly spherical, about fifty kilometers in diameter, banged hard at one end recently, good fresh crater there, quite large and flat. Landed at a spaceport on cracked

blackened basaltic achondrite. Big plates of this overlaid the usual carbonaceous chondrite mounds. Crater rims, low hummocks, scattered boulders, from
pebbles to rocks the size of city hall.

So I was dropped off the ship like a pack of goods
and left on the pad. Shooed off to one side so that
the ship could take off again. Light smattering of dust
and it was gone. I walked off the edge of the pad
onto the dust, feeling the near absence of gravity. A
push with the toes, and off into space—pirouette—
touch down lightly, in a puff of dust. The horizons all
just a short hike away, lumpy and baked black.
Hexagonal cracking on the flat basalt plain: melted
by the sun? Rotation period a couple of weeks, thus a
week in the sun, at thirty million kilometers . . . six
hundred degrees K for the top centimeter, three hundred K for ground under the dust. I nosed around
picking up chunks all burnt and crumbly, feeling like
the Little Prince. Where were they?

Sun began to rise. Breaking over the whole horizon
before me all at once, like the end of an eclipse
when you are standing on the eclipsing body. Adrenaline terror of death by radiation, I dropped behind a
boulder and shoveled the dust over me, insane child
in a sandbox digging deeper in incandescent sand.
Even with eyes clamped shut the world was white on
white on white.

. . . they lived in a structure like an empty cyclo-
tron, dug into the rim wall of the biggest crater, with
narrow slitted windows, heavily shuttered, overlooking the central crater floor, which was cracked and
flat, with the usual central dimple knob. Each room

the arc of a torus, bare, flat-bottomed, curved walls
like the sides of barrels, ceilings bowed down somewhat. The people wear grey cotton pants, grey tunics
or coats, and some of them wear dark red caps. All of
them barefoot. Several days after my arrival I was
taken to the room occupying the largest single arc of
the torus; from one end of the room you couldn't see
around to the other. Once again left alone. Explored
room to both ends—around ninety degrees of the
crater's rim, I guessed.

Returning to the first end of the room I came on a
man sitting on the floor. The usual grey clothes, a
longer red cap than most. I sat beside him. "Why did
you send for me?"

"By your own efforts you have come near to knowing what only Sol can tell us. This we judge to be
your yearning for the grey, working inside you as in
every human being—but in you showing fruit. You,
Arthur Holywelkin, are a sort of . . . you know them
as . . . idiot savant. And we would teach you."

"What would you teach me?"

The old man looked at me. Burnt, wrinkled cheeks;
wet eyes filled with odd humor, anticipating me
somewhere. "The sun is a god, Arthur Holywelkin. The
sun is god."

"And by that you mean?" Feeling let down.

"Sol is a manifestation of the spirit of Mithras.
Spirit controls the radiation emanating from the thermonuclear ball, and that spirit controls all that happens in the space around it. Life began on Earth,
spread through the system, and now engages in
discourse with the Creator; all willed by the thought
of Mithras."

I shrugged, and he spoke of my work. The mathematics of convection currents under the sun's surface,
those that cause the great whirlpools known as sun-

spots; these could not be made consonant with the
model accounting for the curious lack of neutrinos
that escaped from the currents. Now the old Grey
reconciled them for me, drawing out formulas on the
floor with white chalk. For what seemed hours we
conversed in mathematics principally, punctuated only
by "You see," "But," "Then," ". . . yes."

"Who are you?" I said, much later.

"I am Zervan, Father of Fathers. King of the Greys."

I nodded; this didn't answer what I wanted to
know. "And how came you by this?" Gesturing at the
floor covered with the cryptography of our discourse.

"Mithras told me," he said. "Mithras controls me
even as I speak; and you as well."

Nothing to say to that. "With what we have here,"
I said, looking about me, "I can finish my work. The
forms of change will encompass all that we have
observed within the micro-dimensions. . . ."

"Do you understand what that implies?" Zervan
said.

I did not catch his meaning. Even in the heightened state of awareness that I had risen to, in which
the chaotic movement of glints was as clear as a
pavane to me, I could not catch it. I squinted. He saw
into me and smiled.

"We turn to Sol. This is as close as Icarus comes to
Sol, this very day." He stood with the slowest, most
fluid of movements. "Follow."

———————————————

. . . in lock that opened on the central crater plain.
Shutter up, and even with my protective goggles I
was blinded. Total white-out, nothing but hot light. "I
cannot see."

"Look closer. Forms remain." Zervan stood ahead of me. Gradually a world coalesced out of the varying incandescences of white. Chanting from behind me, oddly speeded then slowed down, a chorus of Greys shouting vowels.

It occurred to me I heard from within a daysuit. Speakers in helmet, I presumed.

"Come," Zervan said. He started to the lock door.

"Wait! You've forgotten your suit!"

He smiled, shook his head. Unzipped the grey tunic, pulled his arms out of it, let it fall. Unzipped grey cotton pants, let them fall. Naked scrawny old man, white hair on chest, belly, crotch, legs. He walked to the lock door. "My God!" I said.

The lock door slid up and away. The air pushed by us. Blinded again I reached for Zervan—already gone. Vaporized? I stepped to the slot where the lock door fit. My legs refused to go further. Out there on the crater floor—naked old man, walking slowly toward the shimmer of the central knob. I stepped out after him.

Running after him I expected to collapse and die at any step. Thirty million kilometers from sun, its light only a minute before had been in the furnace itself, and so the radiation must necessarily have been melting my suit my skin my brains my blood my bones, all of me instantly scrambled. But there walked the old man ahead of me, stark naked. Feet on dust six hundred degrees Kelvin. He looked back at me, gestured me on.

Caught up to him. He said, "Do you see now?"

I saw nothing. But the whiteness was reduced, the crater rim encircled us like a wall, we stood on the floor of the universe itself. The sky was the sun, the sun the sky—nothing above the crater walls but roiling white fire, licks of the corona that seemed to

lance down like lightning in a saner world, forming
temporary pillars between the two worlds of white
and overwhite. Panic danced around him: "How can
this be?"

No answer. And he began to fumble at the latches
under my helmet. I struck at his hands and he said "Be
still" and I was still. Suit or no I was broiled to a crisp,
why care? And my limbs refused to move. Beginning
of the end, I thought. He unlatched the helmet and
took it off. Now we faced each other in the vacuum.
I breathed it in, breathed it out. "How . . . ?"

"Mithras shifts the vibrations in this space to ac-
commodate us. All is vibration, you see. Different
vibrations interacting, and nothing material at all.
Mithras can alter the vibrations if it has always been
that way."

This meant nothing to me. And meanwhile he
uncoupled the pieces of my daysuit, pulled them
away from me. Even my boots off. Dust on my toes
like any other dust. "What . . .?"

"All we sense is vibration, nothing is material.
Mithras is a sentient, powerful creator, willing to
discourse with those who learn the way. There is no
choice. Look up."

Up. Neck craned back. Up. White light rumbling
like a great loud generator, twisting, twisting, twisting. Fire. And in the fire, shapes, visions, what was
that—a face?—no—a tree—and music from the crater rim, from every atom in me, but originating from
that tree of sound in the center of Sol's fire.

"You hear his voice. He speaks to you! No chance,
no choice, no change." Zervan's voice a tiny tendril in
the great white tapestry of sound-fire. "Note follows
note in Sol's eternal score, and all our destinies are
written there, billions and billions of years before
these pebbles rolled in the night. And so you see God

eye to eye, he speaks to you, he allows you to come to him naked, without harm; and sends you away with the sound of his voice forever in you." The swirling tree, white glassy currents in the thermonuclear ball, emanating pitches, melodies just on the edge of understanding—if only clear of Zervan's descant—I raised a hand and Zervan fell silent and in a time without time I knew what it was to be a bronze man, immortal, part of the sun for all eternity.

"We must return. Back now, or never again," Zervan said. And destiny moved my feet for me, I stepped away still looking up. "Now you see your part," Zervan said, "your part in the preparation for the one that will follow. Your mathematics the expression of the mind of Mithras. Your orchestra the model of the voice of Sol. And when the one who understands your orchestra shall come—"

"It will be the ninth master," I said, looking down the future as it slipped between the sun's white corona and the white hills of Icarus. "He will come to you, and then on Mars—"

"On Mars," Zervan said,

Clap Johannes slammed the notebook shut. It slid between his shaking hands and fell to the control booth floor. A small notebook on a glass floor inlaid with tiny French horn figures—Holywelkin's Orchestra—Johannes hardly dared to touch it! What to do with it? Fearfully he picked it up, seized it so that it could not burst open in his hands . . . nowhere in the control booth would do. . . . In the end he climbed uncertainly back up to the celesta, slipping several times, once so seriously that he almost lost his grasp on the notebook, and it fell partway open—*No chance, no choice, no change*—banged it shut again, and shoved it back in the brackets against the celesta's inner wall, holding it as if he had a wolf by the ears.

Then down, half sliding half falling, damaging a pulley joint. He didn't care. Out of the Orchestra he fell, and from the storeroom he ran through the hotel, heedless of witnesses, to collapse on the spurious and very transitory comfort of a hotel bed.

♪

bent in her own generator

Margaret heard of this bizarre behavior, and she went to his room an hour or so later to see what was up. She found Johannes seated before a diagram of the inner solar system on his computer terminal, face pale, mouth tight and determined.

"Look here, Margaret," he said without preamble. "When we cross the asteroid belt to Mars we will be traveling very near the aphelion of Icarus, the Greys' world. Icarus will be pretty near its aphelion, crossing the plane of the planets almost."

Margaret inspected the colored display. "Well. It'll be nearer Mars than the sun, but it's still pretty far above the plane, isn't it?"

"I must go there before we go to Mars."

She had never heard him sound so forceful. At the same time it seemed to her that he was terrified; it was a disturbing mix. He stared at her as if to ignite her to the same fiery emotion that burned like a whitsun inside him. . . .

"Tell me what happened," she said.

"It doesn't matter. I have to go to Icarus before the Martian concert."

She shook her head; no one threatened her. "I must know what happened, or I won't allow it."

He burst to his feet. "*I* run this tour! I am Master of the Orchestra! I say where we go!"

Margaret nodded. "All right, then. I must know what's happened, or I will resign, and leave the managing of the tour to you." Suddenly she was angry. "I don't know what those Greys mean to you, and I don't much care. I am trying to run a very complicated tour, and everything you have done has made it harder. Now you're following Grey mysteries, visiting their world—come on, Johannes! Can't you pursue this issue some other time?"

"No," he said. "I can't."

She took a step toward the door.

"I can't, Margaret," he said miserably. "I have to do it now. The music depends on it."

"Tell me."

"It has to do with Holywelkin. He went to Icarus before building the Orchestra. What he learned there is crucial for playing the Orchestra, and for everything I want to do. I can't complete my work until I've talked with them. Do you understand?"

"I do not." Margaret turned aside, to avoid the pitiful sight of the blind man begging. "We don't know enough about the Greys to risk visiting them."

"We will never know enough until we do visit them! You can act in ignorance, Margaret, I've heard you say it yourself. You said we *have* to act in ignorance—we have no other choice."

"Still we choose our acts," Margaret said desperately. "I didn't mean it made sense to do something stupid."

"There is a month before the Martian festival. The Orchestra and everyone else on the tour can go straight there on *Orion*, as you did from Pluto to Uranus. You can discuss the matter of our visit with the Greys here, and come to an agreement—you could be sure I would be safe. You could even come along to see that I'm safe! You and Karna and I could charter one of the asteroid liners and go to Icarus, and then on to Mars. *I must do it*, Margaret!"

"You are creating your own problems," she said, and the bitter cutting tone of her voice surprised her. He was overwhelming her, convincing her against her better judgment, and she knew it, but she couldn't bring herself to change. He was. . . . In her mind she relented a bit; it wasn't completely his fault he was unbalanced. Some strange things had happened to him. Now the Greys. Somehow they had enticed him into demanding this voyage to Icarus . . . something had happened.

"You found something out at the Holywelkin museum," she said abruptly. "You found something there that led you to Icarus."

A long pause. He nodded once. "Yes."

That gave Margaret a funny feeling. Something scratched at the back of her memory, something she had noticed at the museum . . . she sighed. She couldn't remember.

Angrily she walked to the door. Prima donnas she had dealt with before, but this . . . this was something new, something different. Suddenly she felt inadequate to it—a foreign feeling, one she didn't like. "Damn it!" She struck the door open. "In my next life I will stay on Iapetus, and be a traffic cop, and never leave my little street corner."

Chapter Six

‖: **OUT OF THE PLANE** :‖

A small spacecraft left the Grand Tour and arced up out of the plane of the planets, carrying Johannes, Margaret and Karna toward Icarus, the home of the Greys. During the voyage Johannes was withdrawn, and Margaret sensed in him an intense apprehension. Margaret spent her time piloting the craft, playing Go with Karna, and catching up on her sleep. And then a blue soap bubble swam into view, far away in the starry black. They stood before the broad bridge window and watched the bubble grow.

From just outside the sphere of air they saw that the surface of the asteroid was mountainous: ranges folded on ranges, split by canyons and watersheds that indicated a long history of weather and erosion. "That's not how Holywelkin described it!" Johannes said.

"It's been terraformed," Karna said. "Pretty expensive job, too. Nothing left of the original surface, as far as I can see."

"What did Holywelkin say?" Margaret asked Johannes.

"Where did he ever write about Icarus? Why won't you let me read it?"

"I don't have it with me," Johannes said. "He wrote it in one of his notebooks. He said it was a cratered asteroid, a large impact crater at one end."

"Terraformed now," Karna said. "Nice job, too."

"Persia was mountainous," Johannes said.

A shuttle popped through the discontinuity and floated up to them; it moved out of the window's framing, and they felt the gentle bump of the coupling. Minutes later three Greys filed onto the bridge, chattering to each other in their own tongue. One of them had a face like a skull papered with skin, and his cheeks were scarred. They chattered at the three visitors and pointed and led them through the ship to the lock connecting it to the shuttle. Ducking their heads the three visitors pulled through, into the Greys' world.

Descent. In the portholes the sky snapped from black to deep blue. They landed on a short white concrete runway, placed in what appeared to be a high U-shaped glacial valley. They walked through the open door and down a staircase onto the runway. Surrounding the white strip was a carefully manicured green lawn, flat and circular. Beyond the lawn the expanse of shattered, speckled white granite rose on both sides to steep, serrated ridges. The air was thin and cold, the whitsun directly overhead. Margaret shivered as the chill goosepimpled her skin. In the thin air the mountains seemed very close, and Margaret could distinguish with unnatural clarity boulders, cracks, ridge edges, and the jumbled surfaces of talus slopes. There was not a single sound; the air was so still that she became aware of the sound of her breathing, of Karna's breathing. Absolute quiet. Then, off in the distance, down the glacial valley, from over the ribbing of a low moraine, came a floating thread of voices, tiny voweled warbling in echoes off the exfoliated valley walls. And over the moraine appeared a line of figures, trudging across the granite to the landing strip. Grey cotton pants,

long grey coats; and on their heads bright, floppy red caps.
Six of them. Their clothes blended with the speckled diorite
of the granite, rendering them shadows or apparitions; but the
red caps bobbed along steadily, up what might have been a
trail.

Margaret found she was holding her breath, and breathed.
Karna was trying to look in all directions at once, head
swivelling like an automatic scanner's; it would have made
Margaret smile, but she was too nervous. The Greys who had
piloted their shuttle came down the staircase, wearing red
caps that flopped to one side, over their ears. The six Greys
on the trail reached the edge of the grass and she could make
out their severe brown faces: three men, she guessed, and
three women. With the three from the shuttle they walked to
the perimeter of the grass circle, until they were evenly
distributed and facing inward. And so there were—Margaret
counted—ten of them? She counted again. Ten of them.
Where . . . ? Karna looked grim. Johannes was locked in a
gaze with the Grey standing directly in front of him, off at
the edge of the grass. That Grey began to sing in a language
of tones as serrated as the ridges above, while the other nine
Greys chanted vowels in slow low chords. Ten tones, the top
one a jagged ridge in time. Then they stopped and the silence
of that high mountain valley was so empty and pure that it
became a tangible gel containing them, and Margaret could
feel her thoughts roaring in it. Clumps of moss were strewn
like scraps of green carpet over level spots on the banks of
the small stream that gurgled through the jumbled moraine
down the valley—and now she could hear the distant thren-
ody of the creek's voice, where she hadn't before. And there
were small juniper trees struggling for life, flattened by
existence in the wind, humming softly.

The Grey across from Johannes sang, "Welcome to Icarus,
Master of Holywelkin's Orchestra." He pointed down the
valley, back the way he had come. "There is your path—"

And they all froze. They all stopped chanting, the speaker

continued to point like an utterly inert statue, and it appeared that not one of them breathed. Karna took a step toward them. "What . . ."

And then another shuttle popped over a ridge like a great hawk. As it fell toward the strip it grew wings and tilted back to land like a puff of down. It slowed and rolled to a stop just behind the first shuttle. The door opened, the staircase descended: metallic squeaks in the airy silence, *squeak, squeak, squeak, clunk.* Down stepped a single tall man, dressed in grey pants and tunic, his wrinkled face the color of a walnut, framed by a whitish beard. He approached them in an easy long stride. "Do you wish to see the Father of Fathers?" he called, tilting his head in a bemused fashion.

Johannes said, "Yes, I do. But what about these?"

The man shrugged. "I thought they were with you." And, seeing Margaret's and Karna's expressions: "They are not Grey. I have affixed them momentarily to inquire your purposes and theirs."

"We do not know theirs," Johannes said. "We thought they were the Greys come to greet us. No one specified to us what form our greeting would take. Now you come and say you are the true Grey here. How are we to know?"

The man gestured. "Inspect these still figures around you. Their blood does not pulse, their heart does not beat, they do not bleed; yet when I release them they will live. No one but we of Icarus can do that. Now, come see Zervan. He wants to speak to you."

Johannes nodded, and when the tall Grey turned and walked up the glacial basin, Johannes followed him. After one stricken look at Karna, Margaret followed, and Karna brought up the rear.

The trail was no more than a line where the rocks had been walked on many times, until the cracks between them filled with gravel and dust. It led them all up the glacial valley. The sides of the valley rounded in and met at the cleft of a long tumbling whiteline of water. The trail switchbacked next to the stream, so that as they hiked the twisting path they heard the stream's rushing voice recede and return, time after time. Work and the bright whitsun warmed Margaret's neck, then all of her. Wafts of juniper scent were blown out by the waterfall. Blotches of lichen colored the large boulders protruding from the slope, in patches of yellow, red, green, black.

Glaciers carve U's in the valleys they course through, and the bigger valleys fill with more ice and are carved deeper. Side branches of these glaciers are smaller and do not carve as deep, and so where they meet the larger glacier there are discrepancies, revealed when the glaciers melt away as hanging valleys, cirques, and cirquelike heads for every valley branch: waterfalls abound. Now they were climbing up the big valley's side wall to one of these hanging valleys, and when they came to the top of the switchbacks they found themselves entering a broad basin like a giant granite bowl cut in half. Small lakes dotted the bottom of the basin, and a hundred trickles fell down the steep basin walls. In the jagged horseshoe ridge edging the bowl there was a dip somewhat to the left of the horseshoe's middle, and in places on the basin wall short strands of the whitish trail were visible, switchbacking up to that dip. The Grey led his three visitors up the trail, taking the switchbacks with a long graceful stride. Margaret hiked behind Johannes, and began to sweat. She turned her head to speak to Karna, who hiked behind her: "I wonder what the air is made of?"

Karna sniffed. "Lot of oxygen. And the pressure—maybe six hundred millibars? Hard to say. It's thin, though."

At last they came to the dip, and were in a pass. Behind them was their basin—before them another basin, longer, narrower, deeper, a string of finger lakes down its bottom. The ridges rose on both sides; to the left they rose to a thick, tall sawtooth peak. The pass was composed of fat rounded blocks of rough granite, split and cracked in a million ways. Moss grew in some of the splits, and lichen starred the speckled grey rock with color. Margaret felt her pulse tap in her neck. "This is a small asteroid. They've left a lot of open space." The horizons were close, but from their height they saw nothing but range after range.

"There must not be very many people living here," said Karna.

Johannes stood by the tall Grey, observing him in silence while the Grey stared at the thick peak, as if looking for something on it.

In the distant sky a speck winged toward them. "Bird," Margaret said, and Karna nodded. The sky seemed a darker blue than before, and above them the whitsun glared. No wind; no sound of the waterfalls below. Every rock on every slope and basin gleamed individually at them. And the speck flew up the far basin and grew until they saw that it was spinning rather than flapping wings, and then it was too large to be a bird and they saw it was a man, cartwheeling flat on his back through the air. Margaret stepped back, then went to Johannes's side and held him by the arm.

The flying man tilted into a vertical cartwheel and spun up the valley's headwall to the pass. And then he spun in place above them and up one ridge, and slowed his revolutions, and came to a stop floating upright, arms and legs extended outward in the position of the Da Vinci anatomy drawing. He wore only a white loincloth, and his skin was the walnut color of their guide's face. His hair was jet black and he had a hooked nose. He crossed his arms and smiled.

Margaret heard Karna gasp, and it was a sound so unlike him that she tore her gaze from the levitating man to glance over at him. Karna's mouth hung open foolishly, and his face was gray and bloodless. He cried out in Hindi, and to Margaret's astonishment the floating man replied in the same language, his voice high and nasal, like a vocal model for the oboe. Karna stepped past Johannes, past Margaret and her restraining hand. He spoke in a strained, harsh tone. "Who is he?" Margaret cried. Johannes put his hand to her shoulder.

"What are they saying?" she said, frightened. Johannes shook his head, gaze on Karna. She knew that Johannes knew what they were saying, and jerked his arm. The floating man drifted up the ridge, and Karna followed him by leaving the trail and hopping up recklessly from rock to rock. "Karna!" Margaret shouted, and ran a few steps after him. She halted and looked beseechingly at Johannes; but Wright was staring at the tall Grey, his expression as blank as his eyes. Margaret groaned and climbed laboriously from rock to rock after Karna, who was leaping up at a swift clip just below the floating man. The two were still conversing. As she caught up to them Karna skipped up twice and hopped into the air, rising without effort to the levitator's side. Remaining there. Margaret stopped, blood washing through her like boiling water. The two men embraced in midair, pulled apart. With hawklike swiftness the levitator grabbed Karna's wrists and yanked him around, spun him and spun him like a man tossing the hammer, until they were both horizontal and twirling above Margaret. The levitator let go (sudden flash of Karna's surprised face) and they flew off in opposite directions, spinning still, each disappearing in a few seconds over the ranges on the horizon.

Margaret looked back to Johannes. He was walking up the other ridge edge that rose from the pass, accompanied by the tall Grey. *"Johannes,"* she cried, and raced down the rocks, along the spine of the pass, up the other ridge. Johannes turned down a spur trail dropping into the new basin the pass had revealed to them, and she followed him down. Closing on his back she felt a surge of relief and anger. What did he think he was doing? But when she reached him the fear grabbed her again—he seemed tall—he turned. It was her brother. She gasped as if hit and stumbled to a halt, scraping a knee on the rocky ground. The sight of his face, looking just as it had during his life, made her burst into tears. Karl had committed suicide by volunteering for the whiteline jump experiments on Mars; "Karl," she said, and instantly she thought of Johannes and remembered where she was. She squinted and dashed the tears from her eyes, "You're not Karl!" she said furiously, and shouted, "What have you done to Johannes?" She grabbed the figure's shoulders roughly, intending to shake the truth from him, but touching him melted her will, and with a small smile the Karl man touched her cheek. She was crying again. "Where is he? Why did you do it?"

A great calm filled her. "Where is he, Karl?" she repeated, but Karl didn't answer. But it wasn't him. She remembered again, saw that his face was wrong. They were putting her in some kind of trance—she struck the man in the face and he staggered back. It had been a hard blow. "Come on, Grey," she said. "Tell me what you've done with him before I beat you up." She felt light but cool-headed. The man lunged forward and slapped her; she punched him hard, and he rolled away on the ground and got up running pell mell down the steep trail away from her. He dropped like a goat and no matter how reckless Margaret was she couldn't descend the steep rocky trail any faster. She cursed in frustration as her prey reached the basin floor and dashed away. When she reached the basin floor he was nowhere to be seen; big boulders stuck up like houses here and there on the rumpled basin meadow, glacial erratics dropped at random. He could have hidden anywhere. As she wandered down the meadow she noticed the twisted low shapes of the junipers, struggling to hunker down in their little nooks and crannies. Grass patches, mounds of dull heather sparked by flower colors, granite a rich reddish tan, specked with chips of black and white and yellow. She walked down to the basin's crease, where the first pond formed. Around it neat moss lawns tucked into the rock surrounded the dark blue water. And there across the pond, a bighorn sheep, horns spiraling like the shape of all creation: still but alert, head up, ears trained her way. She walked slowly around the pond, keeping eye contact with the bighorn at all times. She had been sent often

as a child to recover hurt wildlife, it was a talent she had.
The sheep had all its sharp hoofs on one flat rock. It clattered
off the rock and then submitted to Margaret's steady approach, until she laid a hand on its bony spine. Then it led
her down the stepped boulders flanking the pond's exit creek.
Little falls over stones alternated with rushing straight spills
until the stream fell into the next pond, a larger one. They
walked together to a patch of meadow grass at the pond's
edge. Clumps of grass, gritty granite sand, alpine flowers
like little fountains of color. A marmot, startled by their
appearance, bounded past them; Margaret caught it up and
stroked it, but it was frightened and jerked out to nip at her
cheek. She patted and cooed and soon it was as calm as the
sheep. A little blood dripped down her cheek. She sat down
and placed the marmot beside her on the grass. The stream
poured into the pond, which appeared to be tilted so that the
stream was higher where it left the pond than where it
entered. Over the smooth sheet of water there was movement. Margaret looked at a particularly large boulder, standing at the pond's mouth; behind it appeared a big light brown
hunting cat. Mountain lion, cougar, puma. Margaret gasped
with delight. Icarus was like the outer worlds, inhabited by
animals. . . . Now the cat circled the pond, each step rip-
pling the fur over its massive shoulders. The bighorn and
marmot watched it, unblinking and unafraid, because Margaret was there. And . . . perhaps there was something about
this pond. The little clicks of water falling, and no other
sound. The granite basin, holding them as in a bowl. Everything she saw, heard, felt, smelled, everything was peaceful.
The cat stepped off a rock onto their little lawn, and touched
noses with bighorn and marmot. It was making a sound like a
deep purr; it was purring. Margaret laughed with delight. It
came to her and licked the blood from her cheek. Its tongue
was like a fine wet rasp. She threw her arms around its thick
neck and hugged it, face deep in the clean-smelling tan fur.
The cat sat, extended forward until it lay sphinxlike on the

meadow. The four of them sat, filled by the rhythmic buzz of the cat's low purr, a cycle of breath that Margaret and the bighorn fell in with; the marmot breathed in double time. The three pairs of eyes watching her were so calm, so calm. Contentment washed through Margaret like a buzz of the purr; she stood and took off her clothes, and sat back down on the rock, an animal among animals. The whitsun's light gleamed on her dark brown skin. She thought, we know we are beautiful because animals give us such reverence. The breeze brushed her skin; the whitsun was warm on her back and legs. The smell of the stunted pines across the pond wafted by, and the cougar purred. A bloom of rock jasmine tumbled into the pond with the stream, and floated toward them. Margaret kneeled and reached out over her reflection to pluck the flower from the water. The bloom had a velvety surface, and its deep pink was all shot with tiny veins of red. An oval green leaf clung to the stem below the flower; it had a waxy surface, and its veins were a darker green than the rest of it. Her dim reflection looked out of the leaf at her, and she frowned; something was not right. She showed the cougar its reflection, forgetting the thought, filling again with the great peaceful harmony that nature in certain eternal moments sings.

♪

There was a faint, narrow trail running up the very edge of the ridge, and Johannes Wright trudged up it after the Grey. The ridge rose at a steep angle; their trail wound around knobs to avoid vertical jumps in the ridge (gendarmes standing watch), and sometimes they walked on ledges in the sheer slopes of steep cirque walls, under the gendarmes' sides. But always they returned to the ridge edge higher than they had been before, and hiked onward, up toward the thick sawtooth peak at the highest point of the ridge.

The whitsun hung in the western sky, pouring light onto them. A series of lakes lay across the floor of the basin below like a string of jewels, aquamarine around their edges, cobalt in their deep centers. Johannes stopped often to look at them and at the curving tiers of scored and jumbled granite. He had never been in mountains like these before, and the immense prospects were overwhelming; sometimes his head swam in the thin air, and he had to look down at his feet and concentrate; one foot after another, trudging it out, step by step, thighs pumping, quadriceps aching like overworked rubber bands . . . sweat pouring down the forehead, stinging the corners of the eyes. . . . Life itself is a moment like this, the soul beat down and held to knowledge: you keep on trudging upward, the goal shifts in and out of sight, always further away than you expected, and the work is hard and unremitting. And the questions are the same as always: What are you doing? Is it the right thing? Should you go back? — Nothing up here but the same answers, stripped bare of all complication: Just walk. Keep hiking. That's all you can do. That is your destiny.

The Grey was faster, and over the next hour's struggle up the trail he drew ahead, until Johannes occasionally lost sight of him in a dip, or around a knob. The ridge widened, became like a rounded road at the top of the world, a ramp to the peak. Hours passed, and the whitsun dropped lower in the western sky. The basins to the east were in shadow.

And then he was there, standing under the final bastion of the peak. An angled slot like a chimney broke the sheer wall of the peak knob, and Johannes pulled himself up it. From its upper end he merely had to hop up a short series of ledges, and he was on top. Nothing higher; the whole world below him, flowing in fractal ranges to the jagged horizons.

The Grey was sitting on a boulder, looking as if he had been there a long time. Not waiting for Johannes, but just there on his own, taking in the view. Johannes sat down and leaned back against a low boulder. He looked at the Grey, and saw that the brown eyes in the wrinkled walnut skin were cold and distant; they seemed to look through him to the rock itself. "Who are you?" Johannes said.

"I am Zervan."

"And why have you brought me here?"

"Why have you come?"

"Because—because Holywelkin came here, before he built the Orchestra. Before he finished his work on the *Ten Forms of Change*. I want to . . ." He swallowed. "I want to learn what he learned."

"What did he learn?"

"I don't know. The Icarus he visited wasn't like this. It was a cratered asteroid. They took him out into the sun at perihelion, with no protection. Naked."

"That would kill him," Zervan said.

"And they—they had communion with the sun. The sun spoke to them because . . . because they worshipped it. You say the sun is God—"

"No," said Zervan. "Icarus has ever been like this. And the Greys do not worship the sun. It is our destiny to interact with it, to use it for its energy. But we do not worship it."

"So you are not Mithraists?"

"No." Zervan shook his head. "Mithraism is long dead. We are Greys."

"And what is that?"

"It is Grey. Very difficult to convey it in your language. We are priests of a knowledge that is not to be revealed. Perhaps that makes Grey an antireligion."

"But you revealed it to Holywelkin."

". . . Yes."

"And you will reveal it to me?"

For a long time the Grey stared at Johannes. "Yes."

"How long have there been Greys?"

"The Greys are older than the Mithraists. They too began in Persia. Do you know the Eleatics? Parmenides, Zeno?"

"They claimed there was only Being, and no Becoming.

That the world was full, an absolute plenum in which change was impossible."

"Yes. And part of what they knew spread to others, to Democritus and Leucippus, and then to Epicurus and Lucretius. . . ."

"And what did they know? What is it you conceal?"

Zervan stared through him to the rock. "It is the nature of reality we conceal. Child, do you understand the implication of Holywelkin's work, or where it stands in the history of human knowledge?"

"I—I am not sure." But all of his fears rushed in at him.

"Bruno, Bacon, Pierre Gassendi, Newton—all determinists, all Greys. Newtonian physics is deterministic. It is true that it fits into the larger framework of the probabilistic system of quantum mechanics. But quantum mechanics fits into the larger framework of Holywelkin physics; and Holywelkin physics is again deterministic. Do you understand?"

"All motion is caused, and therefore occurs by necessity," Johannes recited. It was just as he had suspected, reading Mauring and the notebooks of Holywelkin. . . .

Zervan nodded. "Probabilistic systems already contain the secret, in that they are not random; laws are in operation, but are not known. Thus certain features of quantum mechanics, such as the so-called uncertainty principle, are artifacts of incomplete understanding. When the higher dimensions are taken into account the uncertainty can be bypassed. Holywelkin physics describes the atomic events first postulated by the Eleatics, acting in all ten dimensions. These events are the dynamic fabric of spacetime, and they move without chance. Each event in the ten dimensions of spacetime is determined by all the moments before and after it. And as we are nothing but aggregates of these events, our feeling that we exercise free will is nothing but an illusion of consciousness. Holywelkin obscures this with his later work, afraid of its meaning for human life. But it is nevertheless true. Therefore, those who fully understand Holywelkin's real work . . . become Grey."

"So the world *is* determined."

"Listen to the heretic Grey Laplace. 'An intellect which at a given instant knew all the forces acting in nature, and the position of all things of which the world consists—supposing the said intellect were vast enough to subject these data to analysis—would embrace in the same formula the motions of the greatest bodies in the universe and those of the slightest atoms; nothing would be uncertain for it, and the future, like the past, would be present to its eyes.' "

Johannes stood, feeling the tension over his stomach, the wind cutting at his skin. "That intellect could only be God."

"No. We couple our minds to the artificial intelligence we have built into Icarus, and use the sun's energy to power it. And applying Holywelkin's formulations . . . we see all."

"Not the future!" Johannes said.

"We can. The future, like the past, exists eternally. But the analysis must be made, the calculation, you see. And it is a complex one. We can do it for certain events, and we do do it, sometimes."

"I don't believe it," Johannes said feebly. "So many things happen by chance, are random occurrences—"

"To our perception. But glints move in the absolutely predictable mesh of the ten forms of change. When Holywelkin realized this he tried to deny it, to find a way out. God does play dice with the universe, he joked, desperately; for Einstein's instinct was right, as was that of Democritus twenty-two centuries earlier."

Now Johannes began to understand the eccentric last years of Holywelkin more fully. He too instinctively looked for escape . . . . "But . . . if determinist classical physics rests within the probabilistic system of quantum mechanics, which rests within the determinist system of Holywelkin physics, then it may be like a set of Chinese boxes, so that a time will come when a more subtle physics will find that probabilities rule again, that certain events occur by chance."

Zervan shook his head. "No matter whether the ultimate

entities are atoms, electrons, quarks, glints, or simple geometric points of force, their relationships among themselves are determined by the relationships obtaining before them. This will be true whether human understanding can encompass the relationships or not. And with glints we have come to those basic nodal points of being in non-being; we are on the floor of the universe, so to speak. . . .''

"And so change—" Johannes paced the edge of the mountaintop, unwilling to face Zervan, dodging the implications as he had for months now.

"Change is the illusion of time," said Zervan. "And time is an illusion of consciousness. Consciousness exists in time, and to that extent time is real; but the universe is always there, past and future parts of a whole that is eternally complete. And because the universe is infinite, all moments in time occur forever, in endless recurrence. You and I have always had this exchange; it was fated to be billions of years before these planets rolled, in the eternity of Being."

"And so my future . . ." Johannes said, and then, fearfully: "You know it?"

"It is still being calculated. But we are almost done. When we are done we will communicate it to you."

"Why?"

"That much, we already know will happen."

Johannes struck his head with the palm of his hand: "I don't understand! How can there be no such thing as time, and yet you are still working through, in time, the calculations necessary to foresee my future?"

"Consciousness is trapped in time, at least through most of its existence; it lives in the illusion of Becoming. Why that is, we know not. There are intervals, how can we call them, parts of the pattern of consciousness, that obtrude into eternity. This experience is one that creates Greys, in fact. And this peak is one platform for the experience; we call it the Timeless Peak, and if you look closely you may see others, standing there eternally."

"I see no one," Johannes said.

Zervan touched Johannes on the wrist, and Johannes felt a prickling in the skin there. "Now," Zervan said, "I will grant you the vision of eternity. You will exist there forever."

"But I want to live!"

"Consciousness will struggle on through time. But you will exist here eternally, as you will come to understand."

Johannes stared about him desperately; the whitsun was low in the sky, rumpled mountains extended to every horizon, the valleys were in shadows that gave them all an immense depth, gave him an immense height, and all of it wavering, shimmering. . . .

"Remember," Zervan said. "For your consciousness, the nature of the vision will be exponential acceleration, to a speed far beyond that of light."

"Exponential acceleration," Johannes repeated.

"And you will see the universe itself in its aspect of eternal recurrence."

"Eternal recurrence."

The whitsun dropped like a stone over the western horizon, and the deep blue drained out of the sky. Black night, and the network of stars above. Zervan took his hand, and led him to the edge of the peak, walked off it. They stepped up invisible stairs, endless steps. "We will break through the bubble," Johannes said. "Will we be able to breathe?"

"Look." Zervan pointed down, and Johannes saw they were still sitting on the mountaintop in the sunset, far below. "We breathe not." Johannes realized he felt nothing, that Zervan's voice was merely a thought. A universe of thought, a great *Gendankenexperiment*. The little asteroid beneath them was white and green on its sunward side. Then, as Johannes watched, it pulsed, it stretched out, the crescent of white-green became a band extending across space. And everything blurred, everything fell away. The stars were streaks. There were more of them than he had ever seen. Nearby was what he took to be the sun, Sol, now a bar of light crossing the black space from end to end; and space was filled with other bars of light, each stretching as far as he could see. Looking harder at his solar system Johannes saw the planet-streaks spiraling around the white bar of light, some tight and close, others distant and spiraling more loosely. The gas giants were surrounded by faint helixes of their own. And now the line of the sun curved very clearly, crossing other curved lines. So many stars that the space here was more white lines than black space. He was passing among them. His sun was lost. Some of the starlines were bright red, others were surrounded by hundreds of dull planet-spirals. Double star system a tight double helix, like DNA strands of light. Novas big, scored, translucent cylinders. Black space filled with white curved lines, crowded by them—

Then he was clear. Johannes saw the galaxy below him, a cylinder of spiraling lines so dense in its center that the lines formed a thick endless pillar. The galaxy resembled the sight of a single solar system, except that it was infinitely textured. The spiral-armed shape of the galaxy-in-time gave its time-less aspect the look of an endless white corkscrew; and hidden in it somewhere, invisibly, was Sol, the Earth, all human history.

Other galaxies stretched across the black of space, some close, some far. White threads, scattered randomly. But no. Everything has its causes, and necessarily "becomes" next because it has always been that way: and all of the galaxy threads curved out away from, and came back to, a small white ball far below him. The threads burst away from the white ball in every direction, so that the ball's true size was impossible to see; the threads extended outward, curved back toward the central ball, returned to it. At their maximum reach outward they bowed in graceful arcs, and all of them together made a pattern; the curving white lines appeared somewhat like the outlines of the edges of flower petals. A bit spherical black flower, its petals outlined in white, its center a bright white knob. The universe.

And Johannes kept rising. The only thing in the cosmos moving, he drifted beyond the highest curving galaxy lines. The universe looked like an infinitely petalled chrysanthemum. Spherical white bloom there on its velvet black field, eternally pulsing in and out.

He looked away from the chrysanthemum universe blooming at his feet, and his invisible body reeled, his soundless voice cried out, his mind rebelled; there were more spherical tracery blooms, scattered around him. It was as if he stood on a rolling black hillside covered by white chrysanthemums. A hillside of flower universes, all fixed forever, all recurring eternally, unchanging; he found his universe body choked with harsh, painful laughter. And there above him—a black sky filled with white chrysanthemums. As his vision gained power the white blooms covered the black hillside, filled the black sky, sparked in every patch of darkness; in the endless expanse of infinity every possible universe existed eternally, filling all Non-Being with Being. And he looked up into a sky that was pure white. And the hillside below him was pure white. And around him all was white, pure white, pure white.

Chapter Seven

𝄆 MARS THE 𝄇
PLANET OF PEACE

the ten forms of change

Retrogradation is the reverse ordering of a sequence of notes. From a listener's point of view this procedure completely obscures the original melody; hear the final fugue of Beethoven's *Hammerclavier Sonata* (the mad energy of the universe) for an example of this. *Inversion* is turning upside down—the substitution of higher for lower tones, or ascending for descending lines—as when trees are reflected in a lake. *Retrograde inversion,* then, is the operation that makes a sequence both upside down and backwards. . . .

Augmentation is the arithmetical or proportional enlargement of interval; *diminution* is the arithmetical or proportional reduction of interval; these operations are used to create increased breadth, or increased intensity. *Inclusion* is the expansion of a set of events by the addition of elements. Some forms of inclusion are *interpolation,* the insertion of new elements into a series; *corrective interjection,* the interruption of a phrase to insert an altered fragment of the whole; and *free absorption,* moving one part of a phrase to the background while bringing another to the fore. Other types of inclusion are *prefixing, appending horizontalization,* and *imitation.*

Textural change is the shift of a phrase from one texture (*monophonic* texture is an unsupported melodic line; *homophonic,* a melodic line supported by chords; *polyphonic,* several interweaving melodic lines) to another texture. *Partition* is the division of a phrase by interposed silences, in the same way that phrases of consciousness are divided by sleep. *Interversion* is the diverting of events another way during repetition by changing the internal order of elements; this operation is also known as transposition. And *exclusion* is the shortening or logical simplification of a set of events, by a selective removal of elements. Some forms of exclusion are *decapitation, elision, verticalization, ellipsis, synopsis,* and *curtailment—*

♪

the plot of the irregulars

Back to the world, dear Reader, back to the plane of the planets and our cast of principals. The *Orion* orbited Mars like a third moon, and the tour crew descended to the planet and waited, until some few weeks later they made their rendezvous with the voyagers to Icarus, in the great city of Burroughs.

When Dent Ios rejoined his three friends, and heard their stories about the adventures on Icarus, he was hard pressed to believe them. "You say you met your *grandfather?*" he demanded of Karna; Karna nodded emphatically, and Margaret nodded too.

"My dead grandfather, there in the air telling me to walk up to him. And at the time it seemed like what I had to do, no question about it. And I stepped up and walked on air. Just chose my slope and it became solid."

"Or it was already. Maybe there was some of that nonreflective glass that Anton and Susan are using as stage props."

"Yeah," said Karna without conviction. But Margaret shook her head.

"Nothing that simple," she said.

"Maybe they just heavily drugged all three of you—gases in the air, you know."

"Maybe. But there I was skipping along ten meters above the ground, talking with my old grandpa who's been dead years now, when he grabbed me and spun me around him. He had some sort of fulcrum and I didn't."

"Another sign of trickery."

"He let go and I went sailing off—lost sight of Johannes and Margaret, and didn't fall for kilometers. Didn't ever fall, really—I grabbed the top of a passing pine tree and climbed down!" Karna rolled his eyes.

"Sounds like an interference pattern, creating a layer of zero gee a few meters above the ground."

"Maybe. Anyway, it took me most of a day to walk back to the runway we landed on, across some pretty mountainous terrain. First I met this—well—it would take too long to tell all of it. I met a lot of strange things, dream projections they must have been. Like dreams. When I got to the runway I was exhausted. A Grey met me there and I was going to throttle him, but he told me to go to sleep and I did."

"Drugged."

"Maybe. Then Margaret woke me, who knows how long later, and told me we were leaving. We had to carry Johannes into the ship."

Margaret nodded, and when Dent looked at her she shrugged uncomfortably. "Nothing so unusual happened to me . . . well. . . . Anyway—I got separated from Johannes by trying to go after Karna, and when Karna flew off and I ran back to Johannes, he had turned into my dead brother."

"What?" Dent cried. "A pattern here, I'd say."

"I didn't know you had a brother," said Karna.

"Yes. He came to Mars and volunteered for the whiteline jump experiment. Have you heard of that? They've been dropping little one-person ships into uncapped whitelines, and they think the ships are reappearing instantaneously some light years away. So they've asked for volunteers to pilot these ships, and bring them back to us with all the instruments intact, to see what's going on."

"Ah," Karna said.

"Has anyone come back?" Dent asked, looking shocked.

"No. But it's legal, so . . . a lot of suicides like it."

The two men were silent.

"So I saw him, but I knew something was wrong, and I . . . hit him, and he ran off. And then I just wandered around collecting animals, as far as I can recall. I was perfectly happy doing nothing but that."

"Now *that* doesn't sound like you," Dent said. "You must have been drugged."

"Perhaps I was. But what we *really* need to know is what happened to Johannes! Presumably what they did to us was just to get Johannes alone."

"And what happened to him?" Dent asked.

"We don't know! He won't say!" Margaret clenched a fist and lightly pounded her chair arm, *thump thump thump thump*. "I have grilled that man—I *waited* until he recovered from the catatonia or whatever it was, I waited until we were here on Mars! And then I asked him what had happened. 'We *need* to know if we're going to protect you,' I told him. I begged him, I bullied him, I threatened to quit, I quit, I raved—and all for nothing. He sat there like a lump with those dead eyes and that look on his face that I *hate,* that 'I'm the Master of the Orchestra and I can't be bothered with anything less than the ultimate destiny of music' look.''

Dent laughed despite himself, and even Karna let a small smile twist his features.

"It isn't funny!" Margaret cried, and then relented. "Maybe it is. Anyway, he did his sphinx act until I couldn't stand it any longer, and I left. So we don't know the significance of the trip to Icarus."

"Even if he told us we might not know," Karna said. "He may understand as little of his experience as we do of ours."

"Even so, it would help us to know what form it took. And he was very shaken by it. Very shaken. For a while there I thought he would be catatonic for good."

Their hotel room's holophone buzzed, and Margaret flicked on the audio portion. "Nevis here."

"I want to speak to Karna Godavari."

"Speaking," Karna said.

"I want to see you."

Karna stepped to the phone and turned on the visual. "Here I am. Who is this?"

"This is Charles. We met in Kang La."

"I remember. Let me see you."

The phone's screen flickered on, and the portly figure of their black-and-white-haired informant appeared. "I'm in Burroughs now, and I need to see you."

Karna nodded. "When and where?"

"The Bridge of Geese, at sunset." The image in the phone flickered off.

Margaret jumped to the phone. "Now that is odd. Excuse me, Karna. I'm going to make a call to a friend in the Martian government." She tapped at the console. "Kuan Ch'ing, please," she said to the speaker. Then, while waiting: "Greys are forbidden to live on Mars, did you know that?"

"Charles said something to that effect when we talked to him on Europa," said Karna.

"It's hard to believe," Dent said.

"Downsystem the governments get a lot more bossy, let me tell you," said Margaret. "And for some reason Mars doesn't want to have anything to do with Greys. They give them one month visas very rarely, and when I last talked to Kuan two days ago, none had been granted for some time. So there should be no Greys on Mars. Kuan! Hello."

A very tall Oriental man looked out from the screen. "What is it, Margaret?"

"I need to know if you've let the Greys on planet since we last talked."

Kuan said, "I know that we haven't. I've been keeping track of them since our conversation."

"Thanks. You'll let me know when any of them do come?"

"A large group of them is scheduled to come to the Areology."

"I remember. Thanks, Kuan." Margaret said good-bye and cut the connection. "Now who *is* this Charles? Is he a Grey traveling disguised, or is he something else disguised as a Grey?"

Karna said, "He could be with a splinter faction, as he implied."

"That's right. When we landed on Icarus and were met by one party, and then that group was eliminated and we were spirited away by that single Grey! Now what was going on there? Could they have been fighting over us even on their home world?"

"Sure," Karna said. "I'll bet they were."

"It sounds like it was a pretty desolate place," Dent said. "You never did see a town of any kind. The Greys who met you could have been . . ."

"Anybody," Margaret said. "And this Charles met with the man you saw on Lowell and Titania. So he's not just a solo maverick Grey. He's *in on this* somehow. And here he

is *contacting us.*'' She looked sharply at Karna. ''Could you
get some sort of truth serum into him at this meeting?''
And after a moment they both looked at Dent.
''What?'' said Dent. ''Me?''

♪

the irregulars in action

And so Dent found himself trailing Karna and Yananda as
they walked down one of the immensely broad boulevards of
Burroughs, Mars. Burroughs, dear Reader, sprawling over
Isidis Planitia, is a city of hills like Rome or San Francisco,
cut by a river that splits into a large delta and canal district.
The tour crew's hotel in Burroughs was on the top of one of
the southern hills, and so the three men descended a grassy
boulevard flanked on both sides by double rows of ornamen-
tal cherry trees, their branches thick with white blooms. All
three of the men stared about them as they walked; the
gravity was unusually light, the deep pink sky was infinitely
deep, and it was obvious with every step that they *walked on
a planet.* It was a strange feeling. But Dent was distracted.
He juggled the small dart gun in his pocket; it reminded him
of the tranquilizer gun lent to him by the people on Grimaldi,
although it was smaller, and, he had been told, shot only a
tiny dart. Even the victim would have trouble finding it. Still,
how was he supposed to shoot a man unobtrusively, right out
on the street?

To calm himself he paid closer attention to the passing
scene. Street vendors stood under the trees by their pushcarts,
doing a brisk business in popcorn, hot pies and the like. The
cherry blossoms glowed under the dark pink sky. On the half
dozen hilltops within their view skyscrapers clustered like

rockets, standing a hundred stories tall and more. Hills, as always, were the high rent districts. Big sections of each skyscraper were open to the air, and filled with trees. Each building was fronted with stone of a different shade of the Martian spectrum, which, although narrow, was nevertheless rich: dark purples and veined black-reds were dramatic, the myriad shades of red pleasing, a particular dark yellow soothing. The swift swirls of thin cold air chilled Dent's lungs. Under the stimuli of the engineers the planet itself had outgassed this atmosphere, and Dent thought he could feel the difference. Walking in the light gravity was different too; Dent was sure he looked at least as awkward as Yananda and Karna as he bounded down the boulevard, unable to avoid occasional flights, and even a few falls. The other offworlders on the boulevard looked just as comically uncontrolled. But the Martians flowed as smoothly as creatures in a dream: very tall people they were, towering over even tall men like Dent and Karna; lithe-limbed, with greyhound torsos, and long high-foreheaded skulls; they walked with little dancelike pushes at the end of every long step, and wore thick fabrics of green or blue or rust that fit them closely, emphasizing their greyhound forms. Dent thought them beautiful, and their city ravishing, and as he lofted down the boulevard he managed to forget himself in staring at them, and muttering "A Paris of the mind, a Paris of the mind," so much so that he almost lost Karna and Yananda when they turned down a smaller street at a forking Y intersection.

This street was busier, and Dent was dunned by a variety of street merchants, and political workers waving petitions. Some carried placards or tacked signs to treetrunks, and Dent read over and over VOTE RED, VOTE RED. But the cards that caught his eye were small and black, tucked here and there precariously in the branches of the cherry trees; in green print they said *Green Mars. Green Mars.* Some sort of election coming up, Dent knew; the Festival was a part of it, somehow. Martian politics were byzantine—no one offplanet could ever get the many issues straight, as far as Dent could tell. And the Martians seemed to consider it their private business, holding meetings of their Congress in secret.

The street ended at a T junction, and Dent followed his friends east, downstream beside the river. The blood-colored sun was halfway behind a hill, but as they walked on it cleared the hill and the glassy surface of the water fired. They crossed a bridge, and Karna and Yananda asked for directions. They crossed an island, and on the next bright channel were geese, black marks on the copper surface. A wide flat wooden bridge was apparently the Bridge of Geese, for Karna and Yananda stopped on it and leaned against one of the high side rails. Dent did the same on the opposite side of the bridge. They waited. As the sun disappeared it light- ened in color, until it was a bright yellow point on the hill. The city below was a rusty shadow, sprinkled with yellow streetlights that were not as bright as the salmon sky.

There, across the bridge in a knot of maple trees—a shock of black-and-white hair. Charles stepped onto the bridge, looking wary. Dent leaned over the rail and inspected a popcorn box floating in the murky water. He heard Karna greeting Charles, realized he was facing the wrong direction for the task at hand, and turned around. He sat and leaned his back against the rail, trying to look like a drunken tourist. Yananda and Karna had moved in such a way that Charles now had his back to Dent. Dent fingered the gun in his coat pocket. He had been instructed to aim at bare skin, or else light clothing. But Charles was wearing a Martian tunic of rust bunting, and his pants appeared to be made of the same material. Perhaps a shot at his light socks, revealed between calves and feet . . . or a bare wrist and hand, or the hair on the back of his neck. . . . Pretty small targets, all of them! The gravity of his action frightened Dent, and he began first to quiver, then to tremble. The three men were now deep in conference, it really was time. . . .

Dent took out the dartgun and held it inside his raised left knee. Excellent for concealment, but how was he to aim the thing from down there? He pointed it at Charles's left ankle, fired, opened his eyes. Yananda had jerked, and now he shot a lightning glance of irritation in Dent's direction. Desperately Dent adjusted his aim and fired again. Charles shifted a foot onto the railing and slapped at the back of his calf.

"Mosquitoes around here," Yananda said. "I just got bit myself," with a look at Karna.

"Didn't know mosquitoes had gotten onto Mars," Charles said. "Damned stupid of the Martians, if you ask me. Thought mosquitoes were extinct."

"Apparently all sorts of pests remain," Karna said, sparing one baleful glance for Dent. "Come, let's try the other side of the bridge, here." They crossed and stood behind Dent, who sat on his gun and tried to pretend he was asleep.

"Tell us what the Greys really want," Karna said. "You haven't yet told us that, have you."

"All kinds of Greys," Charles said, sounding befuddled. "Some use Grey to cover smuggling operations. The real Greys don't care. So many of us can be Grey. Even inside the upper echelons there's conflict. That's what they all say. The Lion of Jupiter is in a struggle with the Lion of Mercury, and no one knows where Zervan stands on the matter. No one's *seen* Zervan for years. Makes it so easy for us. . . ."

"Easy for you in what way?" Karna said. Yananda leaned against the railing, blinking rapidly.

"Easy for us. We're going to the Telemann Works, did I tell you that?"

"No, you didn't. Tell us about that."

"All of us are ordered to Earth, to the Telemann Works."

"And who is us?"

"Our group. They'll be looking for me soon—" Expression of dismay, exaggerated panic in his voice—"I have to get back, they'll be looking for me soon!"

"Who will be looking for you?" Karna insisted.

"My group. We leave for Earth and the Telemann Works, but first we have to go see Ekern."

"Ekern?" Karna said sharply.

"The Greys want contact with him now and we have to help. I only joined because I was in trouble, understand? If I had stayed on Europa they would have deep-sixed me for good, I was so far in debt to that woman, I just walked into the nearest crowd of Greys and melted in. I had no idea what part of the Greys they were! It was just chance. Now Mithras protect me, I'm out here talking to you and they'll be after me just like the gangs of Europa, I've got to go! I'm late, I've got to go!" He pulled away from Karna's steadying grasp and staggered across the bridge.

"We're not done talking to you!" Yananda said loudly, but Karna pulled him back.

"Shut up, Nanda. You're drugged too. Dent, get your ass after that man, and don't lose him."

With a loud groan Dent rose to his feet. "Hurry!" Karna said. Dent tried to jog across the bridge after the receding form of Charles, but the light gravity made it treacherous; he almost jumped over the railing into the water. So he loped gently up a narrow tree-lined street after the shock of black-white hair, muttering under his breath at being forced into such a role again. Charles was weaving ahead of him, proceeding quite slowly, and Dent caught up to him without difficulty. He trailed him closely, with little fear of being noticed; Charles was still quite obviously disoriented. It occurred to Dent that he might be able to continue the exploitation of Charles's drugged state, and without pausing to consider it he drew up behind the man.

"Zervan wants to see you," he said into the man's ear.

Charles leaped away, spinning in mid-leap so that he came down facing Dent. His expression was stricken beyond anything Dent had expected. "Come with me," Dent said, fascinated despite himself. "Zervan wants to speak with you."

With a shriek of panic Charles was off and running, down the street and into an alley. By the time Dent reached the alley's mouth, the frightened Grey was nowhere to be seen.

♪

the modern alastor

Since Icarus a bond had developed between them. It had started to grow after the trip out to Fairfax House; but now Margaret and Johannes could sit together in comfort in the endless succession of hotel rooms that contained their lives, and chat or bicker or sit silently as the mood took them. She had carried him down that long mountain trail in her arms, and then roused him and helped him down the valley trail to the runway. . . . He had cried most of the way, poor suffering tear ducts swelling horrendously, so that he had truly become a blind man and she had led him step by step, coaching him, steeling herself against his surprisingly infectious hysteria. And all that wildness broken by moments of calm, a simulacrum of lucidity. "It's the end of Johannes," he had said. "End of all of us. We're just notes in the score, do you see, Margaret? Did they teach you too?"

"No." And off he had gone again, puffed eyes pouring salt tears.

And on the voyage back into the plane of the planets, an arm around his shoulders as he stared mindlessly at the black square of the window, a hand under his head as he slept. . . .

So now they were siblings of a sort: bright feldspar and dark diorite, melted into granite by the metamorphosis of danger. Sitting on the darkened porch balcony of their hotel suite Margaret tried to banish thoughts of the past, and failed. Johannes sat beside her, their shoulders just touched. Below them lay Burroughs, a rumpled blanket of lights, darker in the lowlands, brilliant on the hilltops where the skyscrapers leaped up at the evening whitsuns setting to the west. Over them the duller evening star of Deimos shot upward in its retrograde course like a distress flare.

"What did they teach you, Johannes?" she said. "Can't you tell me?"

"I don't think I can. It has to do with Holywelkin's mathematics."

"I only understand that we can use this work to manipulate the world to—this. To what we see, not just here, I mean, but everywhere."

"Yes. The technology derived from it. But . . ." A long silence. He stood and she could see that he was going to give it a try. "With his mathematics we can see that nothing happens by chance. Everything we do is determined by all that came before."

"Oh that's nonsense, Johannes," Margaret said quickly. "Clearly that isn't true. Physical models of the universe— they come and go. But the subjective reality of chance and uncertainty remains. And that's what is important, isn't it?"

Johannes shook his head. "No! Put it another way—what if it was a human agent? What if some person controlled your life, manipulating it from behind the scenes? You wouldn't be so easy about it then."

"No, I wouldn't. But this idea . . . a mathematical model is only that, Johannes. An idea, no more."

"It's the division Dent spoke of," Johannes said, abstracted and distant. "You can know discursively or by acquaintance. You know these theories discursively, as I tell you of them. But *I am acquainted with them,* now. And the difference that makes, for the future . . ."

"Do you know the future?"

"No. Zervan said I will know it."

"As it occurs you will know it, yes. The Greys," she said

scornfully. "Why should they know any more than the rest of us?"

Another long silence. Finally Johannes said, "I believe their purpose is to hide the true ramifications of Holywelkin's work from the rest of the world."

Margaret shook her head. "I don't. And until we know just what they want, and what they propose to *do*, you should not trust them so."

"I have seen it, Margaret. Now all that remains is . . . music."

He was so distant, sitting there, staring into some part of himself. There was nothing to say to him. "Your composition?"

". . . I don't know yet."

"Your music is important."

"Yes. Sometimes, now, I can't think of anything *but* music."

"You think in music?"

"Sometimes it's the only language left to me. It's frightening. The music writes me."

What to say to him? She felt that he was mad; but his intelligence had not perished on Icarus. Rather had it been concentrated, like chaotic sunlight into a fierce whiteline. Within that whiteline of music he was more powerful than he had ever been in the pursuit of any sane goal; but outside it—the vacuum. "So it might feel to you. But here, on Mars—" Margaret stopped, considered how to say it. "I sense that something different is happening here. If you ask me, these Martians are in the throes of a very quiet and polite civil war. At the festival when you play, they will be volatile, suggestible. Like you were on Icarus. And so—your music—" She halted; she didn't know how to say what she meant.

But he was nodding. "I see," he said quietly. Photoptic cells reflecting all the lights of the immense city.

Margaret held him for a while, let him go, left the room. And when the irregulars came back from their foray she was in a strange state of mind, distressed and impatient. "You shot Yananda?" she repeated. A shame-faced Dent looked at the floor. "So he said Ekern, did he?"

Karna nodded. " 'We have to see Ekern,' he said. But at no point did he make clear who the 'we' was supposed to be. Some faction of the Greys, it seemed to me. But he slid away from that question, even under the drug."

"Some faction of them," Margaret said to herself, "either working for Ekern or else *employing* Ekern. . . ." She glared at Dent. "And you let him get away! Why didn't you keep following him?"

"I—I wanted to see how he would react to the threat of being taken to Zervan," Dent said, crestfallen. "It seemed like a good idea at the time. And it was quite a dramatic response! He simply flew away!"

"Don't say that," Karna said sourly. "Say, he ran off quickly."

"Sorry," Dent said. "In any case, I lost him."

"All right," Margaret said. "We'll just have to search for him. I want all of you circulating during this festival, to look for these faces we keep seeing. Now I've got to talk to a woman from the Martian government."

The meeting dispersed, and Karna and Yananda went to get something to eat. Dent said, "Interesting how many members of the governments are women. All through the system. I suppose since women were kept out of the halls of power for so long, more of them want to wield it now."

"I suppose," Margaret said.

"This makes it nice for the men of our time, as we can assume society will be competently run, and go on to more interesting things."

"Men like you," Margaret replied caustically, and left to find the official.

On the way Johannes joined her. "I want to ask her some questions about acoustics."

The Martian official was very tall. Margaret led the group back to the porch balcony. "We hope you will enjoy your stay on Mars," the official said to Johannes. "It's an exciting time here."

No answer from Johannes; something out there in the city had stolen his attention. Margaret said, "I suppose the audience at your festival will be as large as all our other audiences on this tour combined," speaking directly to Johannes.

"That large?" he said.

"Oh yes," said the official. "For many generations nearly the entire population of Mars made it to the Areology. Nowadays that's impossible, of course, but this year almost four million people will attend."

"They'll all be able to hear?" Johannes said.

"We'll do the amplification following your instructions," the woman replied. "The Olympus Mons slope in the Areology grounds area is a very broad arc of a conic section. For all practical purposes, a flat downslope about six degrees off the horizontal." Johannes asked her a few questions about the air density at the high altitude, and she smiled as she answered his questions. Even her teeth were taller, Margaret thought. Then the official changed the subject.

"This year the Areology is only a week before the planetary elections, so there will be vigorous campaigning by all the parties. It's an important election. . . ." She hesitated, glancing at Johannes to gauge his interest. Difficult to tell with those eyes, as Margaret well knew. "Elections are infrequent, and this one will help to reshape the planet's terraforming policies. . . ." Johannes was staring past her at the city, and abruptly she halted. "This campaigning will only add to the excitement and color of the festival, you understand. There will be added security, and as long as nothing inflammatory happens. . . .''

She was referring to the first two concerts, and perhaps to a couple of the Jovian affairs. Johannes paid no attention to her. Margaret said, "We've had experience with large crowds. We know how to handle them."

"You've never dealt with a crowd of this size before," the woman said coldly, annoyed that Johannes was ignoring her. Or had Margaret slighted the Areology somehow?

Suddenly Johannes spoke: "The more people there the better."

There was an uncomfortable silence.

Margaret watched him—saw that his cheeks were flushed, his fists clenched; he paced by the railing, not meeting their eyes with his own dark ones. . . . He had thought of *something*, by God. Something to do with the sight of the huge city, or the official's description of the concert site. He was humming to himself, producing a sound so strange that it seemed the whirr of his intense vitality. Margaret directed the insulted official away from him, so that she could close the odd meeting by herself.

♪

backstage

Riding down the glass elevator box on the outside of the tour's hotel, Anton Vaccero observed the florid Martian dawn. The sky to the east glowed the color of blood, and a whitsun burst over the horizon brighter than the lost morning star had ever been. Vaccero shivered. A call from the desk had awakened him from disquieting dreams; someone in the lobby to see him. "An Edgar to see you, sir." One of Ekern's messengers, here to charge him with yet another impossible task of acting. And yet within his dread Vaccero still felt the fierce little spark of anticipation central to all metadrama—he was about to be sent onto the stage again by a master playwright, there to do and say who knew what. . . .

No one in the lobby. He stepped outside, walked down the broad greensward of the boulevard. Vendors here and there under the white cherry blossoms were setting up their stands. The boulevard itself was empty, and the grass was gray under the sheen of dew and the dull light of the dawn. Tracks in the frosty dew led across the boulevard to a little copse of cherry trees that stood alone in the center of an intersection; acting on a hunch Anton followed them, keeping an eye out for one of the various messengers, the tall one with the skull face, the woman who had once played Olga in his initiation—

"Ha!"

Vaccero jumped. It was Ekern himself, hopping from behind a cherry tree, red beard glowing in the ruddy light. Vaccero wiped the annoyance from his face and felt his pulse begin its uncontrollable accelerando.

"Master!" he said. "I am surprised to see you here."

"I know."

"On Mars?"

"Yes, Anton. We are on Mars." Ekern laughed, pulled hard at the ends of his graying red sideburns, where they flowed forward into beard. With a jerk forward he grabbed Vaccero by the shirt front, and shouted, "But where is Wright?"

He released him with a shove, backed away, turned and paced around a cherry tree, stopped before the astounded Vaccero once again.

"He is here," Vaccero said shakily. "In the hotel." He gestured back at it.

Ekern waved a hand dismissively. "This much all know, Anton, Anton, I mean, where is Wright's *mind?* What is he *thinking?"*

"I don't know," Vaccero said. "I'm not his confessor, he says little to me. I hardly see him. He spends most of his time in the Orchestra now. How am I supposed to know!" he cried, throwing out a hand to ward off another grab by Ekern.

"I want you to talk to Wright," Ekern said, "talk to him as you should have been all along. You're letting down your part, Anton, your performance is questionable. . . . I want you to talk with him and find out what happened to him on Icarus."

"Icarus!" Vaccero said. "He won't talk about that to anyone! I've talked to Nevis and Godavari, and he won't even tell *them* what happened to him, and they were there with him!"

"Perhaps they are too close to him, and to the experience." Ekern chopped at the air: "Metadrama would be of no interest to the creative individual if there were not challenges like this one. Find your way into his confidences, Anton, negotiate whatever turns or twists are needed, and *be* with him. Learn what he has learned, extract from him this portion of his past."

"But I can't," Vaccero said. "He doesn't talk to me about anything."

"And your vaunted friendship? Your ties that go back to childhood, to schooldays?" Ekern approached him again, his face darkening to a shade near that of his beard. Anton took another step back.

"That never amounted to anything," he said bitterly, and felt the truth of it in his stomach. "The man doesn't have friends, don't you understand that yet? He lives in a world of his own."

"*Not* anymore. He lives in *my* world, on *my* stage, and as he becomes aware of the action on it, his thoughts necessarily follow. But Icarus! Icarus! *I must know!*" He chopped at the air, held his breath. "I must know what Wright thinks happened to him, in order to conduct the rest of the drama most artfully . . . you as my only apprentice must help me in this, if you wish to advance in the order. . . . If you can't engage a subject in *conversation* it shows a lack of ability, of imagination, this is the simplest of manipulations, one practiced by ordinary mortals every day of the week—''

"Not with Johannes Wright," Vaccero said. "You know that. Even ordinarily he is a world to himself, but now—well— whatever happened to him on Icarus, it was a shock. I can give you all his reactions—''

"Not enough!"

"How would you accomplish—" Vaccero began, but Ekern chopped him off with a slash of the hand and a shout:

"Just *do it!''*

And with that he was off striding down the broad boulevard, leaving Vaccero to contemplate his situation in the growing light of day.

♪

composing

Johannes himself woke in the moment when the voices of the chorus split into an infinity of echoes— Quickly he forgot the bulk of the dream. He dressed and left the hotel, meandered through the streets watching the morning traffic pick up and swirl around him. A rosy morning light lay over everything like dust. Poster world. His artificial sight seemed to have been damaged permanently—perhaps over-exposure. So many moments where motion appeared to be arbitrary. There was dust in the air, swirling randomly as a trolley dingdonged by; but looking closely he saw the Coriolis effect, the pull of gravity, the shove of heated air off the grass and the paving of the street . . . causes everywhere, for everything.

Down in the river district the streets were narrower. Walking was like floating. Alleyways in X patterns, blocks in the shape of diamonds so that every corner house was a wedge-shaped oddity, and narrow points in the alleys were bridged three or four stories overhead by broad arches of carved rust stone, with keystones of dark purple. Johannes wandered like a bishop on a chess board, watching the people move. He was a short man and every Martian seemed a giant, some of them gawky beanpoles, some of them fluid greyhound people, with enlarged ribcages and long lithe limbs . . . and they were all in a dance in the dusty alleys, dodging and pirouetting to avoid collisions, stopping to talk, or buy vegetables at a corner stand, or watch the games of chess in the park, or listen to music or a soapbox speaker under a tree, or look at a giant horse (the police were on horses, and many of the street vendors used them); all of them playing their notes in a score written for them . . . eternally. It was difficult to believe. But he remembered in his flesh the experience of the vision on Icarus. And he walked on feeling that he was dancing with a perfect effortlessness.

Down by the river the alleys opened onto a boulevard and then a strip of park edging the river's bank. Cherry trees again, flanking both banks as a line dividing boulevards from parks; a line of white-pink brilliance, blooms bouncing up and down in a slow imitation of the bees among them. Johannes let himself be taken up by a swirl of people crossing the boulevard and entering the park. Once there he sat down under a cherry tree, lay back and looked up into it. Limbs of a tree in two-fifths of a gee, boldly crooking out in every direction. Dust motes in the air like red cells of blood floating in the plasma. The air was full of them, dancing between the jade grass and the quartz flowers and the sandstone sky. Bands of the sun's light slanted down and lit cones of the dust, transforming most of the motes to gold, the rest to metallic reds, greens, blues. Some rose on air heated by his body, others were suspended, others fell from the cooler air of the shadows above the sunbeams into the light, on wafts of the river breeze. Children's voices, over the stream. Dust motes: each was lit by quanta of light pulsing away from the sun. Take the motes as representations of quanta, which were themselves representations of . . . events in the micro-dimensions. Reality was so much different from the material world of the senses. And yet Johannes only understood reality by analogy to something within the realm of his senses. He thought: as we see dust motes, we can imagine quanta of light, and muons and gluons and quarks, and even the glints dancing in every quark. And as we can hear music . . . we can imagine the *movement* in the smallest world, and understand how tones can both *be played* and *have always been played,* because of the idea of the performance and the score. Analogy to the realm of the senses, the five windows in the cave; the dance of music in the air more closely resembled the actuality of the micro-universe than any visual representation possibly could. Music was the clearest and most powerful analogy because it came closest to pure idea. And the universe was a sort of music of ideas. So that it was more than an analogy; ignoring the vast difference in magnitudes, there was an *identity* there. The universe was a music of ideas. And he could write that music.

For a long time Johannes lay on the riverbank looking up into the cherry tree and thinking about what Holywelkin had written in the equations of the *Ten Forms.* As had become his habit during his mathematical studies, he recalled the equations using his own musical notation system, and the mnemonic device became confused with what he remembered, so that the contemplation of the dust motes seemed to lead to an understanding of Holywelkin that was all confused with a continuous music in his head, music sounding clearly as he understood Holywelkin more fully than ever before. As each of the ten forms acted on the wave pattern of sound in his mind it became more complex; the cone of moving dust motes would no longer have been an adequate score, the music was too densely patterned for that. The melody of each particle overlaid the next with a peculiar, dissonant logic, and at times the part of Johannes that was still listening heard only a surging chaos; but Holywelkin's work showed there was order to it: patterns, rhythms, a progression of various harmonies, a thickly textured network of rising and falling musical lines. . . .

Awkwardly he got to his feet, feeling a sudden urgency, and dashed across the riverside road into the net of alleys. Solo glint in dense interference pattern: he had to dance aside and around the growing business of the day, trolley, woman, fruit stand, tree. Once he failed in a moment of difficult execution (But could you say that? he thought as the man railed at him. Isn't that part of the dance?) He smiled at the man and tried to speak and found himself singing a glissando that tried to go both up and down at once, and nearly succeeded, until he choked. "Must go to voice!" he squeaked, and ran on. Out of the alley and onto the big greensward that climbed the hill to their hotel. Climbing, and his thighs remembered Icarus, the music in his head sang and whistled . . . into the hotel. Following the path through the maze of hallways that had always been followed, back to his voice, his home, the other node he was bound so tightly to in the pattern, the singularity that he glinted through again and again.

He circled the perimeter of the Orchestra, looking up into shifting angles of glass and shadow, all reduced to a two-dimensional pattern of black and white, light and dark. The poster world. He climbed into the control booth with the music surging through his every vein and nerve, singing in him and controlling his movement, so that once in the control booth he went straight to the computer and started to program the part of the whole that was most prominent at the time, moving to keyboards for reference to timbre. The part of him that was still listening and watching all this—the part that stood like a third party at the back of his mind, looking over his shoulder—realized that of course since there was no such thing as human agency or free will, since he was performing a dance completely scored and choreographed, he could let the music compose itself. *The music comprehended itself.* Johannes went at the orchestration of the music with an ease and unself-consciousness that he had never felt before. A different recording for each strand of the whole, each equation-symphony programming one trio or sextet or chamber orchestra of its own, all taped for the simultaneous playing, the larger piece that he could *hear perfectly,* as if it were a cathedral he could walk around in and inspect at his leisure. Everything was to be taped before the concert; the musical coursing of the universe through time since the big bang; then successive diminutions of scale, until the composition would represent perfectly April 23rd 3229 A.D. on Olympus Mons on Mars; then augmentations back to the cosmic scale. During the concert Johannes himself would play whatever was destined to come to him; and that illusion of improvisation would be by definition his strand of consciousness in the great mesh of the universe beyond. If he wanted to he could even hear what that strand would be, he could hear the score extending away in both directions eternally in his mind, even as he heard the pulse of it beat by beat, in time. But he returned his attention to the work at hand, programming it accurately, choosing the instrumentation, the tempi, the clefs. Groan of mercury drum, wail of wind machine, all the percussive pops and bams of the world, all the rich timbres that tones and overtones combined to create, employed in each their appropriate moment.

There came a knock at the door. And straightening up Johannes discovered in his muscles what he had not been aware of: the passage of time. Reader, this poor string of words has given you analogies for the storm of thought and music that rushed through the mind of Johannes all that day long; but you know from your own attempts to write down your thoughts what an approximate, elliptic, synoptic and clumsy tool language is for that task; and you can imagine the hours and hours that must necessarily have passed as all this music came to Johannes and was played by the Orchestra.

So his back was stiff, his fingers tired, his bladder full. He stopped to consider; looked at the numbers on the computer screen, heard within him the polyphonic chorus. And he knew that it would all stay with him forever.

The door opened and Dent Ios entered, staring up at the Orchestra without seeing Johannes. Johannes said, "Dent," and climbed down to the piano entrance. Standing on the glass step holding the bench he could look Dent straight in the eye.

"Johannes," Dent said. "We've been learning more about the Greys, and I want to talk to you about it."

"All right." Johannes gestured and Dent stepped up to join him; they sat on the piano bench and looked down at the keyboard and its eighty-eight glass fingers. "What have you learned?"

"Johannes, they are *not* a single coherent organization. There are factions within the Greys, and there are groups pretending to be Greys when they are not. And so Margaret and Karna and I are worried that . . . we think that you shouldn't take to heart whatever happened to you on Icarus."

Johannes smiled a little. "What if I was talking to real Greys? To their Father of Fathers?"

"But how could you be sure?" Dent said. "Wasn't there actually a struggle for you when you landed on the terra? It very well might be that the real Greys were the ones who first met you."

Johannes shook his head. "I know who I talked to. Remember your distinction, Dent, between discursive knowledge and knowledge by acquaintance. Here I know directly. I saw it all with my own eyes. No one but Zervan could have shown me what I saw, or taught me what I learned."

Dent stared at him. "Anything can be faked, Johannes."

"That's not so." Johannes shook his head. "Believe me."

They looked down at the keyboard. Dent said, "With the right drugs, the right sensorium. . . ."

"No," Johannes said. "It's the vision, the knowledge —that can't be faked."

"Anything that can be conceived can be executed. If you can imagine it, then someone else could have too."

"But I can't imagine it! My imagination can't encompass it. It almost breaks me to try."

"And the Greys?"

"They must have different sorts of minds. Trained or grown or evolved. . . ."

Now it was Dent who shook his head. "You can't be so sure. The Greys—they're only human, Johannes. A group that appears truly fragmented to us. And I'm not even sure it's been the Greys you've been dealing with. Some of the Greys are connected with Ernst Ekern, Johannes. They may work for him. They're contacting Ekern and the Telemann Works on Earth."

Johannes laughed. "Maybe he wants an Orchestra of his own. That has nothing to do with me, or with Icarus."

"But Ekern may be plotting to harm you!"

"He can't harm me."

"Yes he can!" Dent said loudly. "And the Greys can harm you too. I've heard what shape you were in when you left Icarus—how can you say they can't harm you?"

A passage of music coursed through his mind, and he could barely hear Dent, barely reply. Don't speak in music. . . . "We . . . will make music, Dent. We will, we must. Same thing. No . . ." He couldn't finish.

"Johannes?"

"I'm tired, Dent. Tired. What time is it?" A little laugh. "It's late. I've been at it for a long time." And still, behind all the words and worries, the rush of sound, the music surging, leaping forward! If only he could tell him. . . . "Wait until this festival concert, Dent. Then we'll talk."

♪

a landscape

A dark pink sandstone sky, banded by pink clouds. Underneath this immense vault, a volcano, the biggest in all the solar system: Olympus Mons. No peaky Fujiyama, however; dear Reader, Olympus Mons is a shield volcano, which has grown over the same spot for a billion years, growing out more than up, so that though it stands twenty-five kilometers above the datum, it is six hundred kilometers across. Its outer perimeter is an escarpment, which in some places is six kilometers tall; above this circling cliff the average slope is only six degrees from the horizontal, in a sinusoidal profile that is slightly flatter near the summit and down near the guardian escarpment. Nestled in the volcano's broad top is a multi-ringed caldera ninety kilometers in diameter, five kilometers in depth.

On the southeast slope of the shield, halfway between escarpment and caldera, there is a small triangular speck. Descend, and see that the speck is a series of terraces in the shape of a fan, with the point of the fan high, so that the terraces spread in ever broader arcs down the gentle side of the immense slope. The terraces are covered with flagstones of Mars's oxidized marble; the entire great courtyard stands out on the volcano's dark lava surface like a piece of bright cloisonné, or a lobate spill of lava from a volcano of a different color. From just above the site wide gradual steps can be seen running down the fan's middle and its two edges, connecting each terrace with its neighbors above and below. Far upslope the top of the volcano gleams, above the new atmosphere. Below the site, the shield falls away in a broad gentle cone to the plateau above the escarpment; and out there to the southeast, far away in the thin clear air, rise three tall bumps out of the mass of Mars, like three peaks of another planet: Ascraeus Mons, Pavonis Mons, and wide-topped Arsia Mons, the trio of Mars's prince volcanoes, facing their Olympian king.

For six hundred and seventy days of the Martian year, this great terraced marble courtyard shimmers under the sun and the whitsuns, empty and unvisited, an insignificant dot on the great cone of lava. Freezing dust typhoons scrape the flag-stones in winter, leaving layers of rime dust and dirty ice to bury the staircases. In Martian springtime comes a spring miracle: lichen appears on the marble, lichen yellow and olive and black and red and green. The dirty snow half melts and the Syrtis grass adapted to Mars grows on the wet dirt by these slushy pools. Seeds blow by and some make landfall, and mosses and alpine flowers grow: gentian and saxifrage, primrose and Tibetan rhubarb, rock jasmine and figwort and stonecrop. Some birds fly up from the fertile plains surround-ing the escarpment, and feed on the insects and flowers. Snow finches and mouse hares share their small burrows; garoks and arctic eagles soar overhead in the hunt for them. In the long Martian summers this marble oasis flourishes as vigorously as any life can at the very top of the new Martian atmosphere.

Now in this summer of the year 3229, dear Reader, on the festival grounds of the thousand-year-old civilization of Mars, crews were setting up tents, pavilions, water tanks, booths, restaurants, lavatories; they were clearing the landing strips just below the lowest terrace, and the tracks that lead from the landing strips to the sides of the courtyard, and up to its various levels. Over a period of three weeks they constructed an entire portable city, on this site that it had occupied for two weeks out of every one of the preceding four hundred and thirty years.

Near the end of this period of construction a small wide-winged plane landed on one of the landing strips, bringing Johannes Wright, Margaret Nevis, Delia Rosario, Anton

Vaccero, and a few more of the Grand Tour's crew to the Areology grounds. They walked in a group up the endless central stairs, past terrace after terrace. The oxidized marble gleamed under a tangerine sun, and most of the tour crew wore polarized sunglasses; Johannes alone stared freely at the scene, wide-eyed and open-mouthed. The rainbow array of tents flapped in the cool breeze. Johannes pointed at them, talking to Margaret in brief bursts. It appeared he was in a good humor; Margaret and the others laughed frequently. They climbed all the way to the narrow upper end of the courtyard, which was extended higher with new terraces every few years, to match the rise of the atmosphere. Somewhat down from the very highest terrace a small lava knob had been allowed to remain, and it poked up out of the marble like a black treetrunk. This was the stage where Holywelkin's Orchestra would be placed during the performance. The tour crew followed Johannes up the spiraling cut steps that led to the smooth flat top of this knob, and looked about them.

For a long time they surveyed the immense prospect, so much larger than anything they had seen before on the tour. They pointed at the three prince volcanoes, and exclaimed over the tremendous distances. Johannes moved away from the rest and stared at the courtyard fanning down and away from him. Eventually he led the others back onto the terraces, and he and Delia went to work, with the others assisting. Margaret stayed with Johannes and took notes; Delia carried a large map of the grounds and meticulously covered it with small dots and initials and notes. Johannes bounced here and there in the two-fifths of a gee, up and down terraces until Margaret began waiting for him at the central staircase; she counted a thousand steps as they worked their way down the slope, then stopped counting. Johannes sang to himself, and his companions laughed as they chattered; only Anton noticed that Johannes had real difficulty returning to speech for his conferences with Delia. Anton approached him and tried to converse with him, but Johannes only sang in a rich glossolalia, that strange border between speech and silence. Once Margaret took him by the upper arm and held him still; his singing dropped to a chanted whisper, he looked up at her curiously, resentfully: "Use the stairs," she said, and let him go, afraid of the look in his eyes.

After a few hours' work they came to the lowest terrace, and looked up at the giants' stairway, the great terraced field of tents and pavilions curiously unpeopled. The lava knob at the top could still be clearly seen. Johannes looked up at it for a long time, singing to himself all the while. Or perhaps he was looking beyond it, to the volcano's top puncturing the vault of the sky. Only the wind stirred, ruffling their hair. Johannes turned, stretched up to kiss Margaret briefly. She looked surprised. Johannes stopped humming and all was silent; the wind died and all was still.

♪

areology

Dent Ios awoke to a low babble, as of water over stones, as if he had slept down by the tapir pens, where the stream fell over the pool dam. . . . He opened his eyes to see the blowing blue nylon of a sunlit tent wall, flapping lazily above him. And he remembered where he was: Mars! The festival grounds! The concert on the slope of Olympus Mons! He tossed aside heavy quilts and leaped off his cot into the cold air, dressed swiftly in bright blue shirt and pants he hadn't worn since leaving Holland. Outside the tent the water sound resolved into the noise of people everywhere on the terraces, talking. Yananda, dressed in a brilliant orange one-piece, stood outside the doorway of the tent: "Good morning!" he cried.

Their terrace was a parade of Martians, all tall, thin, and

long-nosed, all dressed in colorful festival finery. The tight-fitting fashions of Burroughs were not popular everywhere on Mars; here there were men wearing billows and clouds of printed fabric, as if wrapped in one of the tents—women in long dresses, or elaborate pantaloons—and all of them striding with perfect grace through the light gravity.

Dent and Yananda walked with this crowd along their terrace, to the long cafe placed against the railing overlooking the terrace below. They sat under one of the giant speakers that the tour crew had scattered everywhere. Yananda pointed to the east, where a great distance away three shadowed volcanoes stood above the horizon, just below the rising sun.

It is difficult indeed to describe the sheer size of the prospect they had. But imagine you stand on the side of a volcano that is a simple conical mound, broad and flat, but of such bulk that you seem to stand far above the planet, as if in a high altitude balloon—and yet at the same time, the planet rises up to support you. Off to the southeast in the direction of the rising sun are whole plains, canyon systems, and the broad eroded slopes of three other volcano cones, off in the distance so far away that it is difficult to tell that their snowy tops are almost as high as the top of the volcano you stand on. High cirrus clouds cast a pattern of shadow over the broad and broken landscape below you, making a variegated tapestry of rusty tans, one of immense complexity, beauty and size, all seen with an uncanny clarity in the thin air. O to stand on the side of Olympus Mons! Dear Reader, I know you may live in a thatched hut, or in a cardboard shed, or in a crystal palace under the light of Barnard's Star, or across the galaxy; how I wish I could take you to Olympus Mons, so that standing there you might see better the extent of your selves. . . .

In any case, Dent and Yananda stood with the rest of the celebrants on that slope, and so felt the subsequent expansion. Their waiter came and Yananda said cheerily, "I must

warn you that I plan to drink right at breakfast, a bottle of the
White Brother at least. This is a special day for me—it will
be the first time I've ever heard Wright play. All these
months working for him, and I've never gotten the chance to
see him in performance."

"I remember what that was like," Dent said. "But I only
had to wait until the third concert. What has it been now,
fifteen?"

"I lost count—I wasn't around during all those in the
Jupiter system." Soon the waiter brought back two large
omelets and a heated bottle of the White Brother. They began
eating, and Yananda refilled both their glasses often. His low
commentary on the passing Martians had Dent hunched over
his plate: "Look how skinny that guy is! I bet he just slips
through cracks rather than bothering to open doors. And look
at that woman! Dent, look at her!" He imitated leaping after
the woman in question, and Dent imitated holding him back.
"Can you imagine making love to such a woman, Dent? Her
legs are as long as I am altogether!"

"Could lead to problems."

"Not at all! Oh look, she's an election worker."

The woman was talking into a loudspeaker, and Martians
in the cafe looked annoyed. Some passing Martians shouted
at her, but she kept talking: "Our lives depend on a complex
technology orbiting within the coronal zone of the sun . . .
run by a political body whose procedures are hidden from
us. . . . We should be free of Holywelkin devices, which are
not needed on Mars. . . . If Prometheus and Vulcan, Hyperion
and Apollo discontinue sending us energy, the results will be
catastrophic . . . and yet we have no control over this
possibility. . . ."

The Martian diners reacted in a variety of ways: ignoring
her, looking disgusted, arguing among themselves, snapping
up at her. There was tension in the air, Dent thought, a sort
of electric nervousness apparent on the Martians' long fine

faces. . . . Yananda stood and waved at the woman before
Dent could stop him, and she noticed him and walked over.
"Hello," she said. Unamplified her voice was low and friendly.
"Where are you from?"

"I'm from Oberon," Yananda said. "Originally from
Europa. My friend here—"

"Dent Ios," Dent said. "I'm from Holland, in the Uranus
system."

"Welcome to Mars," the woman said. "Are you with the
Grand Tour?"

The two men nodded. "We were listening to you," Yananda
said, "and I wondered which party you represented?"

"I'm part of the Green Mars movement."

"I see. And is that one of the majority parties?"

"No," she said easily. "The majority parties are Red
Mars and the Martian Socialists. We're about as big as the
Grimaldians. But recently we've been working in coalition
with them, and with other groups. Or do you know all
this?"

"I wish we knew more about this election," Dent said,
feeling ashamed of their ignorance, their provincialism.

"No reason to," the woman said, smiling. "It's mostly
internal business."

"But aren't there Martians who want to rule all the system?" Yananda asked bluntly.

The woman smiled. "I'm not sure they would agree with
your choice of words, but there are some who feel Mars is
the center of the system's economics, yes. And they advocate
strengthening that position."

"And you were advocating self-reliance?" Dent asked.
"Freedom from the sphere technology?"

"Yes," said the woman. "As anthroposophists, we feel it
is dangerous."

"Is that why there aren't any Greys allowed on Mars?"
Yananda said, with a slightly drunken smile.

The woman nodded, and Yananda's smile disappeared. "That was one bill the coalition succeeded in passing. And our numbers are growing quickly, so perhaps some day—not this election—but some day. . . ."

Another Martian in a green one-piece called to the woman. She glanced at her and turned back: "I've got to get back to haranguing the actual voters," she said with a polite smile. "I hope you enjoy the Areology."

"We will," they assured her. When she was gone Yananda struck his chest. "My my *my*. She was *beautiful*."

"Yes," Dent said. He looked around at the cafe, the terrace, the great expanse of open sky above them. The center of the system, she had said. Mars, the Earth, Mercury— from the distant edgeworlds they had all seemed the same. And yet when he thought about it, the Martians were their link to the inner worlds, and to the terras across the system in their orbits; and it was the great melting pot of all their cultures, not to mention the historical starting point for many of them. Dent could see many aspects of outer terran culture right there on the festival grounds: the environmental planning, the brilliant compensatory use of color, the intense love of music, the political adventurism; and suddenly he realized that this was, in a very real sense, their home world. "This is the home world!" he said to Yananda, and expected that his companion would laugh at him; but Yananda nodded.

"I know what you mean. Look down there. Listen to that aeolia."

Below them on the next terrace a small building whistled and trilled like a woodwind octet; it was a Vance aeolia, and small apertures in the walls of the building caught the wind and funnelled it through a host of instruments housed inside. Depending on the wind's direction and power, various harmonic combinations were blown into existence, shifting with what seemed to be conscious artistry. Dent toasted the cheerful piping rondo with a glass of the White Brother.

"Karna and the crew must be having a tough time keeping people off that knob," Yananda said.

"At least there is a knob. Without it the Orchestra would probably get overrun."

"True. And no one but the Martians would be able to see it."

They laughed as they looked up the big slope to the black knob near the top of the terraces where the Orchestra stood, a fitting crown to the swirl of color below; it sparked like a statue of gold and wood in the bright morning sun, and Dent looked up at it fondly, proudly, a surge of adrenaline rushing in his blood. No wonder the Martians were tense, excited! They finished the bottle of the White Brother and ordered another one. As they drank they commented on the passing crowd, and guessed the origins of all the people of less than Martian height; they laughed at some of the Martian fashions (a tall silk-and-feather headpiece-and-tunic combination especially), and admired the Nefertiti-like Martian women; and soon the second bottle was almost done. The concert would begin shortly.

"Look!" Yananda said, all his cheeriness wiped away in a flash. "Look there—the man on the stairs, with the red beard. Gray curly hair. Isn't that Ekern?"

Dent saw the man, started. "I've only seen holos, but that sure looks like him!"

"That's Ernst Ekern!" Yananda exclaimed. "Come on." He stood, pulled Martian credits from a pocket and spilled them over the table, hurried out of the cafe with an explanatory wave at the waiter. Dent followed him, hopping up and down to keep the curly gray head in sight among the great crowd on the stairs.

♪

only connect

Margaret was sitting with her legs over the edge of the flattened top of the volcanic knob, looking down at the rainbow slope of tents and people, enjoying the moment of calm that she always felt when she was sure a concert was ready to go and there was nothing left for her to do. Kicking her feet against the ancient rock of Olympus Mons, lofting the fabric of her loose blue pants, checking her watch to see the remaining minutes flick away: all part of her ritual, all made new and exciting by the crowd and the enormous landscape. She felt light in a way that seemed only partly caused by the diminished gravity; it was the view that made her light! The striped-quilt festival grounds squirmed with color, the planet spread its tan plain to the horizon, hundreds of kilometers away, and Margaret grinned, admiring the Martians' sense of place.

Behind her there was an exasperated, impatient shout from Delia. Lazily she turned her head to look; all was well, all was well, no need to shout. . . . Delia was ordering one of her assistants down into the crowd to check a faulty speaker; they both jabbed at the map Delia held until the exact speaker was confirmed. Headphones covering her ears, Delia returned to her console and typed out more test patterns. This time there were a lot of them, with speakers on almost every terrace—a speaker for every instrument in the Orchestra, although that wasn't necessarily how Johannes would use them. The Orchestra looked like a glass tree sitting on hundreds of black plastic roots that ran to the edge of the knoll and stopped as if chopped off by some industrious woodman: the transmitters for the signals to the speakers. They made the top of the knob a hard place to walk over. It was a more complicated system by far than any Delia had ever had to deal with, and it had taken over a week to set up, following the long day when Johannes had made his wishes clear. All those speakers scattered about: "Won't the sound be terrible?" Margaret had asked him. Johannes had shook his head. "Just the way I want it. You'll see." And that was that.

Now Anton was stepping across the transmitting cables, looking as tense as Delia, though he had little to do. Perhaps that was the reason; no need for lights at the Areology. "Anton, come sit with me and look," Margaret called, but he shook his head and continued to pace around the cables, meeting no one's eyes. Margaret shrugged.

Johannes appeared at the top of the stairs cut into the knob, dressed in a rust tunic and tan pants. Karna and Marie-Jeanne were at his side.

As he approached the Orchestra Anton quickly cut in front of him. "Johannes, I have to speak to you."

"Not now." The empty black eyes were looking up at the control booth, and seeing nothing else.

"*Please,* Johan, it's important. It has to do with—"

"Not now, Anton. I can't think about it. Do you understand?" He looked Vaccero straight in the face.

"It's important. *I know what happened to you on Icarus*—"

"No!" Johannes said sharply. He held up a hand as if to ward off what Anton might say. "Just listen to the music, Anton. Do you hear me?"

"But I *have* to tell you," Vaccero said, voice twisted with desperation. Margaret shifted her feet up onto the knob, half rose, worried by the way Anton's voice sounded.

"Just listen," Johannes said, looking up at Vaccero with an expressionlessness so severe that it was an expression, a sort of . . . refusal. "That will answer you, do you understand?" He stepped past Vaccero and ducked into the piano bench entrance; Anton reached out for him and was restrained by Karna.

"He has to concentrate now," Karna said quietly.

By this time Margaret was on her feet, and over the cables to the scene. Anton was shaking, tears fell from the bottom halves of both eyes in a great flood—"Anton," Margaret

said, shocked, "what is it?" But he quickly turned away and
stumbled off across the thick black cables. Margaret stared at
his back, frowning, suddenly worried. *I know what happened
to you on Icarus . . . ?* But he was hurrying down the steps at
the edge of the knob's flat top. She looked over at Delia, but
Delia had missed the exchange. Karna was looking after
Anton, head cocked. Margaret jerked a thumb: "Have someone follow him," she tried to say, but halfway through the
sentence Delia waved up at the control booth, and

*From every direction came a crash, a great wave of
sound.*

♪

the peak

Like a tree growing branches at the speed of light: at the
very moment of that first primal crash Dent knew something
different was happening. He was on one of the central staircases behind Yananda, and they were searching for Ekern
among all the tall Martians who hid him so effectively. The
roar—all of the Orchestra's instruments playing at once,
fortissimo—stopped him. Like everyone else he looked up at
the knob. On the next terrace a giant black speaker wailed an
awful oscillating screech that made it hard to walk, even to
stand upright!—the godzilla and its weird metallic hum, swirling up and down in an octave tremolo. A different sound
from every direction. Stunned, Dent looked around: open-
mouthed faces (he felt his open mouth), frightened eyes,
hands over ears. Behind Dent a treble bass rumbled up and
down its scale, like rain in a dream. Like everyone around
him he ran up the central stairs, stumbling, pushing, leaping
up, making recoveries impossible in normal gravity. Every-

one was moving up. An oboe sounded in his ear, high, thick, reedy, an oboe crying out! Echoes of it came from all over the grounds. He stopped to listen. Another part of him realized that everyone had been running, back then; and now the people he could see were standing still. The terraces above were packed, a field of heads, hair like caps of spun metal in the brilliant sunshine. The penetrating cry of the oboe

Crash trumpets all over the park: the call. Dent closed his eyes. From every direction came phrases in the whole range of audible sound, touching every pitch and timbre. But with his eyes closed Dent heard a pulse beneath it all, insistent and regular, moving through every sound in the cacophony, a rhythm, Dent walked to it, da-da-da, da-da-da, da-da-da, da-da-da, overlaid a hundred times in a thick patterning of the rhythm, but there, definitely there, Dent walked to it as if dancing. A speaker he passed was singing, over the textured pulse two voices sang a melody and Dent's body jerked; it was the song he had loved when he was a boy heartbroken at a girl's rejection—wasn't it? It was gone now, the voices journeyed on but it had had that rise to it, that turn, bringing the whole flood of feeling back. He opened his eyes and looked at the long-nosed faces around him. They were staring at speakers, faces uplifted and vulnerable as surprise, recognition, pain, melancholy, all flicked across them. He met the gaze of an old man with dark wrinkled skin, and knew that they both had heard the song of their first love; somewhere in the weave of melodies some snatch of their own past had been threaded in. Under the instrumental music Dent heard the mass of the audience's voices babbling in the rhythm, voices of wonder, and he said aloud, "Voices are instruments too," but he couldn't hear himself. Faces all flushed, eyes bright, in a physical response to form . . . and all the strands were linking up, merging to five or six melodic lines that tumbled across each other in a wild, thick contrapuntal mesh, all to the rhythm, the rhythm, the dance. . . .

In the control booth of the Orchestra all was calm. Waves of music washed over Johannes as from another world. Nearly every part had been taped beforehand, and he had the leisure to listen, sometimes to listen only. The old orchestrina was really cranking along this time, every thing on every glass arm sawing, blowing, pounding, clanking such that the whole tower was rocking about. All of the keyboards in the booth jumped under invisible fingers, like a convocation of player pianos; it was enough to make him laugh. What bliss it was to know in every vibrating cell that the world was determined, that he need only step through his paces, the thoughts and actions that were implied in the big bang so long ago. To step in the shoes of destiny . . . he had only to add piano phrases now and then, which he did with vigor. Piano Concerto With Mechanical Orchestra, by the Universe. He heard the dense rhythmic music all at once and together for the first time, and it pleased him. So many elements fit together so snugly, and all with such a pulse, such a pulse, such a pulse, such a pulse, such a pulse, such a pulse! With a grin he pounded on the treble bass, both hands in the bottom two octaves, trilling the floor of the sound as if it were the very floor of the universe itself, on which everything else rested. All ten fingers now, play! Play with delight whatever the world says comes next!

♪

Ernst Ekern hid behind one of the huge speakers until the tour crew members pursuing him had passed. When they were lost in the crowd he stepped out from behind the speaker and the curving wall of the mercury drum assaulted him full force, hurting his ears. He climbed to a higher terrace, basking in the awful, patterned cacophony. It was possible to leap up from one terrace to the next! No one else seemed to know it. There was a surge in the music that drove through him, vibrated in his viscera and made his heart pound. It was the pulse he had first heard on Lowell, now elevated to a higher plane. The other members of the order, wherever they were—a turning, falling flute phrase tore at him; it was the melody, it was the melody he was to have played after the dream. . . . With a shudder he listened to another speaker's crescendo and it was gone, buried in the surge of the present chaos. And he had caused this; he had forced Wright to this; he held back a shout then gave way, shouted great bellows—

The cutting phrase returned, rammed home by heavy percussive beats, and suddenly Ekern knew what sounds would come next. He knew it and it came true just as he had foreheard it. He was standing on one of the higher terrace railings, looking over the Martian heads; now the railing seemed more elevated than before, he could see the heads of people on the upper terraces, *below him now*. He saw in a single glance all the speakers scattered over the festival grounds, and he heard the instruments sounding from each of them with the utmost clarity. At first it was wonderful to hear the music so well, to understand the pattern so clearly; he conducted with his arms, pointing from this speaker to that to mark entrances, shouting unheard directions in a tongue-twisting glossolalia. But his vantage point continued to rise, until it was obviously a case of levitation, for the slope was far below him, far below: vertigo. Something was amiss here. Something unnatural was being directed against him. Merely to hear this music was to understand that the future was predestined; had his hoax been true all along? Ekern saw the aftermath of the festival, the vehicles pouring away over the escarpment, planes flying off. . . . Fearfully he clamped his eyes shut and saw the rest of his life coursing onward as inevitably as the tearing violins that now surged inside his skull so wrongly. He was paralyzed, he couldn't speak, he was out of his body, he saw himself weeping on the floor of Prometheus Station, and with a shriek he fell back to the festival terrace and lost consciousness.

♪

Somewhere, from some battery of speakers across the terraces, Dent heard the music he had heard so long ago on Grimaldi, now made whole by its interaction with all the other parts. Something in the way the sound grew louder and softer, shifting from speaker to speaker, made him acutely aware of the physicality of sound, as when one opens a door and the music from the next room grows louder in exact time with the swing of the door. Vibrating air; this thin air at the top of the breathable atmosphere vibrated so purely that he could *see it,* swirling over the great cone of the volcano. All was vibration, patterns of vibration, and everything he could see and hear interpenetrated everything else.

At that moment each speaker spoke with the voice of a single instrument; he could hear each clearly. The sixty strings scattered over the terraces sang together, and across them lunged the metal-on-metal shriek of the Planck synthesizer, from a speaker just behind Dent. The great metallic scrape of life. He heard every speaker there as if he stood before it alone. And as he listened, his attention perfectly tuned, the music multiplied—where before one instrument had sounded from each speaker, now every instrument in the Orchestra sounded from every speaker, and each Orchestra played something different, so that there was a hundredfold jump in complexity. And he was aware of every strand, he vibrated with each of them—

and he knew what was coming next.

Flushed faces split with amazement. A row of tents glowing yellow and red and blue. Because (he felt) he had lived
on Mars all his life, the air was like a gel, a drug, and he saw
everything with aching clarity. . . . He expanded with the
sound until his consciousness encompassed all the Areology;
he was everywhere at once. For a second he thought, *out of
body experience;* then he was just there. Part of his extended
vantage point was immensely high, he looked down on the
festival which was no more than a small patch of variegated
color on the vast side of Olympus Mons. He could see over
the rim of the volcano into the caldera; dark, jagged, ringed
desolation. Looking back down at the patch of order he saw
what they really were, he saw that they were a small colony
of creatures on a planet not their own, that the very air they
breathed was that of an atmosphere (far below him) that they
had created themselves, a thin skin of gas like a houseplant
that had to be nourished and watered and given enough
light. . . . He saw that they were all working together at the
first step of the species' break from the home world, and he
understood that if the first step were taken successfully, with
balance, they could run from star to star all across the night.
All this he saw for the first time, as clearly as he saw the
achingly detailed festival ground below him, where each
person and object was made luminous, its relation to the
whole defined by the interlocking inevitable music that filled
the glass of the air with meshed vibration holding them all.

And now the music multiplied again: now from each speaker
came the multiplicity that formerly had come from all of
them together, so that there was another hundredfold increase
in complexity; and after that, with each pulse of rhythm it
multiplied again, until there were an infinite number of melodic lines. Extension of consciousness into all ten dimensions: the future was set in this vibrating gel as solidly as any
present. Dent Ios saw all time stretched before and behind
him in an endless spiral. For an eternal moment there was not
a thought in his head, just music and the spiral vision.

When he came to, and looked at the beautiful animals milling around him on the terraces, he thought, We're on Mars. *We're on Mars.* It was a spark in his soul, a peak in the music. All the beautiful animals. . . . Dent stirred, he found he was standing on one of the terrace railings, and with a clean standing jump he leaped up to the next terrace, and there was a tall old Martian who looked like his father; Dent *danced* across the terrace to him, three steps and a pirouette, and embraced the man in a crushing bearhug. Off, then, still in the dance. How this gravity let one soar! The music led his steps, he didn't even think of them—Dent Ios was a free man at last, he just pushed off, leaped up, triple-stepped, a likely face, embrace! A likely face, embrace! A woman, her long-nosed Martian horse face so *beautiful,* embrace! And off he spun across the terrace, feeling utterly abandoned, completely a part of the spinning music, absolutely free. A likely face! A likely face! There a brother, leaping to embrace him! And he laughed and looked at the endless succession of terraces below him, and saw that each person he had hugged had danced off to hug someone else, and exponentially the number of dancers grew until all danced, all leapt from terrace down to waiting arms, up to spinning partners, all part of a spontaneous ballet in two-fifths of Earth's gravity, partners all. Partners all. A likely face!

And then the coda began, a shift in structure as clear as the crashing thunder of the treble bass's trilling at the floor of the dance; as in the symphonies of the old time, when with a single chord everything returns to the original key signature, and every listener knows the end is near. Dent was yanked back into time, back onto a terrace railing, into an awareness of his own mortality, a hard thing to experience. He knew the music was about to end. Shaking his head he returned to himself. He had been a Martian and seen the future, he had left himself and become nothing but dance, he had initiated the ballet of embracing—but now he was just mortal Dent again, his mouth hanging open like a dolt. He stared at the people around him, saw tears streaming down faces, figures still hugging each other, he walked light as the touch of a glint over his terrace in the surge of emotion and the great coda. Face examined face (a *beautiful* child), following the music as the pulse slowed at last, the melodies rose up through the final progression of ancient simple chords, tearing up from the crowd to a high end. All the faces wandering aimlessly in a crowd of brothers and sisters never before recognized, never before *seen*—and all the disoriented joy became comical at last and Dent laughed, hugged and shook hands, light as a glint of light, meeting all his long lost kin, all those he had loved for so long without ever knowing it. "I am a Martian," he told them, "I *am* a Martian." Everyone stunned, aware of the music ending, ending . . . cheering for the fun of the noise, to contribute to the music . . . tiny figures up on the knob, embracing . . . dizzily Dent blinked and looked beyond, at the rise of Olympus Mons, and he felt he could reach out and touch the mountain's top, just as earlier he had seen over its rim; he felt at that moment as if he could see endlessly over every point of the compass, touch any place on the planet, and he felt himself fill with love for it was Mars the planet of hope, Mars the planet of promise, Mars the planet of peace.

♪

textural change

Anton Vaccero stopped at the door that said, in dark red letters, EXPLORE THE UNIVERSE.

It was on a shabby, crowded side street of Mareotis, a city to the northeast of the big volcanoes set in a series of shallow, wide, parallel canyons, or *fossae* as the locals called

them. Every district was run down, every side street tawdry
and littered with rubbish. Anton stood before the door—just
an ordinary door—and took a deep breath. His body was a
cold board. It was early evening; he was hungry, he had
trained north all that day and never thought to eat. He didn't
feel it as hunger; he felt it as hollowness. He was the hollow
man. He pushed open the door and stepped through.

Inside it was bright and colorful. A prominent sign on the
wall said, *We Are a Licensed Branch of the Whiteline Jump
Exploration Foundation*. A woman behind a desk at the far
end of the room looked up apprehensively. The room seemed
to telescope down to her. Vaccero approached.

He said, "I want to go." His voice cracked midsentence.
He didn't care.

"Very good," said the woman with a smile. "There is a
three-day waiting period, you understand—"

"I want to go now."

"Well . . . that is fairly common. We'll have to have you
sign these extra release forms." She opened a drawer and
pulled out two packets. "Read these in their entirety, please,
and then sign each."

There were about fifteen forms. Without bothering to read
them Anton sat and wrote automatically: *Anton Vaccero,
Anton Vaccero, Anton Vaccero* . . . empty syllables. Hollow
words for the hollow man.

"Now read this pamphlet, please," the woman said. "You'll
be in command of a complex vehicle, and even though we've
made it simple to control, your survival may depend on
knowing these facts."

"You have no idea what my survival may depend on,"
Vaccero said harshly. The woman pursed her lips, put the
pamphlet in his hand. His fingers closed on it. She walked
into the next room. He let the pamphlet drop to the floor.

She returned, led him into a small chamber. "You'll be
going on the ultimate voyage," she said brightly, with effort.
Perhaps she had had a hard day. "We're more certain than

ever that the whiteline jump will place you without measurable time lapse somewhere from nine to sixty light years away. We get more responses from volunteers all the time, some from people who left over a century ago. It should be quite an adventure."

A memorized speech, made up of lies. Vaccero decided to give her a break, and just nodded. Surely she knew why people volunteered to pilot the whiteline craft. He hated her suddenly, her and her near-tears; she was like all the rest of them.

"Show me where to sit and get me going," he said.

She nodded, blinking. It was probably a hard job. "We're in your craft now. Sit here during the jump." She indicated a big chair, somewhat like a dentist's chair, he thought. What a way to go. He sat in the chair. The woman strapped him in. From the door she said, "The initial acceleration will be the boost down the sled jump and off planet. You'll intersect with a Hyperion whiteline within seconds. You'll know you've jumped when the viewscreen comes on." She left.

He sat in the chair waiting. Despite himself he thought of the festival, the concert. Wright's music. A house built on sand. All of that work, all of that faith, all of that music—all for a lie. Built on Ekern's lies. He tried not to think but it was impossible. He hoped the jump would kill him; he hoped for it more than he had hoped for anything in his life.

Chapter Eight

‖: TIME :‖
PASSES

the irregulars at the wake

A few days later, as the Grand Tour was about to leave Mars for the crossing to Earth, Karna brought the news back from the communications center. Anton Vaccero had volunteered to pilot one of the whiteline probes, late on the evening of the Olympus Mons concert, and he had been launched soon afterward.

Although everyone was shocked by the news, the lighting people were the most affected. On board the *Orion* Rudyard, Sean, Sara, Ngaio and Angela sat stunned in their rooms for a couple of days, ignoring the departure from Mars space. Eventually Margaret and Delia and Karna went down to their suite with their recorders, and as cheerfully as possible instituted a wake. Quickly Margaret found that the lighting people were as troubled by incomprehension as by grief. "But *why* would he do it?" Sara kept saying. "And after the concert made everyone else so . . ."

251

"I asked the same question about my brother," Margaret said brusquely. "And you'll never get an answer now. As for the concert—music affects different people different ways." She tooted on her recorder and they played some mournful off-key little tunes. Anton's elegy. And when they left the lighting people alone again the wake had given their mourning expression, so that after a time it might dissipate; but still no one understood. And it is understanding we want in these matters, understanding more than anything else.

Margaret said to Karna and Dent, "Anton must have had a reason to jump."

Karna and Dent nodded. "That music?" Karna said.

Margaret wasn't listening. "I've put some people to work behind us. One of them tells me there are no Greys on Grimaldi."

"So they were fakes," Dent said.

"Or they might have been Greys just visiting Grimaldi," Margaret said. "But it was Anton who told Johannes about them. He said he had been approached by a Grey in one of those villages, right? But no one else ever saw that Grey. And whoever vandalized our rooms on *Orion* knew when everyone would be in the lounge, where Anton was reading fortunes. And this mysterious Charles knew who among us to contact. I think someone in our group was working for them. And that it was Anton."

Karna nodded. "Maybe Anton was a Grey."

"Maybe," said Margaret. "But if he were, why take the jump just then? No. Anton was trying to tell Johannes something—he said he knew what had happened on Icarus. But Johannes wouldn't listen."

Karna said, "But maybe Anton was a Grey, and knew what happened on Icarus—remember, we were met by two sets of Greys there—or so it seemed."

"Yes." Margaret frowned.

"*I* think someone is using the Greys as a cover for their operations against Johannes," Dent said. "And who's a better candidate than Ernst Ekern? Yananda and I saw Ekern in the audience. And they've hated each other for years, or so you've told me."

Karna shook his head. "It still could be the Greys. No one knows what they want, what factions they're split into. Anton could have been a Grey. So that he committed suicide for some religious reason."

"I don't think so," Dent replied. "They're too convenient a cover. And if you were right, we'd have to postulate two Greys going heretic around us, Anton and this Charles. Also, Charles is connected to the man who attacked Johannes on Titania. No. It feels like a cover to me. And now we know that Ekern is trailing the tour, so I think it's he who's using the Greys as his cover."

"But why?" Karna cried. "What's his purpose?"

Dent was silent.

Margaret shrugged. "Obviously we don't know enough yet. But I have some ideas. I'd like to talk to that Charles about them. . . ."

"We may never see him again after the way Dent scared him," Karna said.

"He'll show up again," Margaret predicted. "And then we'll act."

♪

earth fable

Each hour they came closer to the Earth, and everyone felt it. The point of origin common to them all, the home world—the *home world*! They watched the tiny blue crescent grow in the windows, and in each of their hearts grew a tiny crescent of unease. They were approaching the home they had never seen, a world so big that most of their terras would sink in its oceans like pebbles.

During the long evenings of the approach they told each other Earth stories. One night Delia said, "I went there once when I was a child, with my parents. We visited Alaska because that's where my father came from. He took us in a little hydroplane down the coast south from Nome, just our family, and we stopped in bay after bay after bay. It was early spring, and still very cold. One day we went iceskating on the frozen surface of one of the inlets. It was a clear day and the sun was bright, low in the sky and ringed at times by ice rainbows. And then we came across something none of us had seen before, even Father. Around the shore of the inlet the ice became clear—still thick ice, I mean, but for some reason it was transparent rather than white. We could see straight to the bottom, which was yellowish sand four or five meters below us. And there were big purple starfish all over the sand. Bright yellow sand, bright purple starfish, and us skating right over them.

"Well, one of the clear patches was near the mouth of a stream and the ice turned out to be thin, and my brother broke through. For a while it looked like we weren't going to be able to do a thing about it—Mother was screaming, I was terrified. . . . Finally Father jumped in and just swam and pulled him through the thin ice to shore. So they were both soaked, and really cold. Mother and I had to get the heaters off the boat, and we built a fire and rubbed them dry, and it still took us all day to get them warmed up. Then the next day it snowed, and the storm kept us in our tent for three days. The tent turned into a snow cave. Finally Father piloted us back to Nome through a big swell—waves that almost swamped us, and we knew how cold that water was. And *then*—when we got to Nome, and told people what had happened to us, they didn't even lift an eyebrow! What happened to us was nothing to them—things more dangerous than that happened to them every day!"

♪

approaching: the names

Johannes was seldom seen by the rest of the passengers of the *Orion*. Occasionally Dent or Margaret or one of the others saw him going to or from the Orchestra during the night hours when the lights in the halls were dimmed or turned off; but he would not speak. Once Margaret stopped him by stepping in front of him and putting her hands on his shoulders. She told him what had happened to Anton. He grimaced. "He should have listened. I told him to listen." Margaret let him go on. Other times, when Dent tried to speak to him, he answered in wordless little melodies, and cocked his head at Dent as if surprised Dent did not reply. Dent abandoned the attempts at conversation, and only nodded when he saw him. Dent knew that Johannes was still composing; the Orchestra's computer was scoring Wright's daily work, and Dent pored over the scores note by note, attempting to find the music he had heard on Olympus Mons. He couldn't. On the page it was too dense, too complex to transpose into an imagined sound. Once Johannes walked in on him while he was inspecting the scores from the computer. "Johannes, wasn't there a moment in the Olympus Mons concert when the sound coming from any given speaker multiplied from one instrument to all the instruments?"

"Yes."

"And then that process happened again, so that there was about a ten-thousand-fold multiplication of melodic lines?"

"Using the big bang as the start of the symphony solves the problem of origin," Johannes said, and hummed a bit. "History of universe sung in its largest outline, adequate until our moment of time, when I wanted more detail. Slowed it up, broadened it out, augmento la da ee o say—o la da ee o

say fran ee so eeeeee na,'' and so on, singing with a slightly
pained smile as he took the scores away from Dent.

And they were getting closer. Helplessly they watched the
blue crescent and its white companion crescent, growing in
the windows. Underneath the tiny white swirls of cloud they
could now make out the miniature shapes of the continents,
and the names sounded in their minds as if thickly echoing
choirs were singing them: *Asia. America. Africa. Europe.*
Such rich, bursting, mythic names, each evoking a million
images, each a whole world unto itself! And yet at times,
under the beautiful shifting patterns of cloud, they could see
parts of all of them at once. And for the first time their senses
made them confront a fact they thought they had always
known: the Earth was real.

♪

two martians

Margaret joined the passenger orchestra in the Bellatrix
Room for the hundred and ninety-fourth evening concert of
Orion's plunge downsystem; they played Shimatu's *Double
Concerto for Godzilla and Harp*, and she plucked at her cello
with a fierce pizzicatto, playing the weird dream harp echoes
as if pulling bowstrings, firing arrows at her unseen enemies.
The passenger orchestra was now composed almost entirely
of Martians and Terrans, so that Margaret felt as if she were
playing in a band of giants and dwarfs. She spotted Dent
across the orchestra playing his guitar—in one dream sequence they even had a sort of duet, revolving behind the
solo harp—and so when the concert was over she joined him,
and they walked down to the dining commons to get a meal.

"What's that book you're carrying?" Dent asked.

"A thing on Holywelkin."

"Why are you reading that?"

Margaret sighed. "I'm hoping to understand Johannes better."

"Good luck."

"I know. But it does bring up some interesting points."

After piling salads high over beds of tabouleh they sat at an empty table and ate. "I don't understand that Shimatu," Margaret said between bites. "And it hurts my fingers to play him."

"You have to admit it's sort of fun, though," Dent said.

"Umph. I suppose. Still I like something traditional. Give me De Bruik any day."

"Well—she's good, all right. But you have to give the rest a chance—"

"And it didn't make any difference!" the woman sitting at the table behind Dent said loudly. He looked around—Margaret looked over his shoulder briefly—two Martians, their meal finished, were conversing, oblivious to the rest of the commons.

"It didn't make any difference," the woman repeated. "The Reds won the election, and that's what the polls said would happen all along."

The man facing her said, "There wasn't time for the Areology to change enough votes. It takes time to translate an emotional thing like that into political action."

Margaret and Dent glanced at each other, and Margaret lifted her eyebrows. They looked down at their plates and continued to listen as they ate.

"If it was going to have any effect at all it would have been immediate," the woman said. "The further in the past it gets, the harder it will be for you to remember it. Or believe in it, from what you say."

"I don't agree. If you were there you'd know that you could remember it for as long as you had to."

"Maybe. But it seems to me that in the context of day-to-day life the power of such an experience will fade."

"That's because you weren't there."

"All right! I wasn't there." The woman was annoyed. "Obviously there was something special about this year's festival, but I had to work."

"Yes," the man said after a pause. "There was something special. During Johannes Wright's concert we . . . I saw . . . I *felt* what will come to pass on Mars. I don't know how to put it! I felt it. And—it's good, it really is."

"No one knows the future, John."

"So I would have said, but I *saw* it. Truly! Mars is already the best society in history. And everyone felt that at the same moment in the concert, they *all* saw what I saw. It was extraordinary."

The woman made a sound between her teeth.

After another long pause, the man said, "It's a hard thing to talk about."

"Let's not, then."

"Okay. I'll wait until I can say it better."

"You do that. Are you done eating? Let's go, then."

The two got up and left. Margaret and Dent watched them leave the commons, then looked at each other again.

"Well?" Margaret said, somewhat defensively.

"See?" Dent replied. "Something *did* happen on Olympus Mons."

"I know that. I was there, remember? Believe me, I know it. For a while there I felt like the performance knob was thrusting right out into space! I felt like I did on Icarus. Completely peaceful and happy. But with a wider focus—more aware. I never denied it."

"But you said it was just music."

"It *was* just music. Johannes finally put all the parts of his composition together, and it's a good one. What more do you want me to say? It's a great one, a work of genius. I hope he can do it again on Earth."

"But it's *more* than just that. There is some sort of transcendental effect to it! That music takes the listener outside of time.''

Margaret shook her head. "I don't believe that at all. The mind can enter funny states. You know that, Dent. And music is one of the strongest instruments of mental change.''

Dent nodded. "All right, all right. Say it's only that. I don't really know, and that's the truth. But still, you heard those two just now. That man was saying he thought the whole structure of Martian life might be changed by that concert!''

"And the other one was denying it.''

"Well, okay. But what if he's right?''

"If he's right, then maybe the Greens will start winning the elections on Mars. And Mars will break ties with Earth, and with the whiteline stations, and it'll drop out of the system.''

"Is that what the Greens really want?'' Dent shook his head. "Yananda and I talked with one of their campaign workers at the festival, and she sounded as if all they wanted was to wean the planet from dependence on the sphere technology.''

Margaret nodded. "Independence from the whiteline stations, and from Earth. I suppose it depends on what you think of those goals. I really don't know enough to form an opinion.''

"And neither do I,'' Dent agreed. "But think about what that man just said. And just think—what if Johannes had played three, four, ten concerts all over Mars? What if all the Martians had heard him play like he did on Olympus Mons?''

Margaret shrugged. "Who can say? In the worlds of what could have been, my friend, I frame no hypotheses.''

♪

partition

The crossing from Mars to Earth was going too fast. The members of the Grand Tour had gotten used to a certain rhythm: a week's activity, incessant and exhausting; then a month of rest, leisure, boredom. Around Jupiter, it is true, the ceaseless action of concert-giving had lasted nearly a month in itself; but afterwards there had come the long voyage, and the chance for recuperation. Now they were only ten days away from Mars, and all that had happened there was still fresh in their minds. And yet there, growing in the windows, were the blue-white ball and its big white moon, the binary system with the hypnotic ability to draw the eye, to crowd the window rooms with spectators; and getting bigger every minute, bigger at a speed that seemed to these travelers from upsystem a bit . . . unnatural. Clearly in the steep lower part of the gravity well things had to move faster, to keep from falling into the sun.

♪

dent and margaret

"I want to visit some of the really ancient structures," Dent said to Margaret over another dinner. They dined together now almost every night; it was a habit neither of them discussed. "The Pyramids, Karnak, the Great Wall, Easter Island. . . ."

"I don't know. The United Nations Cultural Affairs Organization is our host, and they're providing all of our surface transportation."

"We're landing at Cyprus, aren't we? So maybe we could make it on our own down to the Nile Valley, eh?"

"Maybe. Those distances are a lot larger than you're used to, Dent. It depends on how much time we have, and how much money. Basically, it's up to the U.N."

"The U.N. has the Earth—" Dent made a closing motion with his hand.

"That's right."

"That might make it difficult for any work we want to do to investigate the Greys—our Greys, I should say."

Margaret nodded. "Karna and Yananda will take care of it. You've been retired from active duty." She gave Dent a hard look, half annoyed, half amused, and he cringed a little. "No more shooting your own side."

"They were standing right next to each other!"

Margaret rolled her eyes. "Karna's got professionals for help if he needs it. You can keep joining the strategy sessions." She got up to leave. "I think I may know what's going on, anyway. We'll see soon enough."

As she walked away Dent stared after her, frowning. Dear Reader, you remember when we first met Dent Ios—when he was the Exemplar of Contemplation—when being "retired from active duty" was the definition of his goal in life. And yet now he frowned; he thought; one might even say plotted; and when he left the commons, he headed for *Orion*'s library.

♪

approaching: the forms

Through the window in the empty Rigel Room Dent watched the blue-and-white ball, now taking up most of the visible space. They were in orbit, over the Pacific Ocean. *In orbit*: they were a little moon of the Earth. Cloud patterns looked like they were painted on the water, and served to show how thin even the Earth's atmosphere was. After living with Uranus in the sky it seemed to Dent that the Earth was not, after all, very large. But the gas giants were gas, while the Earth here was like a big terra. When he considered it in that way it suddenly ballooned into something immense; the Pacific, for instance; that was a *lot* of water. Was there as much water as that in all the rest of the solar system? Tortuga, the Fortunate Isles, Europa . . . he quoted the old haiku,

> "So much to take in
> In this dewdrop of a world
> And yet—and yet—"

and watched as the Hawaiian Islands passed below, like green beads on a blue plate. The world.

Delia entered the room and joined him. "Look at all the spaceships!"

"Um," said Dent; he hadn't noticed. Over the horizon in the black of space there were lines of silver and bronze blips, line after line like the rings of Saturn. "Crowded."

"Except for around Mars and Jupiter, this is the most crowded space anywhere. They even have collisions."

"I heard about that one," Dent said vaguely.

Delia cleared her throat. "Are you wondering what it's going to be like down there?"

Dent smiled. Who had been wondering? "Sure."

"Me too. We're not going to any of the places I visited when I was young."

"Too bad. You should travel to some of them."

"Yeah. But Margaret says we have to go where they tell us."

"Um." The west coast of North America rolled slowly over the horizon, down ahead of them. They watched it silently. "It looks pretty . . . intimidating," Delia said.

Dent watched the Sierra Nevada, tiny white rumples in a brown-green blanket, near the edge of the continent there. That range of rumples was nine hundred kilometers long—longer than the diameter of his home world Holland! Maybe the Earth did look large enough to satisfy him. (That was America down there, America.) Dear Reader—you who may live in a cave, or a closet, you who may have spent all your

life on one planet—you may not have any immediate analogy
for the sensation Dent felt at that moment. To be looking at
the home you have never seen before. . . . . But all of us have
felt the sudden tension, the rush of adrenaline which comes
when we know we must face the unknown; imagine such a
situation from your own past fully enough, and your dia-
phragm will tighten, your pulse will accelerate, in a ghost of
the original apprehension—and then you will know what
Dent felt looking at the Earth.

"Yeah, it's scary," he finally said to Delia. "It's *big*."

Eventually Delia left, and Dent stood in the room alone. In
a little less than an hour he looked down on Europe, the
cradle of technological man . . . another rumpled range of
white-capped mountains showed him where Switzerland and
Germany were. Munich was down there somewhere, then.
And the Telemann Works were just outside Munich. And
down to the south, around the curve of the cloud-wrapped
ball, in the eastern end of the Mediterranean . . . Cyprus.
Dent frowned. There was a good piece of the globe between
them. On the other hand, he could see both at once. . . . He
would have to wait and consider his new plan further.

Karna and Yananda entered the room and Dent jumped
back guiltily. "Look," he said, "there's where we're going
to land!" They looked at him curiously, stared out the window.

"Yes, I suppose it is," Karna said.

Dent muttered a quick excuse and hurried out of the room.

♪

land ho!

Then they were on their way down. Margaret took charge
of the boarding of the shuttle, and everyone in the group

obeyed her orders submissively, glad to become children for the return home.

Imagine it, Reader! The shuttle rocket drops like a dart, it hits the atmosphere and begins to vibrate madly, the windows burn fiery orange and there is a roar that drowns all other sound; your little cylindrical compartment is washed of color, the windows blaze, you shake and bounce under the on-slaught of air; and in each accelerated heartbeat you drop thousands of feet closer to home, the root of every story you know. Imagine the fear of it, the steep exhilaration!

When the windows cleared a ragged cheer competed with the roar. The ocean was still far below them, but it filled one half of the sky, it was almost flat. The shuttle continued to vibrate; Margaret felt as if they were moving at a speed faster than she had ever experienced. She knew it wasn't so, but her senses would not be denied. The ocean was a new blue; the white clouds were distinctly above it now, casting shadows on the minutely wave-textured surface. The people sitting in the center seats stood to see out the windows. Dent leaned over Margaret, hand on her shoulder, and she pushed Johannes's head to the side somewhat, so that others could see past him.

"Land ho," muttered Johannes, looking forward at an angle only he had. Margaret could see only the blue horizon, now perfectly flat. . . .

"North Africa," Johannes said. Margaret leaned and saw the coastline to the right, suddenly curving. "That must be Tunisia," Dent added. "That's where Carthage stood, right down there."

"Landing off Cyprus in fifteen minutes," said a voice on the intercom. "Please be seated and fasten all safety belts."

"Surely we're going too fast!" Dent said.

"Just vibration," Margaret replied. "Besides, we land going about four hundred k's an hour."

"The impact must be something."

"I don't think so."

They were in the clouds, in thick white shifting mist. Then out again, just over the blue sea. Suddenly the roar got louder, the rocket tilted back, and with a thump they hit. Again the windows were white, this time a dim subaqueous blur, like thick clouds. They slowed, stopped. Rocking on water, they looked out at blue sky. Weak cheers. Margaret unbuckled herself and stood.

"It's heavy!" someone said.

Margaret considered it. She did feel heavier than usual. "Earth's gravity is more than one gee," she said, and laughed. The others joined her, and nervous laughter rang in the compartment. "No wonder they're all so short!" Dent said, and the laughter redoubled, it filled them all, Johannes was giggling, Karna roared, Delia and Marie-Jeanne leaned against each other. . . .

Soon they were moving, yawing slightly. Cyprus appeared in the windows to the left. Olive green scattered over a brown slope: an island tall as a mountain, big as a world.

Then they were entering a harbor. Tall metal-hulled sailing ships rocked slightly in their wake. Dirty water reflected brown hillsides. Gray stone walls were topped with flags.

The shuttle stopped. A door at the back purred open. Johannes stood and walked to the door—looked around at his company—stepped up and out. Margaret followed.

It was hot. The sun was a fierce blaze overhead, too bright to look at directly, although Margaret tried as soon as she was outside. It was just as the books said. A dry wind struck them like the air from an opened oven. Dust filled Margaret's nose, she had to squint to see through bouncing red-blue afterimages. The harbor of Kyrenia extended arms of land around them, brown hills covered by olive trees. In the wind the trees' leaves flashed olive-silver, silver-olive. "Come on," said Margaret to Johannes, who had stopped before her. "Walk down onto that dock, there's a welcoming committee for you."

It was true. On the dock a clump of people were watching the rocket. Johannes walked down a broad portable stairway.

The Terrans were short, their skin dark and wrinkled. "Welcome to Earth, Johannes Wright," one of them said. "I am Reinhart Scriabin, United Nations Undersecretary for Cultural Affairs."

"Thank you for meeting us," Johannes said. Suddenly he stopped moving toward the man; behind Scriabin stood Ernst Ekern, smiling broadly. Among the Terrans even a relatively short man like Ekern stood out. Johannes nodded to him. Bolstered by Johannes's composure, Margaret stepped forward to shake Scriabin's hand, ignoring Ekern. The Undersecretary introduced several of his party, while the rest of the crew descended to the dock. Then he said, "It's been decided by the Secretary that the first concert of Holywelkin's Orchestra will be held in Nueva Brasilia, Brazil, for the World Council of the Arts, in one week's time. The concerts after that will be scheduled by the Secretary, at our mutual convenience."

"Please discuss that with our tour's manager," Johannes said, waving Margaret forward and introducing her. Keeping her gaze away from the smiling Ekern, she said hello and got down to business.

♪

walking on earth

Dent Ios walked with difficulty through the streets of old Nicosia. Blake said the senses are the five windows of the soul; at that moment Dent felt as though his little garret slits had been hacked into gaping holes, through which the world streamed. It was too much: he wore sunglasses, his nose ran, he choked on dust, he was skittish with all the jostling in the little narrow streets . . . only his hearing was a match for the

Earth. He heard the music of the open wind, of voices chattering in a score of languages, of trolleys clanking and birds in cages trilling. With his height advantage he could see over the tumble of dark heads to the occasional offworld tourist walking by; he nodded to them as to other swimmers in a stream. Street merchants hawking wares called to him in a liquid English that reminded him of Karna and Yananda's speech; "Free shipping anywhere in the system! Your mother will love you always for sending her something from Earth, O Tall One!" That one almost got Dent, but he walked on. In the alleyways the wind was blocked and it was stifling hot, the air thick with the smells of sweat and cooking food and rotting vegetation and excrement and dirt. The Terrans on the street bustled about rapidly, their foreheads beaded with sweat. They were dark, darker even than Karna and Yananda, for all their lives they had been burnt by the rays of the sun. Dent could feel those rays pulsing on the back of his neck.

Wandering out of the market he came to the edge of the U.N. district, where the streets widened and were banked by long white apartment buildings, each lined by balcony railings of black wrought iron, hanging over the sidewalks. Trolleys and electric cars buzzed by in the center of the streets. Dent joined the crowd on the sidewalk and followed one part of it north, toward the city wall. In the time of the Crusaders Nicosia had been surrounded by a thick stone wall; now only a fragment was left, just north of the center of town. Dent reached it and after paying a small fee he walked up the bowed stone steps of the battlement, inspecting the stone beside him that had been worn smooth by two millennia of passing hands. On the broad walkway at the top of the wall, scattered groups of offworld tourists stared from behind their sunglasses, taking in the view. Below the wall on each side housetop gardens were shaded by vine-covered trellises, and lemon trees in casks. Olive trees shot up like silver-green fountains blowing in the wind. In the distance mountains shimmered, brown and dusty green, and over it all the white-blue dome of the noonday sky pulsed blue and blue and blue and blue. Dent reeled over the flagstones from one stone bartizan to the next, throwing his arms wide and turning in the wind, letting it fly through him and rip at the long banners overhead and the treetops below—staring up at the sky—running his hands over the ancient stonework—hopping a little to test Earth's intense gravity—

"Why look! Here's Dent Ios, drunk at midday!"

It was Karna and Yananda, strolling the battlement together. Dent smiled and waved a hand expansively.

"No one made this wind!" he exclaimed to them. "It moves of its own will. It could grow in strength until it wrecked the city and killed us all, and no one could stop it."

"Let's hope it's feeling friendly," Karna said, eyeing Yananda briefly. "Dent, what are you doing up here?"

"I am being! Oh—sorry—this wind is in my thoughts—I am sightseeing, of course. Why, aren't you?"

Karna shook his head. "We're here to meet that Charles. And—well, it would be better if he didn't see you up here. After the way you scared him last time, he might think we were part of some conspiracy against him, and then we'd never get a chance to talk to him. You understand."

"Besides," Yananda said, and then stopped himself as Karna gave him a look. But Dent got the message, and he came plummeting back to the reality of the tour and its troubles.

"You mean . . . I really am to be kept from helping the investigation any more?"

"No, of course not. You'll be helping us when we confer with Margaret. But we'll gather the facts in the field, Dent. That's what we're trained for."

Dent nodded, feeling affronted even as he had to admit the truth of what Karna said. He had thought to suggest his plan, but now he decided to keep it to himself. "I'll get out of your way, then," he said, and walked over to the battlement steps without another word. Back on the city streets he found himself becoming more and more annoyed. A part of him was happy to be out of the dangers of the action; but that part of him was slipping away; other forces in him were coming to the fore, and they wanted to help protect Johannes from his enemies. . . . His day of sightseeing was ruined. Every offworlder sticking out of the crowd of Terrans reminded him of the tour.

His neck was burnt. Irritably he wiped the sweat from his forehead and returned to their hotel. "I'm just as capable as any other person, aren't I?" he demanded of his room. He had his *Thistledown* account number, which he had seldom used since the early days of the tour . . . and a few calls gave him the addresses he needed. It was within his capability to put his plan into action by himself. . . .

He could fly to Munich, and from there visit the Telemann Works. Johannes himself had given Dent the clue: "Maybe he wants an Orchestra of his own," Johannes had said when Dent told him about Ekern and the Greys meeting at the Telemann Works on Earth. Dent had looked it up, and found that the Telemann Works was the instrument factory that had done much of the work for Holywelkin in the construction of the original Orchestra. And if Ekern was traveling there . . . well. Dent couldn't be sure what that might mean. But he had his theories, his fears. And if he could go to the Works, sneak into them somehow—find evidence of a new Orchestra—take photos of Ekern visiting—take photos of whatever work was being done for Ekern (Dent's plan was a little vague when it came to these details). . . . Then he would have something to *show* Johannes, something to break into this deadly spiral that Johannes and his conception of the Greys had now created between them. Yes—he could do it! He could do it alone.

In each of us the winds of motivation are aswirl. But we have run into this problem before: who among us can propose an adequate meteorology for this weather of the soul? Dent sat in his room for nearly two hours; emotions passed across his face like fronts, he even paced about once or twice in little squalls of indecision. And in the end he packed a travel bag, and called down for a cab to meet him at the front of the hotel. He wrote a short note. *"Margaret—gone to Munich. Meet you in Nueva Brasilia."* He wrote *"Don't worry,"* scratched it out, rewrote the note without it. Signed it. On the way to the cab he slipped it under Margaret's door.

♪

the maze

Ernst Ekern floated just underneath the surface of the rooftop pool of the Magus Diana's villa, just outside Nueva Brasilia. He had arrived just the day before, and already he despised the heat, the humidity, the tame green jungle beyond the villa's park, the gravity. The park itself was a hedge maze, and looking down at it from above Ekern could trace the complicated course it would lead for anyone trapped in it. He closed his eyes, memorized the pattern of hedges as best he could; no doubt Diana would have them all cast into it at some time during their stay. It was abysmally hot, windless and shimmery under the intense afternoon sun. Off in the distance the giant skyscrapers of Nueva Brasilia rose above the tamed jungle like a dream city—and so in a sense it was—dream of the U.N. aristocrats, who apparently did not mind the equatorial stew of heat.

Ekern shoved his sunglasses back up his nose and observed the others in the pool. His fellow playwrights; some U.N. officials, ignorant of the fact that they were attending another convocation; a few nudes, lolling about in the shallows to suit Diana's sense of the picturesque. . . . One of the U.N. people, the ambassador from Europa, waded over from the pool bar with one hand above the water. "Have a bulb of this, Ernst," she said.

"What is it?" He took the bulb.

"It's new. From South America, of course. Called the Anaconda."

"What's in it?"

"I don't know."

Ekern put the bulb down on the pool's blue tile decking. Some of the woman's friends drifted to their end of the pool, and Ekern was congratulated more than once. "Extraordinary Grand Tour." "One of the best in history, I'm sure." He could feel the eyes of the order on him. "Yes," he said with a small smile, "it has gone well so far."

"That concert on Mars," the ambassador said. "We've heard it stunned the entire little planet."

"Yes," Ekern said, and despite himself he quivered; immersion in the water gave him the uncanny sensation of floating as he had floated over the site on the flank of Olympus Mons, and brief bright images overcame even the glarey scene before him, like holos flashing on the inside of his sunglasses, each to be quickly suppressed, that agony on the floor of time—

He picked up the bulb, stuck the open end up one nostril, squeezed. Immediately his head felt colder. "We can't wait until the Orchestra arrives and we can hear it ourselves," one of the women said. "It will be marvelous."

Ekern nodded, concealing his contempt with a large smile. Now he was cool, very cool. Under his forearm the rough texture of the caulking between the blue tiles gleamed in the light, little chunks of pure white as in a painting by Vermeer. . . . "Yes," he said, "it has gone well so far." His eye was caught by a movement at the far end of the pool. Atargatis, slim and brown, dove into the water with a neat clip of a splash. Ekern sniffed from the bulb again. Fluid dark shapes making quantum jumps under the rippled surface: Atargatis came up beside the ambassador, giving her a start. Ekern offered him the bulb and he refused it. "I see you're in your element," Atargatis said to the ambassador, referring to the water world she had probably not visited in years. She nodded, unamused, and Atargatis laughed outright, so that with a curt nod she waded away. Ekern put his chin on the decking and stared at the white city in the distance, and the ambassador's friends slowly followed her away.

Atargatis laughed. "Enjoying the home world, Ernst?"

Ekern felt the coldness behind his nose. "Very bright place," he said, inspiring Atargatis to more laughter.

"I see the locals love you."

"Of course."

"And the Grand Tour proceeds according to script?"

"Yes. They are on Cyprus now, about to follow me here."

Atargatis picked up the drug bulb, sniffed at it, put it down. "I know what happened to your apprentice," he said softly.

Ekern felt his heartbeat quicken. "Yes?" With tinted contact lenses masking his bright eyes, it was impossible to gauge the expressions dashing about Atargatis's face. . . .

"He took the whiteline jump," Atargatis said slowly. "Didn't you know that?"

"I knew," Ekern lied. "But how did you discover it?"

"I have my ways. He jumped into a whiteline. Was that part of your play, Ernst? Did you truly know what happened to him?" He laughed again, loudly this time. People at the other end of the pool turned to look at them.

"I knew he would commit suicide, and I knew when," Ekern said coldly. "The method—that was his improvisation, obviously."

"Of course, of course. You are as clever as Fowles, Ernst. Every part of the tour is under your control always."

"That's right."

This brought forth more peals of laughter from Atargatis.

"Be quieter, or they'll come down here to listen to the jokes I tell you."

"Jokes indeed," Atargatis said. "You are using materials for your metadrama that you don't fully understand, Ernst. Do you realize that?"

Ekern stared at the man coldly. "You don't know what I understand."

"Oh but I do! I do. More things occurred on Mars that were out of your control than the death of Vaccero. The concert on Olympus Mons—"

"I was there," Ekern interrupted. "I saw what happened."

"But do you understand it? You are unleashing certain . . . forces, Ernst." Suddenly the man's mobile face was serious, even grim. "The Greys exist for a real purpose. They are like us in that sense. They are not a joke. Now they have been exiled from Mars, and that concert. . . . Well. They conceal what they know from humanity for the good of *both* parties, understand? If Wright has learned what they know, and if he reveals it to all, then you won't be in control of the results, Ernst. No one will. Your play will burst to chaos."

"That won't happen." Ekern stared off at the glaring green jungle, trying to read Atargatis, his words, gestures, laughs and grimaces. . . . He appeared deadly serious; and what did that mean? He had to enlist the man, control him, use him. "With your help, we break him here. After this he won't reveal anything—he won't have the power no matter what he knows."

Atargatis's mouth twisted down. "Perhaps." He tossed the drug bulb over the railing.

"You will help?" Ekern asked, involuntarily allowing a trace of tension to push at his voice. Why this stupid fear?

Atargatis nodded. "I will help." A small smile: "We are all actors in each other's metadramas, are we not?" Then he was grim again: "I only hope we are not too late."

Then he swam away, over to the small circle of members

of the order surrounding Diana. Diana was watching him—
with a quick shudder Ekern turned again and looked down at
the hedge maze in Diana's broad park. Light green grass,
dark green hedge, both manicured to a geometrical perfection. . . . He noticed that one of the hedge lines was unbroken. He followed it around again. Yes. No way to the center
of the maze. He closed his eyes, opened them, waded off in
search of another bulb.

♪

flying over earth

The tour crew left Cyprus in a big jet-powered airplane.
Looking down at the island after a loud, vibrating, frightening ascent, Margaret saw that it might perhaps be as small as
the maps showed it to be. While on Cyprus she hadn't quite
been able to believe it. But now she saw the curve of the
shoreline, the tops of the inland mountains, and it seemed at
least possible, if not likely, that the other features of the
Earth's surface were scaled in proportion to Cyprus as the
maps showed. That was the meaning of ocean, continent;
they were bigger even than this giant island, this island that
would hold twenty of the hemispheres on Iapetus . . . so that
Iapetus, she now knew, was a small island indeed.

Almost all of the crew had drugged themselves to avoid
motion sickness on the jet flight across the Mediterranean,
Africa, and the Atlantic. Margaret stayed to herself; she
thought people were strange on the turbulence drugs. She
missed Dent, and missing him she worried about him. She
had dispatched a couple of the security people to Munich
when she found Dent's note, but if they couldn't find him
. . . he would have to take care of himself. Their timid critic

(her friend) taking off on missions of his own; their musician withdrawing ever more, day by day it seemed, until he was as likely to sing nonsense as to speak—Margaret sighed. Long tours always became difficult; but this one was a category unto itself.

It was a very bumpy ride, and Margaret moved down the jet to speak to Johannes, to keep his mind off the vibrations if they were bothering him. On the contrary, he appeared to be enjoying himself. Upon questioning he smiled, looking through her like a blind man. "It's like traveling in a drum, rat-a-tat-a-tat." Margaret nodded shortly and looked past him out the window. Cyprus was gone. The finely rippled blue sea rolled under them. It seemed the vibrating jet was very fast. Then, as they crossed Africa, and passed over field after field of grain, out of the sight of any ocean, it seemed that the jet was slow. Very slow.

When they arrived in Nueva Brasilia there was still a week before the concert was to take place, and Johannes said he wanted to get away from the crowds in the big U.N. city. The new capital was isolated and inland, far from Macchu Pichu or Cape Horn, the places he wanted to visit. Margaret explained this to him. Despite her explanation he decided he wanted to travel south, in the direction of the Cape. Margaret chartered one of the hydroplanes that ran up and down the coast of Argentina. "Some of us will have to come along," she said to Johannes.

"Of course," he said, as if there had never been any question about it. Margaret sighed and began organizing the trip. In the end Karna, Delia, Sean, Sara, Rudyard and a few others joined them on the speedy train to Buenos Aires, and they boarded the chartered hydroplane together.

♪

at the telemann works

Dent's airplane arrived in Munich late in the evening; Dent debarked quite sick and disoriented. It was difficult to find assistance, call for a hotel room, find his way to the taxi line at the airport entrance, check into the hotel, and climb the short flight of steps to his room. Once there he collapsed on the bed and told himself that the vibrations were only the reverberations in his middle ear, that he was at rest at last. Very discouraged, and heartily sick of Earth's antique modes of transportation, he fell asleep thinking that his madcap adventure had all been a horrible mistake. . . .

Several times in the next few days he had good cause to repeat this judgment. He took the train out to Zorneding, a town to the east of Munich, and from the town center took the tourist bus out to the Telemann Works, a large complex of industrial buildings set in the woods south of town. Dent was one of only three offworlders in the small group of tourists that followed the English-language guide through the giant complex; he stood behind the other two as they moved from one building to the next, and said nothing. They were shown how the metal was rolled, shaped into tubes, bent into the intricate curves of horn tubing; they stood on balconies and looked down into workshops where craftspeople assembled the string instruments; they watched electrical engineers and computer specialists as they tinkered with the hardware of synthesizers. Every step in the making of musical instruments was shown to them in turn, and despite his ulterior motives Dent found it fascinating. Still he kept a close watch on their progress through the complex, and surreptitiously marked out a rough map on the pamphlet he had been given at the beginning. There were at least a score of long buildings in the complex, but it was a thorough tour, in the Germanic style; they visited seventeen before they were through. As the guide was leading them back across the parklike grounds,

Dent spotted one near the edge of the complex that he was sure they had not visited. "I wonder what's in that one," he said to the pair of Titans, and just as he hoped, one of them sung out to the guide, "What's in that building there?"

The guide looked at her questioner briefly, and then said to them all, "Telemann Works is often contracted by other instrument makers to build special projects, which they wish to keep confidential. The special projects are created in that facility, which is guarded twenty-four hours a day."

"So," Dent said, staring at the building with the rest. Further curiosity would be perfectly natural, he thought, and with a gulp he started to ask the guide another question, but one of the Terrans beat him to it:

"Can you tell us who you're building an instrument for now?"

"Often these contractors are out to get a jump on the rest of the musical world—you understand," the guide said easily. "Therefore that information is confidential, I'm afraid." And then they were back to their starting point in the visitor's center, and she bid them farewell. Free to wander the center's museum, Dent did so for a while (the serpentine and the hurdy-gurdy looked like lovely instruments), then went out to the picnic grounds. He bought cheese and wine from the concession there, and took them to the far corner of the picnic area, where he had a view of the forbidden building. "Well," he said to himself, "that was relatively easy." He was pleased with himself for his detective work. On the other hand, there were the posts of an electric alarm system placed around the special projects building. And the entire complex was surrounded by a high wire fence . . . so . . . what was he to do? He stared off into the ancient hardwood forest, ate his lunch. When the tourist bus arrived to take them back to Zorneding, he got on it, utterly at a loss.

In his room that night he mulled it over. He went for a walk in the nearby English Garden, and watched a small brass band play ancient tunes under a tall pagoda, and considered it some more. Nothing occurred to him, and he grew angry at himself. All the way to Munich, to confirm that the Telemann Works did indeed make musical instruments! And yet he couldn't break into the complex; that simply wasn't within his competence. . . .

The next day he returned to the Telemann Works and took the tour in French. The names of the instruments were beautiful in French. As they returned to the visitors' center he wandered off to look in the door of the forbidden special projects building, as if out of random curiosity. A worker opened the door to leave the building; peering in Dent saw a hallway and another craftsperson. Then he was collected by the guide, who patiently answered Dent's mangled questions while he was led back to the picnic grounds.

So much for that. The next day Dent bought a pair of binoculars, and packing a lunch and the tranquilizer dartgun he had kept since the debacle in Burroughs, he rented a car. The small electrically powered thing was slow and easy to drive, and the autobahn between Munich and Zorneding was nearly empty. He drove into the parking lot at the Telemann Works, then waited until no one else was around, and walked back out the front gate. A low knoll to the south of the complex was covered by very climbable oak trees, and he selected one and ascended it. Climbing a tree reminded him of his boyhood, when he had climbed maples, a real challenge. A good network of branches gave him a seat, a foothold, an armrest for the binoculars, and a leafy view of the forbidden building. He settled down and watched. Occasionally a craftsperson went in or out. He ate lunch, then watched the workers enter or leave until it was nearly closing time. His car was one of the few left in the visitors' lot, but no one noticed him drive away.

There were five more days until the concert in Nueva Brasilia. Feeling foolish, Dent booked a flight for the fourth day, and then returned to his perch in the oak tree. His back and bottom got sore; craftspeople went in and out of the forbidden building; he got bored. Certain individuals he decided were officials of the company (a small building housed them), and occasionally they visited the forbidden building, but . . . Dent ground his teeth and kept on watching, refusing to think about what a fool he was being. Ironic that Dent Ios, having made his momentous decision, should follow a course of action that would lead him to such a lot of pure, motionless contemplation. . . .

But on the afternoon of the third day a man arrived in a rented electric car. He went past the visitors' center to the executives' building, carrying a large briefcase. When he emerged again a group of the executives were with him, and they led him directly to the forbidden building. Dent shoved the zoom on his binoculars to highest magnification, and held the glass firmly on the man. Long narrow face, bony cheekbones; Dent trembled, held himself steady, looked again. The man looked up his way, as if aware he was being watched, and Dent looked him straight in the eye. Red Whiskers. Dent's branch swayed under him. He struggled down from his perch, nearly fell, slowed his progress. The gravity here was enough to bring one to harm. . . . He slipped between trees, hopped into the parking lot as unobtrusively as possible, and hurried to his car. Inside he tried to compose himself, to slow his heartrate by deep breathing. He went through his plans, and checked the dartgun to make sure it was loaded. Some mix of tranquilizer and truth drug. Well . . .

The man was escorted out to his car by a pair of the executives. He was still carrying the briefcase. Dent started his car and when Red Whiskers drove out, he followed. He kept his distance on the country road leading in to Zorneding, then on the autobahn he closed on the man's dark green car. As they drove into Munich Dent became more and more nervous. He kept cars between them to avoid being too obvious, then closed up when the fear of losing the man grew to something like panic.

Down in the old quarter of town, near St. Peter's Church,

the man drove slowly over a cobblestone street and pulled up
to a curb. Dent drove past him, double-parked his car and
leaped out. Red Whiskers was already walking the other
way, briefcase in hand. Dent skipped down the sidewalk, his
heart racing like the percussion in De Bruik's *Madness*. He
took the dartgun from his pocket, hid it inside his coat flap.
Now he walked behind Red Whiskers. He hesitated, then
remembered the attack on Lowell, the kick to his ribs. He
aimed the dartgun at the man's neck and fired five times,
click click click click click. Red Whiskers exclaimed, turned
around, saw him, looked confused. Dent glanced around; no
one watching. Red Whiskers was reaching into his coat
pocket. Dent shoved him and he tumbled back, sat down
hard. He could barely lift his head. Dent put the dartgun back
in his pocket, grabbed the man's briefcase in both hands,
tugged it away from him. The man could only mutter feebly,
head back on the pavement. Dent raced to his car. Someone
shouted. He leaped in and pushed the accelerator to the floor,
nearly ramming a car ahead of him. His heart was beating too
fast, he could feel the pressure of his blood making his eyes
pop, his hands tremble. Around a corner, another, another
still. The image of Red Whiskers struggling feebly on the
sidewalk came to him again, and he groaned; he might have
killed the man! Who knew what that many darts would do?

He drove to the car rental and returned the car. Walking
back to his hotel with the briefcase he recalled that Red
Whiskers had seen him. So it was at least possible that he
knew who Dent was. Name tracing. . . .

In his hotel room he tried opening the briefcase. It was
locked. Some sort of composite material . . . he broke it by
beating it with a chair. A few more stabs with the chair leg
and it broke apart to the extent that he could pull out the
papers it held. He spread them over the bed.

They were diagrams. Blueprints for Holywelkin's Orchestra.

When he realized what they were, and what they implied,
he became more frightened than he had been even during the

attack on Red Whiskers. One of the documents named the Holywelkin Institute as contractor. And . . . his name was at the airport, on the reservation list for a flight to Nueva Brasilia. . . .

He packed his bag, checked out of the hotel, went back to the car rental, rented another car. The rental people provided him with maps; he told them he was going to Zurich, and then when he got out on the autobahn, he headed for Stuttgart.

♪

the patagonian shore

The size of everything was wrong.

The people were too small. All his life Johannes had had to look up at people, and now looking down at the Terrans he felt odd. It was like visiting a nation of children. He stood on the bridge of their chartered hydroplane and watched them curiously day after day. Old wizened children.

And the sky was too big. Each hemisphere on Pluto, and each outer terra with its bubble of air, presented the observer on the ground with a small blue dome, sometimes one through which stars shone. On Earth, however, the sky was an immense solid blue dome which leaped overhead in a shape like the pointed end of an egg. And it was so blue! He who lived in a world of blues found the final blue at last, and from the bridge of the hydroplane he watched the sky and felt that there was a part of his brain that had been waiting all his life to see that color. He thought, I have stepped out of doors for the first time in my life! Or for the second; Mars with its violet sky had been a world, but a world made, while here was the world given.

And it was such a *big* world. A giant among Terrans,

Johannes was dwarfed by Terra itself. The surface of the endless poster-blue sea seemed a perfectly flat plane. For the first time he saw how intelligent men in the earliest days of history could have thought the world flat. He watched, feeling as triumphant as Archimedes, as a rocky headland that the hydroplane had passed was pared away by the distant horizon, until it disappeared under the blue. A sphere, a sphere!

But not a Holywelkin sphere. The Earth's own mass was enough to generate this oppressive gravity, and the bare bones of physics gave him the tools to calculate that such a gravity implied a very great mass indeed. "The Earth is *big*."

He spent the days of their sea voyage on the bridge, and no one—not Margaret with her questions, nor Delia with her solicitude, nor Karna with his heavy jokes—climbed up to bother him. They planed over the waves until they came to a long bare shore: endless steep beaches, backed by low grassy hills. Here Johannes had the hydroplane stop (it rocked in the water like any barge), and they were ferried onto the Patagonian shore. It was late in the afternoon. While the others made camp Johannes walked south down the ridge of grassy dune at the top of the beach.

The sun was low over the westward hills, big and orange, flattened a little. It was possible to look briefly at it. The rush of an atmosphere over a world turning: a cool offshore wind held up choppy waves that approached the beach at an angle and pitched over just meters from the sand. Sunlight pierced the waves before they broke, making them green and translucent. He scuffed the thick beach grass. From the top of the beach dunes he could see up and down the bare shore for a long way; in both directions the beach extended to headlands made russet in the shadows of the hills. To the west the air was like honey, the hills were dark. The wind was picking up. The roar of white water sluiced up and down the steep shingle, rolling pebbles and fragments of shells that were

pink and spiny: a music there, a perfect rhythm, range of
pitches, rich timbre. . . . Toiling up the loose sand of a dune
he felt the blood pound in his neck and thighs, flush through
his skin. All in time together. In time . . .

From a dune somewhat taller than the rest he could see his
friends to the north, scattered up and down the beach. They
had just started a fire, and his eyes were drawn to the yellow
spot in the dusk. Three of his people were clumped together,
blue and green pantaloons flapping in the wind; they looked
alien to the landscape, too tall and shiny for the long harsh
shore. Europeans had landed here long ago; no doubt they
had looked just as alien on this prehistoric beach as his
friends did. The Europeans had met natives of the region
living as they always had, wrapped in furs, black with grease,
brandishing spears and yelling in fear and awe. Watching
from their little ships the Europeans had thought them more
beast than humankind. Johannes looked inland at the dusk-
shadowed hills and considered what it would be like to live
on this coast—up in one of the clefts in the hills, more likely,
or next to one of the marshes tucked behind the beach. Going
out every day to check snares and stalk small mammals and
birds. Collecting shellfish, making nets, fishing in tidal ponds,
tanning skins, building huts, weaving baskets, stringing ornaments of shell. He imagined them hunched around a beach
fire, watching flames cast their glow on the breaking waves.
The crackle of wood against the cyclic roar of water; the
smell of salt and woodsmoke; faces burnt by radiant heat,
backsides cold. . . .

And there, around the fires on the beach, among human
beings who could be mistaken for beasts; there in the voices
and hands of those short brown civilized creatures, with their
minds as powerful and active as any in the Holywelkin age,
music had begun. Around some small precious fire they
talked in rhythms, at different pitches, and hit sticks together,
and doing it they felt that old dust in the blood pick up and
fly through their bodies, impelled as it had been only in

moments of danger, fear, triumph, ecstasy—moving just as fast as they could chant, moved by the apprehension of beauty in sound. Sunken bloodshot eyes glittered in the firelight, gazes met with joy at a new world found, and cries of exultation joined the chant, became a part of it. . . .

The full moon was rising over the sea. How fat it appeared on the horizon, compared to the little white coin it was when overhead! Johannes stared at it, looked up and down the beach, looked behind him; he wanted to see everywhere at once. How he wished for his eyes. . . . In the moonlight the hills behind grew new shapes and shadows. The wet sand of the steep beach glittered white, and the headland to the south gleamed gray, visible again. Johannes stared and stared, his throat constricted, his face hurting: "How could they ever have left?" he whispered. Waves answered.

He took a deep breath, walked around. Then back up the long beach toward the fire, feet sinking in the loose sand between clumps of black grass, hands in pockets for warmth. Silhouettes crossed the yellow spot of fire: small hard people in furs? Men in helmets and breastplates? Though he knew they were only his friends, goosebumps rippled over his arms; against the leaping yellow blaze they looked wild.

He rejoined them. As the moon rose, laying a path of broken moons over the sea, they talked and laughed, ate burnt food, sang chanting songs that made Johannes grin. He was congratulated more than once for the idea of coming there. He did not tell them that it was inevitable, out of his control and none of his doing; no need for that, in this time and place. (He saw how the Greys might have begun.) The fire bounced in the wind. Every transient lick of flame, he thought, burned by necessity; it was determined by all the history of the cosmos up to that point. That was what his vision on Icarus meant, if he believed it. And after Mars, how could he believe otherwise? Unless . . . but he knew it was so, he could feel it. Necessity ruled all. Even those first humans, inventing music on these bleak hills by the sea, had been moved to it by forces acting through them—the music had sung them. Patagonian, Portuguese, Plutonian, they were all the same in that. "Good night," he said, and carried a sleeping bag up the beach. Sand for his bed, a tuft of grass for a pillow. The others sang on as the music continued to course through them. And yet . . .

♪

interversion

They came just before dawn, as silent as those first primitives would have been. Johannes didn't fully awaken until the tape was slapped over his mouth, and he was lifted up in his sleeping bag and slung over someone's shoulder. Karna had been sleeping at his side, and they were forced to silence him too. Johannes saw him slump down suddenly, knocked out by a tranquilizer. Then they were off into the dark, both of them carried by pairs of dark figures. A rough jog down the beach, and then into a craft of some sort. It lifted into the air noiselessly. Two bulky figures, heads cropped—Greys!—lifted Karna up and tossed him out the door of the helicopter. It was difficult to breathe so hard through his nose.

They traveled for a long time. There were several figures in the dark around him, speaking an occasional phrase in a language he didn't recognize.

They came down in high mountains; the Andes, he guessed. He was pulled from the craft, and the sleeping bag was stripped down and wrapped around his legs. It was cold. There was an orange gleam over a rise. At first he thought it was a big fire. They walked in that direction, carrying him. He lifted a hand to tear the tape away but was restrained.

The light came from a volcano in full eruption. Fiery lava

leaped out of a roiling crater, ran in sinuous channels down a slope. He was carried to the rim, and he quaked with fear— they would toss him in—

On the rim's edge was Zervan. Except he looked different in this light. "Well met," Zervan said. "You must play for us at a certain time and place. No choice, no chance." They moved along the rim to a large black catapult, holding in its arm a sphere generator like a great bomb. "Come," said Zervan, climbing onto the large square top of the generator. Johannes was lifted onto it, and joined by a few more Greys. Zervan reached to his face and pulled the tape away with a single rip. "Prepare for the descent," he said.

"A Holywelkin sphere will not withstand lava," Johannes said, voice wavering.

"We strengthen the wave-weave," Zervan replied. "Fear not—this will not be the first time we have made the descent. And now the Master of the Orchestra will play at the sacred singularity." He indicated a guitarp, resting on its side on the generator. He looked at one of his assistants. "Downward!"

The sphere snapped into existence around them, holding them fast to the generator; the catapult flipped them into the lava.

The lava was held off, forming a bowl below them. Long arms of fiery molten rock leaped into the sky, splashed on the sphere, slid down its sides. Inside the sphere it was glarey orange, and faint shadows flickered over them. Zervan smiled at Johannes. "You see, the sphere is strong enough. As for propulsion—" He waved a hand, and they sank rapidly under the surface of the lava.

Now they stood on a box inside a bubble walled by varying shades of light orange; currents of white or of dark orange twisted over the sphere, making strange patterns. Two of the Greys sat before a computer screen, which presented them with a rainbow of colors. Zervan indicated it. "By this map we navigate down the channel of molten rock, and through the crust. Soon we will be in the mantle, where our passage is not so constricted."

Johannes swallowed convulsively. Surrounded by crushing, chaotic, superheated liquid basalt, which was held away by nothing more than a discontinuity. . . . It was hot. Dazed, Johannes sat on the deck of the generator, legs still tangled in his sleeping bag, as they continued down, down, down. The magma swirling against the sphere became a yellow brighter than gold. The Greys talked among themselves. The color of their sun-sky continued to lighten. Time passed.

They were in a bubble of white light, blasted by it. Johannes could see deep into Zervan's irises, and he saw through the tiny pupils to the pulsing retinas inside. He was pulled to his feet, and almost fell. The guitarp was thrust into his hands. Zervan's white mouth was harsh in his white face.

"We stand now at the center of the Earth. On Icarus your destiny has been calculated, and here we give it to you, as you perform the music only you can perform, only at this time, in this place. Your destiny—"

"I don't want to know!" Johannes cried, but all of the Greys were singing wildly in a language he suddenly understood, and filled with terror as if all his blood had turned to adrenaline, he *knew,* the concert in Brazil, the ceremony in Terminator, Ekern's posturing—

He played to fight them off. The white bubble blazed around him and he struck the strings brutally, yanking strings out of tune, filling the dissonant runs and the fisted chords with all his fear and fury, striking at the singing Greys with bolts of musical lightning in revenge for Karna and for the unwanted knowledge of his fate (and still he knew it), making music appropriate to the place, filling it with all his wild fear and furious anger, with stark   white   power

"*Fly!*" Zervan stepped back, stumbled, fell off the generator, sprawled for a moment at the bottom of the sphere, only a discontinuity away from the white chaos. He scrambled back onto the box moaning at the deadly music Johannes bashed from the strings. "Flee!" he screamed at his Greys, but they were groveling on the deck, heads wrapped in their arms. Face twisted with terror, Zervan pulled himself up and struck the guitarp from Johannes's hands. It clattered to the deck with a final twanging dischord. *"Fly,"* Zervan shrieked, striking the huddled navigators, "Fly, fly, fly!"

The navigators returned to their posts. They began the ascent. The sphere was spun and twirled, washed about in the huge tides of the mantle. The Greys crouched above the navigating screen, talking rapidly in their tongue. Johannes had already forgotten the language (if that had been the one he had understood), but he knew from their voices that they were lost. Of course it would be harder to ascend than descend; once they lost their bearings it would be impossible to find one of the pinpoint cracks leading up to an active volcano. They would bounce against the wall of the Earth's crust until they died, trapped inside the molten Pellucidar.

After a long interval the flow around their bubble became orange again, its glow seeming almost dark after the brilliance of the core. The Greys chattered with excitement. Johannes could feel the pull; they were caught in an upward current. Dark streaks flashed by as they rose, the Earth was pushing them out with incredible velocity—

They shot out into the black night sky, up and out. Blackness, blind blackness, a sudden rush—the sphere crumpled, he was falling through air, over the edge of the world he could see the dawn approaching—falling, falling—he had a parachute, he was falling alone through the cool air of the predawn sky, hung under a white parachute, and below him was the coastline, the beach he had left, a pinpoint of fire.

And when he awoke from the dream (sand in his eyes, bitter taste in his mouth, the smell of cold charcoal in his hair, his side stiff and cold, the sleeping bag twisted and wet with sea dew), he got out of the bag and crouched down by their dead fire, knees in his armpits. His face hurt, his throat squeezed shut, tears ran down his cheeks. The sun was not yet up, but the immense vault of the sky was lit. There was a chill onshore breeze, and small waves swept in at a sharp angle to the beach, breaking swiftly across it. Shivering, Johannes snapped twigs for a fire and stared out at the broad ocean. He knew the dream had been more than a dream. And he knew all his future: he remembered it just like his past, rolling out before him like a tapestry in a spiral gallery, on and on and on to its end in the sun.

♪

"a world lost, a world unsuspected"

Dent Ios arrived in Nueva Brasilia after nearly a full day of traveling, with only an hour to spare before the concert's beginning. During the entire flight from Stuttgart, across Europe, the Mediterranean, Africa, the Atlantic, and the Amazon basin, he had been desperately afraid that he would be late, as he had been on Pluto; between that fear and increasing motion sickness it had been a miserable trip. But the flight was on time and from the airport to the the city center was a quick trip by taxi. Once there he had no trouble finding the amphitheater to get a ticket to the concert from Marie-Jeanne. He was set. And in his luggage were the plans for a second Holywelkin Orchestra, commissioned by the Institute. Ekern's doing. So as Dent walked out into the great complex of central plazas he was tired but triumphant—and a little frightened. His body still vibrated from the long jet journey, and everything looked wrong. The proportions of the city were wrong. The buildings were done in an ugly imitation Martian style, white marble towers that were much too tall, separated by plazas of white marble that were much too wide. Ugly city of the bureaucrat aristocracy. Banks of lights had been placed on top of some buildings, and in big rows against the bases of others, and now they snapped on

one by one. The white slabs of the buildings were perfect
mirrors for spectralite and polychrome, and as Dent watched
a broken Cubist city of light sprang up around him, assault-
ing his jangled nerves and his precarious sense of balance, so
that he went into the nearest floor level bar and fought
through the crowd to order a bulb of some calming drug. The
bartender had not heard of any of the drugs Dent suggested,
and he had to describe the effect he wanted, all over the loud
clamor of the excited Terran customers, who were raucously
preparing for the concert. He went back outside, closed his
eyes so that only the Infra lights fenced in his sight, and
sniffed deeply as he pushed the bulb up one nostril. The
plazas pulsed with radiant color, everything was badly dis-
torted; Dent hated it. Between the disorientation and the
heavy gravity he could barely walk. Something wrong with
this dead city, he thought. Trees look like shrubs, the people
like ants . . . who built this place, and for whom?

He negotiated the crowd as best he could and relocated the
concert site; there was a bowl the volume of a very large
building, hollowed out of one of the central plazas. Throngs
of people were descending into this bowl, to sit on curving
benches. Some sort of giant imitation Greek amphitheater,
Dent thought, lit by altered light of all description, so that his
perspective bounced with every blink and sometimes it even
seemed the bowl was a mound that was somehow (violet,
green, pink) still below him. There was time still and he
wandered away again, feeling sick. Perhaps the bartender had
misunderstood . . . in fact it was obvious he had—some sort
of hallucinogen or . . . Terrans swept by him as if in the grip
of invisible tides, laughing, dressed in single-piece suits of
ersatz silk (or perhaps it was real), suits that were belted
anywhere from armpit to thigh, with flaring puffs of silk at
ankle and wrist. Their hair was in every case short and
glossy, every face was carefully made up with cosmetics—
mannequins, slightly too small! Dent gawked like a fool at all
the painted laughing faces. There was a speaker; they were

. . . yes, distributed around the outside perimeter of the big bowl, and then elsewhere in the plaza. The slab towers were sure to echo badly. The effect would be somewhat like that on Olympus Mons—but no. Inversion of that soundscape, with the sunken bowl in the middle. They'd never get that acoustic configuration again. But the speakers would be surrounding them; that was something. Still, a concert depended so much on its setting. And Olympus Mons . . . they wouldn't see anything like it again. Terrans thronging, Dent had to dodge one merry group, throng throng, damned throngers. "All you governors of Earth, damn throngers," he muttered. "In this Age, to think there's an aristocracy still . . ." It disgusted him. It was like static electricity in the air, the careless disdain these rulers of Earth had for the concert, and suddenly all the fear of Earth—yes, fear!—that everyone on the tour had felt, washed through Dent at last; it was such a huge place, and so *old*—its sheer precedence was overwhelming. Perhaps if he were to sit down—feel better. Into the bowl. He sat in one of the upper tiers. An usher came and ushered him to his correct seat (trouble finding his ticket), still in the upper tier but on the other side. He sat with relief.

In the bottom of the bowl was a holo image of the Orchestra, beams of light converging from the surrounding towers to form it. There stood Margaret near it, her hair blue-black like a raven's wing. The floor of the bowl slid away—holo Orchestra floating on air—and then the real Orchestra slid up into its image. Delighted applause. The bowl was only half filled at the most. Apparently the rest would listen from their thronging on the plazas. Speakers were there. . . . The music began, familiar quick clicking weave, the first loose ends of the grand tapestry. The talking continued, all around him. Dent groaned; wouldn't they listen? "*Shhhhh!*" Chatter, chatter. Too much of that sniff. Dent pulled the bulb from his coat pocket, examined it, dropped it on the floor. It rolled down to the next tier and someone there gave it back to him. Listen! But he didn't say anything to them. He was afraid of them.

The music was so slow. Here, for this audience, it was too slow. And the different strains, coming from every part of the plaza—bouncing around off the towers—so that when the moment came and each of the speakers played the entire Orchestra, it was too dense. Cacophony. And at the same time diffuse, diaphanous—millions of gossamer strands, a sound like cobwebs on your face. Overwhelmed by the response of the Terrans around him—sharing it—Dent thought, Get to the good part! The good part at the end! People were talking. The crew was sitting down at the bowl's bottom, tiny crouched figures looking around them, confused, apprehensive, frightened. Like Dent their response to the music had been appropriated by the Terrans'. "Louder," Dent mumbled. All this talk around him. Although the music did seem rather . . . jumbled. Find the pulse of it, the *pulse*. Now each speaker voiced a hundred Orchestras, in the gyre of interlocked melodies, and the pulse caught them all up, so much so that it seemed all possible pitches and timbres were being played at once in rapid runs, and only the rhythm, the dance of it, was within human apprehension. And even then only with a lifetime's music to teach one how to listen; for these throngers, these rulers? Noise. They didn't want to be taught anything. And yet too quiet, volume itself might overwhelm them, what was Johannes thinking?

There—there—the part where it all came together: trumpet shout of triumph, shift of chords announcing the coda, back into time over the thundering at the bass end of hearing, yes! Yes! That got them quiet, damn them, that shut them up and made their hearts quiver and their stupid aristocrat minds wonder what they were witnessing! Yes yes yes! That made them listen!

Over. Over? Yes. Hesitant applause, many voices. Lights broke his sight everywhere, he saw behind him and before him all at once. Streaming up out of the bowl, all the voices, the glossy perfect hair like caps of jewels. Dent stood and climbed out, hunching his shoulders. Chinese lantern world,

"Oh! Sorry! Excuse me!" Illusion towers like lightning bolts, people staring at him. Into a bar. "I need a *clarifier*," to the bartender. "I am *too shattered*, I need something to clear my head, a laser or the like. Do you understand?" The bartender understood. "Try this," she said with a smile. "Anaconda." Dent paid for the bulb, took it, sniffed hard. Both nostrils. Immediately his brain froze. He sniffed some more. Much better vision. Back outside. Lifeless revelry; it shocked him to see all the mannequins jerking about and laughing. Crushed by the burden of the past, so that there was no strategy by which a culture could become original, have worth: these pathetic governors had no culture but the sterile creation of images, juxtaposed together without sense, without history. And yet this was the Earth! The real world! The terras were so much dust, no more than projects, little experiments in space. If an artist from Pluto failed to move the culture of Earth, who was out of the center? Dent grimaced. Johannes had hit Earth as fast as a free glint, but with as much effect: fly right through. Never even noticed. And so the Earth—humanity's home—dead. Laughing mannequins. History ended.

New clarity of vision. Immense clarity. Across the bowl, Margaret's face over a circle of Terrans, light years away. Dent strolled over to see what was happening. He stood at the outer edge of the group. Cultural Under Undersecretary, et cetera. Many congratulations, coming from right and left. There was Ekern with his smarmy self-satisfied expression, standing right by the Under. Dent circled the group and approached Margaret. "Where's Johannes?"

"I don't know." Margaret was furious. She knew what had happened.

Ekern heard them. "But this party is for him," he said, smiling. Redbeard . . . the boss of his foe Red Whiskers, certainly. The red whiskers a sign of it.

And that thought sobered Dent like nothing else could have. He took a deep, deep breath. "We should have him brought to us," Ekern was saying. Dent stared at him, looked away. *I've got you,* he thought, I know your plot. He had to get away; Ekern would notice there was something wrong with him. " . . . Has asked us to do six more concerts in the continental capitals. We can happily comply with his request, can't we Ms. Nevis?''

"Johannes will decide that.''

Dent turned, pushed his way through the growing crowd. Idiot faces. "Excuse me, God damn it.'' The expression on her face: whew! Enough to kill them all.

Over there—"Marie-Jeanne!''

"Hello, Dent.''

"You know—do you know where Johannes is?''

"Uh—he's still in the Orchestra, Karna said.''

"But it . . .'' Falling motion with hand.

"Yeah.''

"How do I get to where it is?''

"At the bottom of the amphitheater there are stairs leading below.''

"Thanks.'' All right, remember that. Back into the bowl, down to the bottom. Huge bowl, hundreds of tiers. At the bottom, a sort of stage trap door, stairs leading down. Down into gloom. Quiet, dark, around a corner. Afterimages bounced in Dent's sight over the dimness. It was dark like a cave.

Ahead of him stood the Orchestra. A wedge of light from a hallway off to the side fell on it. Some streaks, rich brown wood of the double basses, gold gleam of the French horn bells. Dark. Little night light at the heart of it. Stop. Dent stared sadly, swallowed hard. "No defeat is made up entirely of defeat,'' he whispered, but couldn't remember the rest of it. What could he say? Be quiet, don't intrude. (Between us all, that discontinuity.) Little night light on the solitary. Lit the nest in the tree in the cave in the side of the world. . . . A plucked string sounded clearly. A swirl of mercury dipped down, up. Down, up. Breath through a flute.

Dent turned and walked quickly away, back toward the surface.

Chapter Nine

‖: MERCURY :‖ AND PROMETHEUS

onward

Margaret endured the rest of their stay on Earth with a bad patience. When Johannes asked her to arrange for their early departure she was happy to oblige, and she got a particular enjoyment out of telling the U.N. Cultural Affairs people that their plans were cancelled. Once into space and well on their way to Mercury, she called Karna and Yananda and Dent aside and led them down a few floors of the *Orion*, to an empty conference room. *Orion* was only half full now, so that empty rooms were easy to find; and seated before a window facing aft, they could see that only a few ships followed them. For many, the Grand Tour had ended on Earth.

But not for them. Dent spread out the collection of documents he had stolen in Germany. Karna and Yananda had of course heard of them from Dent already, many times. "The infamous plans," Yananda muttered, fingering through them and drawing out a diagram with more print than most. "Dimensions. Is the Orchestra that big? I suppose so."

"Listen," Dent said, after they had perused the documents for some time. "Margaret tells me that in Lowell, right after the first concert, Ekern came down to crew quarters and took Johannes away for a talk. Johannes never told you what they said, but afterwards he was very distracted.

"Now I was attacked by a man on Lowell, who was also the man who attacked Johannes on Titania. The same man was seen when I trailed our so-called Grey informant Charles. And now I find him carrying these plans for another Holywelkin Orchestra, commissioned by the Institute—which means Ekern. Only Ekern would have the power to do something like this without all the members of the board of directors knowing.

"Now—wait, Karna, I'm not done yet—Anton told Johannes about the so-called Greys you saw on Grimaldi. Those Greys led Johannes to the Fairfax House on Iapetus, and from there he went to the Holywelkin museum, and then he wanted to go out to Icarus. So the source of that strand was Anton, who was working for someone. And Anton, like all the rest of you, was hired for his job by Ekern! Both strands lead back to Ekern. The Greys appear not to have *any* direct involvement."

"No," Karna objected. "I think we met true Greys on Icarus. Nothing else explains what happened while I was there. Nothing."

Dent frowned. "Anything that happens can be explained in more than one way. And I think it's clear that Ekern is behind all the interference on this tour. He has some plot to ruin Johannes, and maybe the Orchestra too, and then this second one will be ready when it has to be."

Margaret nodded. "Dent makes a good case." She saw the blush of pleasure on his cheeks, and grimaced. "It may not explain Icarus, but it makes it pretty clear that Ekern is behind a lot of this. And so we have to act."

"But how?" Karna said.

"Well," Margaret said slowly, acknowledging the difficulties. "We should start tracking Ekern. His ship *The Duke of Vienna* is somewhere in that pack." She waved out at the reduced tail of their *Orion* comet. "He'll be on Mercury with us. One of our people should follow him always. This will probably lead us to the others we should follow—Dent's nemesis, and anyone else he meets privately. We follow those too. Meanwhile Marie-Jeanne will keep the bodyguard on Johannes at full alert. Close physical protection at all times, no matter what he says."

"What he says . . ." said Dent.

"I know. We'll have to talk with him. If we can convince him that Ekern is behind these events . . . it may change everything." Margaret hesitated. "Dent, you and I will talk to him."

"If we can."

"You and I! And other than that—" She let out a long sigh, suddenly tired. "We have to *act*. Now that we know what's going on—"

"Maybe," said Karna heavily.

"We have to act."

♪

the anomaly

Dear Reader, Newton's inverse square law of gravitation—

$$F = -G \frac{Mm}{r^2} \hat{r}$$

where M is the mass of the central body, G is the universal constant of gravitation, and F is the gravitational force on the body of mass *m* at a distance *r* from the central body, and the unit vector *r̂* moves away from the central body, so that the negative sign indicates that the gravitational force attracts *to* the central body—is a marvel of physics, a law of tremendous power and elegance. Taking into account the fact that all the bodies in the solar system attract all the others (so that the total force on any planet is $F = S + P$, where *S* is the attraction of the sun and *P* is the perturbing force of the other bodies), the elliptical orbits of all the planets can be calculated very precisely. All of the planets, that is, except for Mercury. As Le Verrier showed in 1859, Mercury's perihelion has an anomalous advance; the gravitational perturbation of the other planets accounted for part of the advance, but Le Verrier's work made it clear that Mercury's perihelion advanced forty-four seconds of arc per century faster than could be accounted for by the inverse square law of gravitation. And this was a serious discrepancy—a true anomaly. Various explanations were made, according to different strategies. Some ignored the anomaly. Others proposed that there were bodies perturbing Mercury's orbit that were not known; thus the proposal of the existence of the planet Vulcan, orbiting too close to the sun to be seen, and later (as Vulcan could not be found), rings of coronal dust, or asteroids. Others proposed subtle changes in the inverse square law, adding factors to the equations that would account for the anomalous advance. None of these changes in the law were satisfactory.

None, that is, until Albert Einstein revealed his theory of general relativity in four lectures in November of 1915. One of the four lectures was devoted to the Mercury anomaly; as Einstein explained, Mercury's orbit had an anomaly because there was no such thing as absolute Newtonian space. Laws of physics are dependent upon our position in space and time—and Mercury's perihelion advanced more quickly than it should because Mercury, being so close to the great gravitational mass of the sun, *moved in spacetime that was sharply curved by that gravity.*

So, as the Grand Tour of Holywelkin's Orchestra rocketed down the gravity well through the new asteroid belt to Mercury, they dove over the steeper part of the well's final curve, where spacetime was perceptibly, measurably different from the spacetime inhabited by those further away from the sun. And in this different curvature of the fabric of the real they found that the anomaly was everywhere.

♪

exclusion

So Dent and Margaret went to Johannes to talk to him. They found him in the Orchestra, sleeping on the floor of the control booth. Margaret clicked her tongue off the roof of her mouth. "For hours and hours he sat, and never hit a single key."

"Only when he's asleep," Dent said, not understanding her comment. "When he's awake, he's playing." He leaned over, shook Johannes gently by the shoulder. The man awoke with a start, a groan, a fearful blind stare around him—

"Johannes," Dent said. "It's just us. Margaret and Dent. We thought you'd need some food."

Johannes nodded, sat up stiffly. "We will go to the commons together," he said, and giggled.

Dent looked to Margaret, who was scowling. "Wake up, Johannes," she said impatiently. "You need food." She took him under the arms and pulled him to his feet. They ducked down the glass steps and out of the Orchestra.

In the commons Johannes would eat only apples. Afterwards Dent undertook to speak with him.

"We know who has mounted this assault on you during the course of the tour."

"Do you?" Johannes said, with an ironic smile. His artificial eyes seemed never to focus on either one of them; it made Dent nervous to try to meet his gaze.

"It's been Ernst Ekern," Dent said. "We are certain of it. Even your encounters with the Greys have been staged by Ekern."

Johannes stared through him, then shook his head. "You don't understand. I have had encounters with the Greys that no man could stage."

"But we have the evidence," Dent insisted, pulling out the notes he had made for their talk, and the reproductions of the plans he had stolen.

"It doesn't matter," Johannes said. "What I have seen could only have come from . . . the Greys."

"Nonsense!" Margaret said bitterly. "You're just easily impressed."

Johannes stared at her, looking surprised at her anger.

"*You* went and talked with Ekern that night after the first concert," Margaret went on. "You know what he said there, how that fits into the rest of this. We don't. And still we can see his hand everywhere in this thing, now. He arranged for the attack on you in Titania, and the meeting you had with his own fake Greys on Grimaldi. . . ." She recited the sequence of events that Dent had so recently reconstructed in an emphatic voice that Johannes couldn't ignore. Dent was certain that her anger would break the wall of indifference Johannes had built around himself; but when she was done, he just shrugged.

"No matter what Ekern may have done, it has nothing to do with what has happened to me," he said. "It's impossible, don't you see? I know it because of . . . what I know. And because of the music. Ekern is too small, too ignorant—"

"But look what he's doing!" Dent exclaimed, desperation shifting to anger. "Look—" He shoved the diagrams for the Orchestra onto Johannes's plate. "*He's having another Orchestra built.* He plans to destroy you and the real Orchestra, don't you see? Everything you have learned has come from him. Even the parts that you think transcend him, he set the conditions for . . . and after that, they came from you yourself.''

Johannes shook his head. "Not from me, I tell you.'' But his eyes stayed on the diagrams, and he picked one up. Dent glanced at Margaret while he inspected it; she was staring at him furiously, mouth twisted into a scowl.

"Do you see?'' she asked him when he put the blueprint down. "Do you see the shape of his plan? He's going to have another Orchestra ready when you're done!''

"Yes," Johannes said blankly. He was staring through them, black eyes focused for infinite distance. For a long time he just sat there and stared. Then he said, "It's rather comforting, isn't it.''

"Oh for God's sake," Margaret snapped.

"Don't you be self-righteous with me," Johannes said. He pointed a shaking finger at her: "You were on Icarus—you know just as well as I do that Ekern had no part of what happened there. To pretend that you do believe that is just an attempt to escape the truth. *But I can't escape.*''

"Or you won't," Margaret said weakly.

"Anything that can be conceived can be executed," Dent repeated. "It only takes the right drugs, the right sensorium—''

Johannes just shook his head, still pointing at Margaret. "Where did the music come from? No. You know more than you pretend, Margaret Nevis. You're just too frightened to admit it.''

"I'm frightened of an attempt on your life," Margaret said viciously, but her face was pale.

"Look," Dent said, trying to calm them down, "let's talk about the music for a while, Johannes. Tell me again how it connects to Holywelkin's work, and . . . and what happened to it on Earth.''

And so Johannes spoke—but the sounds that came from his mouth were nonsense tones, a fluid quick babbling. He looked right at Dent as if Dent were supposed to understand, and sang nonsense. "O lee ba doo eeen a free la la—" Dent swallowed, his stomach knotted with fear at the sight; he put a hand across the table and it was taken up in Margaret's, squeezed.

"Glossolalia again," Margaret said.

Johannes babbled on, oblivious to her commentary. Eyes bright as a bird's he looked to Dent as if for an answer, head tilted; Dent choked down a cry, stood. Margaret stood as well, and circled the table to put a hand gently over Johannes's mouth. "Let's go back upstairs," she said wearily.

They took him back upstairs to their floor, and released him in his room. He sang on. Dent watched Margaret's face twist into a scowl so fierce he thought she might hit something, or start to cry. He didn't know what to say. "It must be part of his music."

"Damn his music," Margaret said.

"I doubt he can help himself at this point. I think he's just trying to speak to us, and it comes out this way."

Margaret shook her head. "I hope he comes out of it. He's got to function on Mercury."

But he didn't come out of it. He wandered the halls between the Orchestra's room and his own, singing wordlessly at the crew in a language of vowels, or sometimes shouting abuse at them, but in a harsh melody that strained the edges of his tenor range. Naturally this upset everyone, and even when Johannes was sequestered in the Orchestra, the rest of them holed up in their rooms, as nervous as the subjects of a mad king. Dent felt it at every meal, in every concert and conversation; the tour had been going on for months, under difficult circumstances. People were at the ends of their tethers, faces pale, eyes ringed with dark exhausted skin, voices tired or vibrating with nervous tension. Then one day Johannes seemed to come out of it; he spent a morning in the dining commons chatting with the lighting crew, and across the room Dent watched them pretend that all was as it always had been. But as he left the commons Delia crossed paths with him in the doorway, and he said hello: "Johannes," she exclaimed, "you're feeling better!" And he struck her across the mouth, shoved her into the wall, shouted incoherent roars, banged her against the wall until the others dragged him off. Karna had to protect him from attack by his own crew. He spoke only in his private language, and no one understood him. Dent held one of his arms as they walked him down to the Orchestra. Dent was shaking with distress at his friend's behavior, and desperately he tried singing the melody that had poked out of the *Ten Forms* on Mars, the melody so close to the one he had loved in his youth. Johannes stared at him with a lunatic gaze, and laughed. Even his laugh seemed a wild descant to some wild song. Against his own will (for he had been determined to continue until Johannes acknowledged him in words), Dent stopped. And they let him duck up into the Orchestra, into his cave. Dent dragged back to their floor with the rest of the distraught crew, feeling depressed and angry. I went to great lengths to get you those plans! he wanted to say. I actually did something! But it would have been talking to an empty house.

One evening, while returning from his solitary supper, Dent got into the elevator and found Johannes already in it. He nodded.

"How are you, Dent?"

He was careful not to make Delia's mistake. "I'm fine, thank you. Listen, I flew from Cyprus to Munich to look for something at the Telemann Works. I chased a man who once beat me on Lowell, and sedated him with a dartgun, and took his briefcase from him. He was working for Ekern, apparently. And he had commissioned the Telemann Works to construct a whole new Orchestra."

"I doubt it can be done," Johannes said calmly. "Holywelkin built much of it by hand."

"He left plans, though. And my real point is, Ekern *is* plotting against you! I went and found proof!"

The elevator door opened and Johannes held his hand over
the light to keep it open. "So you ventured out and found
these plans, and now you think you know the truth. But that
isn't necessarily so, Dent. Think about it. Forget your pride
in your accomplishment, and think about it clearly."

"But I have!" Dent said. "And I think if you would tell
me all that you know or think you know, I could help!"

Johannes shook his head, and led Dent out of the elevator.
"That's because you don't know. Come on, Dent. Leave me
be for a time. I want to rest from all this—even from your
help."

In the tone of his voice, in its music, Dent recognized a
mood he had often felt, and he had to acknowledge it. They
walked down the hallway in silence, side by side. As they
passed the "Bull Room," as it was now called, they heard
two voices humming in harmony. They stopped, looked in
the door. A circle of people, seated around a single candle.
The voices were ending a bridge passage, shifting back to a
major key as they returned to a theme; it was "Greensleeves,"
played on a single recorder. Dent located the player, Marie-
Jeanne, sitting with her back to them. Karna sat beside her,
with a guitar bumping her shoulder; then there was Delia,
with another recorder, Sara with a flute, Sean with a guitar,
Nikita with a fat bass recorder. Margaret was sitting on the
far side of the circle, holding a big four-stringed guitar.
Marie-Jeanne played. She had a clear tone. Dent fell under
the spell of the sturdy, sweet old melody, a tune continuously
popular for over sixteen centuries. Something in it made him
smile; his family had sung it for a winter's song, when he
was a child. Johannes nudged him with an elbow and they
stepped over and sat behind the circle.

"Greensleeves." They played it as a sort of canon, taking
turns with the melody, wandering away from it into Renaissance interludes, coming back to it at different tempos, different keys and moods, but always back to the simple melody
at its center, again and again, until Dent was in a sort of

trance. Someone in the candlelight handed back a guitar to him, and he played the tune in a duet with Delia, strumming the chords that the others hummed as accompaniment. When it was Johannes's turn, he took the recorder from Marie-Jeanne and played it with utter clarity, avoiding embellishment of any kind, but expressing the lifts and drops with a cleanness and accuracy of pitch that was like a perfect grace. Dent played the accompanying chords with all the sweetness he was capable of, trying to *speak* to Johannes with every chord, to tell him that *this* was what music was, and *this,* and *this*—just this perfection of melody, harmony, volume and timbre—not any complex metaphysic, but just this elegant power, this power that was as much power as humans should ever want or need. But Johannes knew, surely; his playing showed that he knew, Dent thought, there was in it a very ordinary, reedy sanity . . . or so it seemed. Margaret must have felt something similar—something—well, that was the thing about music—it spoke so powerfully, but in a language that could not be translated—so that Dent knew what she felt most exactly, but could only sing to himself the emotion. She wanted Johannes to know it too, Dent saw; she was speaking in music just as he had so often recently, and speaking directly to him. And Johannes knew it, too. She sang the melody all the way through, with no words, only vowel tones; and every lilt she put in the old tune left its mark on Johannes's open face. She had a contralto voice, slightly husky, slightly Russian even in vowels. The second time around she sang the final verse with the ancient words:

> "Thou couldst desire no earthly thing,
> But still thou hadst it readily;
> Thy music still to play and sing,
> And yet thou wouldst not love me.
> Greensleeves was all my joy,
> Greensleeves was my delight;
> Greensleeves was my heart's one song,
> Yet I sing all alone of my Greensleeves."

Then the others joined in and sang along, mixing verses and languages, fitting together the harmonies that had stood at the heart of music for so many years. And Johannes sang with them. After that each round had fewer players; and finally Marie-Jeanne was left to play the last time alone, a single recorder piping in a darkened room, rustling the candle flame at the top of its paraffin spire. When she finished they sat together silently for a long time.

♪

terminator

Fall with the Grand Tour down the gravity well to swift Mercury. There it floats, big in the windows, the sunward crescent brilliant as molten glass, the night side just a rust shadow against the vacuum. In the shuttle craft, before landing at a spaceport on the nightside, look out the window and see on the planet's surface a tiny band of silver wires extending out over each horizon. Know, Reader, that this band circumnavigates the planet, like a narrow wedding ring tossed over the northern hemisphere, defining a latitude. And in the dawn terminator, where white and black clash in unrelieved contrasts, where the mounds, crater rims and escarpments stand ablaze under the white corona of the rising sun, while the valleys and shaded slopes are as black as anywhere on nightside—in the dawn terminator a city rolls over the dozen cylinders that form the planet's encompassing band, rolling at the same slow pace as Mercury turning on its axis. The city Terminator is a monument to a technology long since superceded; in that sense it is like the tent city Utopia, Mars, or the sublunar city of Tsiolkovsky, or certain ancient cities of Earth, such as Dubrovnik or Macchu Pichu. In the Twenty-second century the city provided the power for much of the rest of civilization. Exposure to the sun caused an expansion in the alloy cylinders that not only drove the city forward onto the nightside; resistance to this pressure could be converted to energy and microwaved across space to Mars, Earth and Luna, and the lost one. In the Holywelkin Age this energy was no longer needed, and most of the generators were shut down. But the city rolled on, moving at just under four kilometers every hour, circling the planet once every eighty-eight days.

When the Grand Tour landed on the baked plains of the spaceport, the crew saw Terminator loom over the eastern horizon like a big green lamp, or a Faberge egg lit from within. The sunward side of the city was a tall curving shield, called the Dawn Wall; extending away from the Dawn Wall was a long clear oval dome, covering the rest of the city. Under the clear dome they could make out red tile roofs, and the tops of hundreds of trees. They were guided into a small car that drove them over the flat plains to the city's tracks, which they now saw were giant silver cylinders, standing ten meters above the surface on short thick silvery pylons. The car drove into a small station placed permanently on the edge of the outside cylinder; they were ushered upstairs to a broad platform with one flat wall, and when the city strolled by, the wall slid back. They stepped over the juncture of the two floors, and stood in Terminator.

♪

into the maze

Ernst Ekern was also in Terminator, pacing through the narrow streets and staircase alleyways that connected the terraces of the interior slope of the Dawn Wall. Diana had rented one of the villas on this slope for the order, but at this point Ekern could scarcely stand the company of his fellows. He had arrived on the shuttle from *The Duke of Vienna* just hours before the tour crew, and after locating the order's villa and greeting the other playwrights, he had made his excuses and ventured into the streets alone. First he hiked up to the highest terrace, just under the Great Gates of the city, which were set in the top of the Dawn Wall to let shafts of sunlight in on ceremonial occasions. On this highest terrace, Ekern had been told, the Orchestra would be placed during the concert. He looked across the tile rooftops of the city and tried to imagine performing for such an audience. A whole city . . . impossible. He descended the narrow stairs of an alleyway again. Troops of lithe little monkeys swung from tree to tree. The stone steps of the staircases bowed in their middles, where centuries of feet had worn them down. The marble streets were bowed in the same way. Every villa on the slope of the Dawn Wall had an extensive, overgrown garden, with huge ancient trees spilling onto each other: magnolias, oaks, cypresses, willows, eucalyptus, pine, juniper. . . . The city was a rolling garden, with almost half of it terraced up against the Dawn Wall, so that many of the street corners and plazas had vistas across a variety of tree greens, and the oranges and tans of roof tile. Colorful old town.

But Ekern was not pleased. Terminator was a city full of Greys. He regarded them with distrust. There were too many Greys here. Every third or fourth person he passed was dressed in the light grey pants and tunic, hair all cropped, eyes attentive but at the same time vacant. He would have to approach some of them, find the Lion of Mercury, ask questions, even favors. It would be a test. "What *are* you," he muttered as he passed a knot of them. "Insects you are, with some insect knowledge to scare the weak-minded."

Still they knew something. And it was not the knowledge he had put in their mouths (or so he hoped); he had used them as an empty sign, but they signified something of their own as well. And his design . . . under the vacant stares of individual Greys he felt his design waver unsteadily, threaten to fly apart in his hands. He had written the lost journal of Holywelkin for Wright to find—written it in a frenzy of invention and pleasure, calculating the effect on the musician and on him alone. All well and good; he considered it his masterpiece. But now he recalled the bizarre dreams that had haunted him during the composition of the journal: dreams of walking under a sky of fire, of confrontations that smelled of danger, with strangers who frightened him though he never knew why, in terse tense conversations that he could never quite remember. Had he really written the journal, or had he been merely the conduit? Had the dreams dictated the tale? Had Holywelkin actually visited Icarus, and done all that Ekern wrote down, so that Ekern had "invented" the truth? Or had someone tampered with his dreams, as he had tampered with Wright's? Dream suggestion was a chancy business, each dream was a wild steeplechase over the ground of the stimulus; but it could be done. Ekern had done it himself. And he did not doubt that someone could do it to him; someone like Atargatis, say. Or, more likely, the Greys themselves. The Greys, working in a circular fashion, rendering metadrama out of the metadramatists, exerting the highest control possible. . . .

He nearly collided with someone standing still in the street. A Grey, looking up at him curiously. "I—" But he could not speak to the man. The possibility that he was part of some larger drama. . . . *We are all players in each other's metadramas.* Who had said that? He stumbled away, found a plaza, sat on the fountain's rim at its center. His pulse was fast, his skin hot; he felt a bit feverish. The spray from the fountain was cooling. "A clamp on this hysteria," he said between his teeth. "We must act!"

Dogs frolicked in the basin of the fountain. In the corner of his eye—he turned to look—Jan Atargatis, in the company of a Grey. They had seen him. He stood, waved. They approached. Atargatis smiled his quick bright smile. Ekern nodded stiffly at them, squashing all his fears.

"A beautiful city for the worship of the sun, is it not?" Atargatis said in greeting.

Ekern agreed, saw his opening. "Still, not as appropriate as one of the power stations. On those the sun worshipper has ascended to the highest altar."

"It's true!" Atargatis cried. "Are you planning a visit, Ernst?"

"I would like very much to visit," Ekern said solemnly. He made a tiny bow before the Grey, who wore a floppy red cap. "Have I the honor of addressing the Lion of Mercury?"

The Grey nodded. "Welcome to Terminator, Master Ekern."

"Thank you. I want . . . I want to take the Grand Tour to one of the power stations."

"You anticipate our wishes," the Grey said quietly.

Atargatis smiled. "Which one, Ernst? Vulcan, Apollo, Hyperion, Prometheus?"

The Lion of Mercury said, "He will come to Prometheus."

"Prometheus will do very well," Ekern said stiffly, and held fast to his calmness until the laconic Grey left.

With an ironic smile Atargatis said, "Your apprentices are dying off on you like flies in this play, aren't they?"

"What do you mean?"

"Don't you know? Your apprentice Bloomsman, the one who looked like Death—he was found murdered in Munich."

"Ah." What to say, what to say? "Atargatis, you must help me in this drama."

"It does not appear that you need my help," Atargatis said, smiling still. "Or at least, not from this point on. I have convinced the Lions here to let the tour onto Prometheus. You should be pleased—the Greys have not let others onto one of the stations in as long as I can remember." And with a playful slap to the arm he was gone, and Ekern was free again. He sat back down on the fountain's edge, and plunged his hands into the water, trembling slightly. Who were these

Greys? And how far up in their councils did Atargatis really move? And what did they know, thus to control access to the power stations? And *what was happening to his play?* Who controlled it, if he did not?

♪

johannes on mercury

Johannes follows a party of city officials up the stairways that pass for streets under the Great Gates of Terminator, onto the narrow highest terrace of the city. The officials turn left, his body turns left, he follows. The concert is to take place later that day. The officials explain that this is Solday, a holiday in Terminator when the Great Gates are for a time opened. "I see," Johannes hears himself say. They lead him into a long chamber below the Great Gates; Margaret and Karna and Marie-Jeanne and Delia accompany him. The chamber is walled on the sunward side with a black glass, a filter. Off across the planet's black surface the sun is eternally rising. Only the corona is visible, thin pared crescent extending more than half the horizon from north to south. It hurts Johannes to look at it; the room feels hot. Even through the black glass the glare is too intense, it is a rainbow of white fire, and he turns and leaves. Outside on the terrace there are flowerbeds and hanging vines spilling over the wall to the terrace below. Margaret and Karna approach and Margaret says something to him. He hears himself reply but does not understand what he says. Margaret appears satisfied. The concert is to begin soon and he hears the music of it, sounding clear as a fresh memory. Some changes to be made. He walks to the terrace's edge and looks out over the city. Rooftops of dull brown, blue trees everywhere. Birds flitting from tree to tree. Out beyond the city's glassy dome with its faint curved reflection of the town, the long silvery tracks extend off across the black waste, faintly lit by the city itself. Destiny's track made visible at last. There the Orchestra stands, on a promontory of the highest terrace, out over the city, visible everywhere. The sight of it fills his head with the music to be played and he follows himself to it. Exchanges with the crew mean nothing to him now, and helplessly he must nod at Margaret and climb into his home. How many times he has climbed up these glass steps, taken the turn to the right around the godzilla, back left and up to the control booth. Home again, home again. Here one might almost feel as if . . . as if. . . . He cannot complete the thought. Electronics board shows the speakers are on and he pulls out some keyboards, makes some preliminary tests for volume and the like. Pianissimo oboe tones, sustained as if to tune the Orchestra, filling the city. The curved oval dome creates a strong resonance without a particular echo; it's an ambient sound with tremendous possibilities. Johannes pulls out the French horn keyboards and plays chords. Dominant, tonic, dominant, minor, seventh, ninth, huge spreads, simple thirds and fifths, dense horn choir chords, fifteen horns droning through the harmonics of history, filling the dome of this egg city . . . but this is just the speaker test. Who knows how long he has been playing. Below him at the sound control board Delia is pointing up at the Great Gates. They open, and two tall, narrow shafts of brilliant light appear, like panels of gold leaf extending through the air just under the dome, hitting the curved surface at the front end of the city and disappearing into the vacuum. The air is filled with a yellow talc that gives the sunbeams a blinding solidity. The crowd below cheers. Johannes peers between instruments at them; streets and parks are filled with faces, each one a little thumbprint of sensibility, of human frailty and misperception. Except that almost half of them appear clothed in grey tunics and pants, and their faces, luminous in the new light, have a serenity that Johannes cannot understand. A sharp shaft of emotion pierces his breast—some great gate has opened—and even from behind himself he can feel it stabbing. Suddenly he knows the time has come to play. He turns down one switch and the Orchestra begins the *Ten Forms of Change*. The glass arms bow away at the violins and cellos, glass fingers depress the valves and fill the stops of the wind instruments, glass feet kick the drums, a whole forest of puppets jerk into action, and below a whole forest of puppets take it all in. Without his "improvisation" the *Ten Forms* is a stately passacaglia, the original theme rendered ever more complex with each repetition; in this weave, under the twin bars of tangible light, the audience appears completely entranced; a model city filled with tiny still figurines. Dead little figurines who for the moment have forgotten their illusions of free will, having given themselves up to the inexorable music. Johannes feels the stabbing again. "Can't I stop this?" he hears himself say, and watches his hands in a sudden flurry pulling out the keyboards, dragging the volume stops out to their maximum (Delia's shocked face turning up from her console), playing them—one, then the next, then the next, carelessly and without thought. What does thought matter when it will all be as it has ever been? But then he makes some mistakes and becomes angry. He laughs anger now. "Why should we have to try at all? Could it be that music is all that remains to us, the only true expression of our free will? And is it this that accounts for music's power, the felt knowledge that speech in this language is the only thing we create freely? So it feels to me now, so it *feels* to me—" playing as hard as he can, ignoring the context of the *Ten Forms*, ripping through it with great shrieks of the godzilla, the artist as anarchist, and yet, and yet . . . it reminds him of something, some music he played a long time ago, in a fever, in a dream . . . he cannot remember. But the feeling tells him he cannot escape, that the illusion of free will exists not just in music but in all human action that works in ignorance.

And he is doomed to know. And that itself is a sort of music; there is a music that says that, too. Johannes sees the arc of his life, Pluto to Mercury, planet by planet, and vacillating between despair and fierce rebellion he finishes the concert, playing that arc out helplessly.

♪

Stepping out of the Orchestra Johannes enters a world of marionettes. Something seems to have slowed the passage of time for them and they stand like blocks, barely moving their eyes to stare at him. Some effect of the music, apparently. He passes among them and Margaret stirs herself, says, "Johannes!" in a strangled voice, follows him. "What was that, Johannes?" He walks on. She stands in front of him; he walks around her. She lets him pass and hurries to Karna, shakes Karna awake, shakes Dent awake. Dent cries, "Johannes! Explain to me! Explain!"

But across the terrace, there at the door to the window room, stands a Grey of considerable importance. These days Johannes can tell entirely by their demeanor. The man wears the greys and the red cap, his hair is brown and clipped short. Johannes follows him into the room and walks to the black glass window so that he can stand with his back to the fine arc of the sunrise. The Grey's eyes in the strong light are a light liquid brown, incredibly vivid and full of life. A world of color in a single iris. Karna and Margaret appear hastily in the doorway, carrying weapons. Johannes waves them back with a sweep of the hand. Tendons there are tired; there must have been some unusual efforts in the concert somewhere. Karna remains in the doorway, watchful as he leans against one wall.

Johannes says, "I know what I will say. I will say, Even if

the universe is ruled by necessity, why should I know the future?''

And the Grey says, "In the vast reach of infinity, every possible combination of being must have been realized not only once, but an infinite number of times. This is the principle of eternal recurrence, which is proven by Holywelkin's work and by all the work we have done since then. Thus the past will be returned to and the future has already been, not only once but infinitely, and in every possible combination of cause and effect. To know this is to know the reality of the universe. Thus this universe in which your art reaches its full potential is played out, over and over. You have always known what you know.''

"And the way that we *feel*?''

"Part of the illusion of time.''

Johannes thinks about this for a while. "So you are not sun worshippers.''

"The sun is powerful.''

"And Holywelkin never went to Icarus.''

"Did you think that he had?''

"Don't you know?''

The Grey shook his head. "Are you omniscient?''

"No,'' Johannes said. "But there are things I know that I shouldn't.''

"I'm not sure that's possible,'' the Grey said.

"So . . . Ekern deceived me.''

The Grey nods.

"But why?''

"Perhaps Ekern suspects what the Greys know. To learn it directly would change the consciousness he values; thus he sends another on the quest for knowledge, and learns indirectly, so that he is still—''

"So that he knows discursively, and not by acquaintance.''

The Grey nods.

Johannes laughs bitterly. "He may be mad, but he is no fool.''

No answer from the Grey. Johannes watches the sunlight flicker on his face: mark of coronal flare, or Mercurial hill. "Come outside," Johannes says, unable to control his despair. Out on the terrace the city is visible, all its citizens now in motion. It looks like chaos, but its ant-people weave a pattern determined eternally: look, that ant has only two streets to choose from, and all its history makes certain it will choose just the one and not the other (it does); it is like its city, rolling over its tracks forever, again and again and again.

"And music?" Johannes asks, curious about this art that has consumed his life.

"Music," the Grey says, "is an expression of the universe, related to ideas as ideas are related to things. And at the same time that it speaks this universality, it is also most distinct and precise in form. In this it resembles the geometry that Holywelkin made such use of. All possible manifestations of human experience may be expressed in music, but always in their form only. You might say that music expresses the soul of experience, not the body. This deep relation that music has to the true nature of things makes it a language capable of the most distinct and accurate description of the universe; and this is why your audiences have reacted to your music as to the truth that they have always known. Though they cannot explain the music, they know that it has revealed to them all the possible events of life in the world, and knowing that, they glimpse the truth of Holywelkin's work, the work upon which all this world rests. This work is the truth that the Greys have always known, and so your music has for us a special interest. We have kept our knowledge from humanity at large, but we have always known that it would come to this knowledge eventually; some of us on Icarus have known that it would come to this knowledge through the ninth Master of Holywelkin's Orchestra."

Johannes sniffs, swallows, sighs. "I did not know what I was doing."

The Grey smiles brightly, quickly. "No. But now you do, and it is fitting that you finish the tour by coming to Prometheus Station and playing for the Greys there."

Johannes shrugs. "That is what will happen?"

"Yes."

♪

So when Johannes returns to the Orchestra and his busy crew, he tells them of the added concert.

Margaret shouts, "We can't go down there!" She is clearly shaken still by the concert just passed. "We can't afford the energy to get back up from those stations!"

"The Greys will transport us, both down and up," Johannes says.

"It's crazy to put ourselves in their power!" Margaret is furious. "I won't do it!"

"We fly to Prometheus!" Johannes says loudly, and looks around at the crew. In the white heat of his anger they quail; none can stand and deny him. Only Margaret, shifting and nervous, dares oppose him at this moment when his power is suddenly unleashed:

"It's crazy. We don't know what they want of you." She flares up: "I'm damned if I'll do it! You can go if you like and I can't stop you, but if you do, I'm finished! I quit!"

"Quit, then," Johannes says, and with a searing glance recaptures the rest of the crew. In this wild surge of his will they cannot disobey him:

"We fly to Prometheus! From Pluto to Prometheus, outermost to innermost, and the tour will be complete." He climbs into the Orchestra unopposed. From the control booth he hears the crew begging Margaret to stay with them. For a long time she will not reply. Then:

"One more," she says grimly. "Then we're done."

The chill runs all through him. Eternal recurrence: but each time she says those words, he will feel that chill.

♪

the irregulars' last hope

Dent had a plan.

"Listen," he said to Karna and Margaret. "We've got to do this. If we don't we'll never know for sure what Ekern is up to, and Johannes will never listen to us."

"I don't think Ekern matters anymore," Karna said gloomily.

"Ekern matters," Margaret said. "He got us started on this road, and he and a small retinue are already on their way to Prometheus."

"And he left his ship in orbit here," Dent said.

"So the Greys took him down?" Karna asked.

"Yes," Dent said. "Apparently they take everyone down; you need special ships to rendezvous with the stations."

"I believe it," Yananda said.

"I don't like them. . . ." Margaret said, voice strained.

"I tell you, it's the Greys," Karna said. "They're behind even what Ekern's done."

"I don't agree," Dent said. "Ekern could have staged every encounter with the Greys that we've had! We don't know anything about the Greys. But Ekern . . ."

"Ekern is part of it," Margaret said. "The Greys may be something else entirely, obscured by what Ekern has done."

"So we do this," Dent said.

"Yes," said Margaret.

So when the tour shuttled back up to *Orion*, and made the transfer to the Greys' little spaceship (it was just big enough to hold the Orchestra in its hold), Karna and Yananda and Dent stayed behind. Dent approached the little man: "Johannes," he said, and looking at the musician's unseeing eyes he cringed. Would Wright understand him at all? "Johannes, we're going to stay on *Orion* while you go to Prometheus Station."

Johannes cocked his head. "You are?"

"Yes." Impulsively Dent leaned over and gave the man a fierce hug. "We can help you best up here."

"I see," Johannes said, voice empty and clear. "Goodbye then." And Dent had to watch speechlessly while he pulled himself away, into the lock and out of sight.

♪

falling

All during the descent to Prometheus Margaret fretted. She interrogated the Grey assigned to take care of them on the small ship. "Where is Ernst Ekern?"

"I am told he is in Prometheus Station already."

"Who allowed him to go there? Who is in control down there?"

"The Lion of Prometheus decides who comes and goes." This said with an ironical twist on the word *decides*.

"Now why should that be?" Margaret demanded. "How did some damned religious *cult* get control of the system's biggest energy station?"

"All the four energy stations have the same capabilities," the Grey said.

"Don't get clever with me. I asked you: how did your cult get control down there?"

"We operate the generator," the man said. "No one else knows how."

Margaret scowled. "I wonder what happened to the normal people who knew how, don't you?"

"They became Grey."

And down they plummetted, until the time came when
Margaret and the rest of the tour crew had to be led to
couches of a peculiar substance, where they lay and gasped
under their own weight—under the force of the acceleration
of the Greys' ship. Struggling for each breath, faces twisted,
they lay pinned to their couches and watched the abstract
patterns on the viewscreen overhead. "How fast?" Delia
cried.

"I don't know," Margaret said. "Ask the guide. He'll
say, as fast as we need to go."

Sean said, "The power stations orbit just above the solar
flare zone. They have to really fly to keep from falling in.
I've heard it's rare. For a ship to dock with them."

"But we're special," Delia said.

Margaret, already scowling under the acceleration, hissed.
Their viewscreen was half filled with green light, half with
black, in a gridwork of faint blue lines. The sun and the
vacuum, two halves of the world. Near the edge of the green
half a bright red dot blinked. Their destination, no doubt,
swimming on the sea of thermonuclear fire. Margaret pulled
herself off her couch, crawled toward their quarters. Passing
the midships storeroom she heard the sound of the Orchestra;
Johannes was still at work on his music, following the creaks
and bings created by the twisting of their acceleration gravity. Margaret shoved the door open and stuck her head in the
room. "Don't you see that you and you only make that
music!" she shouted. "It was clear as can be during the
concert on Terminator!" Now the music had fallen away to
the light rustlings of the mercury drum. Encouraged, Margaret shouted on: "You set up the music for the Orchestra and
maybe you wrote it inevitably, maybe it was the music of the
spheres, but then you *improvised* across that taped music,
damn it, you ripped and tore right across it to affirm just

exactly the free will I've told you about! You're an idiot if you don't see that!''

Faint maunderings of the balloon flute, oscillation of mercury. Gravity's music. No other response. Disgusted, Margaret pulled the door shut and continued crawling on her way. Let him sleepwalk through his dream if he wanted to.

♪

last crossing

Days passed and the acceleration of the ship only increased, until there was no question of leaving the gel couches. Breathing was difficult, faces were contorted like rubber masks. In this ship without windows they could do nothing but squirm and gasp and watch, through squashed corneas, the blurred image of the viewscreen. According to it the universe was a simple duality; half of it was fire, half empty space. They were so close to the sun that no curvature in its representation was evident; they existed between two planes. So far as they could tell by the screen, they were not moving at all—only the steady intense pressure told them of their increasing speed.

"Out there," Margaret said. "The red dot. Getting closer."

And finally the pressure let up. Sean went to the viewscreen's console and learned how to shift the screen to the optical view. Obviously very heavy filters were in use; the roiled dull brown surface of the sun thrust a million twisting arms of flame at them. The line separating the brown sun from black space was a jagged saw of brown flame. And in the center of this muted composition rolled the bright cone of Prometheus Station.

The sunward side of it—the open end of the cone—was a

brazen torus, a wheel rolling loose in a madcap orbit. Sunlight blazed against this torus, and was broken down and transformed to whitelines in it; then the newly created whitelines were aimed at the singularity sphere—the tip of the cone— where they were directed to their ultimate destinations. Thus in appearance the station was a thick wheel, with spidery spokes and a tiny hub where ships arrived and departed; much more prominent than this material hub, however, was the ghost hub pushed out to the side away from the sun, the singularity sphere, which was a bright confluence of white light even through the filters. Connecting the torus to the singularity sphere was a flickering cone of "spokes," made of the shifting gleams of whitelines. Margaret knew from her reading that the singularity sphere was a good distance away from the wheel, and because of the broad shape of the cone of whitelines connecting the torus and the sphere, she could see in a sudden snap of perspective that the torus was immense. And outside the bright tip of the cone, a broad fan of blurred starlight: one quarter of the world's whitelines, each lancing off across the solar system to its end in one whitsun or another. Even Margaret was moved; here rolled the origin of humanity's power, an immense white wheel with its white hub punched out to the side, hurtling in a haze of energy. And the Grand Tour chased it down.

All through the evening their rate of acceleration dropped, and they inched closer to the great wheel at a slower rate. "The way this tour's been going I don't doubt we're caught in Zeno's paradox," Margaret muttered. But very late in the night hours their Grey guide came to their quarters and asked them to move to a small shuttle craft. "Your belongings are over there already." Margaret felt that his calm voice concealed a great deal of smugness, but she only nodded at him and led the rest into the shuttle. There they were strapped to couches, and when all was ready they were flattened back one more time as the shuttle shot across the space between ship and station. Then all gravity disappeared; they floated against their restraints and looked to the door of the shuttle. It opened and yet another Grey entered to greet them. This one was as tall as a Martian, with a scraggly red-gold beard and cropped red-gold hair under the floppy bright red cap that some of the Greys wore. Margaret, Johannes and the rest were freed from their couches, and they pulled themselves into a small transfer chamber. From there they were led into an elevator that descended for a long time. They emerged in a big hallway that curved ever up, in both directions; it was the central passageway of the torus, an empty, flat-bottom white tunnel. By the curve of the floor Margaret got an accurate sense of the size of the station at last; the circumference must have been nearly twenty kilometers.

They were led up the hallway, and passed two groups of Greys walking the other way. The hallway was marked by occasional long black windows that filled the nightside wall and half the rounded ceiling, so that through them they could see the cone of whitelines and the singularity sphere, and overhead, the other side of the torus. Though the sun burned behind the unbroken wall on the other side of the hallway, Margaret felt its glare.

They were led into an interconnecting suite of chambers that was to be their quarters, and allowed to rest. The suite had one small window in the nightside wall-ceiling, and through it Margaret felt the sunlight curving, striking her, filling every corner of every room, hurting her eyes, penetrating every cell of her. She surveyed her crew; their pupils were tiny pinpricks, their faces were suffused by the light, and she could see all the marks of the strain of the last several months, the deltas of wrinkles, the reddened eyes, the pale skin. Only Johannes appeared fresh, his face unlined, his artificial eyes as dilated as ever. Black bottomless eyes, showing nothing, seeing nothing. . . . "Like living in the door of a blast furnace," Margaret snarled, and took the room next to the one Johannes chose. The red-haired Grey who had welcomed them appeared in the door of the suite.

"Master Wright?" he called, and Johannes poked his head out of his doorway. "The Lion says that with your permission he will schedule your concert for—"

"Tomorrow," Johannes said, and disappeared into his room.

The Grey said, "Yes."

Margaret went into her room and shut the door. Dark: but wasn't that light, spilling in from under the doorjambs, from the intersection of wall and wall? She closed her eyes hard and still saw the light streaming in.

♪

the other orchestra

Early on that morrow, Dent, Karna, and Yananda took a small shuttle from *Orion* to one of the space stations that slowly orbit in Mercury's shadow. There Karna had arranged to rent a skeletal little spider rocket. They got into their spacesuits and were led to one of the launching chambers. "All ready?" Karna asked, voice clear and calm in Dent's ear. Dent cleared his throat nervously, said, "Yes." They climbed onto their rocket, a spindly four-legged metal thing that looked to Dent like the bottom section of a music stand. It had no interior; passengers sat in the vacuum at the control panel, and the craft consisted of no more than the main rocket, an array of side jets, the landing legs, and the seats bolted around the control panel. Nervously Dent sat in one of the seats and strapped himself down. "It's awfully small," he said.

"That's why we chose it," Yananda said. He finished strapping down his box of tools.

Karna waved a hand back at the launch center terminal.

The door at the top of their bay opened, and with a bump they were catapulted gently out of the launch center and into space. Stars glared around them in every direction but one, where the black circle of Mercury blocked off the sun. Down at the sunward edge of the planet Terminator was just visible, a speck of greenish light that shone on the fine silver wire of the tracks. "My," Dent said. The big double wheel of the space station gleamed behind them. Karna began to fiddle with the controls, and the rockets vibrated the little skeleton. They spun slowly, stopped spinning, spun the other way. "Good," Karna said.

"You know where *The Duke of Vienna* is?" Yananda asked.

"Hope so." Karna activated the main propulsion rocket and Dent's head was pressed back in the seat. For a moment he saw on Yananda's face the mirthless grin of acceleration. Then they were coasting again, and he could lift his head and look around. There above them arched the orbit line of spaceships, tightly bunched so they could all sail in slow Clarke orbits to stay in Mercury's shadow. "It's near the beginning of the line, almost in the sunlight. . . ." As they approached the line the ships became variegated metallic shapes, pinpointed by the glow from windows and running lights. "That big one is *Le Havre*. *Duke of Vienna* is just two ahead of it." Karna began to work in earnest at the control panel, and their craft swerved neatly into the orbit line ahead of *Le Havre*. The big rockets of the ship before them were dark black holes, like eyes. "That's the *Positron*," Karna said. "Right around it, our ship. We're going to have to hope Ekern's people are keeping a loose watch. The bridge on their ship doesn't have a direct view aft, and we'll approach them from behind keeping ourselves right inside the radar image of the *Positron*. Then we land on the hull. While we're approaching stay quiet."

With a series of spurts from all of their rockets (their ship vibrated like a silent pipe organ, Dent thought), they rounded the *Positron*, passing just a few meters from its hull, and curved in ahead of it. *The Duke of Vienna* was a good distance away, perhaps five kilometers. Karna made a small *tkh* sound between his teeth. Slowly, ever so slowly, they drifted across the vacuum toward their quarry. *The Duke of Vienna* grew bigger, they passed its rocket vents, decelerated to a speed that nearly matched the larger ship's, until they drifted no more than two meters from the big hull. Yananda unstrapped himself, climbed over the side. His boots stuck to the bright surface of *The Duke of Vienna*, and he pulled their craft to it. The four legpads touched and stuck. Karna released himself from his chair, and gestured for Dent to do the same. Other gestures clearly conveyed that Dent was to move very carefully.

There was a lock door several meters along the hull, and Yananda floated there to place what looked like a giant's stethoscope against the hull. Dent climbed down one of their craft's legs to the ship's hull and tested out the grabpads on his feet and forearms; he was barely held to the metal, and so he moved very carefully indeed. Karna slinked over to the lock door, which was recessed by a step into the hull. Yananda pulled away from the stethoscope and gave Karna a go-ahead sign, so Karna lifted a small packed-light jigsaw from Yananda's box of tools, and went to work on the wheel of the lock door's handle. Suddenly Dent became aware of his breathing. It was all he could hear, it seemed to fill all the space around him; when to breathe next? This was when they were most vulnerable, straddling the outside of the ship like this. . . .

Karna turned the handle and then pulled the outer door open. He ducked into the lock, which was large enough to hold all three of them easily. After they had closed the outer door and Yananda had completed his search for alarms, Karna went to work on the inner door. Everything at this door took longer. Finally he looked up at both Yananda and Dent, and nodded. Yananda pulled dartguns from his box and passed them out; he kept two for himself, one in his suit's chest pouch. Karna checked to see that they were ready. Dent nodded, felt the blood hammer through him; the incredible speed of his pulse reminded him of his assault on Red Whiskers in Munich, but he banished the memory to attend to the action at hand. Yananda was twitching from side to side like a cat—

Karna shoved the door open and leaped through the round opening, and Yananda dove in after him. Dent pulled his way through. An amazed young woman stood in the doorway of the room they had entered, staring at them. Both Karna and Yananda had shot her with darts, and she slumped back onto the wall behind her. Dent stared at the two little red darts protruding from her torso, feeling the heat in his suit. He was sweating, his moustache was wet. Imitating the other two, he pushed the button on his arm that caused his faceplate to slide down.

Yananda's face was shiny with sweat. "This was the right lock," he said as he looked around. "The only big storage chamber is just down the hall from here. If Ekern left only a skeleton crew aboard—"

"Let's go," Karna said. He and Yananda slipped out the room's main door and Dent trailed them, pushing off with his toes and grabbing the wall railing for pulls, just as Yananda ahead of him was doing. They flew down one broad hallway until Yananda pulled on Karna's leg. "Around this corner," he mouthed. Karna aimed the gun, yanked himself around the turn in the hall. Dent heard the click of the dartgun; by the time he had pulled himself around the corner the guard before the storage chamber door was stretched out insensible, a dart hanging from the skin of his bare forearm. Yananda took the man's hand and grabbed the forefinger, placed the fingertip on the door's handle. It clicked open and they maneuvered the unconscious body into the room with them.

The room was well lit, and nearly filled by Holywelkin's Orchestra.

Dent stared at the arc of cellos immediately above him, mouth open. A second Orchestra, replica of the unreplicable, standing there like a mirage.

Karna floated around it, examining the room. Yananda took a small camera from one of his suit pockets and began taking pictures. "Room's empty," Karna said. "And no security cameras that I can see." He looked up at the glittering statue—the boxes of the synthesizers, the broken staircase of trombones, the copper burnish of the tympanis suspended far above. "Good copy," he said, at a loss.

"It's exact," Dent said. "Ekern used Holywelkin's blueprints for the thing. So now there are two of them." He saw details he remembered from the original: the hedgelike tangle of flutes, clarinets, and oboes, the funny way the cymbals hung in their glass arms, the collection of boxes and instruments hiding the control booth. "Johannes has got to see this. We've got to send news of this down to Prometheus—"

"We can send these pictures," Yananda said.

"We've got to tell him!" Dent said. "The concert on Prometheus is Ekern's last chance to do something. Something's going to happen down there, oh," his mind raced into a nest of ominous possibilities, "we've got to get word to him *now!*"

"Calm down, Dent," Karna said. "We don't have a radio."

"But this ship does. We could take it over like we did this room." Suddenly he was sure what their course should be. "Come on, they won't be ready for us. We've got to try— Johannes has to see this!"

"We've told him before," Karna said. "You already told him about it—"

"No!" Dent exclaimed, dread filling him. "*We have to show him.*"

Karna glanced over at Yananda, who shrugged. After a moment Karna nodded. "All right. We can try. But we're going to have to hurry, and pay close attention. If those people we knocked out have been found—"

"Let's just hurry," Yananda said tensely.

They left the second Orchestra's chamber and slung themselves down halls and around corners, moving forward in the ship as fast as possible, heedless of meeting crew members. Dent banged into the walls at every turn, he nearly dislocated a shoulder on one, but he hurried on, ignoring the pain. Trailing the other two he passed a door that was opened by a woman who started to speak—he shot her and was gone before she even began to drift back. He felt light-headed, and unnaturally powerful—they could race through the sparsely inhabited ship at will, putting anyone they encountered to sleep for eight or more hours. He had a purpose at last—

He crashed into the stationary Yananda, piling them both into a wall. Yananda shrugged him off. "Radio room," he whispered. Karna had the giant's stethoscope to the door. After a moment's wait—they were breathing hard—Karna opened the door and shot a surprised radio operator. He pulled the man away from the radio. "Make sure the bridge doesn't monitor this transmission," he said to Yananda, who crouched before the control console. "And hurry."

"Wish they'd fire up a little gravity in this ship," Yananda said. He flicked a switch, turned a dial. "There. *Duke of Vienna* to Mercury Four, *Duke of Vienna* to Mercury Four, come in please."

". . . *Duke of Vienna*, this is Mercury Space Station Four," said a voice from the radio's speaker.

"Mercury Four, we need a link up to Prometheus Station, we wish to transmit to Prometheus Station, thank you."

A pause. "I'm sorry, *Duke of Vienna*, Prometheus passed behind Sol a few minutes ago. They'll be out of direct radio contact for another forty hours."

"Can't you bounce it?"

". . . Only from Vesta. The delay would be about an hour and forty-five minutes."

Silence. Karna said, "Send it." Yananda got out his camera and plugged it into the radio. "Mercury Four, bounce the following message for us, please.'' He looked at Dent, then gave the operator a short description of the picture's origin.

More silence.

"Too late?" Dent said weakly. A dreadful singularity in his stomach pulled at him, inward and inward, toward implosion. . . . Without willing it he slammed a fist onto the radio console and shot up toward the ceiling. Karna grabbed him and slowed him down. "Too late," Dent choked out. "Too late again! Too late! Too late!"

Karna squeezed his shoulder. "Let's get out of here while we can." He pulled Dent from the room.

Once again they flew down the dim halls, tranquilizing a single crew member they passed. It seemed to take much longer getting back to the Orchestra chamber than it had to get to the radio room.

Without discussing it they pulled inside the big storage chamber to regroup. All three of them were silent. No one seemed in any hurry to leave once they were safely inside. Light from the ceiling rebounded from the polished surfaces of the instrument tree, rich brown, bright brass—

"Now what?" Yananda asked.

Dent felt his fists tighten. He grinned involuntarily, as if accelerating. "This room is soundproofed, isn't it?"

"For God's sake don't play the damned thing," Karna said sharply.

Dent shook his head. "Isn't it?"

"Sure," Yananda said. "Look at the walls."

Dent drifted over to the door to make sure it was completely closed. He touched down and floated back to the Orchestra, circled it, eyed it closely. . . . Climbing it was like climbing a tree. Balancing on a glass knob at the end of one branch, he stepped onto the top of the harpsichord, about halfway up the statue. He reached up and grabbed the slide of the lowest trombone, pulled it out and twisted the glass arm holding it until it came free in his hand. He held it up for Karna and Yananda to see. They watched him closely, faces blank. He looked around the room. Then he swung the slide into the neck of a violin, *crack!*

Splinters of glass and wood flew through the Orchestra, and a few floated across the room. Dent himself rebounded away from the statue, but he was holding onto the glass knob with his free hand and he pulled himself back. The neck of the violin sagged away from its body, severed and hanging by the four tangled strings. Dent looked back down at his two companions.

"Eh?" he croaked.

He whipped the slide through the air and blasted another violin and its glass carriage to smithereens.

"*Eh?*" he cried, vision blurred. "*Eh?*" He shook himself back to clarity, and spherical teardrops joined the bits of glass floating in the air. He looked back down. Karna leaped in the air, a stiff expression on his face, and made a lazy arc up, twisted, and with a vicious kick shattered a brace of clarinets. Black wood and silver keys everywhere. Lengths of glass spun away blinking under the light. Yananda methodically pulled loose a trumpet, secured his feet in the body of a cello so that he stood out from the side of the thing, and holding the instrument like a hatchet he chopped hard at the other cellos under him, *crack, crack, crack, crack!* How delicate the thing was, how complex and various! Karna kicked off from the ceiling and lashed out with his boot again, blasting a French horn free of its glass so that it spun wildly across the room, like a big gold soccer ball. Yananda moved on to the trumpets, and he made a lot of noise clanging his trumpet against the rest of them. Karna practiced weightless savate on the little white box of the celesta, up near the ceiling, *crash, crash, clang!*

Dent grasped the trombone slide with both hands and got down to work.

♪

retrograde inversion

Now, dear Reader, to say that two events occur at the same time is no simple matter. In the Newtonian universe, there is an absolute gridwork of space and time, within which the material phenomena of existence fluctuate; and measuring against that gridwork one can of course say that any two given events are occurring at the same absolute time. In the curved continuum of the Einsteinian universe, however, there is nothing *but* the material phenomena of existence; there is no underlying gridwork to measure against, and so you cannot say two events separated by space occur at the same time, because there is no clock that can encompass both of them—their time is inextricably bound up with the other three dimensions that locate them. This idea was expressed long before Einstein, by Heraclitus: "You cannot step in the same river twice."

But in the Holywelkin universe that we inhabit, Reader, the absolute gridwork has returned, has moved *within* the material phenomena of being; every event is fixed to all the rest in a newly discernable pattern, and this great Whole ticks along hadon by hadon, everywhere the same. So that once again it becomes possible to say two events occur at the same time.

And I *will* say it: Dear Reader, at the same moment that Dent and Karna and Yananda entered the lock of *The Duke of Vienna*, Ernst Ekern, inside Prometheus Station on the other side of the sun, left his chamber. And in the same moments that the three intruders floated through the halls of Ekern's ship, Ekern himself walked the curved hallways of the great torus, passing Grey after Grey; so that from here to the end, you yourself can time the simultaneity.

As Ekern walked the curved hallway, he was shaken by the sight of so many Greys. Nowhere to look where there wasn't a Grey. He had provided "Greys" for so much of the tour—and yet to Prometheus he had brought only the rest of his order. They were wearing grey and walking the hall as well, following the groups of chanting mystics, so that every fiftieth face he saw was familiar, smiling a little tucked Mona Lisa smile; but then he saw the smile on every other face that passed him, faces watching him from the corners of their eyes until he wanted to smash one of them with his fist, in warning to the rest. At one point or another on the great wheel were the quarters of the station's governor; Ekern knew the number and yet as he checked the numbers on the doors he passed (they went from 1 to 360), it kept slipping around in his mind, 66 or 99 or 369, no it was 99, 99, 99. Here he was at 180, working his way down the small metal plates next to every door, and the face of Iris, one of the members of his order, passed him for the second time in five minutes, impossible though that was—it would take over an hour to circle the station even if running. Ekern stopped his progress and considered chasing her down, forcing the truth of the situation from her. But that would be part of their plot. He was in control here, he disdained all attempts to disturb his concentration for the final act.

At room 99 the door was open and a whole suite of rooms was revealed, Greys in the window room standing before the darkened glass looking out at the whiteline sphere and singing a lilting chorus in a language Ekern had never heard before; and two rooms down another windowed chamber, smaller, empty and lit only by the strange flickering light of the newly created whitelines. Not empty; against the wall hardest to see stood the station's governor (Ekern had been greeted by him on his arrival) and Atargatis, Atargatis staring at him coolly, both of them still as if part of a tableau.

With a distinct exertion of will Ekern determined to wait them out. He stood and stared at them; they stared back. Ekern stalked to the window, looked up at the blur of white over black. He turned on a heel and pointed a finger at Atargatis. "Well?"

"The concert begins in an hour," the Grey governor said.
Atargatis smiled. "Ernst knew that. He wants to know
what will happen, don't you, Ernst?"

"Will you present the musician in your usual fashion?"
Ekern said, battening down the hatred that he felt for his
fellow playwright.

The Grey nodded. "No room in the Great Wheel will
contain all of us. Those who speak to us all, do so from a
sphere that floats inside the cone of whitelines. The sphere is
visible from the window rooms all around the wheel."

Ekern nodded; all would proceed as he had foreseen. This
was the customary way that the Lion or any other speaker
addressed the population of Prometheus. He had learned this
long ago, he had counted on this, and now it was confirmed.
Now Atargatis and his bright smile could be stared down
with impunity. *What did he know, what did he think he
know? What was his real standing with the Greys if he was
the Lion of Jupiter, what was his relationship to this Lion of
Prometheus, what . . . ?* Ekern's mind spun along an upcurved
hallway of questions, and choking off the whole avenue of
thought he resolved to choke Atargatis if he could, to murder
him in the most dramatic fashion possible, this meddler in his
work—

He found himself outside the quarters, in the big white
hall, floor curving up in both directions. Back to the order's
window chamber, away from all this indeterminacy. Past the
faces left and right, hurrying onward, ignoring the interpene-
tration of his order and this mysterious order of strangers.
How could they be in control here, at the station providing
the power that made all civilization possible? What were
they? What were they?

And there stood Johannes Wright before him, dressed in
grey tunic and pants. Ekern shook his head convulsively but
the sight remained. Because of the odd black eyes Ekern
could tell nothing from Wright's face, not even whether the
meeting was something Wright had sought. In any case there

he stood. Ekern shifted his feet, squinted for signs of a weapon. No weapon; only those eyes.

In the white wall of the curving hallway there was an open door. Wright walked to it, looked back at Ekern. "Come along," Wright said. Helplessly Ekern followed him, and they entered the room.

In this room a great curving black window formed half the ceiling and all of one wall. Ekern stood in the room's center. He looked up; over him beyond the transfer hub arched the giant torus, on which other black windows alternated with the blazing squares emitting the new whitelines. Through the black windows the population of Prometheus would observe the Orchestra, which would float in a strengthened bubble that only the Greys could weave, inside the cone of space created by the converging whitelines. Now these lines flickered between torus and singularity sphere, giving the silent room its only illumination. Ekern glanced around, jumped— there in the corner slumped a figure in grey, head tilted to the side so that it was almost buried in its grey hood. The head shifted, the face looked up slowly, as if it were a corpse reanimated: Diana. The Magus Diana. No recognition in her flickering eyes, only an idiot stare. Ekern pulled his gaze away from her, forced his heart to pound less violently (it was working to escape from his chest, to burst free), and looked at Wright again. Wright paced back and forth under the dark glass of the window, turning in to mark a little crescent around Ekern. It reminded Ekern of something he could not call to mind, something long ago, in a different age of this his ageless life—

"What have you done to her?" he asked.

"What have you done to me?" Wright said.

Ekern's heart made another escape attempt. He stared up at the whiteline sphere, rolling along with them out there in the streaming sunfire. Threats, attacks, kidnapping, drugging, tampering with dreams—lies, deceptions, illusions of every kind—what had he *not* done to him? Looking down at

the little man Ekern stroked his red beard and shrugged
slightly. What could he say? It was a question beyond answering, he would have had to answer it with his whole life.

"You thought you were going to deceive me," Wright
said quietly, his eyes as shiny as the dark glass he was staring
at. "You thought to lead me toward a secret that doesn't
exist, you thought that the Greys held an emptiness at their
center that you could fill with your own fear. That they were
an order similar to your own little one." Wright looked over
at Diana, slumped in the corner. Then he looked out the
window again. "Or you thought you could discover the
Greys' knowledge without exposing yourself to it directly, by
using me as your probe. Isn't that right? But you worked
from fear, and ignorance. You don't know what they know
on Icarus. You don't know what happened to me on Icarus.
Isn't that right? You don't even know what happened to
Holywelkin on Icarus. The journal of his that you wrote, and
hid for me to find—what made you write what you did? You
don't know. You don't know what you cast me into, do you?
Nor do you realize how far you can be pulled along with
me. . . . If you had been on Olympus Mons, you might have
learned."

Ekern cleared his throat. "I was on Olympus Mons."

The black alien eyes stared through him, and he shivered.

"Then you know," Wright said.

"Know what?"

Wright laughed shortly. He paced to Ekern's left side.
"You know that I could tell you all your future. I could sing
to you in the language I have learned and forever after you
would step through every step of your life like a mechanism."

"No," Ekern said, stepping back once. This was his own
dream come true; in the long months of planning, of reading
Wright's notebooks and their sources in Holywelkin, he had
invented this horrifying determinism—in the months when
the dreams had compelled him to write the false Holywelkin
journal, when his mind had perhaps been invaded and *not his*

own—"No—" The little black-eyed man pursued him step by step, his heart was going to leap out his throat, he had to play his part here, Diana was on the floor watching—if it was still Diana—

Then Wright opened his mouth and a melody rebounded. Ekern came to with his hands clamped over his ears, wedged in the corner across from Diana. He could not remember how he had gotten there. Fear, fear pulsing in every vein with every hard knock of his heart. . . . Had one of his plays turned on him and become real? Had he by some awful chance guessed the truth of the Greys?

"What—" he croaked. "What have you done. Why have you done—"

Wright turned away from him, and then with a jerk pointed at him, with a forefinger that seemed to extend all the way across the room. "There is no such question! Note I never ask you why you led me down this road. Your whole life led you to it, each act determined by all that came before. Our destinies lead us step by step, and you, pathetic in your illusion of control, creating a weird simulacrum of the truth, step in the utter darkness of ignorance. I might force the truth into you, but if I did, it would be because I have always done it. And so it gives me no satisfaction. Why . . . why always has the same answer. I'm done with you." He turned toward the door, mouth twisted with disgust. Almost at the door he stopped, rushed back at Ekern:

"When this is over you will have no Orchestra, you will have no metadrama, you will have no future, *you will have nothing as you understand it now.*" He straightened up, took a step back. "I give you that in return for what you give me. You will be master of nothing." He walked to the door, disappeared.

"G-good work," Ekern muttered, as much for himself as for Diana. "You r-really had him deceived. He thought you believed him, there. And so he will think—he will think he has broken through to the real. Good performance. Good performance.'' But his whole body shook, he remembered the moment on Olympus Mons when he had seen something on Prometheus Station, something very like this, something that this was, perhaps, the prelude to.

"Break through the real,'' Diana whispered, staring through the black glass at nothing.

♪

cut is the branch

And if you are Johannes Wright, following yourself and your shattered senses around the curved hallways of Prometheus, you will forget the encounter with Ekern, you will succumb to the death of feeling that has been creeping up on you ever since the visit to Icarus, and all that occurs to you will be perceived but dimly, as if you are the unwilling witness to someone else's dream. You will proceed to the room where Orchestra is being transformed into spaceship, you will feel the sunlight burst through the cracks around closed doors, bend around the hallway that seems part of the underlying synchrotron, smash and rebound against the walls surrounding you. . . . Sunlight will become the visible manifestation of the blind force driving through everything, driving everything to movement, and you will begin to understand the Greys in a detached way that explains nothing. In sun's light is the power of the dance.

You will come to a section of the hallway roofed in glass; spiral staircases lead from the floor of the station's curving hallway up into this chamber, which is filled with computers, display boards, control consoles and their blinking lights, a maze of silver pipes, a forest of bulky tall boxes. In a cleared area above you you will see the Orchestra, resting on the big square shape of a sphere generator. Figures in grey will scurry around it, bolting the instrument down to the generator, wiring a control box for the sphere into your booth. Your body will turn away from that sight, it will pace of its own accord in a widening spiral, a gyre contained by the circle of the hallway. In sun's light is the form of the gyre.

Margaret will appear, and you will regard her as you would an important figure from your childhood. She will join you, she will say, "Don't play this concert, Johannes."

How will you speak of it? "I have to," you will say.

"You don't have to!"

"I do."

"But why? Why?"

How will you speak of it? "Why anything?" Because there was, in the beginning, a big bang under certain laws, the thought experiment of some unimaginable god working its way out, and in the infinity of time and space it held in its circle of eternal recurrence. . . .

"If you don't talk to me about it now," Margaret will say grimly, "then when will you?"

You will regard your old friend with an understanding generated by the timbre of her voice, its anxious hoarse buzz. "On Icarus, and then on Earth, I was taught the true nature of time and space, Margaret. It is there in Holywelkin's work and I stood on the verge of knowing. And then I knew."

"Ekern has pushed you to this extremity. What you think you know is just his insanity."

"Impossible. Ekern may have led me to the Greys, but then he was left behind. This transcends him. You were on Icarus, Margaret, you know that."

"Maybe so." She will have to admit the truth of that. "But no matter what the Greys know—no matter what you think you know, you can't be sure of it. That's what it means to be human. Our powers are finite, our ability to know is limited, and all our truths are relative." The dense texture of rasps in her voice will rise in pitch as she grows more

insistent. "That's what it means to be human, Johannes!
We're trapped in our selves, we are not gods."

"Being human is enough to know it."

"It is not!" she will exclaim angrily. "To destroy yourself
for something you think you know is foolish arrogance.
Holywelkin's math, the knowledge of the Greys, all our
models are no more than models. They're no more than stabs
in the dark, and a new one will replace the old as sure as
anything. How many times have they fallen through? A
determinate system held in an indeterminate one, which is
enclosed by a determinate system of new power—which is
then found to be part of a larger, more comprehensive model
that is indeterminate. And so on through history. This determinism you believe in so strongly is just the model of the
moment—and even less than that—it comes from a *misreading*
of Holywelkin. Think about it, Johannes," she will say
desperately, voice tearing, "if the true reality is a timeless
whole, determined forever, then *where does the illusion of
succession come from?* Why should our consciousness be
moving forward into the future, when everything else in the
universe is static and complete? It's absurd! The mistake you
have made, Johannes, you and whoever led you to this, is to
spatialize time. You are thinking of time as just another
dimension of space, which Holywelkin's equations can map
precisely. But it would be more accurate to *temporalize
space,* to speak of a timespace continuum rather than a
spacetime continuum, to admit that there are many more
possibilities than actualities, that contingency exists everywhere in this indeterminate world of becoming," and meanwhile, all the time she is saying this, you will be standing in
the crystal halls of eternity, watching past and future curve
up and away in spirals extending off immovably, forever.
How will you explain that to her? How can you explain
yourself and still protect her illusions, which, flimsy as they
are, make her life bearable? Soon she will shout at you, she
will pummel you with her fists, and all you will want to do is

calm her, comfort her, thank her, tell her that you love her, in a language that you will be fast forgetting. You will understand the impossibility of any discourse about your acquaintance, the real.

"You don't listen to people, Johannes, and it's going to be the end of you. You didn't listen to Anton, you didn't listen to Dent, and now you aren't listening to me."

You will say, "I am listening to you, Margaret. I am listening as hard as I can. And I answer with my music, always. I thought my music would make it clear." Your body will have difficulty making these words and you will be stopped short, realizing that in every crucial moment of your life you have chosen to speak the language that is more expressive and powerful than any other, but which *no one understands.* "I asked Anton to listen to the music."

"He did."

And a great blackness will sweep through the corridors, blocking for a time the blast of indirect sunlight. You will be lost in this darkness. . . .

"Don't talk," Margaret will say in a new tone, her hand on your arm. The pained dissonance of tightened throat muscles around the vocal cords . . . the blackness will subside, leaving you trembling slightly. Lights will blink from your home overhead, and the two of you will stand in silence together for a long time, shoulder to shoulder, looking up at the Greys who will move so slowly and so ceremoniously around your home.

"What are they," Margaret will say, flat revulsion in her voice.

"They are many things," you will say. "Few of them know what they are."

"And do they worship the sun?"

"They use the sun." You will gesture up, and Margaret will follow your gesture to stare at the Greys who will be forming a circle around the Orchestra, chanting in response to the voice of a red-capped Grey standing on the sphere generator.

"They stand between our civilization and its source of power," Margaret will say. "They can become the high priests that they think they are."

"Perhaps."

"You would think the Earth would intercede."

"Earth doesn't care."

"But the outer terras?"

"These Greys rule them all."

"Not Mars, though. Mars could be free."

"Perhaps . . ." But you will see the circle of Greys look down at you, calling you with their chant, and the blackness will sweep through the room again, and your body will straighten up, step back. "I have to go now," you will whisper.

"Will they have control of that sphere when it's outside?" Margaret will ask, and you will realize that she has understood nothing, that the word *control*, the word *will* that we use so often, the word *time* itself, all refer to ghosts of our consciousness, and through the blackness you will say, "No—I will control it at that time." And with a quick ducking nod your body will move through its paces in the dance, it will start to walk past her toward one of the glass staircases. She will reach out a hand and hold you by the arm, supporting you, as always: "Please," she will say, "don't," and your body will whisper through the constricted throat, "Margaret," it will plead, "I can't bear not to." In her desperation she will keep her hold on you, attempt to stop you; but with a single glance she will fall back, her face twisted with fright. And with a shudder you will walk helplessly away, up the crystal corridors of eternity.

♪

the unacknowledged legislators of the world

For Margaret it was like conducting a conversation with a machine. She had never seen Johannes behave in quite that way before; all his quickness of speech and fluidity of expression were gone, and what was left was slow, calm, insect-eyed—utterly estranged. Sometimes when he answered her there was such certainty, such *conviction* in his face that she became frightened. Had he penetrated Ekern's game to something deeper—some fundamental truth underlying human senses, known only to the highest echelon of the Greys? She remembered the transcendant peace she had felt by the pool in the mountains of Icarus, when every object had chimed together in one large chord of being. . . . But no, she thought, such mystical moments were not beyond the human realm, they were a state of feeling, experienced many times in many places, and even if Johannes had experienced one more profound than hers, it was not enough to justify becoming an automaton. Her fear shifted to anger at his folly, at his complete indifference to anything she could say. Such calm, slow, measured speech! How could he bear to be such a creature? But that thought in itself was frightening. . . . Those eyes—what in other people were the windows to the soul, were in him black walls, barriers that defeated her every effort at penetration, connection . . . banging her head against a wall, useless, frustrating, painful. Her friend was mad. She should have stopped him.

As he walked away from her, and turned up the glass spiral staircase to the level above, she watched him. Watched his back; suddenly she remembered when he had turned around her brother. All her muscles were tight. Then he was up on the clear floor of the level above, surrounded by Greys. She couldn't stand to watch. She took off down the hall and up the endless white curve of it, white floor, white walls, white ceiling, with frequent breaks in the walls to the left for doors that gave onto rooms walled with black glass, black glass burst to light by the sun that was actually on her right. . . . She was disoriented and did not know if she was walking the shorter arc of the circle to their suite, or the longer. The concert would begin soon and it was important that she get back to her people before it did. She looked at the small numbers embossed by the doors . . . 279, 280 . . . and what was their suite number? Nearly zero. She hurried on. Now in the rooms to her left there were groups of them, chanting "uhhh, uhhh, uhhhhhhh." From every open door came the sound. Now and again she passed a small group of them in the hall, hurrying in the opposite direction, red caps bobbing comically, and each one that she saw increased the tension in her jaw muscles, until it felt as if her teeth might explode. These *people*! What *were* they? "Ekern led us into this trap, and he made up a lot about the Greys. He may even have made up the metaphysic that has Johannes so frightened— he may have taken us on Icarus and drugged us and put us in a sensorium and run us through all that, it's possible I suppose. Or the Greys may be a mystical order of some sort, and it was they who took us on Icarus." Gasping as she hurried down the halls. "But in the end it doesn't matter—all that metaphysical crap—because in the real material world, these Greys have us all in the palm of their hand! A cabal ruling the world in secrecy—and not exactly in secrecy, even—rather with a sort of contemptuous open control—say nothing, merely act—the world can remain ignorant or not, they don't care!" Bitter hatred welled up in her and she had to stop for a minute and lean against the wall of the corridor, feeling cold in the blast of invisible sunlight. Here she had solved the mystery to her satisfaction, and there was no one left to tell it to, nothing left to do with it. . . . Her friend was mad, she and her companions were cast in a maelstrom, swirling over a vast whirlpool of light, pierced by billions of glints per second, nailed to the wall. . . .

By the time she returned to the crew's suite, Johannes was already in their view. Above them in the black window the wheel of the station arced up and around and back to them; the sunward side was a brilliant white band. On the night side black windows alternated with the white gates of the synchrotron, where the streams of glints poured invisibly to the round ball of the singularity sphere, as in the Ice Cream Cone Theorem of Reimann where all lines converge at a single point. Deep in this cone of sunwashed space floated a shining white bubble: a sphere of some unusual weave, reflecting the sun's light, so that the Orchestra within it could scarcely be seen, a flicker of black tracery and no more. From their viewpoint it appeared to hang upside down. Speakers in the two sides of the room pulsed with music, a quiet mesh of sound. And perhaps we have come far enough together, dear Reader, to be able to describe this music adequately; particularly since, as it seemed to Margaret, the music expressed all that was happening at that moment. You know that chords have density: within a given span between the highest and lowest note (an octave, ten octaves), there are a certain number of notes bunched; and the more there are, the denser the chord. Now Johannes was playing tall, dense chords, a cluster of notes at the lowest audible pitches—perhaps this was the sound of the sun; then an ever-revolving series of harmonies in the middle range of hearing, changing the character of the entire chord in modulation after modulation—the station, perhaps; and at the highest reaches of human hearing, and beyond, tremolo notes flying in and out of nothing—just as the whitelines did to the eye. So these chords shifted again and again, reminding Margaret of early music, of that other Johannes, the Bach of the organ music, except that this tall, slow, simple changing chord was more ethereal, lighter and calmer than any music Margaret had ever heard. She listened to it closely, with a grim attention to every note. Across the chord, she noticed, the faintest melody danced; a single oboe, nearly drowning in the quietly insistent wall of sound, played up and down the full extent of its range, in and out of the chords, fluttering, swooping, crying out in a subdued way that could barely be heard. Could only Margaret, with her fierce attentiveness, hear that voice? Did she alone understand who that was, singing under the giant chords generated by the world around them? She found she was trembling, she walked to the wall beside the door and leaned back against it, looking up all the while. The Orchestra's protective sphere was a tiny white gossamer bubble out there, blinking in the light. Behind her was the brooding roiling mass of the monster sun, tugging at them all, dominant, tonic, dominant, a world of fire, a gravity well, a fountain of light, a god. The music changed and changed and changed, inexorably; at the top of the chord the serene swirl of the mercury drum recalled to Margaret the Martian symphony, and she shivered hard, cold in the harsh light.

She was the only one who noticed that in the lazy spinning of the brilliant white bubble there was a certain drift. Shimmering within the bubble like the faintest black web, now upside-down, now on its side, now upright, the Orchestra was drifting deeper into the cone, in toward the singularity sphere where all the whitelines found their direction. The chords shifted up continually, in a progression slow and majestic and serene, but Margaret heard that oboe cry out in falling arcs of muffled sound, falling, falling through the rising chords that were one sign of the Martian coda. One could hear in the weave of sound that it would end soon. She thought of him out there alone, looking back at the wheel of fire with its black windows, each a rectangle hiding hundreds of grey figures. . . . She was cold, cold, cold. The coda pressed on her like ten gravities, the metamorphosis of the chord accelerated, rose in pitch so that there were no bass notes anymore, and few in the middle range—

"Look!" Sean cried. "He's moving toward the singularity!"

A deathly frozen stillness as the crew stared up; only the chords moved—

"They're killing him!" Delia cried, but Margaret shook her head.

"No," she said. "He's got control of it."

"No," Delia moaned.

"He's going to fall into the singularity!" Sean said. "It's not much further—" Other voices cried out—

"Quiet!" Margaret said, and they all jumped. She had shouted it. The music was arching up, the tones of certain instruments peeling up and away out of the range of the audible, and Margaret focused all her mind on it, thinking *hear, hear, hear,* and then, captured by the unearthly beauty of the falling upward, hearing, hearing, only hearing. The Orchestra, now nothing but obscure tracery in its blinding white bubble, drifted to the point of the cone, spinning lazily. From the corner of her eye Margaret saw Delia's upturned face, blind like a fish, open-mouthed—

And the oboe fell in with the rest of the attenuated high chord, singing a single note along with the rest, a beautiful simple major chord, floating with only the lightest vibrato, the oboe so lost in it that Margaret felt it spoke only to her, a light high voice with its thick reedy timbre hidden in the center of the final endless chord.

Afterwards the members of the crew argued about the actual moment of the end. Some said that the white bubble dropped into the singularity and disappeared without a trace; others claimed that when the bubble was still outside the singularity it burned away, so that the black tracery of the Orchestra was outlined perfectly for a moment, before flaring into the white fusion. Margaret, her eyes clamped shut, saw nothing. She only heard the music; and as the others gasped and everything stopped, frozen still for that one moment of time, the final chord still sounded clearly in her ears, and she caught her breath to hear it—but it drifted out and away, sounding as if it came from outside the window, from inside her mind. And then it was gone.

♪

And they were alone, and left to start up again as best they could. Delia was weeping; Sean and Nikita, distraught themselves, put their arms around her. Others stood about the room like statues, staring up through the window still, as if they could not believe what they had seen. Marie-Jeanne held herself up against the wall, tears rolling down her broad cheeks. . . . Margaret, unsurprised and aching with cold, could not feel anything. For a long time they stood scattered in a stunned silence.

The door to their suite opened, and Ernst Ekern walked in.

His eyes protruded, his face was flushed a bright pink, and his curly graying hair was in disarray. He swayed unsteadily on his feet as he surveyed them, sniffing and breathing wildly. He lifted a hand, as much for balance as for their attention, and spoke.

"Cut is the branch that might have grown full straight—" But his voice broke, and he had to stop. He took a few steps toward Margaret, staggered, stopped, looked out at the singularity sphere.

"You killed him," Delia said.

"I killed him!" Ekern repeated, and laughed stridently. "He killed himself, didn't he? Rode Holywelkin's Orchestra out into a singularity, so that now he is projected out to all the whitsuns in this quadrant of the solar system! At this very moment he shines on a thousand worlds! Was it not a magnificent death? Can you imagine Johannes Wright dying a better death?"

Silence. Margaret stared at him closely, thinking of those whitsuns.

"I'm glad he took the Orchestra with him," Sean said bitterly.

Ekern stopped short in his drunkard's walk, looked to see who had spoken. "Took the Orchestra, you say. Do you think I would let him destroy Holywelkin's Orchestra?" He started walking again, circling the room with erratic steps. "I knew he was going to do this, you see. I knew it all, I have known it for years. He was not entrusted with the real Orchestra, you see. I had another made." He looked around at their faces, shouted, "He toured with a copy! I kept the real Orchestra for myself, for myself alone! Now Johannes Wright is dead, and *I* am the Master of Holywelkin's Orchestra! Cut is the branch—" His voice broke again, his breath caught in his throat like a sob. "Now I am the Master."

Margaret stepped in front of him and stared down at his livid face. He looked up at her.

"Get out of here," she said.

"Don't tell me what to do!" he shouted furiously. He took a step back, lowered his voice until it was tight, furious, knotted. "In fact, Nevis, your job is done. I'm in control here. You little people—you'd better leave, yourself."

Margaret hit him in the face, hard.

He stumbled back, collided with the wall. She followed him. Only his harsh breathing broke the shocked silence in the room. He looked up at her, hysterical anger contorting his face. Margaret felt some heat leak into her at last. She could see he wanted to kill her then and there. Her fists were painfully bunched, her teeth were about to burst; she welcomed the chance to fight, she wanted to hit him again, over and over, and she saw that he could see that in her eyes. She stepped toward him, and the fury on his face changed to panic; with a moan he turned, and slipped out the door.

Margaret slowly straightened out her fingers. Her right hand hurt. She flexed it repeatedly, feeling a stab of pain each time. All her feeling was in that hand. Marie-Jeanne was holding her. Rudyard looked stunned; Margaret put her left hand on his head. She pulled the corner of her mouth back wryly for Sean and Nikita, who were still supporting Delia. "Why did he do it?" Delia said as she wept. "Why did he do it?"

Margaret made her way to Delia, taking care to touch every person on the way. Hand to hand. Hand to head. She pulled Delia to her feet.

"He had trouble with his vision," she said shortly. "Come on, now."

She led them all down the hall. Up one of the elevators to the shuttle center at the hub. The Greys there looked surprised to see them. "Put us out on the ship to Mercury," she told them, ready to kill. But the Greys were like machines; they did what she said passively, faces blank. They were locked into a shuttle, fired out of Prometheus Station into space. Guided to the small ship that was sailing just above the great wheel of the station. Once inside the little ship Margaret went to the bridge. "To Mercury," she ordered the crew. "Now." Again they were automatons, subservient to her will. They nodded. "Set up our couches on the bridge," she said, and they did. The tour crew lay on the couches; the Greys reset their own chairs so they would be supported.

"To Mercury," one of the Greys said, and the acceleration began.

The pressure was pain; Margaret could see it in her crew's faces. "Did you record that concert?" she asked Delia.

"I recorded all of them," Delia said. "Every single concert, all the way down the system."

"And so they can be transcribed and scored, and played again. By ordinary people on ordinary instruments, as a communal act."

Quickly the force of the acceleration grew. The throbbing in Margaret's hand lanced up her arm, through her heart. The bridge was hushed. Her thoughts were broken and confused. To fill the aching silence she said, "Johannes is dead, and scattered through whitsuns all over the system. When the story of his death becomes known, all the worlds lit by those whitsuns will change. The people of those worlds will learn the legend, and act accordingly.''

The acceleration continued to mount. She was pinned to her couch, her poor hand throbbed, tears ran back into her ears. With a furious thrust she elbowed herself up from the couch, held herself out where she could stare at her companions. ''And we will stay together to see that his music gets played, by full human orchestras.'' Sean and Delia and the rest twisted awkwardly to look at her, not understanding. ''It's *Mars* I'm speaking of, do you see?'' she cried, fighting for breath. ''Mars can break free of these Greys, I tell you, and Johannes will help them do it. You all remember the Areology. *We'll make it happen again.* We'll play his music and get them to join, in Burroughs and Syrtis and Argyre, and on Olympus Mons.''

The acceleration increased at an accelerating rate, and she collapsed back onto her couch, she was crushed into it. The little rocket trembled as they powered away from the sun, faster and faster, faster and faster, faster and faster. Gasping for air, face smashed back against her skull, Margaret said, ''Back to Mars.''

And so dear Reader this tale ends and in the last throes of exhaustion I place it in a whiteline jump—where it emerges you know, I know not. But now you have read it, and in your brain a whitsun burns forever.